MADAME GRAY'S CREEP SHOW

Compiled & Edited

By

Gerri R. Gray

A HellBound Books Publishing LLC Book
Austin TX

A HellBound Books LLC Publication

www.hellboundbookspublishing.com

Printed in the United States of America

Also by Gerri R. Gray:

The Amnesia Girl
Gray Skies of Dismal Dreams
The Graveyard Girls
Blood and Blasphemy
The Strange Adventures of Turquoise Moonwolf

Contributor to:

Ghost Hunting the Mohawk Valley
Beautiful Tragedies
Demons, Devils & Denizens of Hell 2
EconoClash Review
Deadman's Tome Cthulhu Christmas Special
Mixed Bag of Horror: Vol. 1
Night Picnic: Vol. 3
Coffin Bell: Vol. 2
…and others.

CONTENTS

FOREWORD
By Thorne & Cross

Alfred Hitchcock once said, "For me, suspense doesn't have any value if it's not balanced by humor." Over here at the old Thorne & Cross Horror Ranch, we take that quote seriously. Unrelieved tension loses its punch rapidly, but when you distract your readers with some small amusement, a literary pratfall as it were, the horror returns with a vengeance. It shocks and it rocks.

Gerri R. Gray edited *Madame Gray's Creep Show* with the same philosophy in mind. People love being scared, and humor and horror go hand in hand. A good horror story is like a ride on a roller coaster. You get into the car, and your tension grows as you ratchet up that hill until you can hardly stand it, and then, suddenly, you're screaming in freefall. You take a sharp curve and you shriek and wonder if the car is going to go off the rails into the ocean, and when it happens again, you think you might die, but when you don't, your screams turn into laughter that releases all that wonderful tension.

Sitting down with a good scary story is a lot like that; you know you're not in any real danger despite the shadows lurking beyond the lamplight. That noise upstairs? It's *probably* just the cat, right? These things add atmosphere to that horror story in your hands and make it all the more terrifying.

Immersing yourself in a horror story is all about enjoying the thrills without having to clean up after the serial killer or the slime monster. There are no fingers to sweep into the dustbin, and your sheets won't get bloody. (Unless you're *really* kinky.)

All too often in daily life, too much terror can bring you down and make you feel blue. Your brain begins going numb, but stopping to smell a rose or watch the antics of a mime can provide a little welcome relief. A *little*. But horror provides *great* relief from unrelenting reality—and when the horror is good it makes you giggle when a bee flies into someone's eye while they smell that rose. It makes you laugh out loud when a huge sheet of glass falls from a skyscraper and slices the mime in half. These things may not be funny in the traditional sense, but they're *horror-funny*. And *horror-funny* is a special kind of funny.

Within the pages of *Madame Gray's Creep Show* you'll find all sorts of things to tickle your fevered fantasies and make you cringe and shudder in the most delightful ways.

Good horror scares and titillates, sure, but great horror can make you giggle and squirm as well. It awakens that shivery cringe that hits you square in your groin and squeezes and creeps its way up your spine. You know the feeling. The one you secretly crave in the darkest part of your evil little heart.

When Gerri compiled this anthology, she looked for stories that make you shiver and snicker by turns. You'll find all sorts of stories that all have one thing in common: they're scary and they'll make you smile—at least as long as you keep in mind the fact that Alfred Hitchcock considered *Psycho* a comedy.

Within these pages, you'll find all sorts of horrors and, in one way or another, each will give you a chuckle, no matter how depraved your sense of humor. *Wormbreath* will delight you with its O. Henry-esque twists. *Crows in the Attic* will give you the inside skinny on evil dolls and bag ladies, and if you've never fixated on pink toenails, you will when you read *For a Good Time*. There's a wig in *Bad Hair Day* that will curl your short ones, and if you are in the mood to squirm—really squirm—you must read *The Wonderful Thing inside Schmidlkofer's Chest*. There are many more marvelous stories here, too: You'll find morality tales, surprise endings, and the answers to questions like "Should I really walk into that deserted house in the woods?"

So welcome to *Madame Gray's Creep Show*, where the weird, the wicked, and whimsical walk side by side, and the price of admission includes a few sleepless nights spent turning the pages...and checking on those sounds in the attic...those creaks on the stairs...Here, kitty, kitty?

Tamara Thorne
Alistair Cross

INTRODUCTION
By Gerri R. Gray

Ghoulish greetings, and welcome to *Madame Gray's Creep Show*.

To satiate your hunger for horror, I—the one and only Madame Gray—have prepared for you a smorgasbord of twenty-three terrifying treats, each one simmered to blood-curdling perfection and seasoned with just the right amount of gallows humor. From murder and madness to monsters and the macabre, the stories in this anthology are guaranteed to push the boundaries of horror to the next level, and beyond!

Now, if you'll excuse me, I have an axe to grind.

Literally.

But before I descend to the dungeon to sharpen my playthings, I'd like to take a moment to thank my publisher—the cracking and ever-bodacious James H. Longmore—for allowing me the opportunity to edit and compile a third horror anthology for HellBound Books. As with my first two HBB anthologies—*Graveyard Girls* and *Blood and Blasphemy*—this collection of creepiness has been a diabolical delight to put together. I've enjoyed reading every story that was sent in—even those that unfortunately didn't make it into the book.

I would also like to thank Tamara Thorne and Alistair Cross of the illustrious scream team, Thorne and Cross, for writing the foreword to this book. You guys rock!

And last, but certainly not least, I'd like to express my sincere gratitude to all the infinitely talented writers whose work grace the pages of this anthology.

With all that being said, and without further ado, let the creepfest begin!

A PLUME NOVEL
By Scott McGregor

T he lineup must've been three hundred people long. It began at the table where the author sat, stretching all the way outside the building and down the sidewalk. I was hardly surprised by the turnout, considering who attended to sign autographs.

"I can't believe I'm about to meet Randy Plume," a fan in front of me said.

I couldn't believe it either, having waited in line for two hours. In my hands rested what I believed to be Plume's three best works of fiction: *Vampires of Sabbath*, *Jewels of Blitz*, and his magnum opus, *Edge of Shadows*. They all itched for a signature.

It wasn't far-fetched to say that Plume was on his way to becoming one of the best horror writers around the world, rivaling the likes of King and Barker. Plume succeeded in merging elements of suspenseful originality with metaphorical commentary onto the confines of paper. His characters read intensely genuine and empathetic, and his use of description triumphed over the works of Lovecraft. The strangest fact to note of Plume wasn't what lied beneath his book covers, but his age in relation to his success. He was only twenty-eight, five years older than myself. His first novel, *Iceman,* was published when he was nineteen. Since then, he has sold seven, soon to be eight best sellers in America.

To really read one of Plume's novels was like integrating yourself into the domains of the fictional world, trapped in a harmony of unease and paranoia, while also simultaneously perplexed by satisfaction. An even more impressive observation to make about Plume's work was the distinction of each novel, both in storytelling and craftsmanship, like each novel was written by a different author.

When I heard Plume scheduled to promote his new book, *The Relinquished Fees*, in the Portland Public Library, I set aside all my other responsibilities to attend the meet and greet. The day arrived, and when he came into my view, my stomach jerked.

For years, I've stared at his photograph, but a picture was nothing compared to the real deal. He wore formal attire, black pants and blazer with a red dress shirt, the top two buttons undone. He was clean-shaven, with freshly cut auburn hair. By all accounts, he was a handsome man, and he demonstrated a form of sophistication I yearned for. A kind of confidence provided with the success of a best-selling author.

And now, after years of admiration, I stood face to face with him.

"Hey there," he said.

The word *hi* would have been an appropriate response, if I had let it leave my mouth. Instead, I stood there silent, frozen in what seemed to be a staring contest between Plume and I. His smile loosened, and I knew I made him uncomfortable.

"Mr. Plume is a very busy man," said a stout, neatly dressed man who stood behind Plume, voice croaky. "Please, get on with your business."

Plume turned his head and said, "Godfrey, don't be rude. These are my fans." He faced me again. "Don't mind him. Manners have never been his strong suit."

"It's okay," I mumbled.

"Books?"

"Oh. I don't have any. I don't have any published, I mean. I've written a few. One... I mean... I've started one, I guess."

Plume laughed. "No, I mean the books in your hands. You want those signed, right?"

"Yes... sorry." I handed my novels over to my idol—back to who they originally belonged—and stood there blushing, eyes glued to the floor. Could I have made a bigger fool of myself if I tried?

"Who am I making this out to?"

"Allen."

"So, you're a writer, huh?"

I nodded.

Plume scribbled down his signature on the first book. "I could tell the moment I saw you. You have that look."

"Yeah, I write sometimes." By sometimes, I meant three hours a day, studying and harnessing my craft in preparation to join the big leagues with Plume. My novel, *In the Depths of Night*, was a project currently in development, only three chapters written. The story was going to be about two backpacking college students who face the demons of their past in a single evening, right after stumbling upon an abandoned and haunted resort. The idea itself might not sound like much, but it was mine.

"So nothing published, huh?" He signed the second book.

I shook my head, thinking *he probably thinks I'm just like all the other amateurs.*

"Sir, the lineup must keep moving," Godfrey insisted.

"Give me a moment, would ya?" He signed the third book. "Tell you what, Allen, why don't you send me some of your stuff on my website submissions page and I'll give it a look. Just make sure you leave your phone number somewhere in the story for me."

"Okay…"

Plume handed back his works to me, and I walked away astonished, saying to myself, *did that really happen? Did Randy Plume say he'd read my work?* I opened up my copy of *Edge of Shadows* and stared in awe at the lovely signature left me.

For Allen,
May all your wishes come true! I look forward to reading your work.
-Randy Plume

* * *

One month later during my break at Barnes & Noble, I received an unexpected call.

"Hello?"

"Hey, Allen," a familiar voice said. "It's Randy Plume. We met at my book signing, remember?"

"Yes," I sputtered, trying not to sound too excited. How could I forget meeting my idol? "What can I do for you?"

"Look, I just got done reading those chapters of *In the Depths of Night* you sent me. Sorry it took so long. I've been incredibly busy. I wanted to tell you, well, this is exceptional material."

I felt a punch to the gut in the most soothing, orgasmic way possible. "Really?"

"Yes, really. Say, are you busy this evening? I was wondering if perhaps you wanted to get together and talk more about your novel in detail. I think I can help you get to where you need to be."

"I'm not busy. Not at all. That sounds awesome. When and where?"

"How's my place, say, eight o'clock sound? I live on 3303 Hillcrest Drive, but that's our little secret."

I scrambled around the room to find a pen and piece of paper. "3303 Hillcrest Drive at eight o'clock. I'll be there. Wouldn't miss it for the world."

"Wonderful. I look forward to picking your brain."

* * *

At eight o'clock on the dot, I arrived outside of Randy's estate. I guessed it to be twenty, maybe even thirty times the size of my apartment just from the external view. In his driveway sat a glimmering—and what I guessed to be very expensive—sports car.

I rang the doorbell, and seconds later, Godfrey opened the door and stared at me with his froglike face.

"Oh, hi… I uh—"

"Mr. Plume will see you in the living room," Godfrey said.

Godfrey escorted me through the house, and I found Plume sitting on a sofa, sipping on a glass of booze. "Ah, Allen, wonderful to see you. Please, have a seat."

I took a seat on his luxurious couch and said, "Mr. Plume, you have a lovely home."

"Please, call me Randy." He patted me on the shoulder, then, poured me a glass full of whiskey. "I hope you like Dalmore."

"Oh, I don't drink…"

"Come on, have a drink with me. One writer with another."

Although I can't say I enjoy the taste of any sort of alcohol, I couldn't help but smile at the notion of Randy Plume wanting to share a drink with me. I took a slow sip of the whiskey and coughed.

"So, Randy—" I choked, uncomfortable calling him by his first name, "I've been meaning to ask, how do you go about your writing? Do you prefer laptop or pen? How many words do you normally write a day?"

"Some days… most days actually, I write close to nothing. Other days, I have pages and pages of material appear before me. All my work comes from a Tinex word processor. You ever see one of those?"

"No."

"I figured. They're a model not available in the public market, but I managed to snag one for myself back when I was in college. The novels just write themselves with one of those." Randy gulped down his drink. "But enough about me. You're the man of the hour. How long have you been working on this story you've got?"

"About, I would say, three months," I lied. It was closer to two years, but I kept that knowledge to myself. I had every chapter of *In the Depths of Night* planned. Hell, every scene and line of dialogue was sketched out in my head, but my insecurities kept me from writing it down.

"Novels can be a daunting task," Randy continued. "However, what if I told you there's a way you can have your novel written out by the end of the night?"

I almost sprayed whiskey out of my mouth with laughter. "Wouldn't that be something?" As I set down my glass, a wave of dizziness overthrew me. My hand slipped, spilling half of the whiskey on the table. "Oh, I'm so sorry, Randy. I guess I can't hold my liquor very well. I didn't mean to—"

I collapsed onto the ground.

* * *

My senses returned in waves upon my awakening. First, the smell of metal lingered, then, the sound of what I guessed to be tongs clicking. I felt something damp run down my forehead, warm and thick. My vision blurred, steadying myself out of blackness and confusion. The first sight I made out was Randy beside a computer. Lines of manuscript were sprung onto the screen, and a small part of me giddied to learn Randy began his next novel. Until my vision cleared up, and I saw what appeared to be the lines of my opening chapter I sent Randy a month ago. I tried to move, but remained still, looking down to see my arms and legs strapped to a chair.

Then, I heard him say, "Ah, I'm glad you're finally awake, Allen."

"Mr. Plume? Where are we?"

"Please, call me Randy."

The dampness from my forehead dripped onto my arm, and I saw that my sweat was dark, and red, and not sweat at all, but blood. "What's going on?"

"Godfrey, are we just about ready?"

"Almost, sir," the croak said from behind.

"Allen, you must be wondering why I've strapped you to a chair in my remote, rather bleak workplace. Before we get into that, I want to tell you a story. I take it you've read my first novel, *Iceman*, correct?"

"Yes?" How could I not have read *Iceman*? It was a compelling tale of a post-apocalyptic ice age, and it was the book that launched Randy's career and turned Plume into a household name.

"Well, what if I told you that *Iceman* isn't strictly my property, Allen?"

"I'm don't understand."

"Back when I was a freshman in college, I had a best friend named Neil Robertson. Like me, he wanted to be an author, and the two of us engaged in a little friendly competition. At least, it started off friendly.

"As time went on, I came to understand that Neil was a much better writer than I was. I often tried to surpass him. I read bullshit self-help books to harness my craft. I tried to copy the styles of other icons like Poe and Lovecraft. I even borrowed ideas given to me by other amateur writers, but none of it mattered.

"By the end of our first year at college, Neil had finished his first novel-length piece, and that story went on to be called *Iceman*. I learned, instead of trying to surpass someone who was clearly superior to me, I should merely take their work for myself. So I did, and that novel went on to launch my career."

"You hired a ghost writer?"

"Not exactly. I never paid Neil to use his property. In fact, he doesn't even know *Iceman* belongs to him. Not anymore, anyways."

"I still don't get it."

"This is rather tragic. You are someone I have enjoyed talking with. You're a bright, passionate young man. I see a lot of myself in you, and you don't deserve what's about to befall. After much analysis, you have the proper craft of a true storyteller, however, I think you lack the proper motivation to truly make it in this industry. You're not willing to do whatever it takes to become a successful novelist. So that's why it's time for us to get down to business. Allen, I want to own exclusive rights to sell your story under my name."

"Wait, that's why you wanted to meet with me? You want to, what, patent my story?"

"Did you think I met all those fans out of the courtesy of my heart? I was on the prowl for new material. You won't believe the number of terrible stories I've slogged through this past month. Trivial pieces about haunted cell phones and derivative serial killers. So much of what I've read is muddled with clichés and tedious prose. But your work? Oh, I could not ignore your work. You have integrated a new sense of internal horror. The tone is so sickeningly... personal. You should feel proud of the story you've crafted. I could never come up with something this stellar, and that's why it must be *mine*."

The words I had wanted to hear for years presented itself in the worst nightmare possible, and I countered back, "You can't have it."

Randy laughed. "I don't believe I said you had a choice in the matter."

"For fuck sake, Randy, I've only written three chapters. You can't have my story even if I gave it to you, because it's nowhere near completion. Months... years away from being what it should be."

Randy patted his computer engine twice and said, "That's where the Tinex processor comes in. The whole of your story, with fascinating characters, intricate details, and hauntingly good atmosphere, has been written in your mind, even if you don't know it. It all lies within your head, and it just needs to be... extracted."

Extracted. The word hung around in my mind like a frame on a wall. My imagination puzzled together dozens of different scenarios to learn what he meant by that, none of them pleasant.

"Sir, we're all hooked up and ready to go," Godfrey said.

"Very good." Randy rose from his seat towards a mirror in the corner of the room. "What I'm about to show you, Allen, will shock you. It will horrify you, far more than anything my novels have put you through."

He rolled the mirror in front of me, and my eyes witnessed to the most disheartening image of my life. The reflection revealed Godfrey standing behind me, as well my peeled back skin and exposed brain, hooked up to a mechanism from above. Three tongs held my hair back, and five cords with needled tips dangled an inch above my showcased cerebrum. Worst of all, the mechanism wired straight into Randy's Tinex processor.

Then, I did what any sane person would do when faced with such a grotesque reveal. I screamed. I screamed so hard it incited a cringe out of Randy.

"Your reaction is to be expected," Randy winced. "I've only had one writer who didn't shriek when I showed him this. Quite honestly, I do think there is something wrong with that man. Clint Burston, the one responsible for *Vampires of Sabbath,* which many of my fans have gone on to quote as *fucked up.*" Randy sat down again. "I'm afraid we've reached the part where I take your story, Allen. You need to understand, none of this is personal. I just need another bestseller."

"And then what?" I snapped. "You going to kill me? Is that what you do to all the writers you steal from?"

"Of course I'm not going to kill you. I'm not a psychopath. Besides, if I did, my sales would go down. No, I'm going to erase your memory of this event. I'm going to relinquish you from your idea, and I'm going to delete this wickedly unpleasant moment from your brain. You won't remember a thing. You'll still get to live a healthy, albeit mundane life and continue to appreciate my novels."

"Randy, please, don't do this." I continued to squirm in the chair as I begged, desperate for any sort of escape, but it was pointless. I was completely trapped.

"I could put you asleep during this process, but I find writers are most creative when they're awake, don't you agree?"

Randy pressed the *enter* key. The needles drove into my brain, and my head cocked back in anguish. First, it felt like someone sucked on the inside of my mind with straws. Then came the electrical, agonizing stream. My body shook violently, and my nails dug into the crevices of my palms.

Through all the pain, I kept my gaze towards the computer screen. I saw twenty pages, then thirty, forty, fifty… three-hundred-and-sixty-five pages of manuscript written out in a matter of seconds. After two years, *In the Depths of Night* reached its completion.

The voltaic sensation stopped. I gasped for breath, vision fuzzy.

"Allen, I regret to inform you that your services are no longer required."

"R—Rand—dy," I stammered, drool pooling down my lip.

"Hey, you're more than welcome to come to my next book signing."

He pressed *delete*.

* * *

"Look what came in," Jane announced, tossing a hefty box onto the front counter.

I immediately registered the name Randy Plume on the label and opened up the cardboard with eager haste. "I've been waiting for this for weeks."

Jane giggled at my enthusiasm. "You always get so excited when a Plume shipment comes in."

"Can you blame me? His work is exceptional and beyond our time. He manages to integrate frightening surrealism with a mix of social commentary, and he—"

"Slow down. No need to go full fanboy."

I pulled out a copy of *In the Depths of Night*, the ninth book in Plume's bibliography. "Isn't that something to behold."

"Tell me, what's this book about?"

"It's about two college students backpacking across the country, and in the middle of night, they stumble upon a deserted resort. At least, it seems deserted, until a bunch of ghosts appear and hallucinate them. They're then forced to face the demons of their past in a single evening." I took a moment and stared at the cover, appreciating the craft of a mastermind. "Plume is such a genius. I don't know where he comes up with these ideas."

"Didn't you meet him last year for a book signing?"

"Yeah…"

It was true, I had met him, evidenced by the signatures within my books, but I can't remember what the encounter was like. God, how could I forget meeting my literary idol?

I had his autograph memorized. *For Allen, may all your wishes come true,* he wrote to me, followed by, *I look forward to reading your work.* I'm still not quite sure what he meant by the latter half of his note, but I can hope he thought I looked like someone who might be a successful writer like him.

I hope one day—a day that may never arrive—I can come up with an idea as clever as a Plume novel.

THE WONDERFUL THING INSIDE SCHMIDLKOFER'S CHEST

By Scott Bryan Wilson

When Schmidlkofer was eighteen he got his nipple pierced while on spring break at Panama City Beach. Sometime in his twenties, having "grown up" a bit, he took it out. After that the nipple always felt kind of hard underneath the skin, but he developed a habit of squeezing it unconsciously, something that he didn't always realize but everyone who came across him certainly noticed (shopping for a toothbrush; waiting for his order number to be called at Burger King; in line at the DMV). There was something comforting to him about the act, and at night he would watch TV, eating chips with one hand and squeezing the nipple with the other, usually all warm and cozy under his Snuggie. He'd get little shocks that did not feel good but that also weren't entirely unpleasant. He always assumed the hardness was scar tissue from the piercing healing over, but one night he was watching the new episode of a reality show about forced horse impregnation when his nipple felt different.

It was sore, but also squishier, but in a dry way, like it was full of sand. He looked down and saw that it was inflamed and red and throbbing from where he had been squeezing it. There was a grayish sheen to it, and it looked like a mushroom was bursting from his chest. He went into the bathroom and splashed some water on the mirror to wipe off the toothpaste stains and then wiped the water off with some toilet paper. He pushed his chest as close to the mirror as he could, and saw what looked like a piece of string sticking out of where the piercing used to be—the head of the mushroom, as it were. He found some tweezers and pulled on it. It was coarse like a hair, but white. The string came out a few inches, then, suddenly, with a little tug, more than a foot. His stomach roiled, and he felt a little light-headed, but he resettled his feet and took a deep breath and kept pulling. A few drops of blood trickled from the hole and the string turned pink but it just kept coming. When there was about ten feet of wet, pink string coiled in his sink like floss, he said enough is enough. He had scissors in the medicine cabinet, so he cut the string and immediately shit himself and passed out.

When he came to, he had a throbbing headache from where he'd banged his head on the toilet, and his nipple felt like it was on fire. There was dried blood all over his chest. Worse, there were several new mushrooms, a little colony of them there. This he found more disturbing than the pink floss he'd pulled out. It was like a tiny mushroom village.

He was late for work, and he had a bunch of meetings today.

He showered to get the blood off, got dressed, got on the bus. He had to stand the whole ride. The urge was there to play with his nipple, but he was suddenly very conscious of it, and—literally—stayed his hand. His company was taking bidders for contractors who would build out a new infrastructure for the metadata in their repository system, and the day was going to be filled with back-to-back meetings as the contractors made their pitches and gave demonstrations of their programs showing the cross-sector functionality and how it leveraged the power of targeted something-or-other.

He always made sure and held a pen in his right hand while he was at work because that was his nipple-scratchin' hand, and if he had a pen in it he wouldn't manipulate his nipple while sitting at his desk or in a meeting. He was staring at the presenters but otherwise wasn't paying the slightest attention to the presentation. No one gave a shit what he thought and no one would ask him anyway. He was there so that his department could have strength in numbers; he was supposed to vote however his boss did, if it came down to it.

He did eventually notice that the presenter had stopped talking and everyone was looking at him. It took him a minute to realize that they were also talking to him, asking him if he was all right, with looks of disgust on their faces. There was a rasping, flapping sound coming from inside his shirt, and he looked down and excused himself.

In the bathroom, he saw in the mirror that his shirt was moving, as if popcorn were silently popping under it. There was a sound like a squirrel digging in a plastic bag. He removed his shirt and saw that there was a small hole where the string had been, and it was now full of brown bugs that were colonizing the mushroom bumps that were crowded in the hole. The sound was louder with his shirt off so he put it back on and left work without taking his things. He hadn't brought his lunch today because the company was ordering sandwiches so that everyone could keep sitting through the meetings instead of leaving for lunch. The sandwiches were always cold, with too much bread. They always ordered veggie wraps in addition to the other sandwiches but no one ever ate them, and sometimes if no one was looking he just took them himself for dinner. He wasn't very hungry anyway. He had a seat on the bus this time and his heart was racing because he was very nervous because he knew that if you had bugs inside your skin then something was wrong. He could feel them burrowing into the tissue and muscle and when he looked down he saw that blood was now seeping through his shirt. His heart was racing and he was trying to be calm and concentrate on his breathing. While he couldn't describe the feeling, it didn't necessarily feel wrong, though that did not make him happy about it.

When he got home he rummaged around under the kitchen sink and went back into the bathroom and when he removed his shirt he got light-headed again when he saw that now the hole was twice as big as it was an hour ago, but fully populated with gray and olive mushroom bumps and the skin around it was all peeled back but there was a spiral indentation, like a quarry, over his heart. There were a hundred brown bugs crawling and digging and scratching in the mess. He expected blood but mostly it was very dry and flaking, like a sunburn. He took the bug spray he'd taken from the kitchen and emptied the can all into the hole, the bugs going into a frenzy as the spray hit them. He began to choke because the room wasn't properly ventilated and he couldn't breathe.

He passed out from the fumes and when he woke up it was dark outside. It was the sound that woke him—a frantic buzzing. He stood up and turned the light on and his head felt like ginger ale as he saw in the mirror that his chest hole was now black from thousands of bugs. He swiped at them with both hands and they burst into a cloud, but he was able to swat fast enough to clear them so that he could briefly see his skin. He used both of his hands and he gathered up the skin around the hole and squeezed like he was strangling someone, and crushed-up bugs starting squirting out of the center of the hole, others fighting to get out. There were popping sounds as the mushrooms exploded, and thick yellow slime oozed between his fingers. He was now kneading his chest hole, crushing everything that moved, swiping between squeezes, the pain unbearable but he had no other option. Eventually the bugs were either all dead or flying angrily around the bathroom, and he took his tweezers and rooted around in the hole a little bit, inspecting the folds between the unpopped mushrooms, trying to see if there was anything left, like a doctor digging for shrapnel, and could see that there was something still in there. Dropped the tweezers, used his finger, started pulling the hole apart, digging around with his finger, the hole getting wider, the entire space so abused that it was now numb and he could no longer feel anything, and mentally he was so checked out at this point that it was as if he was operating on someone else. He began to slowly pull the hole apart as if working some Play-Doh, until he could get a finger and thumb inside himself, and began using the forefinger to scoop out the black eggs that filled the recesses of the hole. Scoop them out and flick them into the sink, the toilet, against the wall, the mirror.

When he woke up he was on the couch, the TV on, a show called *My 600-Pound 90-Day Fiancé*, about morbidly obese mail-order husbands. He could smell vomit and realized that he'd voided his stomach contents all over himself and the couch. His ears were ringing and his head felt as if it were full of helium. He couldn't bear to look down at his chest. He knew it would be a horror show beyond his imagining.

He just wanted to sleep—he wanted to die, really—but if he could just sleep he would be able to exist without this hole in his chest and he could escape and maybe he wouldn't wake up.

The doorbell rang and he wasn't expecting anyone or any packages but he also received so few (no) guests that just the idea of someone knocking on the door was enough to brighten his day, even though he knew it would be a Jehovah's Witness or a political canvasser, but he didn't want to be rude or pretend that he wasn't home, so he threw on his Snuggie that he kept draped over the back of the couch and went to the door and there was a policeman there and he asked if everything was okay sir and Schmidlkofer could hear the buzzing again, knew that he'd missed some of the eggs, that they were hatching inside him, he could now hear a squeaking sound as new mushrooms grew and rubbed against one another like balloons, and the police officer asked if he could come in, and once inside he pushed Schmidlkofer onto the couch and stood across from him on the other side of the filthy coffee table and began thrusting his crotch and working his hips and popped all the buttons off his shirt as he began to flex and gyrate, now swinging his shirt above his head in a giant arc like a lasso, and from his holster he took a bottle of baby oil, which he squirted all over his chest and began to smear into his skin, suggestively, his torso waxed, and leered like a wolf over his sunglasses and said, "Oh yeah, oh yeah, oh yeah," now toweling between his legs with the shirt in a steady rhythm to unheard music as Schmidlkofer sat and watched and hoped the police officer wasn't going to arrest him for having a hole full of bugs in his chest.

* * *

The stripper was realizing that he had gone to the wrong address when he noticed that the man on the couch no longer appeared to be breathing. This concurrent with the fact that it looked like he had a newborn kitten or puppy under that blanket he was wearing. There was a kind of buzzing and rattling sound coming from under it, like someone shuffling a sheaf of paper. He stopped dancing, sizing up the man's unmoving expression, not taking his eyes off him as he reholstered his baby oil, grabbed his clothes, took his sunglasses off so he could see. Tried to remember if he'd touched anything coming in. Bundling his clothes in his arms like a john whose client has just died underneath him, he stole a bowl of change sitting by the door as he used his shirt to turn the knob so he wouldn't leave prints. As he closed the door behind him he took one last look in, and the man had not moved, but the puppy or kitty was now playing so violently under the blanket that it appeared as though the man were moving, the papery rasping sound now so loud that the stripper could no longer hear the techno running through his head, the music to which he danced his way through life, and that would be his soundtrack until death.

FOR A GOOD TIME
By Cooper O'Connor

P epper couldn't stop thinking about the blonde with the small mouth. He steered the car along the lonely roads that looped through the New Hampshire forest and rolled over the picture of the girl in his mind. *It's a shame*, he thought with slow and muddy thoughts in whose deep water his conscience had long ago drowned. Pretty girls shouldn't be left to close alone. You never knew who might be standing outside your door.

He wondered what she looked like now. It'd been five days, and five days can do a lot to a body. He bet she didn't even look like the pretty young thing whose lips he'd wanted to kiss oh so bad.

He was the last man who'd ever lay a kiss upon those lips. Who was the first? A dark smile warbled to life on his face and he dreamt of the girl, maybe around twelve.

Cute, freckled, pigtails. It's the fourth of July in the local park, and she can smell the briquettes of the nearby grill. The lights boom boom flash in the sky before sparkling down back to earth in trails of gold, green and blue. Her heart is beating fast because she knows the boy she sits beside is going to kiss her. When she turns to him, she can see the fireworks in the reflection of his eyes. He's nervous but he smiles and squeezes her hand. Her stomach rockets up as he leans in. His movements are awkward and his intent is obvious. She closes her eyes, and instinct takes over. Her neck arches, her head tilts, her mouth parts. And now his lips are on hers, pressing softly. His tongue is unsure what to do, and she tastes the faint trace of butter on his lips from the corn on the cob they'd eaten earlier. Something awakens in an electric flash within her, and she knows that something has changed for her, maybe forever.

And Pepper thinks of those same soft lips, the same soft mouth his tongue had snaked across then wiggled into five days before. She'd tasted like strawberries. He wondered what he tasted like to her. Cigarettes, he supposed, and warm beer. He took pride knowing his lips would be the last things she would ever taste. Her entire life was book-ended by these two kisses: two ends of a bridge suspended above an abyss. It was as if she had come into existence with the boy under the exploding stars, and she ceased existing when she met Pepper. And now all she'd ever taste again was dark earth and dead leaves. The only touch, the slither of pale worms though her lips. He felt a stirring his lap. He thought about pulling over, but decided against it. It'd been a long day of driving and he needed to keep moving, anyway. He felt better with every mile he put between himself and the girl's body.

He never even knew her name. He had stopped along a stretch of road, just like the one he currently drove upon, rested his car under the heavy boughs of a pine and stepped into the convenience store to take a leak and grab a snack. She'd just been about to close. Funny how life turns out. If he'd been just five minutes later in getting there, he'd never have met her, he'd never have wanted to kiss her lips, and she'd still be alive. Maybe right now there was an alternate universe where she was still alive, like in the comic books whose pictures he'd stared at (he never bothered reading the words) as a kid. The ones where Superman would go to another world where he was raised by Nazis. Maybe there was a world where she was still alive, where Pepper was five minutes later in arriving at the store, only to find it closed, or where Pepper hadn't been born at all. He had a hard time thinking of himself other than who he was. Pepper was Pepper. He couldn't imagine a world where a version other than the one who'd kissed that girl existed so he discounted the possibility of alternate worlds. It was the deepest thought Pepper had had since childhood. Possibly the deepest thought he'd ever had. And as soon as he had turned it over in his mind, he tossed it aside and hugged to his chest the memory of the girl with the small mouth.

He held her up for the money. She took him to the safe. He made her show him where the videotapes of the cameras were. Once he destroyed the evidence, he had his way with her among the boxes of potato chips.

Her toenails had been pretty and pink. She had worn a toe ring of a kitty cat. He had marveled at how bright her toenails looked as he dumped shovelful after shovelful of dirt upon her broken, lifeless body.

She wasn't the first, of course. There had been others. The redhead with the green eyes. The brunette with the chest tattoo. The fat one with the small tank top. The one with the glasses. August was rolling up into September and his summer vacation was coming to a close. He'd left a trail of bodies (some found, some unfound) in the forests of New England. He'd kept to the back roads, dressed in unidentifiable tourist regalia: a *Mount Washington* hat, dozens of five-dollar shirts of airbrushed moose and wolves he'd taken from gas stations. He was of average height and slouched forward when he walked. He carried about him an unwelcoming cloud that caused people to dislike him without ever knowing why, but that feeling lifted as soon as he left the general vicinity. What made him evade the police these past three months was not ingenuity on his part but the gift of having been born completely forgettable. You might remember parts of the whole (the puffy, pockmarked cheeks, the crooked teeth, the wisp of a moustache) but you'd never be able to remember enough of the pieces to put the puzzle together.

In the far distance of the road, a faint spark flickered to life the deep black. He passed a sign. *Rest Stop Ahead*, it read.

He pulled the car into the rest stop, killed the ignition and jerked the E brake. He stepped into the night air and stretched his lanky body to the treetops above. His was the only car there. It had been a lonely drive the last few hours. He hadn't seen many people, which was fine for Pepper. After all, he wanted to continue to hide in the deep forests of New England for as long as possible. It was better than the city life. They always caught you in the city. Too many cameras. Too many witnesses. Out here? Everyone's too trusting. They made life easy for Pepper.

He walked into the rest stop bathroom. A dim light, almost green, sputtered above a row of rusty sinks. The wall-length mirror was tagged with graffiti. The floor tiles were wet (rest stop floor tiles always seemed wet) and peppered with dirt. A few flies buzzed around an aluminum trashcan that smelled of old diapers and tuna fish.

He pushed open the handicap stall and closed the door. Pepper always took the handicap stalls. It was one luxury in life to which he treated himself. And if some handicapped asshole ever made a stink of it... well, let's just say girls weren't the only ones that had gone missing in the New England woods this summer.

He slid the tiny bar into its hole, locking the door in place. He unbuckled his pants, sat on the toilet and winced, realizing he should have wiped it down first. The seat was not only cold but wet. Growing up, Pepper's stepfather told him you could get THE AIDS from sitting on wet toilet seats. Said the homos shot their spunk just so good-natured Americans could get THE AIDS, too. Said the homo spunk waited there and wiggled their way up your butthole.

Normally, Pepper always wiped the seat first. In fact, he usually pulled out a wad of toilet paper so the homo sperm wouldn't wiggle their way under his fingernails. But it was late and he was tired and could only pray he wouldn't get THE AIDS.

As he sat there with nothing better to do but wait, he pulled out a joint from his *Bah Habah* fanny pack and lit up. He took a few hits, let the smoke fill his lungs and extinguished it. He didn't need much and besides, he didn't know when he was going to get his next score so he needed to conserve what grass he had.

While the hazy, lightheaded feeling filled him up, he looked around the bathroom stall. In typical rest stop tradition, it was a feeding ground for graffiti. His lips pulled back over large, uneven teeth, revealing a smile. He chuckled at the writing on the wall. He wished he had a pen so he could add to the bathroom library. Something simple. *Pepper was here.* Then everyone who read it would wonder who Pepper was. It'd be like being famous.

Among the diagrams of male genitalia were the following daily bathroom inspirations:

"U R Gay!"

"Sing a fucking song even if you don't know"

"Bumby wuz here."

"I want to fuck my girl's friend. Dam!"

"White girls give the best blow jobs"

"Clutch customs!"

"Don't let ride get ugly"

"Conduit ate your hamster. Deal with it."

"What is Ja. Boo. Da."

"You know fucking RAW (w/o condom) is the best." Beside it, someone had added, *"And you have AIDS."*

Then his eyes landed on, *"Call Me For a Good Time."* A number was scribbled next to it. Pepper couldn't tell you how many times in his life he'd seen that or similar invitations tagged or scratched onto bathroom stall walls, and he didn't know what was different about this one. But there *was* something different, so he pulled out his cell phone, laughing as he did it.

"My step daddy said you only live life once," he said to the flies that buzzed just beyond the wall. "Hope it's a chick that picks up, right? Don't want to call no 'mo."

He dialed the advertised number, thinking it would go straight to the voicemail of some vengeful boyfriend's ex.

"Hi!" said a voice. It sounded young and sweet and full of life. He thought of the girl with the small mouth and pink toenails. She had been full of life once. Before she met Pepper. "I can't answer your call right now. Just leave a name and a message and I'll get *right* back to you. I promise! K' bye!"

The phone issued a beep.

He was just about to leave a message when his phone died. He pulled it away from his ear and looked at it.

"Call Ended," it read.

He shrugged. Whatever. He didn't know what he had expected. Sure, there was the off chance that some chick would have picked up and would have promised what was written on the wall, but rest stop fantasies are just that, he supposed: fantasies.

A few moments passed. He focused his attention on squeezing the weight in his gut out of him. He needed to stop eating the fast food shit. It was clogging everything up down there. He squeezed so hard, the blood thundered in his eardrums and he barely heard the door to the rest stop open with a squeal.

He looked at his phone to tell the time but remembered that it had died during the call. He thought back and tried to remember what the console of the car had told him last. He was pretty high but a sober Pepper was not much more intelligent than a stoned Pepper and chances were he wouldn't be able to remember if he hadn't smoked up. If he were to give a ballpark estimate of the time, he'd tell you it was somewhere between eleven and two.

He listened while the soft flap of flesh against the wet tile slapped towards the stalls.

Is someone walking on the floor barefoot, he wondered?

The footfalls grew closer and closer. Pepper hoped the other person would be quick. He never liked going to the bathroom if someone else was there. Hell, he couldn't use the urinal at all if someone else was in the room. And being all blocked up down there, he needed all the privacy he could get.

The footfalls stopped in front of his bathroom stall door.

The hell?

The person knocked, only once. It was a sharp, hollow crack in the otherwise still night.

"I'm in here," he said. "Pick another one, man."

The person cracked against the door again.

"You deaf? Someone's in here."

The person paused but Pepper could tell he was still there. Then the person knocked again, this time with more force. It was enough to make the stall door shake in its hinges.

"Hey, get the fuck out of here, man!" Pepper said. Pepper tried to peer through the crack in between the door and the frame, next to the graffiti tag: *Rage Against the Latrine.* He couldn't see anything. "I'm trying to take a shit!"

That's when Pepper looked down.

A gust of fear swept through Pepper, and he froze on his spot on the wet toilet seat.

The feet were pale, grub-white with thick black dirt that caked the spaces between the toes and ringed the toenails. The pink toenails.

And there, on one toe, a little kitty cat ring.

The knock came again, this time more forceful. The latch strained. Pepper watched as the screw rattled in its place. It wasn't screwed in properly. With one or two more blows like that, the door would fly inwards, and Pepper would stare into the eyes of the...

No, he thought, *it can't be. It can't be.*

Another blow smashed against the door.

His final images of his life were of the sad, squalid little writings of lonely men on the bathroom wall. If he were a smarter man, he'd appreciate the rather fitting fact that his end came in a bathroom stall, as his stepfather used to threaten to flush him down the toilet like the little shit he was.

Boom!

The door rattled. The screw threatened to pop out.

Boom!

And he couldn't...

Boom!

He couldn't stop…
Boom!
He couldn't stop thinking…
Boom!
He couldn't stop thinking about…
Boom!
The blonde with the small mouth.

LEFT-OVERS
By Rob Santana

N o way I was staying in that prison. My blessings on Chef. He arranged my escape, having shared my outrage over the charges brought against me by the local District Attorney, that over-zealous, vote-seeking bastard. Ten to twelve years, tops, for selling pot to "minors?" Come on. My clientele had consisted of young men—age range: eighteen to twenty-two. Give me a break. I wondered who ended up with my stash.

After a lengthy court process, they slammed me in with a bunch of desperadoes and low-lifes, the kind you cross the street to avoid. Every other night a fight would break out in the shithole they called a cafeteria, mainly between guys with razor blades tucked underneath their tongues. After eighteen months of fruitless calls to lawyers, I planned my breakout.

But how? With Chef I could commiserate. He hated the judge, hated the system with its micro-town mentality that kowtowed to local politics. Smithville, population 1,776: the last place you'd want to relocate to after a narrow escape from eager-beaver cops in a much-larger town.

"Doug? I can help you," Chef had whispered. "Ain't fair, a good-looking boy like you servin' time for selling feel-good weed." That's how it began. Chef was a guard.

"Help how, Chef?"

I waited out his north to south appraisal of me, his tongue rolling across his lips. The man was pushing forty but looked more like the Crypt-keeper.

"Security's pretty lax here past midnight, and I'm the guard rappin' his night-stick against the bars about then," he said, a glint in his red-veined blue eyes.

"You mean you can—"

"Ohhh, yeah, sonny. The ol' look-the-other-way routine."

That's how small this hick town makeshift prison was, if you could call it a prison.

Chef gigged as a part-time cook with his lady friend for some crappy diner (*his* name for it). He took pride in his pies. "You'll never go back to standard pies once you try one a' my special pies," he winked. All I cared about was getting the hell out. But how? He explained it to me as if I were a five-year-old. I didn't like the part where I had to first allow him free reign with my lean, six-foot frame. *Please.* But it was only for one time, he promised. He mostly just kissed my neck and felt me up. I would've drawn the line at nasty stuff, but he never did insist. Poor lonely fool.

I had a cell to myself, thanks to a warden who wouldn't lock me up with a murderer or a rapist, so the decamp would be easy. I could hear two inmates snoring as Chef unlocked my cell and had me follow him to a back exit.

"Keep goin' straight from where I point. You'll end up on a road. Young man like you shouldn't have no trouble hitching a ride. But before then it's all woods, a whole mile of it, maybe more. Ain't no other way."

"Thank you, Chef." I would have walked ten miles.

"Oh, one other thing. I was told there's an old house situated along the path. You just might run into it, but no guarantee. Personally, I think it's bullshit. Just keep walkin' a straight line. Here's some money, case you run into a phone booth or a bus."

Chef handed me two twenties. What a generous guy. My car had been impounded and they snapped up my wallet. All I had on was government-issue prison garb. As we edged towards an opening in the fence, an outside guard stood watching Chef.

I was in shadow so he hadn't noticed me. Chef lowered his hand and waved me off as he distracted the guard for a cigarette. I scampered into the woods. No looking back. Creeping along a heavily wooded area in mid-August was not my idea of freedom.

* * *

After a mile-long trek slapping at mosquitoes and dodging thick renegade branches, I came upon a sight that made me smile. There it was, the house Chef mentioned, an aging two-story den situated in a cleared-out area, its rear facing a wall of yet another wooded landscape. Its isolation confused me. Who builds a house smack dab in the middle of a forest? In my frazzled, exhausted mind, I imagined Smokey the Bear stepping out for a smoke.

I bounded towards it, careful not to step on branches that would announce my arrival. Fat chance, though. Middle of the night. One light on, top floor, which made sense. You never knew if an escaped convict would make a beeline for a house in the middle of nowhere.

Just as I reached a cleft that led to the gray dwelling, another light switched on. I stepped back and hid behind a fat ancient tree.

The front door opened. A silhouette stood under its frame like a still from a photograph. Maybe thirty seconds passed before I could make out the faint glow of a cigarette wedged between his fingers. He drew on it lazily. The faint sound of a woman's voice made him swivel his head towards it.

Okay, so the place was occupied by a couple.

I guessed their age range to be early to mid-thirties. The man was tall and gangly. From my vantage point he sported a shock of long, black shaggy hair and a scraggly beard.

Another voice. From inside.

Sounded like a kid.

After a few puffs, the man ditched his butt and shut the door. His cigarette break was over. No smoking allowed inside. I edged towards the side of the house. On closer inspection, its exterior was crumbling, on the verge of structural collapse. Decay was imminent. I noticed the window just above me and chanced a peek, making use of a filthy derelict milk box to stand on. I could hear them as they sat at a wooden table that reminded me of the Old West. The walls surrounding them were black and a single naked bulb illuminated their gnarled faces.

I needed to gauge these people's personas before summoning up the spunk to knock on their door.

So I listened.

"Brett, he can't go on this way. I'm losing sleep over that boy."

Brett.

"He's insatiable," Brett said. "What we got is a boy who's insatiable. Hell, didn't he down a plate-full of ribs this morning? Polly? Look at me."

Polly.

"Good thing it's Saturday," Polly said. "Can you imagine having to wake his little ass up for school after a sleepless night?"

I reared back. *Whoa.* What school? Was there a bus stop nearby? A car? I scanned what I gathered to be their 'front yard.' No vehicle. Just a large green dumpster partially hidden under a cluster of vines and assorted debris.

I pictured ants and sow bugs having a field day foraging under the cluttered ground. It was hard to imagine there might be a bus stop or another building nearby. I peered to my left. Just an endless chain of trees and shrubbery on the horizon.

Talk of food reminded me that I hadn't eaten since yesterday morning. I was famished and desperate.

I had to risk it.

I took the four creaky wooden steps that led to their door and knocked.

I heard Brett mutter, "Well, I'll be." Footfalls. The door swung open. Brett stared down at me. I spewed out my mentally rehearsed lines, nearly stammering.

"I'm so sorry to trouble you, sir. My car broke down about a mile from here. And I sorta wandered off in the wrong direction and, well, I'm kinda lost."

Polly's head popped into view over Brett's shoulder. Her eyes widened for a second. She and Brett exchanged glances.

"I'm real sorry to bother y'all," I added, my belly growling in punctuation. I wanted to slap it for comic relief but held back. This wasn't the time for levity.

"Uhh, where exactly did you lose your car?" Brett asked, his eyebrow cockled. My brain jammed on me.

"I was driving cross-country," I said. "I didn't notice any road sign when it happened. It's an old car. Shoulda known better, I guess." I shot him a shit-eating grin. The couple traded glances again and Brett widened the door. I was *in.*

Brett's craggy face was lined with crevices. His hair spilled over his shoulders. He had thick brows and bumpy jowls, a hippie version of Nixon. His black t-shirt was rumpled but his jeans looked pressed, at least. As for Polly, her stare was unwavering. I felt any moment she would call the police. A cordless phone lay atop the kitchenette's counter. She had enormous, black doll's eyes. Her hair-length matched Brett's. Were they twins?

She was thinner, looked slightly taller, and unbridled about wearing a short blue pajama top that barely concealed the soiled crotch of her white nylon panties.

On a much younger woman it would have looked erotic. I regarded the chair that matched the décor of the dining room, or whatever it was, hoping these hicks would offer me a seat.

"You look put out. Sit here," Brett said. "Hungry?"

Next stupid question.

"Yes I am, actually," I said, totally self-conscious about my prison uniform, which, come to think of it, wasn't that much of a give-away. It was gray and dull, with classic shirt pockets. I sat at the table and Polly finally spoke.

"Where you from, Mister?"

"Boston," I lied, hoping they'd never set foot there.

"Uh-huh," she said, open-mouthed, her lower lip wrapped over rotting teeth. She might've been pretty at one time.

"Yeah, I been on the road," I added, as if they'd been expecting me to fill in the blanks. "I'm on vacation and thought I'd venture out, see America."

"See America?" she asked. I felt like an idiot. Brett padded to the kitchenette and hovered over the stove. A minute later Polly served me a cold hunk of what looked like ham, and a fork on a plastic dish. It had been cut up so I could prong at it. Brett sat down across from me while Polly hovered behind him. "It's edible," Brett said, studying me like a surgeon.

"Oh my, he's too-" Polly began, then stopped. I stabbed at a pig piece and brought it to my mouth, so famished I ignored the rancid under-taste as I chewed and swallowed. There was an odor I couldn't place coming from somewhere in another room.

"We lack for a microwave, so excuse the nippy," Brett said. "You got any money?"

Oh, boy, here it comes—the inevitable segue to hard-core inquiries.

"Just some loose change," I said, hoping they wouldn't press the issue.

"Don't matter, does it, Brett?" this from Miss Thing. I could have kissed her. Her tone suggested a mild scolding.

"I'm guessin' you left your wallet in the car," Brett said.

"I did, matter of fact. I don't carry much on me as it is."

I focused on the meal in front of me. The color seemed 'off.' I could sense Polly's burning gaze. "How long've you guys been living here?" I asked, finessing a change of subject.

"So you left your car on the road, a ditch, what?" Polly asked.

"I, yeah, rolled it behind a billboard."

"Oh, smart move," she said, more to Brett.

"You got family?" Brett asked.

"I'm single." If I'd told them otherwise, they would sure as shit have wondered why I didn't take the wife along on my road trip.

"Single, huh?" He nodded his head back towards Polly. "Me and Polly? Ten years livin' in sin. I mean, the fug we need a piece a' paper to shack up? Right, baby?"

"Ten wonderful blessed years," Polly said, still staring at me.

"You guys planning on raising a family?"

"MAAA!!" a young voice screamed from behind a closed door.

"Lyon, you be quiet over there!" Polly said.

"Ly, get your butt in here!" Brett shouted. What I gathered to be the portal into their bedroom reeled open and a boy, maybe eight or nine, stood there, watching me. His black crew cut was spiky. The kid looked emaciated and his orange pajamas drooped over him as if it were disembodied. I flashed on an Auschwitz survivor I once saw in a photo.

"Lyon, say hello to your new best friend," Polly said.

I frowned. *New best friend?* Were they expecting me to adopt this mess?

Lyon shuffled towards me, his mouth a tight line. I wondered if his teeth were worse than Polly's. He had inherited his mother's enormous eyes and used them to study me as if I were a new pet.

"Who a' you?" he croaked.

"I'm… David."

He turned to Mom.

"Lyon, you be nice," she cautioned.

Lyon renewed his evaluation of me. "You smell."

"Lyon!" Polly barked.

"Well, he'll be fresh and clean soon enough, so don't you worry none, Ly," Brett assured him.

"Yup, he'll have a nice bath waiting for him soon's he finishes eating, son," Polly added. Lyon padded closer to me. A strong waft of perfume dropkicked my nostrils. What kind of mother anoints her son with perfume? I nearly gagged and scarfed down my final stab of ham.

The kid reached over to touch my arm and I twitched. He slid his hand along my triceps and

I began squirming in my seat. If I weren't so bone tired I would've bolted from this grotto in a flash.

"Lyon, 'nuff now. Stop," Polly said. "Go back to bed."

Lyon's hand pulled back and he about-faced.

"Go on," Polly insisted.

The boy, still close-mouthed, gave me one final over-the-shoulder look before scuffing back to his room. What a spoiled skinny brat. I smiled at Polly.

"He has your eyes."

No response.

Brett cleared his throat. "C'mon, uhh... David? That your name? Finish your meal."

I pushed away the plate. "Know something? Not really that hungry. Thanks just the same."

Yet another crossfire of glances traveled between Brett and Polly. Of all the places to hide out in. But then, what did I expect? What family lived like this?

"I'll run up a nice hot bath for you, David," Polly offered. "Would you like that?"

"Yep, get all that crud offa ya," Brett said.

Hell, yeah.

I felt clammy under my damp shirt, although I would've preferred a shower.

"Our shower doesn't work," Polly said, as if she'd read my mind. She turned and headed for the grimy-looking bathroom.

* * *

It turned out I could fit nicely into one of Brett's fresh plaid shirts, and his Dockers caressed my waistband like a glove. Polly, bless her brave heart, had washed my gray boxer shorts by hand and draped them over the kitchen's windowsill. So, with my crotch unfettered, I was primed for a decent night's sleep.

"We got us a cellar you can use to sleep in," Brett said.

No fucking way.

"The idea of sleeping in a cellar, Brett." I shook my head. "I dunno."

Who knew what lurked in a cellar. I thought of spiders and mice crawling over me on the wet floor. Brett's eyes went south. He looked slightly disappointed. He entered his bedroom, shut it behind him, and I could hear hushed whispers. I made out the words, "I can't find it, looked everywhere," coming from Polly. "It's just a piece of fabric, woman," Brett said. He came back out and gazed at me.

"You can use the guest room," he said, pointing to a half-open door. I wondered why he hadn't offered me the room in the first goddamn place. Special guests only? He went back inside. I approached the guest room. I groped for the light switch and flipped it up.

I almost screamed.

A mass of waterbugs fanned out east and west from the unkempt bed and scattered across the dingy white floor. I had never seen cockroaches that big. What amped up the horror meter were the leftovers splattered on the floor. They looked more like dried vomit. I'm not squeamish about upchuck, but those insects made my skin crawl. I backed away, trembling.

"Hey, Brett?"

Brett joined me in the foyer, frowning. "What's wrong?"

I pointed at the circus he called a guest room.

"Ohh, shit, yeah. I forgot to fumigate the sucker. Sorry about that," he said. "No avoiding the bastards, this bein' the sticks and all."

"I mean, Jesus Christ, Brett."

If only beggars *could* choose. But whatever, I opted to lie down on the dining room table. He shook his head. "Naw, listen. The cellar's got a nice clean cot. You can crash there. No bugs or vermin, I assure you."

I wanted to ask him why he hadn't mentioned the cot before, but I wouldn't push my luck. Besides, all I wanted was to sleep and then move on come dawn. I didn't look particularly dangerous, so hitching a ride seemed like a good idea.

I tensed as Brett turned on the cellar's garish overhead bulb. It reminded me of my prison cell. The floor was swept clean and the cot looked cozy and inviting. A shuttered window stood above it. The bars were vertical. No fan, of course. But I could live with the lack of ventilation.

"Okay, so, we good?" Brett asked.

"Much better, Brett. Thank you."

"We'll get some eggs in ya, then I'll walk you to where your car is. I toiled as a mechanic at one time."

I nodded. "Did you, really?" I asked, knowing full well I'd be long gone before he ever got around to waking up. No way I'd let myself oversleep. My mental alarm clock never failed me. "G'night, then."

Brett nodded, then turned and shut the door, its heavy metallic click a comforting sound.

Time to think. I sat on the cot and juggled my options. My cousin Felix, a bachelor, lived just off the border of this godforsaken town. Whatever ride

I snagged could take me to him. No! I would use the money; take a bus to New York. I had friends there, mostly potheads. Yeah, that sounded better.

I scoped out the tiny room and focused on the sheet-rocked wall across from me. It had a small, but not that small, door that reminded me of *Alice in Wonderland*. How peculiar.

I got up and stooped closer towards it. This door had a lock secured by a loose screw. I could easily knock it off its hinge. The smell was familiar. I sniffed and drew back, grimacing. Lysol? I noticed something else. There was a tiny scrawl etched on the upper part of the door. I inched my face closer. The tiny words forced me to squint:

Left-overs.

Then I heard a scratching noise. I looked behind me. The window? No. Please God, not another fucking roach. I dipped my head and gazed into the cot's underside. Only my battered shoes occupied the space.

That scratching sound again.

So faint I couldn't make out its geography. I waited, still as a rock.

Another scratch. Louder, more intense.

It was coming from behind the little door. I tapped on it and the scratching became louder still, more frenetic. Did these people stuff an animal in there?

Common sense told me to back off, slip onto the cot, and drift into much-needed sleep. But the scratching persisted. It would keep me awake.

A pig, maybe?

I had to know.

I pulled off the lock and swung open the door. A chalky human face stared back at me, his mouth stuffed with a rag, his eyes wide and pleading. The overhead bulb illuminated the obscenity below the face. The 'leftover' had one right arm. His other limbs were gone. Sweet Jesus. How long had he been in there? I stumbled back, fighting down the impulse to shout. I stared at the prisoner, my ass frozen to the floor. The sound of a telephone ringing upstairs broke the spell.

I could hear Brett's muffled voice but couldn't make out the wrangle. Screw sleep. I pulled my left shoe over my right foot and had to start over. The butchered man began making strange noises from his throat. Any other time I would've pulled him out, stayed with him, and called for help.

"I'm sorry," I said, and sprang for the door. No go. I throttled its knob and shook it violently. Then it hit me, right then and there.

Chef. The diner. Special pies. Chef calling Brett. "Is he there? Fuckin' A."

So subtle, Chef's off-hand remark about a house I *might* come across, knowing damn well I'd be looking for it.

I pounded the door like a madman, my heart pumping acid. "Brett!" Top of my lungs. Feet clomped down the stairs. The moment the door clicked open the captive squirmed out of the hole, plopped onto the floor and slithered towards me, using his arm like an oar.

I was too petrified to scream. The door whooshed open and I couldn't pull back in time to avoid the hand towel Brett shoved against my nose.

Darkness shrouded me and I could feel my eyes rolling up my brain.

* * *

As I came to, morning sunlight streamed across the ceiling. The stench of chloroform lingered. I felt a pressure in my arms and legs and looked down at my naked, prone body. I'd been roped like a calf. Naturally I couldn't speak because my mouth had been gagged. Brett and Polly stood watch over me, their heads tilted as if they couldn't figure their next course of action. I ducked and bobbed my head for them to remove the rag from my mouth. Nada.

They just stared at my twitching body.

"He needs fattenin' up," Polly said, as if I were Lyon.

"How do you fatten up a man too scared to eat?" Brett replied, scratching the jungle under his chin.

"Oh, he'll eat," Polly insisted. "He'll eat, cuz, if he don't eat," she bent slightly towards me, making sure I'd hear, "he'll end up in the dumpster as fly food."

I jerked spasmodically and nearly toppled off the cot.

"Take it easy, David," Brett said, in a gentle tone.

Polly went to the door and called out. "Lyon? Come down here!"

As they waited, Brett fished out of his pocket the cash Chef had given me. It was never meant for me to spend; I knew that now. Lyon shuffled in just as Brett handed Polly a twenty.

"Junk food. Lots of it. And a whole chicken."

Lyon loomed closer, looking me over like I was pre-cut prime.

"Can't be helped, David," Brett said. "Our boy here's a special case. Got a taste for it ever since he chowed down a dead baby some bitch left in the woods nearby. Still fresh enough to cook. We was broke then, and desperate. Just eighteen months old, Lyon was. Animal food just wasn't the same after that. Took a liking to your kind. Hope you understand."

I understood. It was God's punishment for my unlawful deeds, for my arrogance and my stupidity and my fear of serving time. Brett grabbed the one-armed prisoner, who began howling, and shoved him back into the hole, slamming its door shut. Lyon, meanwhile, drifted closer towards me until his face hovered above mine.

"Lyon? You like what you see?" Polly asked, as if she'd just given him a Christmas present.

The boy opened his mouth for the first time and grinned.

His sharpened canines looked huge.

THE CROWS IN THE ATTIC
By Carlton Herzog

T he old bag had a thing for dolls. So much so that they overflowed her beat-up, rusted shopping cart. Since she was homeless, she probably considered them her *de facto* family. As relatives go, even makeshift ones, they probably weren't half bad insofar as they probably didn't complain about her smell. When you live on the street for any length of time, you are enveloped in a distinct, noisome vapor that can peel the chrome off a trailer hitch and make a nun go blind. Your constant exposure to sewer gas, urine, feces, garbage and sweat builds up in the pores over the years like money in a bank account and then releases itself into the air as aerosol interest nobody wants.

I wanted to feel sorry for her. I really did. I thought about warning her about the dolls. But I knew better. For her to be carting that many around, they must have surely gotten inside her head and turned her into a familiar. They are insidious little pricks they are, always looking for the renegade human to help them do their dirty work.

I live and die by the credo that the only good doll is the one that is never made. Or is made, but is melted into a puddle of burning, bubbling plastic. That means I take extreme measures to rid the world of the infestation. Like that crone.

I caught up to her in the alley late on a Friday night. She had parked her cart and had arranged he dolls in a protective circle around her sleeping bag. I came up quiet. The dolls, grimy and oily as shit, watched me with their beady unmoving eyes. But they were talking inside my head the whole time.

I wasn't surprised. The word was out in the doll community about me: Killer of Dolls. The police were not my fans either, because I made sure the dolls' familiars couldn't backslide once I had purged them of their evil little armies.

So, the dolls cursed me up and down. But I didn't let it get to me. I swung my bat and brained her once, twice, three times a bag lady. As she lay there with the blood coming out of every orifice in her head, I could hear the dolls screaming in mine about how I was going to hell.

That didn't bother me either. I put on my special gloves to keep them from burning me with their invisible fire, then tossed them all into the dumpster. I threw in the gasoline, lit the whole thing up and had me a devil doll roast. I skedaddled when I heard the sirens.

The invisible hand of Satan is everywhere in the form of dolls. I am one of the few with the mystical acuity to see it. But while I am tuned into deeper realities that make me privy to great truths, I cannot prove them. I am, as it were, seeing in fire but working in clay.

The average person looks at a doll and sees nothing more than a toy or a collectible. They have no reason to look deeper or to suspect anything nefarious. Given the level of manufacturing sophistication they represent, the level of detail, so nuanced and granular, one could look at them with a measure of pride for how far we have come from smearing paint on cave walls in France.

But the average person lives on a placid island of ignorance surrounded by shallow self-reflecting waters. In this post-literate visual age, people don't want to look deeply into anything beyond their phones. The act of reading, which sharpens the mind the way exercise sharpens the body, is studiously avoided. If you want to hide truths from someone, just stick them in a book.

It is that gross incuriousness that has opened the door to the dolls. It has let them seize control of toy factories and multiply like rabbits, so they are in every home and shop, watching, waiting for their moment.

I know this because I can see them move. Not in the sense of gross motion we humans we enjoy, but in the subtle nearly imperceptible shifts of head and eye position one such as myself, endowed as I am with microscopic visual acuity, can detect.

I am not the only who has ever been gifted with such talent. The alchemists knew from firsthand observation that dolls were not what they appear to be. The first mention of dolls as more than mere miniature facsimiles of the human form appears in Count Pierre Lafleur's

Et in Dulcibus Aquis Salsae Repositoria Daemonum (On the Haunts and Repositories of Demons), 1676. Lafleur observed that the very idea for dolls came from the devil himself—to mock God for having created man in His image and to house wayward spirits, namely, those demons who will not bow down, even to the Prince of Darkness. That demographic, he asserted, arose from the offspring of Adam, the first man, after he was booted out of Eden and spent his days fornicating with evil spirits.

In 1880, Cardinal Degas of the Rome Diocese wrote an expansive treatise on the secret hiding places of demons: *Furtivum Latibulus Daemonia.* He gave doll owners and shopkeepers specific methods for determining if a doll was haunted. One could, he wrote, sprinkle holy water or place a crucifix on the suspicious doll. If an evil spirit possessed it, such contact would induce a theophobic response ranging from a mere shudder or tremble to the outright fleeing of the doll from the presence of the holy materials. He suggested that reciting the Lord's Prayer or the Beatitudes in the presence of the doll could induce the same response.

Supposedly, Cardinal Degas spent his last days hunting down and exorcising demon- possessed dolls all over Europe. As the story goes, he came to a doll shop in Frankfurt, Germany. The owner was extremely reluctant to let the Cardinal perform his exorcism rituals. He even went so far as to have the constable escort the Cardinal and his retinue out of town.

However, the Cardinal was not to be denied. He made his way back into the town, broke into the shop, and, judging from the materials laid out when they found him in the morning, attempted to exorcise the demons he believed haunted all the dolls in the shop.

The shop owner found the Cardinal the next morning lying in a pool of his own blood. His head and arms had been torn clean off, and the rest of him hung upside down. The dolls themselves were free of blood, so suspicion fell on the shopkeeper. He was hanged in the village square.

But none is more famous in demon doll hunting circles than the great Prussian scientist Baron Karl Von Hertzog. In his famous treatise *Auf Die Vernichtung der Teufell Puppen* (On the Extermination of Devil Dolls), the Baron describes in intimate detail the number and types of demon-haunted dolls that he captured and incinerated. He also mentions the number and occupations of familiars that he poisoned, shot and stabbed.

After reading Von Hertzog as a young girl, I knew my calling in life could be no other than a ruthless destroyer of haunted dolls and if need be their familiars. At the tender age of 14, I lured a friend of mine into the woods, encouraging her to bring her hellish plastic companion on the hike. I bashed her head in with a stone. Then I burned the doll until it was nothing more than a mass of melted plastic.

I could hear it talking to me in my head. Taunting me, cursing me. Telling me that I would burn in hell for what I had done.

I told no one of the crime. When the police interviewed me, I told them I hadn't seen the treacherous cunt: *No, I haven't seen her. I don't know why anyone would want to hurt her or her beautiful doll.*

Cunning, you need cunning to outsmart the dolls and their demons. And you can't be too careful what you say because their traitorous familiars are everywhere.

When I killed—and I did it often—I didn't think of it as murder. I thought of it as a necessary cleansing of evil from the world. But the more I did it, the more I feared the dolls. I'm not some random dupe or victim to them. I am the one and only, not to be imitated or outdone, living, breathing doll-killer.

To be sure, my truths may seem like unbuttoned musings of a fevered imagination. But have not all the great truths begun in such a humble and insubstantial way? Were that not so, young Albert Einstein would not have pictured himself traveling on a beam of light and then gone on in adulthood to give us the Special Theory of Relativity.

Like Einstein, I picture myself riding on a beam of light, one that that sheds light on a dark truth, namely, that dolls are the unhallowed repositories of demon spirits. And I am therefore compelled to maintain a healthy fear of them.

My doctors say there's nothing healthy about that fear. They call it pediophobia. They say it comes from the uncanny valley syndrome where human facsimiles induce feelings of fear and revulsion in disturbed people.

My doctors all concur that my so-called phobia stems from my mother's and sister's obsessive doll collecting and my father's side hustle as a ventriloquist. I submit that there is no more evidence for that theory than there is for my own, which holds that hollow objects are haunted by demon hordes. But the arc of truth has a history of being bent toward explanations that are comforting and convenient. Alas, mine disturbs the frail and unsettles the weak.

Inevitably, the truth comes out, though not without a fight. The idea of a geocentric universe where everything revolves around the earth is certainly more endearing than that proposed by Copernicus. But egocentricity eventually went the way of the dinosaur. Why? Because the heart of truth is disproof and self-correction.

As you can see from my knowledge of physics, I have a well-ordered, rational mind, one that takes a dim view of the psychiatric profession, the reach of which exceeds its grasp. One idiot thought it would be good therapy to bring a baby doll to one of my sessions. I went ballistic and started screaming. Not because she had brought in a doll *per se,* but because that doll was bursting with demonic energy. The hellish negativity radiated off it in waves and nearly made my skull burst.

I grabbed it away and ripped off its arms and head. Then I threw a chair through the window to create an opening and then hurled the doll bits out the hole in the glass. When Doctor Cyclops, or whatever that asshole's name was, tried to subdue me, I stabbed her in the leg with her own pen. I would have stabbed the bitch again had not the receptionist pulled me off her. Lucky for her, the stupid cow didn't file charges because I would have slit her throat if she had. Why? Because she was a collaborator with the dolls. All those good intentions and professional demeanor baloney were just a cover for her being a fucking familiar.

They committed me to the Trenton Psychiatric Hospital with all the other fruitcakes. They said I had become too disassociated from reality to be allowed to roam free. To prove that I didn't belong there, I spent my time tormenting the other patients. Like the cacomorphobics—you know, the wackos who are afraid of fat people. The wacko cacos not only think that fat people will try to eat them and but also believe that the bellies of fat people are full of hungry monsters composed solely of food. Food babies. How nutty is that?

Not any nuttier than collecting dolls, I can tell you. They even have a name for doll collecting: plangonology. Can you believe that doll collecting is branded a discipline of learned study, an ology if you will, as if it stands on equal footing with other hard sciences? Is there no end to our semantic madness?

Idioms notwithstanding, I hate doll collectors as much as I hate dolls; I guess that makes me plangonologophobic.

I have heard all the goofy explanations as to why people collect dolls. They do it to recapture their childhood, or substitute for live offspring or to fulfill a love of fashion, or to make money—the list goes on.

But if you ask me, they do it from an irrational fear of life. The dolls create a comfort zone, a faux reality where good guys always wear white hats and win; the world is calm, orderly and predictable, and the collector is always in control.

What are dolls but the illusion of rationality in an irrational world? Dolls stay put. They do and wear what they're told. They don't sass you or change their minds at the spur of the moment. They don't steal or kill or borrow the car. They don't cheat on you. They are fetishes for weak spirits to endure the harsh reality of day-to-day existence.

Doll collectors give me the heebie-jeebies. They tend to be anal retentive and obnoxiously committed to maintaining a regimented lifestyle. I speak from experience. Both my mother and sister would have had no problem following Hitler. I can see them in my head at one of his famous rallies. Then goose-stepping to Paris and beyond with all the other animatronic control freaks bent on world domination.

But I digress. The doctors kept me isolated from the other screwballs. Good thing. I spotted some of the dumbasses carrying therapy dolls around with them. They even talked to them. How stupid is that? You know those demons were putting crazy ideas in their already crazy heads.

I can imagine what the dolls were saying to them:

Hey, nutty, when you get out of here, go find a gun shop and get you an automatic rifle. Relax, there's no background checks in this state. Go take that rifle—make sure you get plenty of ammo—find you a mall and have at it. God needs more people in heaven, and he wants you to get them for him.

Those nut ward nitwits would not have enough sense to question the career advice coming from a doll. Why? Because they don't know the difference between fantasy and reality. For the record, I do know the difference between fact and fiction. I resent the implication that I am some drooling lunatic suitable for a straitjacket and a padded room. But that is ever the case for those gifted with the second sight, the ones who can see what lies behind the veil of the mundane.

After I left the nuthouse, I went back home to live with my mother, my two brothers and sister. The boys had action figures and my sister had Lillys and Donnas. They were told to keep them out of sight whenever I was around, lest I suffer another breakdown.

Mind you, I didn't want to live there. But necessity makes strange bedfellows of us all. If I had stayed on that nut ward any longer, I would have killed someone. I didn't have any stomach for living on the street. I had tried it once and had my fill of eating from dumpsters and panhandling. Drugs were not my thing. Nor was doing tricks, only to be slapped around by a pimp or beaten to a pulp by a John. Nor did the prospect of being cut down by AIDS sit high on my street to-do list.

Of course, I did not forget that I was in enemy territory. So, I bided my time and waited. I slept fitfully or not at all. Although I had never seen a doll walk or make a large mechanical gesture on its own, I didn't rule that out as a possibility. I would lie awake at night and listen for any suspicious activity, such as a creaky door or floorboard, or the pitter-patter of little plastic feet.

I started collecting sharp objects—knives, screwdriver, scissors—as well as a hammer, a hatchet and makeshift strangulation wire. I wanted to be ready to dismember any would-be doll assassins and doll collaborators irrespective of human affiliations. I knew that if any members of my family had been co-opted by the power of hell, then it was up to me to liberate them from this existence. By liberate, I mean strangle, behead, impale, stab, and chop before they could under orders from those plasticine princes and princesses of darkness do the same to me.

But even as I prepared for the inevitable battle between good and evil, I comforted myself with the notion that I had three hot meals and a cot, and all the Prime binge watching my soul could swallow. Besides, my siblings and parents worked all day, so I had the house to myself for most the day. Hence, I was free to indulge in whatever wackiness moved me, no matter how perverse or pointless.

It was during one of those self-indulgent sessions that I developed a craving for hard liquor. I burned through what little there was in my father's liquor cabinet but wanted more. So, like any other lost soul possessed by the demon alcohol, I went where angels feared to tread: my sister's doll-abundant room, where I knew she had put some money away for a rainy day.

She kept her door key under a vase in the hall. I retrieved it and entered the room. Not one of the dolls made the slightest gesture to stop me. But they watched me with a laser-like intensity. I could feel the potential energy in those little monsters gathering itself a coruscating aura of evil, pulsing in all the fractured colors of the rainbow and emanating as a colorful kaleidoscope of evil intent.

The little plasticine shits spoke to me in a mephitic chorus of tiny voices that shouted in my head: *So, we meet at last Cassandra. You are a bold one coming into our lair, daring to profane our sacred place. We have reserved a*

special place in hell for you when this is all over.
You might as well give up now, for the outcome is
foreordained. You are damned and belong to us.
There is nothing you can do or say that will change
that.

I was not to be intimidated. I told them to "Go
fuck yourselves." Then I hunted around and found
the money. I headed straight for the liquor store
and bought a jug of Tennessee whiskey and some
wine coolers to wash it down.

I got good and smashed. The booze, as it often
did, gave me a strong dose of liquor courage and
whiskey muscles. I toyed with the idea of throwing
every single doll in the house into the garbage
barrel out back and letting the purifying effects of
gasoline-fueled fire send all those evil spirits back
to whence they had come. Before I could, my sister
arrived home, followed on her heels by my mother
and brother.

My sister, coy bitch that she is, didn't take long
to see that I had filched her cash. To pay me back
in the cruelest way possible, she called me into her
room. When I came to the door, she grabbed my
arm and swung me onto the floor. Then she
screamed, "Thieving bitch!" slammed the door,
and then locked it from the outside.

I was trapped with an army of Lillys and
Donnas. To my sister, her little judo throw meant
nothing more than tweaking what she saw as an
annoying phobia. To me, she had tossed me into
the lion's den.

I flipped.

I went crazy the way I did in the shrink's office.
The dolls, for their part, taunted me, cursed me,
demanded that I slit my own throat or throw myself
out the third-floor window.

That sent me into a berserker rage. I pulled open the window and went to grab the dolls to hurl them out the window. But they were fiery hot to the touch. And when I looked at them, they were glowing with an eldritch flame.

Nevertheless, I used a towel to cover my hand and began unceremoniously hurling them out the window, even as they persisted in their raucous anger. My head began to pound as if someone were driving railroad spikes into my skull. Somehow, they were hurting me without touching me in the same way they were talking to me without moving their lips.

I didn't stop until the last one lay on the lawn. I was surprised that the fire they burned with when I tossed them out the window had not singed so much as a blade of grass or gave off any vestigial smoke that it was out.

By now my sister knew what I was about. She came charging into the room, screaming at me, "Lunatic bitch! I'll kill you for this!"

That was the last straw. The dolls had been too lively for her not to notice. Obviously, she was a familiar who clearly meant to hurt me, so I drove her sewing shears into her eye as she charged me. I drew them out as she staggered around the room clutching her left eye, and then promptly drove them in as deep as I could to her right eye. With that, she collapsed and bled out on the floor.

My mother stood at the doorway holding one of her precious Russian nesting dolls. I knew that she had to die as well. I pulled the shears from my sister's bloody face and made for my mother. But she was not infirm. In fact, she had cat-like reflexes, no doubt a reward for being an apostate to righteousness as a familiar for those fucking demon dolls. She ran down the stairs and out the door.

I ran after her. The chase moved into the street. We weaved in and out of cars as shocked drivers and pedestrians watched in horror. One elderly man got in my way and grabbed my arm. I stabbed him twice in the chest and continued the pursuit.

There was no doubt in mind that my mother had the benefit of some mephitic adrenalin being piped into her system via mystical means at her doll's insistence. How else could she be sprinting away from me like an Olympic runner when she had just celebrated her fiftieth birthday? Traitorous old bitch.

The chase wended its way toward a strip mall. She ran through the parking lot with me in hot pursuit, shouting imprecations as I went. When she came to a coffee shop, she ran inside, through the kitchen and out the back. I followed. The staff and customers stared in disbelief.

She ran down the alley. She hadn't gotten far when three thugs stopped her. I don't know if they wanted to rape her or rob her or both. Not that it mattered. They took one look at my furious looking blood-spattered face and clothes, as well as the blood-soaked shears, and ran for the hills.

My mother had no intention of going down without a fight, hell-spawn that she had become. She picked up a board and held it up to swing at my head. But first, she tried to get me to lower my guard.

"Cassandra, what in God's name possessed you to murder your sister and attack me? You need help. You're obviously intoxicated. Put down the scissors, and let's go home and sort this out. I know that you're afraid of the dolls. I'll get rid of them. So we can put all this behind us."

I was not about to be taken in by her maternal charade of protective solicitude.

"You think you can fool me with your little act. You and Mary are in cahoots with the devil and his army of tiny nightmares. So, I'm not going anywhere with you. I'm going to finish what I started and end you once and for all. Then I'm going to burn that devil's den and all the dolls in it to the ground."

"I'm your mother. I would never consciously do anything to hurt you. Cassandra, honey, the dolls aren't alive. That's all in your head—inadvertent backwash from overexposure to mine and your sister's collecting and your father's work. You can see that, can't you? You have to know by now that you're sick and need help."

I balked. *What if she's right? What if I have gone around the bend and the whole thing is nothing but a bad horror movie playing inside my head?*

I was about to drop the shears and give my mother a hug. But the doll she was holding, the one with all those other dolls inside it, started talking inside my head.

Mommy is tricky like us. Of course, we're alive. How else could you hear us in your mind if we weren't? Frankly, we don't care if you kill her. After all, she's been betraying you all these years, sleeping with the enemy so to speak. If we were you, then we would kill them all just to be sure. Don't you want to be sure?

I couldn't argue with their logic. I don't know what my mother intended. But I made like

I was going to give her a hug. When I stood in front of her, I stabbed her in the one eye, and before she could react, I did the same to the other. I picked up the Russian nesting doll and carried it back home for the bonfire.

It was some blaze. When I was sure it was going strong, I slipped away. Now I live on the run from the law and the dolls. Every now and then, I burn down a toy store or kill a doll collector to keep things on an even keel. So and such is life in the uncanny valley.

DEATH BROKER
By Lisa Pais

F ilming had gone smoothly so far. Establishing shots of the Grand Canyon were taken while the sky was still a veritable paint box of red, orange, gold, and purple. Hollywood could not have created a more picturesque backdrop, and the boys upstairs agreed, stating a green screen and CGI wouldn't cut it. This was why Jonah and his production crew were out here in the first place instead of some air-conditioned sound stage back in LA. And why now, Jonah remained outdoors while the big wigs relaxed in air-conditioned comfort in a tricked-out trailer sipping imported beer and noshing on shrimp cocktail.

They were on location to film the final episode of *Death Watch*, the highest-rated show in *necrotainment*. Jonah didn't know if they had a real shot at an Emmy but then, that wasn't the point.

This was Jonah's baby. If things went well, he'd get a good percentage of the glory. If they went south, he'd get all the blame.

God, it's hotter than the Devil's ball sac out here, Jonah thought miserably for the hundredth time today. Even at this late hour, it was still hovering at 102 degrees, with the heat rising from the ground and burning through the soles of his shoes, good Italian loafers. The leather now smelling faintly of spicy capicola. *Can leather melt?* Another hour and he might find out.

Cameras had been strategically placed, all that was needed now was the oversized super pea shooter which was set to launch a man into oblivion. Hell, they'd even strapped a GoPro onto the poor bastard's helmet. Not that he'd need a helmet, but it made for good showmanship, in a twisted kind of irony. They had a few drones in the air too. A second camera crew waited on the other side of the canyon, while a third had set up camp in the basin along with a retrieval crew. They would capture the spectacle from every angle.

Jonah checked the time, turning at the sound of approaching footsteps. It was the show's host, Dural Fontaine, his crisp white polo shirt a nice contrast to his tanned features. He held out a bottle of mineral water to Jonah.

"Thought you could use this," Dural said. "Gotta stay hydrated."

"Thanks. All set there, Dural?" Jonah asked.

"Just going over a few last-minute facts."

"Don't sweat it, you've got this in the bag."

"Sure, sure," Dural said flashing his easy trademark smile, the one that got him this gig in the first place. "No need to memorize lines when I have this," he added with a wink and raised his tablet, conveniently blocking his view of the cannon and all it represented, as it was being wheeled into position. The human cannonball had finally arrived.

Most people wouldn't have noticed, but to Jonah, the small tell couldn't have been plainer. That, and the fact the host never stopped moving as if to avoid dwelling on the night's big event. Dural's official age was 37, only a few years older than Jonah, though he'd gone through several more cycles than Jonah, who at 33 and with only 3 cycles under his belt, was seen as a young buck. Meaning, Dural had been around long enough to remember the time *Before* and was witness to the cure. He'd enjoyed all the advantages that came as a result, but he also understood the cost and because of this, was often most sensitive just before the director yelled action. Yet he never broke character or his contract. Admirable. Though truth be told, Jonah had felt somewhat unsettled himself lately, the feeling heightened by the day's heat.

Jonah turned his attention back to the set. His career trajectory tied to this moment, everything had to be perfect. The director's voice was transmitted through Jonah's headset.

"Places everyone, we go in two minutes," he announced. With filming about to begin, Jonah stepped out of the frame and Dural took his post in front of the cannon. Makeup artists descended upon the man for a few last-minute touch-ups, though he stood camera ready as always.

Jonah watched the monitor, things looked to be on track. Tasteless in its extravagance, an over the top spectacle for certain, but this is what television had become. *It's what the audience wants. Numbers don't lie.* Words to live by according to his boss.

"Cue the dancers," he heard the director call out. The screen panned over to a group of scantily clad women and a few men undulating in a tightly choreographed routine. Next came the acrobats. Jonah had wanted a couple of gymnasts from the last Olympics but including children seemed inappropriate. Clowns and jugglers in the background rounded out the ensemble. The circus was in full swing. The theme old school, in the vein of P.T. Barnum. They'd even brought in a tiger. Jonah had wanted an elephant too but it was much more expensive to rent and would've blown the already sky-high budget. He needed to keep an eye on profits. "Stay in the black," another quote from his boss. *Probably tattooed to his ass.* Still, Jonah had no doubt this would bring in a huge payday. Competition amongst sponsors for prime air time had been a blood sport of its own.

The camera focused in on the host and master of ceremonies, Dural Fontaine, and the director gave the green light to begin.

"Good evening America, we are coming to you live from the beautiful Grand Canyon where we have a very special event for you. Do you see that cannon behind me? That, folks, is the original Red Rocket Launcher from 2008, restored to its former pristine condition, with a little something extra added. You'd never know this baby was 200 years old, and tonight we will be shooting a man out of it."

Just then Jonah heard a voice in his ear, the panic seeping through the headset.

"I've changed my mind, I don't wanna do it."
Who the hell was that?

The crackle of static garbled the man's next words, but his point was clear. The next voice that came through was that of the young Production Assistant, clear and urgent and somehow sounding equally distressed.

"What do we do?"

Fuck. Whose brilliant idea was it to mic the bastard? Jonah pinched his forehead trying to relieve the tension then tapped the thin wire and spoke into the mouthpiece.

"Why isn't he sedated? They pumped enough tranquilizers into the man to put a grizzly bear to sleep." Jonah waited. "Well?" Still no answer. "Dammit!" He didn't have time for screw-ups right now. Time was money.

Jonah headed toward the set, but the PA—a kid of no more than 25 and no cycles yet—was suddenly in his face.

"What do we do?"

"What the hell do you mean, *what do we do*? We're set to launch in less than a minute. We go. Light the fuse!"

"But...but," the PA stuttered.

It wasn't the PA's job to *actually* light the fuse. They had brought in a licensed executioner from the state pen for that. The assistant, eyes wide and all color draining from his face, stood frozen. Jonah glanced at the director. Should they cut and give the human cannonball another sedative?

The director shrugged.

Well shit... Jonah sighed resignedly.

"For Christ's sake, the bullet's in the chamber. Do your job!" Jonah barked the order, the PA taking the brunt of his frustration.

As for the doomed man, he had been wrapped up like a mummy, not only so they could stuff him in with a bit more ease, but also to keep him from being burned. That cannon had been outside for less than twenty minutes, but the metal was hotter than a frying pan pulled from the sun's asshole itself. It wouldn't make for good television to melt him like a marshmallow before launch. A significant part of the platform for this show rested on the audience votes. The higher the points, the more money the family would be compensated. The compensation, of course, being tied to the thrill of the execution; style over gruesomeness. Though Jonah wasn't convinced there was a difference.

This episode was especially important as it marked the 100th anniversary of *The Cure*. Commemorated in much the same way as America once celebrated the 4th of July, a holiday no longer observed having been preempted. Death had been vanquished. Yet here it was only a couple of generations in and already, the thirst had returned. Death brought meaning. Death brought purpose. It was also important for population control. When the cure was first distributed, it had only been to a select few until a successful lobbyist group had gotten a bill passed that the cure should be for all. The serum was distributed. Everyone was inoculated. The problem now was resources. A moratorium had been placed on breeding, which helped, but it wasn't enough. There were still the occasional accidents, murders, and suicides, more suicides than you'd think. But even that was not enough to reduce the footprint mankind had left behind.

So, a lottery system had been implemented.

Time seemed to have frozen. No one moved, all eyes were on Jonah. A sedative would cost precious minutes. Glancing back at the trailer, Jonah gave the signal. He wanted this over with. The director hesitated then nodded and everything was suddenly in motion.

The fuse burned fast. Then bam, the explosion rang in his ears, temporarily deafening him as all sound was suddenly sucked from the atmosphere like a super-sonic vacuum engulfing him in a cone of silence. The ground shook and he stumbled backward from the blast, arms flailing but he stayed on his feet. The human cannonball shot through the sky like a comet, lighting up the darkness with its trail of red and gold streaking through the night sky.

Jonah hung his head, an overwhelming sense of dread settling over him, invading his body like a flu virus from days of old. The sound of running and cries of "Whoo-Hoo" came from behind.

"Did you see that?" asked Jonah's boss, Nolan Jeffers, who, in his exuberance wrapped a beefy arm around Jonah's neck and put him in a headlock, mussed his hair and then released him. "Course ya did." Followed by a hearty thump on the back. "Looked like a rocket."

"Oh man, he shot out of there like a scud missile," Dickie Eldridge, professional ass kisser, chimed in with the enthusiasm of a kid blowing up a bottle rocket and with just as much concern.

"We should've strapped one on his back and shot him toward Iran," his boss suggested, sounding very much like the overgrown frat boy he was. "That was totally awesome!" Another round of high fives ensued amongst the gathering crowd. "It's a wrap people, party at LaRedo Jim's!"

Amidst cheers and applause, Jonah turned his attention back to the cannon.

"Hey, Jonah, where are you going?" His boss called out.

"Gotta check on something."

"Well hurry up, don't wanna be late. This party is going to be da bomb!" He said and head-butted the air in triumph then strode toward the waiting limo hovering two feet off the ground.

Jonah found the PA. The only other person present who seemed to remember that a man had just died.

"What happened?" Jonah asked noticing the red mark under the man's right eye. "Who did this to you?" The PA appeared to be in a state of shock, eyes focused on something unseen in the distance.

"He changed his mind. He didn't want to do this."

"Who lit the fuse?"

The young man blinked, then slowly shook his head. "He changed his mind," the PA said again, his voice barely above a whisper.

Jonah sighed. "Come on Ron, let's get out of here. There's nothing more we can do." The young man said nothing but turned and followed Jonah back towards the tent.

* * *

Jonah hesitated at the door, trying to come up with an excuse that his boss would buy. He had no desire to attend a party; there was nothing to celebrate. Still, as the producer of the show, he had to make an appearance. It was expected, especially when you work for the biggest network on the planet. Sure, he'd agreed to take on this assignment, had practically begged for it even. So why the overwhelming melancholy? He'd grown up with the lottery system. The concept always remote and a little abstract. With no bearing on him personally, he'd never given it much thought.

"Hey, hotshot, buy me a drink?" Marina sidled up to him, looking perky in every way. She was a goddess. "I hear congratulations are in order. Word is, the show got picked up for another season. You're on your way."

"News travels fast," Jonah answered.

"There he is," his boss called out to him from across the crowded room. A thick haze of smoke gave everything a dreamlike quality. Jonah couldn't remember a time when smoking wasn't legal or ubiquitous—though, before the cure, he'd heard it had pretty much gone the way of the dinosaur. Cigarettes used to kill people. Of course, they weren't smoking ordinary cigarettes these days, not when much more interesting varieties were available along with a new name. Pleasure sticks could give you good dreams, enhance your sex life, and make you look and perform better.

Jonah drifted toward his boss. His only thought was to get through the evening and then home. From the look of it, most people remained in costume, even the clowns, which gave the party a weird 'what happens in Vegas' vibe, though they were in Arizona. He hated the desert. He wanted to get back to L.A. preferring the shiny buildings, the plastic, the hustle, the crowded freeways, even the smog. To him, it represented the norm.

"There's the man of the hour," his boss said and took a drag off his cigarette, then exhaled a stream of neon purple smoke. "Candy, Krissy, show this man a good time." One of the glamazons, Jonah didn't know which one, Candy maybe, hooked a slender arm into his.

"Enjoy tonight," his boss said with a wink. "When we get back to the office, we're going to do some serious brainstorming. We need to up our game. We've got eight more episodes to produce."

* * *

Three days later, Jonah and the rest of the creative team were back in L.A., already seated, when his boss, Nolan Jeffers, strolled into the conference room, looking cheerily confident, causing Jonah's stomach to contract.

"Well boys, *and* girl," he said with a nod toward the only female member of this particular team. "We did well in Arizona, pulling in our highest ratings yet." He paused as if waiting for applause. If Dural Fontaine ever came down ill and couldn't perform, Nolan Jeffers could step in without missing a beat. Might even do a better job. Nolan could sell shoes to a legless man.

"But we can do better," Nolan continued, "and we've got the chance. The network has signed on for another eight episodes. I'd like to thank everyone here for their efforts and a special thanks to you Jonah. Job well done."

"Here, here" and cries of "congratulations" were uttered.

Jonah choked back the rising bile in his throat. No question, Jonah was driven and had done all sorts of things while climbing that ladder of success. He'd even joked that he'd kill if necessary. Who knew he'd eat those words? Jonah didn't know if there really was a Hell but if so, he'd purchased a one-way ticket, first class. Good thing he'd been inoculated with the immortality serum.

"Let's review the footage, shall we," his boss said, though it was hardly a question. The wall screen lit up and there they were, back in Arizona. Most of the crew hadn't watched the final cut. The one that had streamed online and into every household in America as well as the major markets around the civilized and maybe even the uncivilized world. How had humanity sunk so low? Worst of all, he had played a major part in its descent. He deserved to be shot out of a cannon.

The last frame went black. Nolan sat on the edge of the conference table, a tactic employed to make him look like he was part of the team, just one of the guys.

"You all know what a fluffer is, right?" The room went silent then Dickie raised a hand. Jonah rolled his eyes. *Christ, we're not in school.* His boss raised a brow in surprise, and then nodded to Dickie. Apparently, this wasn't a rhetorical question after all.

"Fluffers work in the pornographic film industry. It's their job to keep the guy hard between takes."

"Give that man a gold star." Nolan pointed, then paused. "You can put your hand down now, Dickie. Though you might be our next fluffer." Nolan laughed, so did the rest of the room. Lambs being led to slaughter. He had their undivided attention.

"Pop quiz people. Why the three-ring circus?" Nolan stood up, now assuming the role of professor. "We were putting on a show. The acrobats, jugglers, and clowns were there to whip up the audience. Get them excited about what they were about to witness."

"Wouldn't that be more like a hype-man rather than a fluffer? Like one of those rapper dudes?" Dickie asked. My God, the man didn't know when to keep his mouth shut.

"Yes, Dickie. That is the purpose of the performers. I guess you didn't understand the analogy. Perhaps Jonah could explain it better. Shed some light. What do you say, Jonah?"

"Something was missing?" Jonah answered, not liking the direction the conversation seemed to be heading.

"Ding, ding, ding. We have a winner." The rest of the room looked on, clearly confused as just moments ago they were being congratulated on a job well done. Nolan stood up now.

"Do you know why people like NASCAR?"

Jonah could feel the muscles in Dickie's arm twitch and elbowed him to keep quiet. This time, the question truly was rhetorical; the boss was about to make his point.

"People don't care who wins. Well, maybe a little, especially if they've got money riding on the outcome. But the real reason they watch is the danger, albeit vicarious danger. Secretly, or maybe not so secretly, what they really want to see is a crash. There's nothing more spectacular than when one of those cars zooming around the track at a buck seventy spins out of control, careens into the barrier and causes a big accident. Bonus points if it ends in a fatality." Nolan looked over the room as if daring anyone to dispute him. "Blood lust people. It's all about the blood lust. It's part of who we are as a species." His tone, his demeanor now that of a courtroom lawyer. "That's always been true. Back when executions were held in the village square. Justice was swift and fed the bloodthirsty masses lifting them out of their dull everyday existence."

An audible gulp was heard from Dickie.

"Back to our human cannonball. What's missing?" He pressed a button and an image of the man just as he emerged from the mouth of the cannon flashed on the screen.

The room remained quiet, even Dickie. Nolan spoke quietly too.

"I'll tell you what's missing. The unknown. Where's the danger?" His voice grew louder, his body language more animated. "We crave it. Half the fun of watching a human cannonball is the thrill of wondering if the meat bag will live through it." He was pacing the room now, taking on the role of the hype man, whipping up the crowd. *But who will be the fluffer?* That's what worried Jonah.

"According to statistics," his boss went on, "nearly fifty percent of the people who performed this stunt did not survive. Back in the day, there was some serious math going on to calculate trajectory and measures were put into place in an attempt to make it safer, but let's face it, anything can happen when you turn a person into a human projectile. Our problem? There's no danger. No mystery. The person is already slated for termination, so no surprises there. We drug 'em up to keep it painless. No drama for the audience to feed off."

At this, Jonah winced, remembering the man's last words. "It's too clean," Nolan went on. "We could have shot an actual cannonball out of there for all the difference it would've made." He stopped pacing and in a low voice said, "So people, I'll ask you again. Now that we know what's missing, what are we going to do about it?" He was met with silence. "No one? Really? Dickie?"

Dickie appeared to strain against some internal struggle and Jonah waited for him to crack. When he didn't, Jonah sighed inwardly, a little relieved. Maybe all was not lost, and he needn't lose faith in humanity.

"We could do a more in-depth profile, interview the family," Lauren said, the first to speak up.

"Yawn. Been done before," Nolan said.

"Been done to death," Earl quipped under his breath, garnering a snicker from his toady.

"That might garner too much sympathy," Dickie said.

Jonah looked at Nolan to see his reaction. His boss was looking down at something on his wrist phone. Had he heard or was he intentionally ignoring what Dickie said? All at once the room erupted in suggestions and counter-arguments.

"What if we didn't drug them beforehand?"

"Is that even legal?"

"It would certainly save money."

"What if we used convicts instead of regular citizens?"

"We could up the prize money."

"Spend more?"

"We could make it up in advertising."

"People, we're getting off-topic," Nolan said, interrupting the debate. "I thought I'd made myself clear. You need to keep me hard, keep me interested. Here's what I propose: Live audience. No drugs. Keep 'em wide awake. Sounds like a good beginning to me." On his way out the door, Nolan had one final comment: "Hesitation and a weak stomach have no place here." He gave Jonah a pointed look, his meaning clear. Jonah was being tested, his future at the network in flux and already the sharks were circling, smelling blood in the water.

When the meeting finally came to an end, Jonah went back to his office, creatively, emotionally, and morally spent. His boss would expect big ideas, preferably by lunch. Funny how even with all the time in the world, people still rushed around as if it were a quickly diminishing commodity. Time may be forever, but the mindset hadn't quite yet caught up.

Jonah was online when the pop-up on his computer notified him of a new message. The sender was unexpected. Official business. His hand shook as he touched the screen to open the communication.

Dear Mr. Steidler, it began. Jonah scanned the text but only got to the second line, suddenly unable to breathe.

"I need air," he said to the empty room and pushed away from his desk. His chair rolled backward into the floor lamp behind him. Although the lamp remained upright, the bug farm terrarium on the adjacent table was knocked onto the floor. The loud crash brought his secretary, Lena, running.

"Jonah, are you alright?" she called in her sexy Italian accent.

No. "Yes. I'm fine.

She poked her head inside the doorway. "What happened here?" she asked, indicating the overturned tank.

"I'll take care of it." He bent down to pick up the little creatures, their world, like his, had just been turned upside down.

"What's wrong?" her brow furrowed with genuine concern. She started to reach toward him then withdrew her hand, placing it on her shapely hip instead.

"Nothing. I…I've got to take care of something." He replaced the terrarium on the table, giving it a more secure location. Lena glanced at the acrylic box, wrinkled her nose and asked him when he'd be back, reminding him he had a two o'clock.

"Cancel all my appointments. I'm not sure how long this will take." With that, Jonah hurried off, head down, hoping not to bump into anyone who might ask where he was going. "Sorry," he mumbled in apology after nearly crashing into a woman carrying two large bags of take-out from an upscale sushi restaurant. He turned left, rather than right, to the car park, too shaky to drive. *Walk it off,* he told himself, as if that would help. If that were the case, he'd have to walk all the way to New York.

After a few blocks, he found himself in an unfamiliar part of town. He stopped in front of a shabby building which looked more like a house than an actual business, with its light blue siding and lack of signage. The only indication of its purpose was the red neon letters in the corner: BAR. He hesitated, considering his options. Was this the day he'd start day drinking? Probably wouldn't matter he reminded himself and kept walking past a tattoo parlor and a Chinese takeout. The buildings were becoming increasingly decorated with street art, more people had their hands out, and one man stood on a box screaming the apocalypse was nigh.

Nigh? *Really?* Jonah crossed the street.

A woman approached, pretty, despite the heavy makeup and cheap clothes. Prostitute? He ignored her and kept going, aware that she was trying to catch up and increasing his own pace until he found a coffee shop. At least it wasn't one of those vegan, gluten-free, hormone-free, taste-free joints that used to be all the rage. He slipped into a booth in the back. The woman slid into the seat across from him and smiled.

"I'm Meryl."

"I don't mean to be rude…"

"So don't be."

She had a great smile.

"Look, I'm just not in the mood..."

She cut him off again. "I can see that. Which is why I'm here now."

"Huh?"

She tilted her head and lowered her voice a little. "You got some bad news, didn't you? The worst."

"What are you, some kind of psychic?"

"No, silly, it's all over your face. Maybe I can help."

He snorted. "I doubt that."

"Try me."

Whether it was her openness, her big doe eyes, or the fact that he desperately needed to tell someone, he wasn't sure. Probably a combination of all three. *What the hell, I'm already dead anyway.*

"I received notice today." He swallowed and tried again. "My name was drawn."

She reached over and placed her hand on his. "I'm sorry... Truly."

"Yeah, well… thanks," he said, somewhat stymied by this small act of kindness from a stranger. It seemed to come naturally to her, which completely unnerved him. She reached into her pocket and then placed a small business card on the table, sliding it toward him. "Kinda old school," she said, nodding toward the card. "But there's a number on the other side. Call it. Within an hour you'll hear back. Problem solved."

Jonah picked up the card. It was plain white, just a number. No name. No logo. He turned it over and then raised his brows in question.

"Death broker," she said simply, and then got up.

"Wait, I don't understand."

"He'll explain."

Jonah grabbed her arm. "Why are you even helping me?" He narrowed his eyes. "What's in it for you?"

Her gaze traveled down to where he held her, his grip tight, desperate, then back to his face, her eyes burning into him. A challenge. He let go, another mumbled apology in less than an hour. She sighed and, in that breath, she seemed to carry the weight of the world with her.

"You're all the same," she began. "You always think there's an angle, or that I'm receiving some benefit. Maybe I'm just nice." She raised her brows as if daring him to contradict her.

"No one is just nice. No one does something for nothing."

"Maybe not in *your* world." Her voice became sad. "Call the number. Or don't. It's your life.

* * *

Jonah waited two days before finally calling the number, well aware of the fact he no longer had the luxury of time. When he finally did, he got a voice recording telling him to leave his contact info and, just as Meryl had predicted, Jonah received a call within the hour. The man's name was Breen and they were to meet at Oyster, a flashy and popular nightclub featuring a drag show every evening at midnight. Now that Jonah had set things in motion, he was anxious to get things moving.

The place was packed. He'd turned the heads of both men and women as he made his way through the crowd. This wasn't his scene, but under different circumstances, he might have enjoyed the club and he certainly didn't mind a few admiring looks from either sex quite frankly. Jonah checked his timing device, which also provided him with a constant news feed in addition to internet, GPS, and a personal locator. Hiding wouldn't be an option. Even those who lived off grid—there were still a few—were unable to fully conceal their whereabouts. Cameras and tracking devices were everywhere. For his generation, locators were embedded under the skin and could be removed, but for those even younger, it had been injected into the bloodstream at birth and lodged deep within the heart. Sure, it was nice to say that finding a lost child would be easy, but was it justified to track a person for life? Forever? Privacy was just one of the luxuries exchanged for immortality.

Despite arriving early, Jonah found Breen, thanks to the description provided, already sitting at the bar.

"So how exactly does this work?" Jonah asked after ordering a drink.

"You pay me a sum of money and I find you a willing volunteer."

Jonah looked down at his drink, thinking. After a moment Breen spoke up.

"It's all perfectly legal," he said, as if that's what bothered Jonah. As if that was his biggest concern.

"Bullshit. If it's so legal, then why aren't we in some lawyer's office passing papers, hashing out the particulars?"

Breen raised his hands in surrender. "I just meant, that you can have a surrogate stand in for you. There is no law…"

"I know. That's not what I was thinking about."

"Oh, well then what's on your mind?" he asked, sipping his drink with a straw. "Crisis of conscience?"

Jonah blinked in surprise. He hadn't expected the man to be so perceptive. "Something like that." Jonah swirled the whiskey in his glass but didn't drink. "I just don't get it. Why would anyone be willing to volunteer to take my place?"

"You might be surprised. Different people have different motivations. Not everyone has as much to live for as you do." An accusation.

"You think I'm just some spoiled privileged asshole."

"I didn't say that."

He'd be right though; Jonah knew it. "I am fortunate. I'm not blind to the fact. Not that I didn't work my ass off to succeed," he added defensively. "But it's true. I was lucky enough to be born into a wealthy family, where I received support and encouragement."

"You want to live, simple as that."

"Yes." But it wasn't so simple. The divide between the haves and have-nots had grown wider. Until recently, Jonah hadn't concerned himself with such thoughts, preferring to focus on his own problems and goals, always looking to the future, which for him had burned bright. He didn't know what it was like to live without opportunity or hope. Still, he couldn't wrap his mind around the idea that for some, life was so miserable that death was preferable. Was there no better option?

"Are you in?"

Jonah remained hesitant, wanting desperately to say yes, but guilt, like a rolled-up sock in the mouth, gagged him. *Why must someone die? Are things truly so dire that we must resort to forced euthanasia? Do we not have the technology, if not the resources to care for everyone? And if it is that bad, why choose names from a class of people with everything to live for? Why not round up the less fortunate: the poor, the crippled, the mentally ill, or criminals? Why me? Young and with everything to live for. Am I to surrender myself or condemn another to go in my place like some sacrificial lamb?*

"Yeah, I'm in." *Damn right I'm in.* His anger turned to indignation.

Breen drained his glass and stood up.

"Good. I'll be in touch in a couple of days."

"That soon?" The flame of Jonah's ire suddenly doused and replaced with dread.

"How do you find…" Jonah trailed off.

"Does it matter?"

Jonah wanted to shout, "Yes, of course it matters!" but shrugged instead.

"Look, the less you know the better."

Not knowing was probably better, but he wasn't used to leaving the details to someone else.

"And if you don't find someone?"

"Let me ask you something?" Breen said. "Is it hard to find contestants for your show?"

"Not really. They are well compensated—their families are. They choose to go out on their terms, getting their fifteen minutes and all."

"The network's a regular fairy godmother." Breen chuckled.

"Yeah, something like that," Jonah mumbled feeling even worse.

"I'll find an alternate. Just make sure you have the money." Breen slapped his hand on the bar, the matter settled and added, "My cut is 20%. It's standard and it's paid out separately. Call it a finder's fee."

Jonah didn't know if that was a bargain or a rip-off, though he leaned toward the latter.

"I'll be in touch," Breen said and walked out.

* * *

Four days later, Jonah heard from Breen.

"It's all set," Breen told him, then gave Jonah instructions on how to get the currency into an account. A large sum, though Jonah could well afford it. "Plenty of years left to earn it back," Breen reminded him, "with interest."

With his stomach in knots, Jonah closed the communication and set down his tablet. The news was like a punch in the gut and had not brought the relief he'd expected, and instead left him unsettled. He should have been relieved, and part of him was. But guilt overshadowed any thoughts of his future. He was responsible for someone else's death in a way different from his job with the network, though that was just semantics really. And while he may not be the one to pull the trigger (or push the plunger on the syringe), he might as well be.

Jonah hadn't told anyone. Not even his father. Though he had a pretty good idea what the old man might have said, had he known: "It's not your fault, son. It's the government's doing. They're the ones who inoculated the whole damn populace and then instituted the lottery system. You paid the fee, fair and square." Still, it didn't feel right, and he could only imagine the day his alternate was having.

What a mind fuck. To know that he had taken a life, even if that life was willingly given.

I don't think I'll ever sleep peacefully—or at all—again.

Two days later, Jonah made the transaction. The surrogate was filed with the lottery commission and Jonah's name was removed per official notification making him ineligible to be called for at least another 200 years. What were the odds of lightning striking twice?

This all occurred without ceremony or fanfare. Uncorking a vintage Shiraz, he poured himself a glass and then raised it in a toast.

"To life," he said out loud, although he was alone, and choked down a bitter mouthful. It burned his throat and was as appealing as battery acid. Everything tasted rotten, tainted by his cowardice. *I'm going to live.* The mantra had become an earworm playing on until he was numb.

Unable to relax, he went for a walk in the park. While it may have been an unconscious desire to see her again, he was, nevertheless, surprised to have found Meryl, the woman who'd turned him onto the death broker. He'd been consumed by thoughts of her, powerless to erase the memory of her face, though he barely knew her. For the first time in days, he smiled and headed over, but stopped when he saw the other woman. The pair seemed to be arguing. Then he saw the little girl. Meryl scooped the child into her arms and swung her around, causing the girl to squeal with delight. Not wanting to intrude, Jonah turned and left.

Distraction was sought by reviewing the itinerary for the next shoot and he'd caught the redeye to Paris after his boss had contacted him, clearly not buying the story that he was sick.

"Get off your lazy ass and get back to work," Nolan had told him with a chuckle, assuming Jonah's affliction the result of sleep deprivation from chasing tail. The man could be so clueless.

Jonah had offloaded most of the responsibilities onto his new assistant, telling him to view it as an opportunity to move ahead. In truth, Jonah couldn't face watching another execution and wondered how he'd get through it. Ron, the previous PA, had quit right after the Arizona shoot. *Probably should have followed Ron's lead and handed in my own resignation.*

That afternoon Jonah was in Paris, but his mind remained 3000 miles away. Imagining his alternate in some sterile facility surrounded by loved ones, Jonah tortured himself with thoughts of the doomed man. It was the least he could do. His penance. What was his proxy's last meal? Had he already received the injection that would slow and ultimately stop his heart from beating? Once the official documents were submitted, it was only a matter of days. It was more merciful that way. The person was given a week to get things in order. Two weeks by request, but that was it. Jonah's replacement was named eight days ago.

Jonah found himself at the entrance to the Champ de Mars Park, the Eiffel Tower looming in the background, though somehow dwarfed by the spectacle before him.

"Can you believe this place?" With his characteristic slap on the back, Nolan Jeffers ushered Jonah forward as if they were going to a ball game rather than a beheading. The Godzilla-sized guillotine (*guillotine de monstre*)—or Guillotinezilla, as the staff had affectionately named it—sat 35 feet high on a platform in the middle of the staging area. Built to resemble the Eiffel tower, it dwarfed the real one, which sat in the background. Lights ran up and down the length of the runway to illuminate the blade on its perilous descent.

"It's spectacular," Nolan said with a reverence that chilled despite the heat of the August afternoon. Parting clouds let in the sun and the sharp edge of the blade was caught in its golden rays, glinting as if winking at Jonah. He turned away and looked out at the waiting crowd, his insides churning.

Jonah found Dural Fontaine at the mercy of the makeup team. Face pale, a marked tremor in his hands. Was there something stronger than water in his Evian bottle? Jonah decided to check on the man. Makeup wasn't quite finished with him yet but it explained his color. Like a clown, his face was painted white with rouged cheeks and a penciled in mole. The result garish and the wig and tights made him look like an old queen.

"How you holding up?" Jonah asked Dural.

In answer, Dural held up the bottle and took a pull. "Good, all things considered." Then gestured over to the main attraction, Guillotinezilla. "The mechanism falls like lightning; the head flies off; the blood spurts; the man no longer exists."

"Yeah, that sounds about right."

"That's a direct quote by the man who invented the machine. Dr. Joseph-Ignace Guillotin. It was meant to be a merciful death."

Jonah nodded and gave Dural's shoulder an encouraging squeeze and then walked on, looking to see if everything was in place.

The crowd was held back by an invisible shock barrier. A VIP section in the front marked *Zone d'éclaboussure*—or Splash Zone—had been created. Fifty lucky individuals had won the right to view the beheading close up. A crewmember tossed rain ponchos and plastic baskets big enough to fit a basketball (or a human head) at them. They jumped and cheered, arms outstretched trying to catch the rather serviceable swag, in prelude to the evening's main event.

Other promo items such as tee-shirts, beach balls, glow sticks, and candy were cannon shot into the audience. Rock music blared from giant speakers, the reverb thumping through Jonah's chest. Supersized viewing screens were mounted throughout the park streaming live feed, which would ultimately provide everyone with an unobstructed picture of the big event. Cameras swept the audience, stopping to focus on various revelers, especially girls in tight shirts. Along the perimeter were food carts and souvenir vendors.

Cast members were dressed in period costume. Dural Fontaine was made to look like the Marque de Sade with a powdered wig and painted face. He looked ridiculous. He looked ill. A little person wearing a Napoleonic hat stood poised with his drum near the base of the guillotine, ready to herald in the day's victim. If the other episodes were focused on the unusual, this episode and perhaps this season, in general, had taken a different tone, one far more macabre. This was to be a public execution and while cast and crew might be playing dress-up, it was no different than ones from days past.

This season's theme was old-style executions like an Old West hanging, a firing squad, an electric chair—or the soup de jour: a medieval beheading. To make it more dramatic, a live audience had been added. The price of admission: nightmares for life.

Nolan pulled Jonah on stage. Filming began. Fontaine delivered his lines, admirably considering the man was completely (probably) drunk off his ass. Somehow, he managed to hold it together, though Jonah would wager he'd gotten himself into such a state in order to do just that.

Slow mournful drumming quieted the crowd. The "prisoner" was led to the middle of the stage. Jonah leaned forward, unable to see the face hidden beneath the burlap sack. The "royal" guards, who looked more like Musketeers rather than real militia, guided the blinded prisoner up the steps to the guillotine, and then lowered him into position. Dural Fontaine unfurled a scroll and began to read a list of "crimes," causing Jonah to shift uncomfortably. It's just an act, he told himself. The crimes aren't real. *Are they?* Punishment had never been the show's intent, or the lottery's.

"You have been charged with theft, prostitution and other crimes of misconduct and poor character."

Booing and hissing issued from the crowd, prompted by the network staff holding giant cue cards. An actor dressed as a Benedictine monk, who looked more like he belonged in the Spanish Inquisition rather than revolutionary France, performed the last rites.

"May God have mercy on your soul," the monk intoned, looking directly at Jonah. A prickle of unease crept up Jonah's spine, his insides seemed to liquefy, and he needed to lean against the scaffolding. This was nothing like Arizona. The mood now appropriately somber as the crowd once again quieted, holding its collective breath. The executioner removed the sack, revealing the victim's face.

Jonah gasped. "Meryl?" Her eyes were wild, searching and then she found him, their gaze locked. She had not been given a sedative. Horror struck, he ran forward. Nobody stopped him.

"Why?"

"My daughter," she said.

Jonah was suddenly paralyzed with fear and confusion, though she visibly calmed. He'd paid for this. Well, not this exactly but he'd funded her death nevertheless. She was his stand-in, his replacement, his death by proxy. She could've gone to the facility to undergo a private and humane death. Why choose this? Why die for him at all? She gave him a sad smile, like the one she gave him that day at the bar, and he realized that she hadn't done it for him. He glanced over at his boss. *What had the network offered? How had they found out he'd been chosen?* Nolan met his gaze, a knowing look crossing his features.

A hush settled over the crowd and Jonah became aware that the drum had stopped beating. His breath caught as a rumble like distant thunder sounded. Meryl winked then lowered her head, breaking the spell between them.

"Wait!" Jonah shouted, finding his voice at last. But it was too late. The rope had been cut and the lead-weighted blade was already plummeting toward its target, picking up speed as it descended. Jonah clamped his eyes shut, unable to watch and powerless to stop it from happening. Stunned silence was followed by the sounds of retching and he knew it was done. A moment later the crowd erupted in cheers and applause.

"That was awesome!" Nolan shouted, then draped an arm around Jonah and whispered, "How *you* gonna top that?"

WORMBREATH

By James Dorr

It must have been the lightning that did it. He read in the papers afterward that there had been an unusually savage storm. But he didn't know then. He didn't know much, really.

After all, he was dead.

Dead, he thought, at the time. Pickled. Preserved. Boxed up and buried. Laid on a slab and given the old formaldehyde whiskey shot up the arteries. And, too, there was... well, a certain earthy odor about him. From which he concluded he'd been there for some time.

But how long, exactly? He didn't know that yet, though he found out later.

The problem was, he didn't really *feel* dead as he lay, his eyes dazzled by bright white light when there should have been, he would have thought, only darkness. The bolt of lightning, he figured out later, transmitted through the wetness of grave soil into the coffin where it had exploded. The sound of sizzling. The blue after-flash from the metal grave liner.

All these things he knew—the first things he knew since…

Since he had felt himself being *pulled back* somehow. From what, he wasn't sure.

But where he was, he knew. He, a good provider in life, had at his wife's insistent nagging made sure in advance that all arrangements would be taken care of: The cemetery plot. The gravestone, a simple marble plaque.

"Honey," she used to say, "I'll be grieving when, you know, when *it* happens. Men, after all, don't usually live as long as women. And our daughter, Daphne, well, she'll be grieving too."

"What about me?" he'd say. "Won't *I* feel sort of bad about it too?"

"Oh, honey," she'd say. "You shouldn't make jokes like that. Not about things like that. What I mean is, it *would* be a comfort to Daphne and me if we didn't have to worry ourselves about all those little details."

He suspected later that she'd been having an affair with the cemetery plot salesman who, after all, got a commission from the funeral home director if he could sell his client the whole package. And prior to that, maybe, the insurance broker. But it didn't matter now.

What mattered, rather, was that he knew where he was. And, moreover, he knew *what* he was in.

The wood of the coffin top already splintered, perhaps from the lightning. But cheap wood anyway, thinner than it had looked despite the money he'd had to pay for it.

Maybe they'd cut corners on the embalming, too.

And for the liner, the "Vault of Ages" as it had been listed in the catalog, it was already corroded and full of holes, made as it was from the thinnest of copper. He climbed through it easily, up through the rain-soaked mud above it, taking his time. Not needing to breathe, he found, since, after all, dead men don't need oxygen. But glad enough still to smell the free air, the rain having since passed, once he finally clawed through the surface.

He took stock of his appearance then, standing beneath the "Perpetual Light" spotlight the Happyvale Cemetery provided to cut down the incidence of vandalism. Not too much the worse for wear, he decided, considering... well, he *was* dead.

But as for the grave clothes...

The pants legs were slit in back—that, he realized was for the undertaker's convenience in dressing his corpse—as was the shirt he wore beneath his suit jacket. Ditto his shoes' backs, not to mention the general decay of all his clothing.

But then he heard something.

A muffled giggling.

And realized, sure. He'd been young himself once. And cemeteries, for all their anti-intruder lighting, still were filled with dark, shadowy places that teenagers screwed in.

He followed the sound.

He wasn't sure why at first. Maybe, he thought, he might ask for directions? Where he might find a clothing store open? Or maybe for money to buy new clothing? Or maybe, it came to him, simply because, having been in his grave for how long he still wasn't sure, he was just *lonely*.

Then, all of a sudden, he almost fell over them, both of them naked. Humping away on a thick wool blanket they'd spread to protect themselves from the ground's dampness. Their clothes folded over a nearby gravestone.

The boy was huge—a high school football team fullback, maybe—pumping away, his eyes shut tight, as hard and as fast as if he were scoring a winning touchdown. The girl's eyes were shut tight, too.

He bent to catch himself.

"Ew, Johnnie, your breath," she murmured, her eyelids beginning to flutter.

He couldn't help himself; he bent still closer.

"You forget to brush your teeth again? It smells like you've been eating *worms* or something!"

And then her eyes opened.

And then she *SCREAMED!*

And Johnnie screamed too, his eyes opening as well, pushing himself off her stiffening body. She was dead in a faint now as Johnnie ran, naked, into the lights of the graveyard's main path—the "Street of Heavenly Tranquility"—crossing it, stubbing his toe once and falling, then up to a low spot in the outer wall and, scrabbling, over its top.

Listening, the dead man—he'd need a new name, he thought, since, after all, he was in a sense a different person than he'd been before—heard a car starting, a skidding on gravel. And then, he thought, why not? He'd call himself Wormbreath, taking a cue from Johnnie's girlfriend's exclamation. And he started laughing.

Yes, dead people could laugh, too! Taking the air in and out through his half-rotted lungs, expelling it in great gaseous explosions, he reached to the gravestone, taking his pick of Johnnie's now abandoned clothing. Out of decency, draping his own clothes over the fainted girl's naked body.

Then, leaving in the direction he had seen Johnnie run off in, hearing the awakening woman he'd left behind him start screaming anew—especially when she found what she'd been dressed in—he had one final thought:

Being dead could be fun!

* * *

Oh, he was a joker, Wormbreath was. In life, he had had a job installing home security systems, until his wife's nagging had finally done him in—that's what he thought now. His wife's and his daughter's; Daphne had taken after her mother. But the thing was, now that he was dead he had the run of his neighbors' houses, knowing, as he did, which ones had alarms. And how to turn them off. Which ones had watchdogs and how to draw them away with scraps of meat—sometimes his *own* meat. Which had timed light systems and how to reset their clocks so they would stay off until he was finished.

He knew his victims' habits as well, their comings and goings, in part because his wife had insisted they move to an upscale neighborhood, one nestled between the California beach and the mountains. "For Daphne's sake," she had said when he'd argued they couldn't afford it. "So she'll meet nice people."

And meet them she did. Punkers from high school. Motorcyclists. Surfers—one couldn't call them beach bums insofar as their parents were wealthy.

And now, in college, druggies and hipsters.

He knew now, too, how long he'd been in his grave, checking the newspapers when he'd come out for the ones that had his obituary. Not so long a time after all—not much more than a few months.

But, in those few months, quite a bit had happened.

He found this out after he'd moved back to his own home. In his first weeks after being unburied he'd lumbered east to the streets of Los Angeles, taking up residence among that great city's many homeless. He found he could pass there—his look, his manner, even his *smell* raised few, if any, eyebrows. He learned how to beg, finding a paper cup in the gutter and shaking it lustily, taking care not to shake off any fingers—shaking off fingers, he found, caused prospects to draw back from him—taking care not to breathe too heavily in prospects' faces. He did quite well begging, earning enough to go to the Salvation Army store for a new suit of clothing, one baggy and black, more suited to what he considered his station.

But he had been discontent.

Subsequently he had tried life as a hermit, moving north up to the Santa Monica Mountains for a spell, sometimes pretending he was a Sasquatch and living off tourists. Feeding himself from abandoned picnics—he thought of himself as a sort of neo-Yogi Bear, something akin to an extra attraction—when they ran in terror. But, while good, he found the life getting lonely.

And so he moved back to the Malibu home his wife and daughter still called their own, using the dark of night for cover as he pried his way in through a basement window. The basement, a place his wife never visited—"It's too dirty," she'd told him once when he'd asked her to help him by holding the flashlight when he changed a fuse—and so a place he could unroll a bedroll in, sneaking upstairs when his wife was out.

It was at this time he abandoned shaving.

He tried it upstairs in what had been his bathroom, but found the razor too prone to scrape flesh off as well as whiskers. He'd laughed afterwards when he heard his wife's screams from his basement nest, he having neglected to clean the basin. But more important, he found out also why he still had urges to raid the icebox.

He'd wondered about that. Being dead, after all, he required no food. Also, he'd wondered about his worm breath insofar as, whatever he might eat, he wasn't eating worms. But now he discovered in what once had been his bathroom mirror, seeing the creatures peep from his nostrils, the corners of his mouth, that, of course, the worms had been eating *him*. Eating his body. Breathing their own breath out through its orifices, both fore and aft, along with the other gases his rotting flesh generated.

And now he understood. It worked out okay. If he kept *them* happy, stoking organic matter into his gut for them to enjoy, they in turn helped to keep him together, the longer ones, especially, weaving themselves around and through his varied parts, keeping them tied tight, one to another. The shorter ones wriggling, lending a certain animation to wasting muscles, dancing, as it were, to his neural impulses and, thus, helping keep his body in motion.

It was, in a word, a true symbiosis—an "I'll help you, you help me" kind of situation—as opposed to the parasitism exemplified by his wife and daughter.

His ex-wife and daughter?

He wondered about that as he lay below on his basement bedroll, listening to their TV programs blasting down from above, their conversations when Daphne came home on her college vacations. Of course his wife could legally remarry, if she could find anyone who would have her. After all, he was dead. And his insurance, even though he had been over-insured, wouldn't last long, given her rate of spending.

But there was another way out for his wife, too, he learned from eavesdropped conversations.

His daughter, he found out, was going to be married. She'd bagged herself a rich fiancé in her past term in college. At night he crept upstairs to read the newspapers and found the announcements, the young man in question the scion of an Orange County computer dynasty. An honest young man as best he could tell, one undeserving of the fate planned for him. Unless…

Wormbreath thought. Unless he could do something.

He bided his time. The wedding, he found out, was to be performed at a local church, one plagued by vandals in the past and so guarded by the pit bull collection the minister had since acquired for it.

No chance of success there. He could draw off some dogs, but these were too many. The bodily treats he could tempt canines with would only go so far before there was not enough left for his own use. But, for the reception...

For the reception, his wife had planned an outdoor gathering in their own back yard. And so in the next month he bided his time, not even making his twice-weekly raids on the refrigerator—apologizing to the worms within him, promising them better rations to come—lest his wife grow suspicious.

Lest she hire dogs too.

But dogs there would not be, he found out to his relief. Just an outdoor afternoon buffet, with iced champagne, with cakes and candies, with cold cuts and cheeses and good rye bread—the kind he used to enjoy with pastrami, except his wife wouldn't let him eat it. "It makes your breath smell bad," she used to tell him. An outdoor buffet with all the neighbors, the rich and the richer. And some wealthy widowers—he heard the plotting that went on above him—that his wife, pretending to a gentility that was, in fact, as far from her reach as the moon was from her grasp, might aspire to bag for herself as well.

He almost laughed then. Almost gave himself away as the morning came, as the wedding party left for the church. Peeping from windows he watched the caterers setting their tables, memorizing the lay of the back yard. Making himself ready.

Quieting his symbionts.

And then in the afternoon, men resplendent in their tuxedos. He knew from reading the *Miss*

Manners column that they should be dressed in morning coats, actually, but then this *was* Southern California. The women in cocktail gowns. Vulgar with jewelry. His wife, like a gilded moth, flitting among them. His daughter, complacent.

His daughter, Daphne, already trying to eclipse her new husband, taking so much the ways of her mother.

And then the toast. Then the cake.

Then his cue—an older, well-dressed man saying to Wormbreath's wife, "It's too bad the father of the bride couldn't be here too"—and Wormbreath came forth. Shambling, Wormbreath burst out from his basement lair, staggering, lurching through the shocked crowd, leaving a trail of slime straight to the head table. Straight to the table where Daphne, her husband, her mother and the parents of the groom posed for photographs for the newspapers.

And Wormbreath came forth. And silence gave way to gasps and screaming.

And Wormbreath shambled forth, leaning now over the multi-tiered wedding cake, taking its sweetness into his nostrils where there the cake odor encountered something sour.

The stench that ensued then was more than most of the guests could endure, except for the news and the TV photographers who sensed a story. Who kept on shooting as the smell rose higher. Until it was more than Wormbreath himself could endure.

And so he vomited.

Blew chunks. Barfed. Hurled.

Yawned the Technicolor yawn, except, in his case, it was more in earth tones. Browns and grays, tinged with green putrescence. All squirming and wriggling as it played the cake like an iced trampoline—gorging, devouring, whirling and bouncing.

Crawling up guests' sleeves.

He hadn't had as much fun in his whole life!

Or in his death either.

His daughter was shrieking—she recognized him!—as he just laughed and laughed. "You did this to me, Daddy. Y-you did this to me on purpose!"

The mother and dad of the groom backed away, one whispering as the other nodded. "Of course we'll have to have it annulled."

The groom nodded also.

His wife said just one word. "*Bastard*," she said, with enough pent-up venom to send the older man standing by her side retreating into an also retreating crowd. And then she hit him, pounding again and again on his chest, until she realized, each time she drew her hands back to hit again, that parts of *him* were sticking to her fists.

And then she threw up too as Wormbreath laughed harder—especially when he saw the look on his daughter's face *then*. He gathered the parts of himself back together, taking the worms back in, stuffing them into his mouth with gobbets of half-eaten wedding cake, tables of cold cuts, buckets of writhing, squirming champagne.

And he laughed and belched, and belched and laughed harder as his wife fell in a faint, Daphne trying to hold her up but slipping and falling too, knocking a bowl of sticky punch over them. Staining her trousseau red.

Then it began to rain. Rain, in the afternoon, in California, as if the gods saw justice too. Wanted to join the act.

And then the cops came.

* * *

In the confusion, Wormbreath hid among the garbage, waiting until night to make his escape. He found he had an affinity for garbage. As part of his substance rotted away, a roll in a muck heap would add back all he had lost and more. In short, in the aftermath of his daughter's wedding's destruction, he had discovered a practical sort of immortality.

That is, of course, if one who is dead can properly be said to be immortal.

But Wormbreath was beyond philosophical conundrums by now. He had indeed made an important discovery and, to his thinking, the time had come for him to act on it. And so he made his escape to the mountains, the San Bernardinos, but then farther east, hitching rides in boxcars of garbage, in barges, in trailers. Crisscrossing the country. Camping out in municipal landfills.

And always, at night, visiting cemeteries.

You may have seen him yourself at times, especially on warm summer evenings with thunderstorms brewing. The strange, heaped grave where the ground should be flatter.

The shadow among trees.

The grave markers afterward, tiny metal rods thrust through the ground where it's thin over coffins, often disguised as holders for flags. Even when there has been no holiday. Or, sometimes, also as tie-downs for baskets for bouquets of flowers, even at times when there have been no visitors during the day. No grieving relations who might have left these things.

And you might have wondered.

But Wormbreath is wise now. He long since has understood it *was* the thunderbolt that had caused it, as he had suspected that first night he rose up. That it was the current from God's own sky that had reanimated him. Jump-started neurons. Jolted his brain awake, drawing him back from who knew where he had been? Bringing him back to the first day of his undeath.

Bringing him joy in the humor of life, he, always a joker. If what he now possesses could be said to even *be* life, per se. Properly speaking. But Wormbreath no longer cares.

Call it… *whatever*.

For Wormbreath knows this much: That tiny metal rods will conduct lightning.

And Wormbreath desires to share.

RIPPER ROOM
By Ross Baxter

Jen paused before the entrance door and took a moment to compose herself. Her first job since graduation was a big step, a new chapter in her life. Having graduated with a good degree in criminal psychology from a good university, being employed as a team member in an escape room company was actually a long way from her ideal first role, but she still remained positive.

Pushing open the heavy door, she entered the garish green foyer beyond. She recognized it from her interview, where the two employees had quizzed her for almost an hour and now stood to greet her.

"Hi Jen, welcome to Prime Escape Rooms," called Ian, with barely a hint of enthusiasm. The tall gangly manager in his late twenties ran the Derby operation for the corporate owners in far-away London with an air of bored indifference.

"Yeah, welcome," said Tash, her fellow team member, without any enthusiasm at all. An uber-goth in her early twenties, Tash had said very little during the interview, preferring instead to touch up her own heavy black and white make-up.

"Thanks, I'm very glad to be here," smiled Jen, shaking Ian's half-heartedly proffered hand. Tash did not offer her hand and instead took half a step backwards.

"Have you learnt the scripts for the three escape rooms?" asked Ian.

Jen nodded, clearing her throat. "Welcome to the Ripper Room, located in the appalling slums of Victorian Whitechapel, deep in London's nefarious East End. Death has stalked the streets for many months in the form of the evil serial killer, known as Jack the Ripper. You are trapped in a dark tenement stalked by the Ripper; you have just one hour to solve the puzzles and make your escape before the depraved maniac returns."

"Fine, you can skip the other two rooms," said Ian, already sounding bored. "Now, we have a rule here that the newest member of the team has responsibility for cleaning the guest toilets, and for covering the front desk."

"Okay," said Jen with a shrug, having expected something of the ilk.

"And?" hissed Tash, fixing Ian with an icy stare through thickly mascaraed eyelashes.

Ian face flushed red, his cheeks turning the same color as the many pimples. "And, well, we do have a few strange customers. As they're regulars, we always turn a blind eye to some their antics. There are too many escape room companies in this city vying for a limited market, and we can't afford to ban the few weirdoes' who regularly pay the full room rate of one hundred pounds per hour. So, we let them do what they do."

"Which is?" questioned Jen.

"I'll tell you," cut in Tash, suddenly sounding more enthusiastic. "We have a late middle-aged couple who come in twice a week to have sex on the Iron Throne in the Game of Thrones room. There's also a man who regularly masturbates onto the bloody sheets on the prostitute's bed in the Ripper rooms."

"Yuk," said Jen, wrinkling up her nose. "Who cleans that up?"

"Well, no-one actually," admitted Ian, his face still scarlet. "We think it adds some authenticity to the scene."

"Gross! Can you see it on the cameras?" Jen asked.

"You can, and it's very gross," said Tash. "We just turn off the cameras when the clients go into the rooms."

"Fine," sighed Jen. "Is there anything else you should have told me at the interview?"

"No, and we're both sure you'll enjoy working here," offered Ian, trying not to meet her eyes.

* * *

By the last day of her first week, Jen had seen the couple come in twice for sex on the Iron Throne. Initially she had left the video feed on, but after a few minutes quickly switched it after disgust overcame curiosity. The masturbating guy had not yet made an appearance, for which she was glad.

The final hours of the evening shift passed slowly, with only one party booked in. Ian busied himself with paperwork, and it was Tash's day off, so Jen sat at the front desk and idly passed her time gaming on her mobile phone. The sound of the door intercom startled her.

"Prime Escape Rooms," she answered.

"I want an hour in Ripper Room," came the voice on the intercom.

Jen glanced at her watch; they were open for another seventy minutes so she pressed the button to unlock the door. It swung open and a tall man came through into the foyer, well wrapped up against the cold of the February evening.

"Hi," Jen greeted him, trying to see the face beneath the hood. "The Ripper Room is available, although we close at ten."

"I won't be long," answered a gruff voice from under the hood of his large dark coat.

"That'll be one hundred pounds, please."

"I pay cash," muttered the man, placing a small pile of soiled ten-pound notes on the counter.

Jen picked up the notes to count them. They felt damp and grubby, and she quickly put them away in the till. She guessed he was the masturbating man, although she could not be sure.

"Have you played the Ripper Room before, sir?" she asked, sticking to the memorized script.

"Many times," said the man dismissively. "I'll let myself in."

"Okay, enjoy," said Jen, still sticking to the script, although it now sounded vaguely ridiculous.

She watched him stride down the corridor, and heard the sound of the door to the Ripper Room open and close. Flicking on the screen for the backroom of the Victorian pub, she stared with interest as the man deftly opened the numbered padlocks on the first two doors, and quickly entered the final door to the prostitute's bedchamber. Obviously, he already knew all the codes.

Switching cameras, she saw how he entered the bedchamber slowly, running his hands lovingly through the clothes in the flimsy wardrobe, gently handling the thin neck of the water jug on the bedside table, and then lovingly caressing the blood-stained pillow of the murder scene. Standing by the bed, he fumbled with his trousers, took out his manhood, then worked himself up to release over the bloody bed sheets. Moments later he fastened up his trousers and hurriedly left the room, passing through the foyer and the stunned Jen to leave without a word.

She sat for a few moments in shocked disbelief, before rushing to the office to find Ian.

"The masturbating man was here!" she blurted.

Ian fixed her with a frown. "So?"

"He jacked himself off!"

"Did he pay?" asked Ian.

Jen looked at him in bewilderment. "Yes."

"Then it's fine," he replied with a bored shake of his head, returning his attention to his playing cards.

"How is that fine!" Jen cried.

"We just made one hundred pounds in ten minutes, which pays yours and Tash's wages for a day. If we banned every weirdo we come across, they'd just go and frequent our competitors down the road, and we'd be out of business in a matter of weeks."

"But…" started Jen.

"No buts," Ian cut in quickly. "I told you about this when you joined. Just do your job. If you don't like it, don't come back."

Jen shook her head in disbelief before returning to her lonely seat by the counter.

* * *

The weeks passed slowly and Jen settled into a routine. Her two colleagues largely ignored her, both too wrapped up in their own little worlds to care much about hers. She missed the academic world of criminal psychology, and took to reading papers on the topic during the many slow days. The varied clientele using the escape rooms became a great source of interest, and she started to have hopes about actually writing a paper herself.

Apart from lack of job satisfaction, poor wages and unfriendly colleagues, her main concern related to the masturbating man. Definite that something was seriously amiss with him, she started to search the Internet to see if the bizarrely psychotic behavior had any manifestations outside of her place of work. Using knowledge gained through her degree, she started to search for any peculiar spikes in criminal activity, and anything suggesting a pattern. This was old-school psychology: a tool used by countless researchers in the past to prove links between things such as defeats for local football teams and increases in domestic violence. She concentrated her efforts on rape, sexual abuse, grievous assault and murder, but could find no patterns specific to Derby or the Midlands. After weeks of fruitless work, she finally stumbled upon statistics for suicides of young homeless women in the Midlands. The data shocked her; after cross referencing police statistics from the Derbyshire, Nottinghamshire, Leicestershire and Staffordshire forces, a definite pattern emerged relating to the numbers of homeless women committing suicide on railway tracks. When taken together, the figures suggested a rate ten times higher than the national average.

She knew that autopsies on bodies found on railway tracks were notoriously difficult to undertake due to the catastrophic damage inflicted by the train. Apart from toxicology tests, a coroner could tell very little from the sack of small pieces usually recovered, and, consequently, placing a victim on a railway track ranked as one of the best ways to disguise a murder.

Armed with all her information, she realised she had definitely discovered something amiss. How such correlations could be overlooked by the authorities was concerning, but she guessed it was fairly symptomatic of the regional structure of the UK police forces which encouraged silo ways of working.

As regards the masturbating man, in looking for his attendance patterns at the escape room she quickly discovered that the cash payments made were missing from company banking deposits. Clearly, the cash was simply being pocketed, and had been for almost two years. Whether it was Ian, Tash, or both of them was unclear, but it explained the reason why they turned a blind eye to the depravities of some of the customers. The fraud was of no interest to Jen; her concerns related only to the lack of records to tie into her data. For that, she needed to talk to them.

She chose a quiet time when they were both at work, then she cornered them in the coffee room. They greeted her with the usual indifference when she walked in, with neither acknowledging her presence.

"Hey," she offered.

Ian looked briefly up from his phone, whilst Tash pretended not to hear over the music in her headphones and continued to read her book.

"Do you guys know how long the masturbating man has been coming to the Ripper Room?"

Ian looked up in annoyance. "God, what is it between you and him? It's all you ever bloody talk about!"

Jen sighed. "Well, it's not that either of you ever want to have a conversation or discuss anything that isn't work related."

"If you want scintillating conversation, go and work somewhere else," said Tash coldly.

"Yeah, look, I'm sorry," conceded Jen, trying a different tack. "It's just that I've found some scary data on the recent deaths of homeless women in the Midlands, and I'm just trying to put it into context."

"What does that mean?" asked Ian sharply.

"All I want to know is how long the masturbating man has been coming here?"

"Why?" demanded Tash, her voice suddenly patronizing. "Does Detective Jen think he's a murderer?"

"Yeah, we all know you've a degree in criminal psychology, but that means nothing here. Here you have to work for a living like the rest of us!" Ian yelled.

"Look, I'm sorry. I'm just trying to rule him out," she answered, desperate to keep control of the discourse.

Ian stood and faced her angrily. "Just keep your sick hobbies out of work. It took me ten years slaving here to become manager, and I don't want that ruining because you taint the name of this place with the police. Business is tough enough, and you could ruin the reputation of Prime Escape Rooms not just in Derby, but nationally. You could put us all out of a job!"

"And I like my job here," added Tash.

"Look, you don't belong here Jen," continued Ian, wagging his finger at her as if she were a naughty child. "We both hoped you'd resign weeks ago, but you can't seem to take a hint. I'm just waiting for you to make one simple slip up, then I can fire you. Now get back to work!"

* * *

Jen returned to work the next day determined not to give Ian the excuse he needed to fire her. The tension with her co-workers grew more toxic, with both refusing to either talk or even acknowledge her. Ian gave her extra cleaning duties, although she found the additional work helped relieve the boredom. She made sure she cleaned well, knowing she needed to be there a few more weeks.

The following day was her day off, and she spent the next morning at home correlating the dates the masturbating man visited the escape rooms with reported suicides of homeless women on train tracks in the East Midlands. The results were alarming, with a clear link between both. Elated with the clarity of the data, she immediately packed all the evidence into her laptop case and left the house to make her way to the main police station.

After reporting to the front desk, the experience quickly became far more disparaging than she expected. Despite all of her preparation and the clarity of the data, no one seemed to want to take her seriously. Finally, the third officer to see her, after two long intervals of waiting, appeared to be a little less negative. Jen repeated her story for the third time that day, and showed the summary data to the detective sergeant, who took her time looking over the pages.

Finally, the detective sergeant looked up from the pages. "So, you've a degree in criminal psychology?"

"Yes," Jen said proudly.

The detective frowned and put the papers down on the desk. "I just don't see the link you're claiming is there."

"What?" replied Jen in surprise.

The detective shook her head. "Data can be spurious. It's easy to see patterns by subconsciously making data fit to the story you want it to fit to. We get this a lot; amateur detectives who come here thinking they know more about police investigations than the real police."

"I never said that!" Jen protested. "I just spent time piecing a lot of data together."

"As the old adage goes: 'lies, damn lies, and statistics'," replied the officer dismissively.

"But the link is clear!" Jen blurted.

"I've spent twenty years on the force, investigating real crime. Then you come in here, after three years at some stuck-up university, and arrogantly think you can tell me my job. Well, not this time. There's nothing here for us to investigate."

"What can I do to prove the link?" asked Jen, tears welling in her eyes.

"Nothing, unless you actually see a crime being committed. Leave solving crime to the professionals," said the detective sergeant, standing and indicating the door of the tiny interviewing room to Jen.

Jen left the police station in a daze, reeling at the outcome of her visit. Her high hopes once again in tatters, she made her way back home.

* * *

After a sleepless night, Jen rose, bitter and disillusioned to meet the new day. Unsure of what to do with her life, she knew she needed more time to think. The only good thing about the drudgery of her job at Prime Escape Rooms was that it did give her such time, and she resolved to make best use of it.

Ignored by Ian and Tash, she spent most of her late shift cleaning, booking in the few customers, and manning the front desk. She constantly questioned herself as to whether the scornful detective was correct, but each time came around to her original conclusion of the link between the masturbating man and the smashed corpses on the railway lines.

She was unprepared when the masturbating man appeared at the desk in the last hour of her shift; he normally came at the end of the work, not the start. Silently she took his damp and dirty bank notes, the whole transaction taking place without her uttering a single word. He then slunk into the Ripper Rooms, leaving her sickened and nauseous.

This time she left the cameras on, watching his every disturbing, offensive move. Her nausea turned to anger, and by the time he released his load, she was ready. Leaving the front desk, she burst into Ian's office.

"It's customary to knock," hissed Ian, angrily looking up from his comic book.

"I feel really ill; I have to leave right now," she said tersely.

"Fine, but I'll dock half a shift from your pay!" Ian yelled, as the door closed behind her.

Jen arrived back at the foyer as the dark figure left the Ripper Rooms and headed towards the exit. She saw him turn right into the street and, grabbing her coat, left to follow him.

The street was relatively empty, with just a few late shoppers hurrying home in the fine drizzle. She stayed a safe distance, speeding up every time he turned a corner, then cautiously peaking round to see when he was and waiting until the gap increased again. After leaving the town center, he reached the back streets, seemingly picking up his pace in the empty narrow lanes and through the old ramshackle industrial units, which clustered by the railway lines. It was a lonely area, one frequented by drunks and homeless who often slept under the arches of the nearby viaduct.

Jen saw him suddenly duck into a space between two boarded-up units fifty meters ahead, clothed in the darkness afforded by a broken street lamp. She backed quickly behind a dirty white van parked half on the pavement. Unable to see the hiding space without making herself visible, she crouched down to lay on the cold wet street. Ignoring the icy touch of the water soaking into her jeans, she stared at the space from beneath the van, and waited.

Ten minutes passed, which seemed to her like an hour. Only a lone cyclist had ridden by, seeing neither Jen nor the man hidden in the shadows. Jen started to wonder if the man was still there, but could do little more than wait crouched uncomfortably under the van, ignoring the cold and the stench of old oil and diesel. Then she saw movement at the far end of the street; a figure walking towards them on the same side of the road as the man's hiding place. With growing horror, she saw it was a woman, a filthy sleeping bag under her arm and dank dreadlocks poking from beneath a large cap. Realizing suddenly that she had no plan, her mind whirled with thoughts of what to do. Shouting would only reveal her position, and it was likely that calling the police would produce a half-hearted and late response. Holding her breath with anguish she watched the woman approach the darkened hiding place, then suddenly saw a dark figure grab her and bungle her soundlessly into the alcove. Desperately, Jen squeezed herself backwards from under the van, staring all the while at the dark void hiding the man and his victim. Then the alcove lit up. She gawped in confusion, then realized the masturbating man was taking a picture with his mobile phone. The light illuminated the woman on her back, weakly struggling against the man's boot on her neck. She saw him place the phone on the ground, before reaching down with a wicked carving knife to slice clean across her throat. For the first time she heard sounds, a ghastly, choking, spluttering noise of the victim taking her final bloody breaths through her severed windpipe. Then he forced her mouth apart and sliced out her tongue, stashed it quickly in the pocket of his long coat.

Jen heaved, tasting the acid of bile in the back of her throat. Choking back the vomit, she watched as the man picked up the still-trembling body and carried it in his arms away from her down the empty street. Dragging herself from beneath the van, Jen stood shakily, peering around the vehicle as he paced away. At the far corner of the street he crashed through some bushes to disappear. She realized it was the railway embankment. Unable to move, she continued to gape at the bushes, seeing him reappear a minute later, without the body, and calmly walk off in the direction of the station.

Finally, Jen managed to move her leaden feet, and stumbled forward towards the bushes. Looking cautiously around, she saw no trace of the man. Pushing through the bushes, she saw a rubbish-strewn overgrown embankment, with twin railway tracks at the bottom. In the dim orange sodium light from the street light at the opposite side of the tracks she could see a body stretched across the furthest set of tracks. She became aware of a noise, a gentle rumbling, which quickly increased in volume. The train shot by, smashing and shredding the body, which disappeared from view under the multiple speeding steel wheels.

* * *

Jen awoke the next morning with the same sense of self-loathing and shame she had felt since witnessing the murder the night before. Her inability to act and her failure to save the woman made her sick to her stomach. Having replayed the events a thousand times in her head, she was still unsure as to what she should have done, but felt anything would have been better than just mutely watching.

Confused and upset, she decided to go into work. She thought she would go in and quit, but the idea of leaving brought her no joy; instead, it made her feel she was quitting the women who would continue to be preyed upon. She continued on to work in a daze, hoping her mind would clear sufficiently to allow her to know what to do.

Tash and Ian were deep in conversation when she arrived, with neither even bothering to look up to acknowledge her. Trancelike, she went about her usual chores, finally ending up in the Ripper Room. The layout consisted of two adjoining rooms, linked to a third by a short corridor. As she entered the third room, the prostitute's bedchamber, her mind suddenly cleared, and she knew what she must do.

* * *

The masturbating man showed up as usual for the final session of the day. Trying hard to stop her hands from shaking, Jen silently took his money and he skulked off down the corridor to the entrance for the Ripper Room. She watched him on the screens as he deftly opened the locks to pass from the Victorian pub to the sitting room, and then through the short alley to enter the prostitute's bedchamber. He did his usual routine of running his hands lovingly through the clothes in the wardrobe, fondling the thin neck of the water jug on the bedside table, and lovingly caress the bloodstained pillow on the bed. Unzipping his trousers, he got to work on himself, going faster and faster before finally shooting over the bed sheets. Jen watched him finish and walk to the exit door. Unable to open the lock, he became more and more agitated. Having changed the combination earlier, Jen watched as his attempts proved fruitless as he tried again and again. The entrance to the room proved no use either, it having no handle and heavily weighted to only be able to open one way to prevent customers retracing their steps. After kicking violently against both doors, he picked up the wooden chair, swinging it at the door repeatedly until it broke into pieces, whilst having no visible effect on the exit. It was then Jen screamed for Ian and Tash.

"Guys, come quick!"

Both came out of the rest room.

"What's up now?" questioned Ian.

"There's been an accident in the Ripper Room. Someone stood on a chair to look for a clue near the ceiling and the chair collapsed. I think they're unconscious!" Jen blurted.

"Shit!" cried Ian, looking unsure of what to do.

"You're both first aiders; you go and help and I'll phone for an ambulance," offered Jen.

"Right, come on!" yelled Ian at Tash, running towards the entrance.

Jen watched them rush through the first two rooms and the small corridor to burst inside. The masturbating man rounded angrily on them, incandescent with rage. Ian and Tash tried to open the exit door but to no avail, the man screaming at them. Suddenly, something seemed to snap and the man produced a large carving knife from under his dark jacket. He slashed at Tash, catching her in the ribs, before jumping her falling body to pin Ian against the wall. The knife flashed back and forth, each manic thrust puncturing Ian from groin to chest, spurting blood covering both of them. After a dozen thrusts he let the manager's limp form slump to the blood-soaked floor before turning back to the wounded Tash, who had crawled to the room entrance to desperately claw at the closed door. The killer took the huge knife in both hands and brought it swinging down to bury it deep in the back of Tash's skull. She convulsed and fell forwards on her face, blood pouring from her mouth and nose. With a look of delight on his face, the killer removed her tongue and then started to slowly butcher the corpse.

Jen switched off the screen and called the emergency operator on the foyer phone to report the double murder. After replacing the receiver, she grabbed a sheet of paper and a marker pen and scribbled "I Quit" across it in bold letters, sticking the note on the PC screen. Satisfied that her job was finally done, she put on her coat and unhurriedly exited the building to pass into the busy street beyond.

BAD HAIR DAY
By Gerri R. Gray

A tingle of adrenaline coursed through Gloria's wiry body as she plucked the wig from the fiberglass mannequin head with the disturbingly elongated neck and skillfully shoved it into her faux alligator tote bag without anyone seeing her do it. Her heart thumped with excitement as she casually strolled past Harriet DeGroot, the sour-faced sales clerk perched behind her cash register like a she-gargoyle. Gloria flashed the woman a phony smile before exiting the vintage clothing shop on Bradmore Street with her stolen prize. A feeling of accomplishment caused a wicked grin to tug at the corners of her mouth, out of which escaped a little giggle of delight.

Gloria had long prided herself on being what she considered "an expert shoplifter," stealing whatever small items she could fit into a purse or pocket, and boasting an impressive track record of never having been caught. She began crooking things while in elementary school; by the time she entered high school, her frequent five-finger discounts graduated to full-blown kleptomania.

Unlike some unfortunates who must resort to stealing in order to survive in this dog-eat-dog world, Gloria did not need to steal, but rather she *loved* to steal. The illegal act of taking something from a store without paying for it provided her with an incomparable thrill. However, by the time she arrived home a short while later, the rush had dissipated.

She was paused on the front stoop of her townhouse, fishing through the tote bag for her keys, when she heard a nasal voice call out her name. She immediately knew to whom the voice belonged without having to turn and look. It was Melvin Finkel, her trash-picking transvestite neighbor from next door. As usual, he was accompanied by his incessantly yapping companion, an epileptic Pomeranian he called the Goddess Jennifer.

"Today is a very special day," Melvin announced, his voice grating on Gloria's nerves like fingernails scraping down a chalkboard. "It's the Goddess Jennifer's birthday! She just turned three!" He beamed like a proud parent. "Isn't that just sublime?"

"Spectacular," Gloria replied without enthusiasm, still searching for her keys.

"I'm throwing a little soirée for her, tonight at seven. She just *adores* parties, you know. You *will* come, won't you?"

A birthday party for a dog? Gloria had to fight hard to keep from rolling her eyes. The very idea was ludicrous—the most ridiculous thing she had ever heard. Truth be told, she couldn't stand the mangy little fleabag, and she wasn't overly fond of its owner either. Her mind raced for an excuse to decline the invitation.

"That's so sweet of you to invite me," she began. "Unfortunately…"

"You simply *must* come," Melvin insisted. "The Goddess Jennifer and I won't take 'no' for an answer!" He picked up the tiny yapping beast and cradled it in his arms. "Isn't that right, sweetie-kins?" he said to the dog in a nausea-inducing baby-talk voice. "Daddy's little princess."

Gloria reluctantly agreed to come to the party, despite the fact that she had fantasized more than once of poisoning the guest of honor.

At last she located her keys and escaped posthaste into her townhouse, quickly shutting the door behind her while her neighbor rambled on about the dog's "wonderful" birthday pedicure. Gloria wasted no time retrieving the wig from her tote bag and depositing the hairy thing on top of her vanity table. With her nose wrinkled, she wondered what on earth possessed her to take that particular wig. It was downright ugly. In fact, she was quite sure it was one of the ugliest things that had ever made its way inside her tote bag, which she had also stolen. With its ratty streaks of black and white human hair, it had the looks and all the charm of a skunk's amputated tail.

Emitting a sigh, Gloria knew that her ill-gotten acquisition, like the hundreds of other useless things she had pinched from stores over the years, would soon be relegated to a box or garbage bag in the musty-smelling storage room down in the basement and forgotten about.

With the thrill of the steal now behind her, Gloria poured herself a glass of wine to celebrate and then retreated to her favorite corner of her couch. She slowly sank into a mire of boredom. When her wine glass was empty, she went back to her vanity table and took another gander at the wig. Laughing to herself, she pinned her flowing blonde hair on top of her head and, just for a lark, put on the wig.

I guess I could always wear this hideous thing for Halloween, she thought as she gazed at her reflection in the mirror. Youth's vernal charms had begun to fade from her features, allowing the wig to give her face an almost witch-like appearance.

And then, just for an instant, her image in the mirror somehow changed. Her familiar reflection was no longer that of hers. The face now looking back at her belonged to someone, or some*thing*, else… something with dark hollows for eyes that seemed to radiate with evil. Something that wasn't quite human.

Startled, Gloria sucked a short gasp of air into her lungs and blinked her eyes. The mysterious face in the mirror suddenly vanished, and, much to her relief, her own reflection once again stared back at her from the glass.

As she reached for the wig to take it off, her scalp suddenly began to tingle in a most peculiar fashion; it was as if an electric current were flowing into the top of her head. And then she felt the mesh of the wig cap start to tighten like a boa constrictor preparing to squeeze the life from its prey. She grabbed the wig and tried her utmost to yank it from her head. However, she discovered, much to her horror, it would not come off.

In her panic-stricken struggle with the wig, she inadvertently knocked her tufted vanity chair to the floor and then tripped over it while attempting to flee the townhouse for help. Landing with a painful thud that brought stars to her eyes, she writhed about on the floor for one terror-filled minute that felt like a lifetime before unconsciousness submerged her brain into the blackness of merciful oblivion.

When she finally came to, Gloria found herself on an unfamiliar street dotted with large, stately homes boasting meticulously manicured lawns and circular driveways filled with expensive cars. With her mind wrapped in a dream-like haze, she had no inkling of where she was, how she arrived there, or to where her feet were carrying her. They seemed to have a will of their own.

The street dead-ended at a cul-de-sac dominated by an imposing English Tudor style house set back behind high hedges and a gated driveway. Gloria watched in amazement as her finger seemed to know the right gate code to punch in to unlock the gate. It slid open and she followed the long, Italian cypress-lined driveway to the rear of the house. The back door was equipped with a keypad door lock to which Gloria somehow also knew the security code. She punched it in and pulled down on the polished brass lever. Seconds later she was inside the mansion.

Confusion flooded her brain. Why did she come here, and how did she know the security codes? She could find no explanation for any of it. She had never stepped foot in this house before, let alone this part of town.

Her footsteps echoed eerily as she ascended a carved marble staircase leading to an oak-paneled hall decorated with swords and oil paintings from another century. At the far end of the hall, nestled behind an intricately carved arched door, was a cavernous study filled with towering antique bookshelves contrasted by modern, black leather swivel chairs sporting chrome legs. In front of a trio of leaded lattice windows stood a desk, upon which sat a Tiffany "Venetian" desk lamp from the early twentieth century and a curious bronze paperweight in the shape of a charging boar.

Gloria sat down at the desk and gazed out the windows as she waited, unsure of who or what exactly she was waiting for. The view they afforded her was one of a garden of blue anemones adorned with a white octagon gazebo with a two-tiered pagoda style roof.

The flowers and paperweight reminded her of the story of the goddess Aphrodite and her mortal lover, Adonis. According to the ancient myth, Adonis died in Aphrodite's arms after being gored by a wild boar during a hunting trip. His blood mingled with the weeping goddess' tears and gave rise to the anemone.

Except for the faint ticking of a clock, the house stood shrouded in silence. Time seemed to stand still and Gloria began to wonder if she might actually be dreaming all of this. She felt oddly detached from herself, swept away in a torrent of unreality. It was something she had never in her life experienced and it rendered her fearful.

Suddenly there came the sound of heavy footsteps from out in the hall. Each step grew a little louder as they drew closer. They came to an abrupt stop outside the door to the study, which then began to slowly swing open. Despite the warm rays of morning sunlight streaming into the windows, an icy chill, like a breath of death, seemed to breathe upon the room.

"Marisol?" came a man's voice from behind Gloria. "It can't be. You're..."

"Dead?" Gloria completed his sentence. "Is that the word you were searching for, Jason? Dead?" Her confusion multiplied itself. She had no idea why she said what she did, or how she knew the man's name. The voice that came from her mouth sounded like hers, but the words were somebody else's. "I believe a more appropriate word would be, murdered," she added.

She swiveled her chair to face him.

Jason was standing in the doorway of the room, his arms crossed. A neatly trimmed beard and a dark blue, three-piece Italian suit gave him a rather dapper appearance. His dark eyes met Gloria's and he snarled, angrily, "Who the hell are you?"

"Have you forgotten me already?" Gloria whined with mock sadness. "That hurts my feelings, Jason. It truly does. But I haven't forgotten you."

A scowl came over Jason's face. "Look lady, I don't know who you are or what kind of sick joke you're trying to play here. But this bullshit's gone far enough. I'm ending this, right now!" He took a step back into the hall and turned his head toward the staircase. "Marguerite!" he thundered. "Phone the police! There's an intruder in the house!"

"It's Thursday—Marguerite's day off. Remember?" Gloria announced, matter-of-factly. She then made a 'tsk-tsk' sound with her tongue and shook her head. "You seem to be forgetting a lot of things today."

"Fine. I'll just call the police myself."

Gloria let out a taunting laugh. "Go ahead, Jason. Call them. I'm sure they'd be all too interested to know where you hid my body after you strangled me with that exquisite Christian Lacroix tie I gave you for your birthday…the same tie you're wearing right now, as a matter of fact. Isn't that just precious?"

Jason's mouth dropped open but no words were forthcoming.

"Do you want to hear something else that's precious? Do you, Jason? Well, I'll tell you. You see, I wasn't quite dead when you tossed that last shovelful of dirt over me." Gloria once again laughed as the color began to drain away from Jason's face, only this time her laughter was louder and maniacal, and chilled her to the very marrow of her bones. "I was still alive… just barely, mind you, but still alive. Did you know that, Jason? Did you know that when you buried my body in the backyard, you buried me alive? It's true. You never could do a job right—especially in the bedroom."

Jason's eyes narrowed with contempt, which brought a strange feeling of elation to Gloria. But still he remained silent.

"But be my guest and call the police," she continued, winding down her harangue. "I'll even dial the number for you. And after they dig up the flagstone floor under that lovely gazebo you had built over my grave, guess who'll be trading in those handsome Italian threads for an orange jumpsuit?"

Jason slowly advanced into the room, the pallor of his face now reddening with ire. He shut the door behind him and pressed the button on the knob to lock it. As he slowly made his way toward the chair where Gloria sat, he undid his tie and yanked it from around his neck.

"That was quite a performance," he said, sounding almost complimentary. "For a moment there you almost had me convinced that Marisol's ghost had come back from the dead. *Almost.* I don't know who you are, but if you think you can blackmail me..."

"Go ahead, Jason. Do it!" Gloria cackled. She swiveled the chair so that her back was once again facing him. "You can't kill me twice!"

In an instant, Jason was behind the chair and had his tie wrapped around Gloria's neck, choking her.

"Don't worry, bitch," he growled with teeth clenched. An angry vein pulsated in his perspiring temple. "I'll do the job right this time!"

He pulled tighter and the silky material of the tie bit into Gloria's flesh.

Gasping for air, she reached into her tote bag and extracted a large and ominous-looking hypodermic syringe. She hadn't the faintest idea how it came to be in her bag. However, she knew, almost instinctively, that it was filled with ten milliliters of a chemical drain opener containing liquid lye and sodium hypochlorite. Without hesitation, she plunged the needle into her assailant's wrist, injecting the entire of its deadly contents into his bloodstream.

Jason let out a horrendous yowl as the caustic mixture raced through his veins. He released his grip on the tie and doubled over in serious agony. Within seconds he was rolling about on the floor, his eyes bulging from their sockets and pinkish foam bubbling from his mouth like a rabid animal. Now, *he* was the one gasping for a breath.

Gloria nonchalantly rose from her chair and stood over Jason's dying body, gloating. She couldn't help but to notice that his bladder had released a torrent of urine, which soaked not only his pants, but also the plush, white carpeting upon which he lay. A slowly spreading puddle of salmon-pink slime—some of it streaked with bright red gore—had formed on the floor around his twitching head.

"Marguerite's going to have her job cut out for her when she returns tomorrow morning," Gloria remarked as she fluffed up her wig with her fingers. "Hopefully she can get all those nasty stains of yours out of the carpet."

After awhile, Jason's struggle to breathe finally came to an end. His convulsions ceased and the pink lava flow from his mouth abated and then stopped all together. His once-handsome face was now contorted in a ghastly rictus and had turned a frightful shade of blue.

Satisfied that the man on the floor was dead as the proverbial doornail, Gloria departed the mansion, but not before swiping the bronze boar paperweight from the top of the desk and depositing it into her tote bag. It was an ugly little thing, but Gloria was unable to prevent herself from taking it. Once a thief, always a thief. That was the motto by which she lived.

And so began Gloria's glorious murder spree.

The high that it gave her that fateful day was most exhilarating. You might even say electrifying. She had never before experienced a rush of pleasure so deliciously intense. It was even more intoxicating to her senses than the act of shoplifting some useless trinket from a store. No longer could she imagine living a life without murder. She craved more.

Her next victim—a panhandling street mime in whiteface—met his untimely end when the wigged-out thrill killer shoved him in front of a speeding bookmobile en route to an emergency book club meeting. Gloria tingled with delight and squealed with glee as the tires of the vehicle ran over his body with two loud thumps and then sped away. He died as he lived—without saying a word.

Feeling quite pleased with herself, she proceeded down a nearby alley until she came across a raggedy old man sleeping inside a large cardboard box, a half-empty bottle of cheap whiskey by his side. Giggling, Gloria picked up the bottle and bashed it into the drunk's head. Upon impact, his skull made a loud cracking noise as it split open. Blood spilled out, turning the weed patch of matted gray hair on top of his head the color of beetroot wine. His drooping eyelids flew open, revealing a pair of bloodshot eyes, yellow with jaundice from the progression of alcoholic liver disease. They were fixed on Gloria as if entranced.

Gloria was in seventh heaven. However, she wasn't finished with the old man just yet. Humming a happy melody, she doused his twitching body with the whiskey until the bottle was as empty as her soul. With the toss of a single lit match, she set him ablaze, stepped back and admired her handiwork. A foul-smelling, black smoke filled the alley as the flames licked at the derelict's body, charring his flesh and boiling his eyes in their sockets.

The remainder of the afternoon was spent killing as many people as possible—men, women, even children—it didn't matter much to Gloria. Each kill supplied her with an indescribable rush, each rush greater than the rush before. By five o'clock she had snuffed out so many lives she was no longer able to keep count. It was a beautiful day for murder.

After beating the minister of the local church to death with his own Bible and nailing his body to the cross in the chancel, Gloria was feeling terribly ravenous. She had worked up quite an appetite from all the physical activity of the day and decided to head home for a bite to eat. While her stomach was growling, her mind was busy plotting new methods to put people to death. She could incapacitate her victim with a date rape drug and then saw his body in half like Simon the Zealot. She could capture a longhaired woman and then choke the life out of her with her own braids. If she happened to be feeling old school, there was always scaphism—an ancient and barbaric method of execution whereby the condemned is drenched with a mixture of milk and honey and left to be devoured by creeping things like insects and other vermin. There was suffocation by cow manure, impalement by beach umbrella, rectal explosives, even a poison toothpick like the one that did in Agathocles of Syracuse in 289 BC. The possibilities were endless.

So many fun and creative ways to kill, she thought with a smile on her face, *and so very little time.*

As Gloria strolled past the vintage clothing boutique on Bradmore Street, Harriet DeGroot peered out the shop's plate glass window at her. A wild look filled her eyes and within a matter of seconds she had sailed out the front door of the boutique and was shrieking, "Wig thief! Wig thief!" on the top of her lungs. The long, bony index finger of her right hand pointed accusingly at Gloria. "Somebody stop that woman! She's a filthy shoplifter!"

To Gloria's dismay, passersby were beginning to stop and stare. Some even went as far as to pull out their cell phones and record the drama unfolding on the sidewalk. Mortified, Gloria tried to diffuse the sales clerk's rage with an apology and an offer to pay for the wig. However, after her credit card was declined, the irate DeGroot cut it in half with a pair of scissors and handed it back to Gloria in a huff, threatening to phone the police and have her arrested.

Horrified by the prospect of going to jail, Gloria's immediate instinct was to run from the boutique as fast as her feet could carry her. But then a strange urge took root inside of her, and with an expeditious wave of her arm, she slashed the sales clerk's throat with the sharp end of the cut credit card. Blood immediately gushed out of the gash and the woman screamed out a four-letter word, clutching at her throat in an effort to quell the bleeding and alleviate the pain.

Gloria's hand then dipped into her tote bag and pulled out the bronze boar. With a battle cry of "Eat bronze, bitch!" she promptly bludgeoned DeGroot to death with the heavy paperweight. When she was through, the woman's sourpuss resembled bloody chunks of raw hamburger meat with stark white bits and pieces of bone poking out here and there.

After washing the splattered gore from her face and hands, Gloria left the bloodstained boutique and hurried back to her townhouse. She popped a frozen TV dinner into the oven and plopped herself down in front of the television to unwind with a glass of wine. Just as her favorite crime drama was beginning, it was interrupted by a special news bulletin:

"Police in Haroldsville are investigating a rash of gruesome homicides that began earlier today and have left at least twenty-five people dead," reported the stone-faced news anchor with the laughable bowtie. "Police Chief Dunning has advised terrified residents to remain in their homes and keep their doors and windows locked until the killer, or killers, have been apprehended. As yet police have no motive for the vicious attacks and no arrests have been made. However, several eyewitnesses have reported seeing a suspicious-looking woman in a black and white streaked wig in the area at the time of the murders."

Suddenly, a face appeared on the TV screen and Gloria nearly choked on her wine.

The face was hers.

"A passerby filming an altercation in front of a second-hand clothing store on Bradmore Street captured this image on her cell phone of a woman fitting the description of the one wanted for questioning in connection with today's grisly citywide slayings," the news anchor continued. "Police are asking the public for their help in identifying this person of interest. Anyone with information about this woman and/or the murders is asked to call the police department's violent crime tip line at…"

Gloria turned off the television and, feeling on the verge of hyperventilation, sprinted to her vanity table, where she fixed her eyes upon her reflection in the mirror. Her scalp was now beginning to tingle under the wig like before, and once again she felt herself slowly falling under its malignant spell. She knew she had to resist. She fought against the surging urge to massacre the masses, and she fought hard. It wasn't easy. Not by any means. The power of the wig was not only evil, but also quite formidable. Gloria instinctively realized that she needed to destroy the wig… before it destroyed her. She frantically pulled at it with all her might, but her efforts to remove it proved to be an exercise in futility.

"Damn you!" she screamed, knowing all too well that it was only a matter of moments before the wig would once again take full possession of her body and her mind. Gloria was determined not to let that happen.

Desperate times call for desperate measures.

Gloria grabbed a purple can of Aqua Net Extra Super Hold hairspray and applied a copious amount of the flammable hairstyling product to the wig. She then struck a match and a huge fireball instantly engulfed her head.

Gloria let out a blood-chilling scream that could be heard as far away as the townhouse next door, causing Melvin's dog to break into a fit of barking. The flaming wig released its deadly grip and leapt to the floor as if it were alive.

With tears stinging her eyes, the un-possessed serial killer rushed to the kitchen sink and began running cold water over her smoldering head in an effort to cool the searing pain. A short time later, when she mustered up enough courage to look at herself in the mirror, she felt sickened by what she saw. Not only had the combusting hairspray singed off every bit of her gorgeous blonde hair, leaving her completely bald, but her scalp was blackened and riddled with huge, watery blisters. She then looked down at the wig lying on the floor. To her bewilderment, it appeared to be fully intact and unscathed by the fire. Not one of its streaky strands showed even the slightest bit of scorching.

Gloria felt uneasy about going near the wig. It was not to be trusted. However, she wanted it out of her home and out of her life—and the sooner the better. She grabbed a broom from the utility closet and cautiously swept the wig into a dustpan, keeping a watchful eye on the malevolent clump of hair the whole time. Keeping it at arm's length, she promptly deposited it inside the aluminum trashcan outside her back door. "Good riddance," she mumbled to herself as she slammed the lid shut, relieved that her terrifying ordeal was at last over.

Sleep did not come easy for her that night. Even the softest of pillows hurt her burnt head. It seemed impossible to find a comfortable position. She tossed and turned, her mind plagued with mental images of all the people she had brought death to. But eventually exhaustion overcame her and sleep mercifully ensnared her in its net of dreams. But, as luck would have it, her peaceful slumber was not to last for very long.

"You dirty bitch!" screamed a high-pitched nasal voice that yanked Gloria out of a pleasant dream of shoplifting in Bloomingdale's. She awoke with a start, momentarily disoriented. She felt something strange wrapped around her neck and then, as the sleep cleared her eyes, she saw there was a man in her bedroom. She realized Melvin was standing over her, his beloved Pomeranian by his side. His face was coated with layers of garish make-up and he had on a blue chiffon evening dress. Around his neck was a string of pearls and atop his head was the wig Gloria had thrown out.

"Melvin?" she asked, confused.

Gloria suddenly felt the thing around her neck tighten and realized it was a dog leash.

"I'm Mel-*vee*-na!" the wild-eyed transvestite shrieked in a falsetto voice, causing the dog beside him to bark, excitedly. "And I look better in a dress than you could ever hope to. Bitch!"

Gloria tried to move but found her wrists and ankles were bound tightly to the bed. Fear raced through her body. Her heart pounded like jungle drums in her chest. With desperation in her voice she begged her next-door neighbor to untie her and let her go, but her words fell on deaf ears.

"How *dare* you stand us up! You promised you would come but you didn't. I suppose you think you're better than us; too high and mighty to have the decency to call. Well, your lack of manners upset the Goddess Jennifer so badly she had a seizure! You ruined her birthday party, you bitch! You rotten, evil bitch!"

"Melvin, I mean Melvina. Please don't hurt me," Gloria pleaded. "I'm so sorry. Really I am! I promise I'll make it up to you and your dog. I've had an accident. My head…"

"Lies! Lies! Lies!" Melvin screamed, pulling harder on the leash, which burned a red mark into Gloria's neck. "How should we punish this conniving woman for her wrongdoings?" he asked the dog, which set off a barrage of yapping. He turned back to Gloria and issued a deranged smile. "The Goddess Jennifer says the punishment for you is… death!"

Singing *Happy Birthday* to his tail-wagging dog, he proceeded to tighten the leash around Gloria's neck, blocking the flow of air to her lungs. The minutes passed like dripping molasses and eventually her struggling lost steam and her body went limp. A bluish tint, the color of blue anemones in the springtime, embellished her face. Her bulging, lifeless eyes were fixed in a death stare at the wig on her executioner's head.

Melvin basked in the splendor of his dastardly deed. The high that it dispersed throughout his entire being was most exhilarating. You might even say electrifying. It was even more intoxicating to him than the feel of a Chanel little black dress caressing his manly flesh. He craved more.

And so began Melvin Finkel's glorious murder spree.

ONE HAND FOLLOWS THE OTHER
By Drew Nicks

I t's funny to think that as an "advanced" species, we think we know it all. There are certain rules and regulations, which the natural order runs according to. The moon does not rise during the day. Our lungs prevent us from surviving in the water. And, most importantly, the human body is far from the enigma it used to be. These rules were made to be broken…

Jasper Grant awoke that morning with a queer trembling tingling sensation in his left hand. Not that feeling we've all had of a sleeping appendage, but something far stranger. A feeling as if the hand were no longer a part of his being. Standing, he shook the arm vigorously in hopes of triggering some sort of bodily response, but alas, it was not so. He considered if he went about his morning routine that may jolt the unwilling beast to life.

Brushing his teeth proved to be a handful. Being left-handed certainly did not help his predicament. Toothpaste and water quickly began to spatter the already grimy walls. Dollops of spittle coated his cheeks and ran down his unruly stubble.

Anger ruled his mind as he dressed himself. The right hand had now begun to question itself. It followed the awkward and unnatural movements of its brother. Jasper began to question his sanity. *What in the name of God is happening to me? Why me?*

He stumbled down the stairs like a drunkard at last call. His hands refused to follow orders. They groped along the walls, dislodging the gaudy paintings, which lined the stairwell. With his stilted movements, Jasper resembled Buster Keaton.

Bruised and battered, he reached the bottom of the stairs. With still more than forty-five minutes before he needed to be at work, he contemplated whether he could make coffee. Coffee was a constant. A lifeblood if you will. Jasper was like many of us; he needed that caffeine charge to function. Looking down at his hands he saw them contorting into lewd gestures. The left flipped Jasper the bird. The right balled itself into a fist. Had he not had control of the rest of the arm, he was certain he would have tasted an unrelenting uppercut. He now knew that operating the delicate fobs of the coffee maker would be impossible.

Just then an even more frightening thought crept into his already troubled mind. *How am I going to get to work?* If the simple processes of the coffee maker were out of the question, how smart would it be to drive a car? He'd run across scores of brain-dead drivers at this hour but he doubted that any of them suffered from his current affliction. He had terrible visions of even putting the key in the ignition, let alone pulling into any sort of traffic.

He slumped heavily against the wall, falling to the floor painfully. He felt his hands purposefully scuttle away from the unforgiving hardwood. He began to think of his hands as like rats from a sinking ship. Always one step ahead of impending danger. They seemed to possess a lifeblood of their own but what they lusted for, Jasper dared not guess. With the help of self-pity, he conjured a solution to his work problem. The only foreseeable solution was to take the bus. This was not a notion he wished to exercise, but any other option presented countless unwanted outcomes.

With disdain, Jasper lifted his gaze to the clock above the lintel. This choice of public transport offered him a mere eight minutes to reach the bus stop. Pushing himself from the floor with his elbows, he awkwardly stood. The hands objected, raking their nails into the white dry wall. They bled and tore but Jasper felt none of it. Determination was now on his mind as he fumbled to open the door with his knobby elbows. Success was soon found and he walked out into the dreary gray morning.

* * *

Mindful of his neighbors watching, he quickly elbowed open the picket gate. Seeing its opportunity, the left hand raked its remaining nails across Jasper's face. He let out a quiet yelp of pain.

"Good morning Jasper!" called Mrs. Duncan, noticing her neighbor's unusually early exit.

Jasper whirled to face the little old lady, but before he could respond verbally, his left hand responded for him. It flashed its middle finger to the sweet grandmother of six. He was shocked and ashamed of his foul appendage. He opened his mouth to explain but no words escaped from his gaping maw, only a dull wheezing. Mrs. Duncan scoffed and stomped back inside her quaint pre-war house. *Great*, he thought, *another problem to clear up*. Noticing the pervasive silence surrounding him, he realized that time was of the essence if he planned on catching the bus.

With seconds to spare, Jasper made it to the ramshackle glass hut that passed for a bus stop. He was thankful that no one was there. Hoping to calm himself before the inevitable circus the bus would prove to be, he took a seat on one of the heavily stained benches. He could smell piss. Thick and abundant, the stench filled the air like a fog. He couldn't breathe and neither could his hands. They writhed about spasmodically at his sides like a pair of epileptics. He had to get out. The hands proved to be faster than he; grasping sharply the frame of the ramshackle hut, they heaved him headlong onto the cold asphalt. He only briefly saw the bus' headlights bearing down upon him.

Jasper heard the horrid squeal of brakes and the unmistakable sounds of a cantilevered door opening. When he opened his eyes, he saw the bus' tire only a mere three inches from his face. He also saw the angrily tapping boot of the, no doubt, furious bus driver. Jasper tried to crawl his way back out towards the sidewalk but the hands would not allow it. They clung madly to the front axle and refused to be moved. Suddenly, Jasper felt some unexpected help in the form of a strong, meaty hand gripping deeply into his calf. It wrenched harshly at his leg. Jasper cried out in pain but still the hands would not dislodge. After a few more yanks from the rugged hand on his calf, his hands finally disconnected but did nothing to resist the violent dragging, which presently befell their possessor.

When Jasper got to his feet, which is to say, was forced to his feet, he looked deep into the eyes of the tiny, furious man who stood before him. Fire red hair, emerald green eyes; the bus driver resembled a very angry leprechaun.

"What are you? Some kinda' fucking moron?" screamed the bus driver. "I almost killed you!"

Jasper waited a moment to answer. He knew he could not tell the angry man who stood before him the truth. The more he thought about it, Jasper wasn't even sure he knew the truth. All the while, during this scolding, the hands fought for supremacy. He used his arms to keep the hands behind his back.

"I'm so sorry," Jasper apologized shakily. "I tripped. I didn't mean to. It's been a hard day already."

The bus driver looked him over in the oppressive gloom. He looked at Jasper's jittery eyes and the unusual movement of the hands behind his back. Though the driver did not know Jasper, the disheveled appearance of Jasper's clothes led the driver to believe that there must be family problems. He'd been there.

"No buddy," the driver replied, unhanding Jasper's collar. "I'm sorry. Problems with the missus?"

Jasper thought how best to answer this query. The hands continually fought to voice their opinion.

"Yeah," Jasper said. "Something like that."

The bus driver quickly turned and climbed back on the bus. Jasper stood dumbfounded for just a moment. He looked up and down the fog-shrouded street. The area still seemed to be devoid of any other people. Jasper now questioned whether it was even worth it to go to work. He wasn't sure he'd be able to play off his offensive hands in the office. His thought train was quickly broken:

"Hey buddy," called the bus driver from the still open door. "If you want a lift, we're already five behind schedule. Get on!"

With no argument and no other options, Jasper climbed up the rickety stained steps of the old city bus.

* * *

Inside the odorous confines, Jasper felt no more at ease. At each side of him the hands fought tooth and nail to break free of their placement behind his back. Jasper scanned the rows of seats, hoping against hope that he may find a row with no other occupants. This scenario seemed unlikely. The center aisle, which was standing room only, was jammed full like a can of sardines. People of all types clung to the handrails unwilling to cede their position. Beneath his feet he felt the bus shudder to life and he toppled to the floor. He wondered how he would right himself, when he felt the unnatural movement of the hands upon the sticky floor. He hoped that none of the other passengers would pass judgment but, as he glanced about the sea of staring faces, all he saw were expressions of disgusted derision. The hands did not help matters as they grasped for handholds. They quickly found purchase on the calves of fellow riders. The right hand tightened with all its might upon the leg of a young woman riding with her two young children. She screeched and batted at the hand, which so perversely grasped her. Jasper's face turned beet red and he tried to wrench the hand free. It would not let go. It seemed to have found something it liked. With all the force he could muster in his arm, he pulled the hand free and quickly righted himself with his elbows. He scuttled madly to the back, hoping that few had seen the unsettling scene that had just played out. He had never been a lucky man and now proved no different as all available eyes followed his route to the lone unoccupied seat.

He slouched down awkwardly in the seat while his hands seemed to sniff the air. They undulated uncomfortably towards the passengers who sat on either side of him. He fought them viciously, trying to force them to stay at bay. The woman who sat to the right of Jasper offered him a shy smile. The vagrant who sat to the left of him stared coldly into his eyes. Jasper forced himself to stare straight ahead. He thought that perhaps if he just stared ahead the hands would be at a loss. Perhaps if their possessor paid no attention they would find no power. In this thought, he was sadly mistaken. The right hand began to grope the woman's leg. Lightly at first, but soon the motion became aggressive. She smiled for a moment before her expression turned to horror. The hand would not stop. Despite his best efforts, Jasper could not get the hand to cease. Soon the vagrant put an end to this:

"You wanna fucking die?" yelled the vagrant. "I am the angel of death!"

Jasper felt an angry set of hands clasped around his throat. In a way, he was glad that these hands did not belong to him but that feeling was short lived. He felt the life slowly dripping away from his already shattered frame. Without warning, the left hand shot to life and lifted the vagrant high in the air. Slowly, the vagrant began to wheeze and turn blue. Judging faces around Jasper turned to horror as they witnessed this attempted murder. The crowd stood frozen, unable to stop the madness unfolding in front of them. The abrupt screeching of tires called an immediate end to the insanity. Before he knew what had happened, Jasper found himself curbside. He still tasted the bus' stale fumes as it rapidly pulled away.

* * *

Fifteen minutes later, Jasper stood in front of the offices of Pearce & Fredericks. He tried to catch his breath in the gloomy air. He felt hot and ashamed of what had happened but knew there had been nothing he could do to prevent it. Glancing to the clock, which adorned the front facade of the cold brick building, he quickly ran inside the cheap revolving door. The clock's hands read 8:05.

Racing through the front reception area, he only vaguely heard Tara calling a good morning greeting. He ignored it and ran into the obtrusive faux red velvet elevator. He instinctually reached for the rows of bright buttons without thinking.

Soon the hands found a new playground as they swept their greasy digits over every button. This would be the longest elevator ride of his life. Jasper sighed but knew there was nothing he could do.

After an agonizing ten-minute journey, the elevator doors shrugged open on the thirteenth floor. He looked out to the frosted glass windows, which confirmed that he had indeed reached the accounting level. Clumsily, he staggered from the elevator. He wondered just what the supervisor would think of his tardiness. With Herculean effort, he pushed open the glass doors with his elbows and found himself again in the workaday world.

No one in the clinically organized office seemed to notice Jasper's entry. In fact, it seemed to Jasper that his coworkers seemed to notice nothing at all. They all stared intently at their blinking computer screens. *Home free*, Jasper thought, before he stumbled his way to his desk. Along the route, the hands proceeded to act like a pair of kleptomaniacs. They snatched and grabbed at anything that appeared interesting to them. While Jasper tried to prevent them, he did so with little effort. The truth was becoming quite apparent to him. He was beginning to accept the unlucky hand in life he had drawn. In fact when he passed the desk of his closest work cohort, Christopher, Jasper did not even fight the hands as they swiped the red Swingline stapler sitting prominently on his desk. He did not seem to notice.

Jasper sat down in front of his idly blinking computer. He now realized the mistake he had made. How was he to get any work done with hands that would not cooperate? Resigned to this unnatural existence, he slumped down in his chair. He hated himself. Hated what he had become. Hated the madness that seemed never ending. Quite suddenly, he felt a tap on his shoulder. It took all of his right arm's strength to prevent the hand from lashing out at this unseen assailant. Jasper swiveled his chair around and saw the unusually serene face of his supervisor, Bill.

"Can I speak to you in my office, Jasper?" asked Bill, casually.

Without argument, Jasper stood and followed his unassuming supervisor. Just as he made his way along the putrid green carpet, he noticed that Christopher was looking at him. He smiled casually at his cohort. Christopher smiled back and offered out his left hand. Before Jasper could do anything, his right hand firmly shook Christopher's left. Strangely, the hand let go without the sort of vulgarity that had ruled the day.

"Good luck," Christopher said with a wink.

"Thanks," Jasper replied tonelessly.

Jasper took the long walk close behind Bill. He did not relish what was to come.

* * *

Jasper stood rigidly on the bridge with his hands firmly behind his back. As he looked over the eighty-foot drop, he wondered if there were any way the hands could alter this outcome. At this point he didn't care. Jobless. Useless. He knew there was no other way out. He knew what Bill was going to say to him before their "friendly chat" even started. His work ethic was slipping. His appearance was shoddy. The work he did turn in had to be redone. Before Jasper even walked into Bill's office he knew the game was up. The tardiness only drove the point home. *There is no other way*, he thought.

Jasper stepped atop the railing, which separated him from pure happiness. He knew the only way to end this madness was to be rid of the hands and life itself. He breathed deeply before he stepped across the threshold to the great beyond...

He knew he should feel nothing but still somehow he clung to life. He opened his eyes and gazed back to the bridge. The hands, feeling their impending doom, had clung to the railing. Jasper screamed with unadulterated rage. Even death would not come easily! He rocked his body back and forth like a pendulum, knowing that the hands could not hold on forever. With each swaying movement he saw the hands weaken. One by one, fingers began to lose their grasp. When it finally came to two snow-white pinky fingers grasping futilely to the cold steel, Jasper threw his whole body weight into a pendulous swing.

He felt like he was flying. He felt like he was free.

* * *

Christopher awoke that morning with a queer trembling, tingling sensation in his arm...

THE IMP OF THE PERVERSE
By Carlton Herzog

Whenever I feel squirrelly or blue, I head down to Sid Samhain's Dark Emporium for a dose of unmitigated perversion. In that occult hermitage there is a world of unholy visions and black silences filled with creatures otherwise touchless and unshowable, a secret theater of deformities, freaks, and otherworldly things known only in whispers and fairy tales. A horrorcosm where I might study the troubled book of what I have done and yet may do, a reflector more revealing than anything I can find in any mirror.

One day as I was poking around his dusty tomes, I spied *Evil for Dummies* tucked away behind jars of giant floating probosces, presumably from the Jimmy Durante collection. It offered step-by-step instruction on creating mystical mayhem with curses, potions, and summoning spells. Eager, and convinced that I was apt, I took it home and immediately studied it.

My first spells went horribly wrong. When I tried to foresee the future, I came away with a rheumy, near-sighted third eye. When I tried to bulk up my arms, I wound up with tentacles that tried to strangle me. The *coup de grace* of failure involved a love spell that had me fleeing from a pitchfork-wielding mob of pink-hatted feminists shrieking *"Alba masculos interficere"* in their best rage. Let me say that there is no sensation more painful than the tip of a pitchfork penetrating three inches into a doughy tender gluteus. It makes a root canal seem like a walk in the park.

What was I, the would-be mystical master, to do? *Evil for Dummies* was mute on spells gone awry. So, I called Sid's customer service rep, Creepy Pete. He didn't mince words: "You're trying to punch above your mystical weight. Stick to the basics."

He graciously walked me through the first three chapters. Thereafter, my spells were efficient and poetic: I turned my obnoxious blabbermouth wife into a chipmunk, my mother-in-law into a pig, and my bullying neighbor into a chicken.

I even managed some serious levitation. Were it not for the flight of crows that used my head for pecking practice, I have no doubt I might have reached the stratosphere or beyond. Every time I got above house level, they would appear from out of nowhere and Kamikaze me until I dropped like a bag of dirt. Who knew they could be so territorial about airspace in a residential neighborhood?

Following my aviation debacles, I decided to turn my newfound mystical power on my bosses. I created an inter-dimensional portal on the workroom floor. It sucked three of them away without so much as a whimper, and they haven't been seen since. Suspicion immediately fell on me because I am the archetypical disgruntled postal employee. The guy everybody assumes that will go postal sooner or later. That I am a card-carrying, tee-shirt wearing member of the Satanic Temple didn't help. But since nobody could prove anything, all I got was a letter explaining the postal policy on mystical portals in the workplace.

If the letter proved anything, it's that the Postal Service has a rule for everything, no matter how trivial or ridiculous. To wit, "While it is not the Postal Service's intent to interfere with its employees' creativity, order must be maintained on the workroom floor. Unauthorized entries and exits created by rank and file members are not permitted, especially when they involve extra-dimensional or extra-terrestrial excursions while employees are on the clock." That somebody wrote those lines with a straight face is hard to believe. But the Post Office is a universe unto itself, where physics takes a back seat and magic opens the show.

But postal management wasn't the only one concerned about my activities. The Devil and his minions had an issue with my weaponizing magic against those who are not magic literate. So, he sent the Imp to set me straight

One minute I'm delivering mail, as smug and self-satisfied as I can be, and the next choking on a cloud of noxious green smoke. As my vision returned, I saw a little man-shaped thing, no more than two feet tall, with a forked tail, cloven feet, and horns grinning at me.

The Imp said, "Well, if it isn't the inimitable mailman scholar. How's it going, Mr. Wizard? Turn anybody into a fire hydrant lately?"

I stood there slack jawed.

The Imp kept leering at me until he finally spoke: "Here's the deal, Voldemort. It's one thing for two necromancers to beat on each other with magic, and quite another for a necromancer to beat up on a mundane. One of the finer points of evil etiquette not discussed in *Evil for Dummies* is something called the Fairness Doctrine, which holds that combatants must be more or less equals for the fight to be fair. Otherwise, we look like bullying thugs. Hardly the kind of PR you want when you're trying to turn people to the dark side.

"Now the Prince of Darkness, that Spirit most Foul, a.k.a. Little Horn, whom I represent, doesn't offer that kind of advice to just any Tom, Dick or Harry. However, he sees you as someone who shares his contempt for God and man. A kindred evil spirit if you will."

I didn't hesitate. "I hate my bosses, my co-workers, my customers, my wife and kids. I even hate myself, but I'm not sure why."

The Imp said, "I love it that you're a self-loathing human. So, you're open to any kind of malicious mischief I suggest, yes?"

I said, "Absolutely! What do you have in mind?"

The Imp said, "I know you hate your boss Finnegan. Who wouldn't? He's a fat blob of a man who looks like Popeye if Popeye only ate at Popeyes. I have it on good authority his mother said *Beetlejuice* three times right before she gave birth. It is your Darwinian obligation to get rid of him since he gives your kind a bad name."

I asked, "You want me slit his throat? I will. Just say the word."

The Imp said, "Calm down, Caligula. Any idiot can stab somebody just like any idiot can own a gun, and God knows many an idiot does. Slashing and shooting are common and obvious. We're looking for insidious evil, not splatter punk. I want you to crawl around inside his head. Start fiddling with the dials and switches. Find the ones that will make him off himself. That will earn you your wings as a social assassin."

I said, "I get it. Mental murder, manslaughter by mind."

He continued, "For a social assassin to be lethal, he or she needs to debase the victim's social standing to the point where suicide seems logical and practical. That's the tried and true method of social media bullies. So, you need to prime the pump. Become the person whose words determine social worth and standing. You can't crush somebody's spirit and public image to the point of suicide unless people see you as a leader whose approval makes or breaks people. For that, you need to be clever and witty."

A few days later, my co-workers and I were gathered near Finnegan's desk where the time clock hangs. The Imp whispered some lusty limericks in my ear, which I dutifully recited aloud for all to hear:

There once was a lady from Wheeling
Who claimed she lacked sexual feeling,
'Til a cynic named Boris
Simply touched her clitoris

And they scraped her off of the ceiling

I followed that with:

There once was a man from Belair
Who was humping his wife on the stairs,
'Til the banister broke,
So he quickened his stroke
And finished her off in mid-air.

My co-workers loved the limericks. Finnegan did not. He told me the workroom floor was no place for sexual innuendo. Then he ragged on promiscuous people in general for doing nothing more than enjoying life's physical pleasures. He quoted Bible verses about the wicked and the wanton. I couldn't take it anymore. Neither could the Imp, who said, "We need to cut out his tongue."

Mind you, he didn't mean actual elinguation. Rather, the mute button in Finnegan's head that hopefully was near his body's off switch. One day, as Finnegan was playing the role of the humble, self-effacing planet on legs and asserting that he needed to get into a gym, I told him and everyone else within earshot that "the only way you will ever get into a gym is if you screw a guy named Jim." The stunned look on his multi-chinned face was priceless.

But I wasn't done. Not by a long shot. I wanted to make sure that horse was dead. I tried to induce a stroke with two more salvos: "Finnegan, the only time you will ever get a pussy wet is if you drown a bag of cats." At that point, he was beet red and swaying like a thin tree in a strong wind. I fired my second salvo in

171

the hope it would kill him: "The only woman you will ever make happy is the woman who digs your grave."

Close but no cigar. He went home for the day and didn't return until a week later. He came back more rotund than ever with a chip on his shoulder to boot. He took every opportunity to bust my horns over trivial things. And he started getting frisky with insults. Would the phrase *frisky ball of lard* be oxymoronic or just ironic?

So there Finnegan was on the workroom floor, smelling like garlic and sweating like his blubber was melting. I tried to dodge him the way a small ship does an enormous iceberg. I had almost gotten past his pulsating globular presence, when out of nowhere, he said, "Hey Bulimia Joe, the Olsen twins called. They want their eating disorder back."

I gave that a seven out of ten. Mind you, I thought that his little burst of bile was a one and done scenario. But the prick was really gunning for me. Mind you, he wasn't subtle about it. The next day, for example, he said, "The people of Somalia have more meat on their bones than you do."

That one made *me* laugh because it came out of the blue with no set-up. I shot back with "What's the matter, not enough butter on your blubber sandwich?"

The bittersweet back and forth continued. A few days later, I told him I needed more time given the workload. He told me to "stop being a cry baby and just do it, you damaged little climber."

Finnegan was a natural born imbecile, so his newfound bravado had to be coming from a budget Cyrano de Bergerac, who was most likely another manager. Or his oleaginous mother. After all, pinguid bullfrogs don't hop far from the birth pond.

Everything came to a head one day. Fatso Finnegan was yelling at me for taking too much time to deliver the mail. I told him where to go and then pointed out that his belly was like a coal mine in Chile—a dark, dank hole filled with 70 people who think they're going to die." I thought I had him on the brink. This was the tipping point I had been waiting for and I unloaded my nuke: "The only difference between you and Hitler is that Hitler knew when to kill himself." That adipose, addle-headed, human moon around whom light bends because he's so dense suspended me for two weeks without pay.

During my hiatus, the Imp and I plotted his Flabbiness' murder. I wanted it to be food. Something on the order of Terry Gilliam's belly explosion in *The Meaning of Life*. However, I had to settle for something less dramatic and disgusting.

It played out as follows: Every Friday night, Finnegan blobbed and wobbled his elephantine frame over to the Feed Bag Bar and Grill for all the All You Can Eat Buffet. I acquired some aconite, or wolfsbane via the Net. When ingested, it causes cardiac arrest. The only way to detect it is by an in-depth autopsy utilizing mass spectroscopy. But in Finnegan's case, the odds of a heart attack would be attributed to the high cholesterol associated with eating Volkswagens.

On that fateful Friday night, I entered the Feedbag in a red dress, blond wig and heels. For the record, cross-dressing is underrated. It really brought out my feminine side along with some predators who dig thin, masculine women.

I proceeded to dine. As Finnegan began inhaling his supper, I called the front and had them page him to the desk. When he lumbered away, I minced my way up to his table and liberally sprinkled the wolfsbane on his meat. He died of a heart attack while driving home.

Some may say that my hatred of postal managers is pathological, the sure sign of a deranged and twisted mind. My response to that assertion is that postal managers are like the lilies of the field: they toil not and neither do they spin, but somehow they command six figure salaries. Salaries that my efforts in rain, hail, sleet, snow and driving heat provide. Salaries that should be going to educators.

I thought things would improve with Fatso Finnegan out of the picture. I was wrong. They simply replaced him with another Kryptonian deformity.

McGinley slithered into our office in true serpentine fashion. Another shining example of managerial recruitment that consists of flipping over rocks and hiring the first thing that slithers out. I could be wrong, but I think I saw him in that abysmal chasm Adrien Brody and Jack Black fell into in *King Kong.* You remember: a bestiary of slimy, slithery poly-legged carnivores, some insect, some reptile, eager for a taste of human flesh.

That's not a forced comparison. McGinley slid about the workroom floor as a small bald man with a squamous face. He had scaly skin and spoke with a hiss. The only thing missing was a forked tongue lathered with venom. His beady unblinking reptilian eyes were devoid of all sentiment save contempt. Doubtless, he had been bullied as a child. Now he used his supervisory power to bully his betters. He walked around with a ruler, measuring the height of our socks to ensure they comported with the dress code. He constantly inspected our shoes, our hats, and our shirt tucks. A true martinet. A little man who wanted to be bigger. A man worth killing for good reason or no reason. A man whose only good would come from not being born.

The Imp hated him on sight. The Imp laid some heavy truth on me: "This McGinley character is truly evil because he's mean for no good reason. It's one thing to use underhanded, immoral and lethal means to get something you need, and quite another to be a dick for the sake of being a dick."

I said, "You're a dick."

The Imp said, "Not to everybody, and not for lack of a good reason. We—the fallen angels and our minions—got screwed big time. Satan had a small policy disagreement with the Almighty and the next thing we knew we were sizzling and crackling like bacon for all eternity. Seems a little over the top, wouldn't you say? Considering He made us and knew we were going to do it before even we did, you must admit the whole eternal damnation thing seems that much more ridiculous. Think about it: If your kid sassed you, would you throw him in an oven set to 5000 degrees?"

I said, "I see your point. Let's see how Old Slippery pans out."

To continue the Gold Rush metaphor, McGinley didn't pan out. Instead, he rode me like a rented mule. Called me every name in the book. Like any good psychopath who knows enough to isolate his victim, he would always do it when no one else was around. However, he did not realize that I was seething with murderous intent and I had a pint-sized green demon in my corner.

Eventually his luck ran out and his isolation strategy backfired. He showed up on my route late on a Friday. He wanted to hand me more work, but not the necessary time to do it. I could hear the Imp whispering in my ear: "Wait for it; wait for it; wait for   it—now!" So, one minute we're arguing; the next I was bashing McGinley's brains in with my electronic scanner.

Sidebar: Postal scanners are virtually indestructible, a modern equivalent of Thor's Hammer if you will. They can crack open a skull with such force you can see brain. Or lack thereof, depending on the gray matter content of the victim.

When the first blow connected, McGinley let out a groan and slumped over the bumper of my truck. He tried to talk but all that came out was a gurgling sound and a trickle of blood from the corner of his mouth. As I rolled him into the truck, he suddenly came to life. I hit him again with the scanner. He fell to the ground, blood gushing from his split skull. I hoisted him up by his armpits and dragged him up into the truck over the mail trays. Bloody letters. Bloody truck. Dead body. Not how I saw my day ending.

I remembered that I kept large trash bags in the truck. Duct tape too. Part of my moonlighting gig. Don't ask. I stuffed McGinley into a trash bag, and then slipped another bag over that one and duct taped the whole mess. Mummification on the cheap.

The murder had taken place at the end of a cul-de-sac devoid of houses. It's where I go to eat lunch in peace.

The mail he had intended to give me was still in his truck, as were the accompanying packages. But the mail in my truck, soaked through and through with his red sap, would have to be burned.

I retrieved the clean mail from his vehicle. I delivered it as if nothing had happened. I planned to finish the day, lock the truck, then come back at night, take out the body and clean up the blood. From watching *CSI*, I knew that it was virtually impossible to get rid of the blood evidence. It would show up if they used luminol, a chemical that reacts with hemoglobin. There was stuff to get rid of blood evidence, but that required the addition of liquid nitrogen. Where was I supposed to get a tank of liquid nitrogen?

At that moment, the Imp, my fairy god devil, popped in with some sound advice. He said, "Try fire. Mail trucks are nothing but metal on the inside. Sneak back after hours and use a propane torch to cook every inch of caked blood. Down the road, you can repaint the inside."

Nothing like having a supernatural *consigliere* to steer you in the right direction. I got myself together and finished up what I could. I clocked out, and came back at three a.m. I parked my car across the lot down a few hundred feet from my truck. I planned to drag the body across the street, then along the grass behind the other trucks.

I got out of my car. But all the icy calm of the planning stage melted. I was so nervous I dropped my keys on the ground. As I reached to pick them up, I heard a weird whistling that grew louder and louder. I thought of the legend of the banshee, the Irish spirit whose wail means death is coming. I looked up and saw that the sky was getting bright; so bright the entire parking lot was bathed in light.

Then it hit. There was a series of concussions and brilliant flashes of light. A blast of hot air blew me off my feet and back into the bushes. As I was flying backwards, I could see mail trucks flipping end over end, and others rising into the air.

I hit the ground and rolled downhill into a stream. I heard two rushes of air followed by two crashes as mail trucks fell on either side of me.

I thought terrorists. War with China. Alien invasion.

I started to walk forward, my legs and hands shaking. I came to the top of the little hill and the first thing I saw was an upside-down mail truck teetering on the roof of the annex. There was a smoking crater where my mail truck had been. I looked inside and saw my truck flattened into a pile of smoking slag. McGinley's body had become one with the earth and the truck.

There were craters and fires everywhere. The parking lot looked as if it had been shelled by artillery.

As my wits returned, I remembered that a meteor passing through the atmosphere gets hotter than the surface of the sun, and the kinetic energy of the impact would obliterate anything in its path.

There was still the issue of McGinley's truck parked on the cul-de-sac. I gathered my wits and high-tailed it over there. I wasn't exactly sure what

I could do to get rid of it. But when I arrived the point was moot.

The meteor that struck the carrier annex was part of a shower, a shower that had vaporized McGinley's truck, the cul-de-sac and several nearby houses.

As I sat there marveling at the flaming cratered landscape, I reflected on the issue of luck. I hadn't received so much as a scratch, and all the evidence against me—McGinley's body and truck—had been obliterated. I had gotten away with murder. And that was better than any casino or lottery luck by a mile.

I wondered if luck were a product of mere chance or a force that operates in human affairs? If it's a force, then is it a particle or a wave or both? Is it an energy that is conserved? Where does it come from? Can you describe it with an equation or a particle model?

The foregoing questions might seem silly, but given the attention devoted to its presence or absence, its goodness or badness, they are a legitimate line of inquiry. After all, everybody has an opinion on their luck or lack thereof. And I suspect everybody has a different definition of it.

The Imp certainly did. As I sat there marveling at my good luck, he appeared grinning from ear to pointy ear.

He said, "Say pal, I think somebody up there must like your work. It's not every cold-blooded killer who gets divine intervention in the form of a meteor shower. What are the odds of that happening at the exact time and exact spot needed to incinerate all the evidence of the crime? The Old Man ain't so bad after all, is He?"

I said, "It's like He signed off on it with invisible ink."

The Imp said, "I'll let you in on a little secret. God knows He made a huge mistake when He created your kind. The Bible is an extended and painfully circuitous memoir of His regret for doing so. How else do you explain the mass drowning described in the Flood, the volcanic incineration of Sodom and Gomorrah or the coming barbecue of the whole planet in *Revelations*? Or, for that matter, why He sits idly by while you massacre one another in civil conflicts, genocides and world wars? He hates all of you and wants you all dead but is too lazy to do it Himself.

So, in effect, you're doing the Lord's work, one dickhead at a time. Don't feel bad about it. Sooner or later, everybody dies. You're just greasing the wheels."

I liked the sound of that: the Lord's work. Has a nice ring to it. Of course, the Imp has been a bit vague about what's waiting for me in the afterlife. But I'm having too much fun to care.

A few weeks later, the Imp helped me acquire some Honduran sand fleas. You know, the kind that carries the incurable flesh-eating disease, leishmaniasis. It won't kill you. But it will leave you with enormous weeping sores so enormous you'll want to kill yourself.

I use them on my mail customers—you know, the ones who are real dicks. I put the fleas in their mailboxes with their mail. It only takes one bite and the rest is, as they say, medical history. Who knew the Lord's work could be so diabolical and fun?

WHAT THE PEEPER SAW
By Kelli A. Wilkins

Eugene crept across the dune, crouching low to conceal himself behind several jagged rocks. The roar of the ocean waves crashing against the shore masked his heavy breathing. Gritty sand trickled inside his loose tennis sneaker. He ignored it and smiled.

There, now he'd moved even closer. He stood within ten feet of them, and his view was much better. The full moon illuminated the beach, yet provided many shadowy hiding places. The couple didn't suspect he lurked here. He had waited for hours in the hot, muggy night, watching, like always.

Summer was the best time of year for watching. During the day, nubile young women came to the beach and sprawled out in tiny string bikinis that exposed more flesh than they covered. Tourists came to Freeport from far-away places like Boston and New York, so there were new girls to look at every week. He loved going to the beach and seeing all that tan, taut skin baking in the blazing sun. The college girls half his age basked in the heat, tanning every inch of their almost-naked bodies.

Nighttime was fun, too. Once it got dark, he strolled up and down the beach, listening to the wild parties taking place inside the summer houses. These were parties for the popular people—parties he'd never be invited to. But years of watching had taught him that couples left the parties and got naked at the water's edge. Cold ocean waves splashed them and damp sand clung to bare flesh. He watched them, all of them, from his secret place.

Eugene turned his attention back to the couple on the blanket and focused on the curvy girl.

"You don't think it's creepy being out here like this?" she asked her date.

Eugene licked his cracked lips and held his breath. After what had happened last month, would the girl get scared and insist they leave? If so, could the boy convince her to stay? He checked his watch in the moonlight. It was a few minutes before twelve. The couple had been drinking beers and talking for almost an hour. He'd hate for them to leave now, before he got to see. He strained to hear their words over the breaking waves.

"I mean, jeez, Stan, two people were murdered over there." The girl turned her head toward the dunes. "What the—? I thought I saw something."

Eugene froze. The girl had looked right in his direction, almost as if she knew he was watching.

After a second, he relaxed. He didn't have to worry about getting caught tonight. His powers were at their peak during a full moon. Everyone believed what they saw on television and thought the full moon brought out lunatics and werewolves, or that it caused madness in the mentally deranged. But he knew better.

The moon gave him the ability to vanish at will. Cloaked in its pale light, he could slip into the shadows and come and go as he pleased. His moon powers had proved themselves last summer when the police almost caught him peeking in a bedroom window. He'd strolled right by them and they never suspected a thing.

A bead of sweat trickled down his back. So much of the game involved waiting. What if something went wrong? What if the girl saw his wire-framed glasses reflected in the moonlight? That happened on television all the time—that's how people got caught. He removed his glasses and tucked them into his shirt pocket. He really only needed them for driving. Even without them, he was close enough to see clearly.

Stan tilted the beer can to his lips. "You're jumpy because of the stories. Now you're seeing things. Don't be afraid, Lisa." Stan rubbed Lisa's bare arm. "Don't worry; you're safe with me here."

"But we're not supposed to be out on the beach. It's so… deserted. You didn't tell anyone we came out here, did you? If the cops catch us…"

"No, I didn't tell anyone. Nobody saw us leave the party, either." Stan trailed his hand down Lisa's back. "Just relax. I'm here to protect you." He nuzzled her neck. "Besides, it's better to be alone. We wouldn't want anyone to interrupt us, would we?"

Lisa leaned forward and kissed Stan's bare chest. He let out a deep groan.

"No, of course not. I just said it was creepy, that's all," she replied. "Those other kids were out here having a good time and look what happened. They got killed by some maniac."

Eugene grinned. Did the thrill of danger excite Lisa? He'd read stories about women getting all hot and bothered when they were afraid. He knew first-hand that the risk of discovery always increased the titillation of watching.

"Nah, it wasn't a person. The cops said it was an animal. Probably a wild dog or a coyote that came out of Wolf's Neck Park." Stan shrugged and sipped his beer. "But that was last month. It's over."

"The newspaper said their throats were ripped open," Lisa said. "The police warned people about being out at night, and they even set up a curfew. They wouldn't do that if they weren't worried."

Eugene nodded. Lisa was right. He'd been following the story closely. Once a month for the past three months, people had been found dead on the beach—but the local cops covered it up. The mayor didn't want out-of-towners to hear the news and change their vacation plans. Tourists came here to eat lobster, buy antiques, and look at lighthouses, not get attacked by animals. That would be bad for business.

The first killing happened about two miles away. A middle-aged man was found with his throat torn out. A month later, two kids came across the mangled remains of another man. Last month, a twenty-something couple was discovered ripped to pieces not far from here. Everyone along the beachfront was worried, and the locals were extra cautious about leaving their homes after dark.

Tonight, Eugene had barely gotten out of the house. Mother had tried to stop him. She didn't like him "wandering around" at night anymore. She wanted him home so she could keep an eye on him and watch everything he did. He'd yelled at her and stormed out. There was no way in hell he'd stay inside tonight. After all, tonight was a full moon.

Mother never understood that he *had* to come out and watch, especially on hot, steamy summer nights. The beach was deserted in the winter, and he was forced to stay inside, watching inane television programs until his mother went to bed.

But as soon as she was asleep, he'd creep into his tiny basement room and stare at the dirty magazines he'd picked out of the neighbor's trash. These beautiful blue-eyed women liked him. They didn't laugh at him or call him a disgusting pervert. He envisioned the big-breasted women smiling and inviting him to rub them. When he touched himself, he imagined it was their hands wandering all over his body, urging him on.

The women on the beach were the same way. They enjoyed putting on a show. One night he'd reveal himself to a girl and she'd invite him to touch her...

The sound of Stan's voice snapped him back to reality.

"Come here, Lisa. I'll take your mind off of everything."

He watched Stan caress Lisa's breasts through her T-shirt before pulling her down on top of him. Eugene slid his hand across the growing bulge in his shorts and bit his bottom lip. He wanted to be Stan, to be lucky enough to touch Lisa. He'd never had a real girl. Even when he got up enough courage to talk to girls on the beach, they laughed in his face—or worse, they called him a stuttering old creep.

His heart pounded as he watched them undress. Lisa's topless body covered Stan's and she bent her head over his neck. This was it! They were going to do it...

Eugene closed his eyes. The sound of waves crashing along the beach filled his ears. He reached down past the elastic waistband of his shorts and started stroking himself.

Stan moaned loudly, and then let out a little yelp. Eugene worked his hand faster. He ached to see Lisa's body writhing in the moonlight, but forced himself to wait a few more seconds. He wasn't quite ready yet, and if he lost his erection...

He heard a piece of driftwood snap in front of him and he opened his eyes. His hand froze in mid-stroke. Lisa stood before him, naked.

He licked his lips as he gawked at her round breasts and perked nipples. A few seconds later, he tore his gaze away and looked at her face. *What the hell?*

Lisa had transformed into some kind of animal. Fresh blood was smeared across her pointed snout, and clumps of sand mixed with blood and gristle were matted in her hair. Her lips were drawn back in a snarl, revealing sharp yellow canines.

He tried to scream, but only emitted a feeble squeak. The thing that used to be Lisa growled at him. He glanced across the beach. Stan lay motionless on the blanket, a dark stain pooling around his neck.

The creature clamped a clawed hand around his throat.

Eugene closed his eyes.

He didn't want to see any more.

LUCKY STAR
By Brett O'Reilly

"Another?"

Chase contemplated the glass in front of him, and the last swallow that lurked at the bottom. Strong stuff—stronger than he was used to. But it had taken the edge off the ache in his knee.

"Sure," he said. "A smaller glass though. I'm driving out of here tonight."

The bartender arched an eyebrow. "So a half-pint?"

"Yeah, whatever," Chase shrugged and gave the championship ring on his finger a twist, a souvenir of days gone by. Much like the wedding ring on his other hand. On another day he might've wondered why he was still wearing either. In the moment however, he'd reached a point beyond caring, helped along the way by the honey-lager. One more and he'd split this podunk town, try to pretend it never existed, that he'd never been.

Not that he'd ever succeed. Vaughn, Perry, and the others would make sure he didn't.

"Excuse me? Sir? Are you... are you Chase Dempster? The hockey player?" The voice was husky, yet feminine.

Unable to help himself, Chase jerked slightly in surprise. He turned to find two women standing a few feet away, watching him.

"Hi," they said in unison, grinning. Both gave him a small wave.

He guessed the younger, a blonde, to be around twenty-eight or twenty-nine; the older appeared a youthful fifty, her hair silvery-gray, a few soft lines etched in her features. Possibly mother-daughter, though doubtful. The blonde's face was crafted of pale Scandinavian lines, whereas the gray-haired one had a darker cast to her.

The blonde let out a squeal a younger Chase would have found enticing. "Eeeeeeh! It is him! It is Chase Dempster!"

The older woman, whom in Chase's youth would've fit his definition of a 'silver fox,' spoke with the voice which had first called for his attention. "We're sorry to bother you, Mr. Dempster. We're just really big fans. That and we don't get many celebrities passing through Darkwater."

Chase flashed the duo his most inviting smile, thankful he'd never left any of his teeth on the ice. Unlike his career. Thankfully, he'd earned his championship ring before blowing out his knee.

"Oh, no trouble at all," he replied. "Always a pleasure to meet some fans." The two women smiled again, filling Chase with old, familiar warmth. Out of the corner of his eye he glimpsed the bartender's sneer as the latter pulled a draught from the tap. Chase ignored him.

The blonde piped up again, "I can't believe it! An honest-to-goodness Stanley Cup champion! Would you like to come sit with us, Mr. Dempster? We'd love to… get to know you better." A nervous smile accompanied a nervous gesture towards a table near the door of the bar. There, a redhead and a brunette, both in their mid-thirties, were watching excitedly and waved when Chase turned their way.

The thought, *a set of assorted flavors*, ran through Chase's mind, followed by a spur of insecurity. Twenty-five years ago he would have been delighted at the possibilities. Now, age, a busted knee, and a broken marriage had left him more than a little bruised.

"Come, Mr. Dempster, come sit with us!" The brunette waved him over as the redhead snatched a chair from another table. The blonde and the older woman waited impatiently for his decision. The bartender shook his head as he placed Chase's beer on a vacant coaster. Chase was pleased to note none of the ladies paid the bartender any mind, or even seemed to notice his presence.

"Well..." Chase hesitated, "I only stopped in for a quick one, and I still have to find a motel for the night."

"Oh! That wouldn't be a problem, Mr. Dempster. I own the Darkwater Inn, a few blocks away. I have a few vacancies at this time. I'm sure I could set you up in a room. On the house." The silver-haired woman smiled coyly at him.

Chase blinked, surprised, but also intrigued. A bit of the old Chase Dempster rose up: the one from before he'd met Stephanie Chambers, the one which had disappeared long before she'd served him with papers stamped with 'irreconcilable differences.'

"Well," his Texan drawl slipped to the fore, "It would be remiss of me to turn down such a generous offer." He glanced over at the table where the other women waited. "If it's not too much trouble, that is."

"Of course not, Mr. Dempster. Please, join us." The two women escorted him over to the table where their friends squirmed like excited schoolgirls about to meet their teen boy band crush.

A quick round of introductions was made. Kathleen of the husky voice and silver hair was clearly the matriarch of the quartet. Blonde Katrina of the squeaky voice was next; all bright-eyed and bushy-tailed. Chase was tired just from watching her bounce in her chair. The brunette, Kari, was the chatterbox of the crew; Chase noticed she was also the only one who wore a wedding ring. Self-consciously, he slipped his own off under the table, dropping the gold band into his pocket with only a slight measure of guilt. *Stephanie's choice*, he reminded himself. He'd been willing to work things through.

Which left Katherine the redhead. Chase was fond of redheads; his estranged wife was testament to that. And Katherine had everything he liked about redheads in spades, from the touch of freckles on her cheeks, to the slight rasp in her voice, to her sparkling emerald eyes. In fact, Katherine could have easily passed for Stephanie as she had been fifteen years ago.

Maybe this side trip didn't have to be a waste of time, after all. Again, Chase felt a little of his old self returning, like a call back to his glory days.

"What brings you to Darkwater, Mr. Dempster?" Kari, the brunette, peered at him with interest.

"Please, call me Chase. I'm not sure if you know, but since I retired from the ice, I've been working as an NHL talent scout…"

The foursome nodded in unison. Chase found it a little eerie.

"Currently I'm with the new Seattle expansion. I got a tip the other day that one of your local teams, Darkwater Diamonds, might have a 'diamond-in-the-rough' so to speak, so I drove up to take a look. Of course, it turned out to be a bad tip; I didn't realize the Diamonds were a beer league."

He grimaced at a group of middle-aged men dressed in denim and flannel, who cheered as one of their number balanced a stack of empty beer mugs on his forehead.

All four women shot the inebriated hockey crew a look of derision. "Definitely no 'diamonds-in-the-rough' there," snorted the redhead, "You'd be lucky to find a cubic zirconium in that bag of rocks."

The quartet guffawed, and Chase chuckled.

"Are you all on a team yourselves?" Chase asked, noting their matching black and pink Runback jackets.

The silver fox gave Chase a smile that left him a little light-headed, though he admitted to himself it might just be the beer.

"Yes, we are. We're the Darkwater Divas. The local women's curling team. I'm the team skip. Kari's the vice, Katherine's our second, and Katrina's our lead."

"That…is a lot of K's." Chase struggled to keep them all straight, as he took another pull from his beer.

"Yeah, people started calling us the Special K's," Kari remarked. "Only they started putting the emphasis on 'special' 'cause we can't seem to move past the first round of a tournament."

"Except, I feel our luck changing," winked Katherine. "After all, we have a Stanley Cup champion among us! A bona fide NHL star!"

"And not just a star," squealed Katrina, "but a Star! From Dallas!"

Everyone, including Chase, gave a surprised laugh. Kathleen grinned at him, "Looks like you're our Lucky Star, Mr. Dempst—I mean, Chase. Can we buy you another beer?"

Chase glanced down at the glass in his hand, surprised to find it empty. "Why that would be very kind of you," he said graciously. He raised his glass and waggled it at the bartender across the room, as he silently thanked the gods of hockey that not only had he been allowed to keep his teeth, but that his Darkwater excursion hadn't been a completely wasted trip. Even if he wasn't lucky to land some female companionship for the night, at least he had some now. It had been a long time since he'd felt that kind of warmth.

* * *

Chase woke up with a dull throb in his knee and in his temples, and instantly regretted drinking so much beer. Thankfully, his bladder wasn't troubling him at all. Another thought followed: *What if he'd lost control of his bladder while he was unconscious?* Reflexively, he reached for his groin, only to be stopped short. Lifting his hand twice more produced the same result, which he found duplicated when he tried to lift his other hand.

Touched by panic, he tried to sit up only to find himself restrained across his chest. Reason slipped away as he struggled against his bonds, which also ran across his thighs and secured his feet. Even as his rational mind stepped aside for instinctive terror, his senses categorized other facts: the light around him was diffuse and distant; he was fully dressed, and in fact, warmly dressed; the air was cold on his face; and finally, he wasn't alone.

A squeaky voice spoke in the dim light. "I told you the restraints would hold. We've had to deal with bigger men than him at the hospital."

Chase turned his head towards the voice as a murmur of approval rose from three others. In the dimness he could make them out—the Darkwater Divas—standing there watching him with an eagerness he was beginning to think he'd misinterpreted the first time around. All four wore dark, hooded robes straight out of a Hammer horror film. Still hazy from drink and adrenalin, Chase asked the first question that came to mind.

"What's with the robes?"

"Do you like them?" Kari asked. "I picked them up at the Halloween store that pops up every year. I know it seems kind of cliché, but they really provide a sense of unity, I think. Like our own uniforms."

"But what about your curling jackets?" Chase's wits started to return to him. Looking around, he appeared to be in some kind of ice rink, one that was much narrower than a hockey arena.

Three rows of bleachers lined the walls, with no glass to separate the ice from spectators. The muted light came from overhead fluorescents dimmed down to the point where Chase couldn't be sure if there were anybody there in the stands. For all he could tell, the five of them were alone.

Katherine's slight, sexy rasp answered him. "We thought of that, but we didn't want to take a chance on getting blood on our jackets. We're still wearing them underneath, though."

The mention of blood drove a cold spike of fear through Chase. He raised his head and took a second look, this time focusing on his immediate surroundings. Brown leather restraints bound him to a white-sheeted hospital gurney. From underneath a patch of white gauze on his hand, a trail of clear tubing ran to a large white box mounted on an IV pole, its surface covered in dials and digital displays. From the box, two more lines of tubing ran upwards to the top of the pole, where two empty IV bags each hung in separate plastic cases with transparent covers.

A third snake of tubing led out of the fly of his unbuttoned jeans to another bag on a second IV pole; this third sac was nearly bursting with yellow fluid.

"Oh my God!" gasped Chase. "What are you...you...you drugged me!"

He didn't expect the reaction he got. All four women burst out laughing.

"Oh, silly boy," cooed Kathleen. Or was it Katherine? No, that was the redhead. The silver-haired one with the husky voice was Kathleen. "I admit, we were going to. But we didn't need to. You, dear man, cannot hold your beer." She gestured to the IV bag of amber liquid.

Comprehension widened Chase's eyes with horror. "You...you stuck a catheter in me?"

"It's alright, Chase. Katrina..." the diminutive blonde waved enthusiastically from beneath her Halloween-store robe, "is a nurse. She knew what she was doing. We couldn't have you staining the gurney, after all."

"I have to have it back by six," Katrina squeaked. "That's when the morning shift starts."

Chase dropped his head back on the small pillow. "I don't understand. What is happening here?" He looked questioningly at Kathleen.

"Kari will explain. It was her idea. She should get the credit." Kathleen nodded at the trio and the brunette stepped forward, almost tripping on the hem of her robe.

"Hi Chase. To explain: you see, I actually got the idea when my husband was watching a documentary on ice sports. You see, there's this whole thing about the 'lucky loonie.'" Kari hiked up her robe and fished a gold-colored Canadian coin from out of her pocket. "You see, it started in Salt Lake City in 2002, when a loonie was buried in center ice. That year both the men's and the women's Canadian hockey teams took home the gold, and Wayne Gretzy donated the loonie to the Hockey Hall of Fame.

"In Turin 2006, loonies were buried at each end of the ice in the curling rink. The men's curling team took their first ever gold that year.

"Then came 2010. Canada won twenty-six medals, fourteen of them gold, setting the world record for most gold medals won by a single country during a Winter Games. Given, it was Vancouver that hosted, I have no doubt there were loonies hidden everywhere.

"So you see, I had this idea that maybe we could do the same. Turn our losing streak into a winning one."

"Only it didn't work," Katherine interjected.

"We didn't win a single game," offered Katrina. "If anything, it got worse. Everyone else started having great luck. Against us."

Kathleen jumped in. "It became pretty clear that we needed something different. Something new. And then, Kari found the book." She raised an old, thick book bound in brown, cracked leather.

"You see," Kari started again, "My son got into the occult for a little while—honestly, Brad and I were just so happy it wasn't drugs."

Another appreciative murmur passed between the four women, as Chase wondered how he'd missed the signpost on the way into Darkwater that read: '*Now Entering the Twilight Zone.*'

"Anyways, I was going through all his books one day—my son Tony's, not my husband Brad's—to try to understand the appeal. You see, if you understand their hobbies, you can connect with them better," another nod of assent from the group, "and then I found the answer to our problems."

"The ritual," Katrina chipped in.

"The ritual," repeated Kari. "This one book, the *De Vermis Mysteriis* had—has," she glanced at the book in Kathleen's hands, "a ritual to bestow luck on anyone who performs it." She took a deep breath. "Only it comes with a catch."

"It's a blood ritual," said Katherine. "Basically, instead of putting a loonie in the ice, we mix the lifeblood of a sacrifice into the red ice paint that the curling rings are painted with. That, we hope, will give us the luck we need to win."

"Which is where you come in, Mr. Dempster," Kathleen said. "We were going to use one of those idiots from the Diamonds. We were waiting for them to get drunk enough to lure one away without anyone noticing. Then Katherine spotted you at the bar."

Katherine took over, her voice laced with excitement, "I knew the minute I recognized you, it was meant to be. I'm sure one of those imbeciles would've worked fine, but a former NHL star!"

"And a Stanley Cup champion to boot!" Kari beamed at Chase.

"Hold on! Hold on a second!" Chase tried to keep the frantic edge out of his voice. "Why don't you take my ring? My Stanley Cup ring. You can bury it in the ice and it'll be like a loonie, only an actual championship token. You're bound to change your luck. And you don't have to sacrifice anyone. Especially me. Please. Take it. All yours. I give it freely."

A thoughtful silence fell across the rink. Chase lay statue-still, ears straining, a desperate prayer cycling through his head.

"He's got a point," said Kari. "Technically, the ring would probably work."

Chase allowed himself a sliver of hope.

"I don't know," Katherine said doubtfully. "We've gone to a lot of work to set this up. The gurney, the robes, renting the rink all night...I had to get Bob to reverse the motor on the rapid infuser without him suspecting anything..."

Chase decided he didn't like redheads anywhere as much as he used to.

"It would save us a lot of other work, though," Kathleen mused. "We still have to dispose of the body. And we didn't plan for his rental car. We would need to figure that out, still. Taking the ring would save us a lot of hassle."

Chase flushed with thankfulness when he saw Kari and Katherine had begun to nod in agreement. His gratitude was cut short when Katrina spoke, her squeaky voice filled with a surprising conviction.

"We can't take just the ring. He knows who we are. We have him strapped to a hospital gurney in the middle of our curling rink, with an IV and a catheter in him, and a circle of candles all around the ice."

Chase couldn't help himself; he strained to spy the candles on the ice.

Katrina continued. "Conspiracy to commit murder may not be murder, but we're still committing a felony. If we let him go, there is no way in hell he doesn't turn us in. And even if he didn't, we have no guarantee the ring will work. Whereas if we take both his ring and his blood..."

Chase shuddered as the foursome exchanged glances, pondering their teammate's words.

"We do already have the body disposal figured out..." Katherine commented.

"Between the four of us, we should be able to figure out how to return the car without too much suspicion," Kari suggested. "We've come this far."

Kathleen studied each of the Divas in turn, nodding. "It's settled then." She gazed down at Chase. "I'm sorry, Mr. Dempster. Please understand this isn't personal. We do like you, and we are fans. We're just tired of being on the wrong side of the backline."

She glanced up. "Kari, why don't you start lighting the candles? Katrina, you have the athame?"

Kathleen opened the leather-bound tome to a dog-eared page.

Katrina strode over, pulling a slender black-handled dagger from underneath her robe. Spotting it, Chase began yelling for help.

"It's no use," Katherine told him. "The building is soundproof, we're here after hours, and Darkwater's too small a town to need night security. We have the whole rink to ourselves."

"Besides, Chase," Katrina joined in, "we're not going to stab you through the heart or anything so dramatic. All we need is a little nick for the ritual. The rest we'll collect with the rapid infuser that Katherine's boyfriend modified; that's the device on the IV pole. Normally it transfuses blood into you; Bob's rewired to pull the blood out of you. Though Bob doesn't know that. It'll be quick; the infuser can pull as much as a thousand milliliters of blood in a minute. I promise you, it won't hurt at all. It will be like going to sleep."

"Please, you don't have to do this," Chase begged them. "I can pay you. I have money; I've made some good investments. And I promise—I swear—I won't tell. Not a soul."

"We don't want money though," chided Kari, who had returned holding a barbeque lighter. "We're all quite comfortable, financially. What we want is to win."

The quartet took up positions at the four corners of the gurney, Kathleen and Katrina near Chase's head, Kari and Katherine down at his feet. Katherine carefully pulled the IV pole with the box-like humming machine a little closer.

"Are we ready?" Kathleen asked. The others nodded. "Let's begin."

The four women closed their eyes and each held one hand out over Chase, palms down. As one, they began to chant.

"*Si vocare te gelu de altissimis tenebris premuntur, Walker ventus.*"

(From the darkest ice we summon thee, wind-walker.)

Chase gaped at his captors in disbelief. Then it occurred to him: a joke. It was all a joke. An elaborate prank set up by Vaughn and Perry and the others. It had to be.

"*Ex gelida vocamus te vastitates saeculi, silentio ab Alba.*"

(From the frozen wastes we call thee, Silence of the White.)

Chase's head whipped around as he tried to scan the outer edges of the ring. Were they there now, in the stands, having a laugh at their fellow talent scout? Or watching from the warm comfort of a nearby hotel room through the eye of a hidden camera?

A sickening thought occurred to him. *Was Stephanie in on this?*

"*Wendigo forti, audi nos causa.*"

(Mighty Wendigo, hear our plea.)

Angered and a little frightened at the thought of his frigid, soon-to-be ex-wife conspiring with his peers to turn a stupid snipe hunt into something so much more elaborate and cruel, Chase barely registered that Kathleen had unzipped his parka down to the chest restraint, and was in the process of undoing his shirt.

"*Offer te ad nos sanguinem hominis huius gustum,*"

(We offer thee this man's blood to taste,)

Kathleen snatched Chase's attention back as she held his shirt and parka apart, exposing a small portion of his upper chest. Katrina reached over, balancing the tip of the athame on his pectoral, immediately above his heart.

"I get it now, I get it! You're funny! You guys are real funny! You really had me going!" Chase shouted furiously into the empty rink.

"*Nos offer munus suum animam tuam,*"

(We offer his soul for thine boon,)

"You can call it off now!" Chase's voice carried over the foursome's chant. "I'm wise to you! Not funny anymore!"

Then he saw it. A figure, cloaked in shadow, dark and indefinable, in the stands. Watching.

"Stephanie!" he called. "Stephanie! Is that you?"

"*Ithaqua, dona nobis gratiam tuam!*"

(Ithaqua, grant us thy favor!)

"OW!" Chase cried out, jerking in his restraints. The cut left by the athame was shallow, not much deeper than a scratch, yet it seared with icy fire. Blood welled up and struggled to move beyond its exit. The pain in his bad knee was long forgotten.

At the foot of the gurney, Katherine reached over and pressed a button on the humming machine attached to the IV pole. A loud beep was followed by the low whir of a motor. A stream of crimson shot up the IV tube from under the gauze patch on Chase's hand. The stream disappeared into the bottom of the machine and reappeared at the top, where it funneled up and began to fill one of the two empty IV bags.

"What? No- no, this has to be a joke. It has to be...a sick, stupid prank." He spied the figure in the stands again, a malignant stalagmite in the empty rink. "Vaughn! Is that you? Perry! Perry, call it off! Call it off! Stephanie..." A wave of dizziness pulled the words away from him.

The IV bag filled at an alarming rate as the chanting continued.

Chase again looked at the thing in the bleachers, seeking if not succor, at least some clarity. The shroud lifted its head and Chase stared into burning eyes as cold and ancient as Polaris itself. Above its terrible gaze sat a crown of antlers, majestic and corrupt.

Chase understood. This was not Stephanie, here to witness a final humiliation before cutting him out of her life. Nor was it Vaughn or Perry, reaping the fruits of an elaborate stunt. No, the thing in the bleachers was here for him. To collect. It wanted him in a way that no mortal ever had.

Terror surged through Chase's veins and arteries, replacing the lifeblood that drained from them.

"*Nos offer munus suum animam tuam! Ithaqua, dona nobis gratiam tuam!*"

(We offer his soul for thine boon! Ithaqua, grant us they favor!)

A bitter cold settled into Chase, a cold born of outer darkness and eldritch winds. A cold not felt in his dying physical frame, but in the depths of his soul. The first IV bag filled, which prompted the infuser to switch to the second sac without hesitation.

He was dead before the second bag swelled to completion. To his horror, he did not die alone; however, when Kari looked to see what he was staring at, all she saw were empty stands.

* * *

The Special K's, as they'd rebranded themselves once they started curling on the international circuit, beamed at each other as medals were placed around their necks. Gold for their country. Gold for the pride of Darkwater. Gold for Kathleen, Kari, Katherine, and Katrina.

In one unified motion, all four reached up to gently touch their breastbones, above the gold medallions. To their millions of adoring fans, it was a gesture of patriotism, of camaraderie, of heartfelt gratitude for their finest achievement. To the Special K's, it was simply reaffirming their lucky talismans were still there, underneath their curling jackets.

It had been Kari's idea, after her husband Brad had watched a documentary about Angelina Jolie. Ms. Jolie and a former lover had worn vials of each other's blood around their necks; this had inspired the four women to create their own versions, using the lifeblood of their Lucky Star.

Outside in the darkness, the wind howled through the city of Milan as the light of Polaris, the North Star continued to reach across the void.

THE STIFF AND THE DEAD
By Josh Darling

He had at least fifteen, maybe twenty years on me. The Father's black shirt framed his white priest collar. The collar was a few shades lighter than his pale wrinkled skin. In the past, I'd held two other online auctions for this sort of thing. The first time, a thrill-seeker millionaire showed up. The second time, a devil-worshipping freak was at my door. It made sense. Dollars and cents. After all, Annabelle Jane Montgomery was five years old. I remember reading a story online about Jared, the Subway deli spokesperson busted as a kiddie toucher. He'd sent a friend a text saying something like *boys or girls, I don't care; it's the fact they're kids that turns me on.* I didn't want to ask The Father if that was true with all pedophiles.

In my vestibule, The Father presented me with a leather satchel.

It was heavy. That surprised me.

Placing it on the hallway table, I opened it. There were bundles of bills. None were new or fresh. The money was old and soft, like the man in my doorway.

I thumbed through the banded stacks of bills.

"You don't trust me?" he smirked.

"Given what this money is for, no." I returned to the cash.

He interrupted my counting with, "Have you been here long?"

I thumbed through another stack of hundreds, "I've been in Litchfield my whole life. I took over the family business when my uncle died. This looks good, come in."

I didn't think about where I should put the bag.

I seldom receive cash.

Closing the door behind him, he followed me. Despite the wear of years on him, The Father had some pep in his step. His cheeks were flush. From behind his closed-mouth smile, he hummed an upbeat tune.

I stopped at my basement door. "That a gospel tune?"

"Katy Perry's *California Girls*."

"Never heard of it; I mostly listen to folk music."

From my black slacks, I pulled the basement key and unlocked the door.

A few steps down, I turned; he was still on the landing.

"Close the door behind you," I said.

"Don't want them getting out?"

"Worse. I'd hate for anyone to get in."

"At this hour?" The Father said.

"Would you prefer to *not* take every precaution?"

Humming with his head bobbing in time to the tune, he pulled the door closed.

He followed me to the bottom of the stairs.

Where she was.

I didn't care about her.

Seeing Annabelle Jane Montgomery's small, naked body, he drew in his breath, making an *oh* sound.

"Can I touch her?" he asked.

"Yeah, but there are some rules."

He darted to the girl.

Annabelle laid, eyes closed and relaxed with the overhead work light washing out her skin.

He touched her lips with his fingers, then her chin, then down the middle of her chest, his fingertips curving into the air before reaching her bellybutton.

His hands trembled. Clasping them together, he held them to his lips.

The bag full of money strained my arm.

Money was money, and Annabelle Jane Montgomery was dead.

Better her than a living child.

I'd been in her position once, but I was living, and it was not as clichéd as a priest. That's probably how I got to be this age and alone. The experience was necrotic poison, killing every relationship I'd ever had.

What did it matter?

As of now, I was rich.

"Before I go upstairs, let's talk about some rules."

"I don't understand." His head shook as if startled out of a good dream.

"In two days, she's having an open casket funeral. Please, be gentle with her and don't create more work for me. I can fix a lot, but there are limitations to what I can do."

"How could I hurt something so cute? I just want to love her. Can I ask, how did she die?"

"She had a defective heart valve no one knew about. She died on the playground in the middle of recess."

"Poor baby." Leaning over her, he kissed her lips. It was a tiny peck, like a grandparent kissing a sick grandchild. His hand slid around her neck, encircling it. His tongue pushed passed her lips.

I wanted to vomit.

"Be careful with her neck, you're likely to break it."

He nodded.

I coughed, "And please don't touch her eyes or cheeks. I've put eye caps in and I don't want to do anything twice."

"Eye caps?"

"They're like contact lenses with ridges on them. They keep the eyes closed and prevent a sunken eye look depending on how long of a wait there is before the funeral."

I'd yet to sew her mouth shut. I didn't know what the highest bidder might want. I can fix anything, but I'm not looking for extra work. Enough years as a mortician and cleaning up knife wounds to the head becomes no big thing.

This massive old guy was going to climb on my stainless-steel table and mount the body of a five-year-old dead girl; it was an awful thing to think about. I pulled the overbed table away from the work area. I'd already laid out the injectors and needles I'd need for embalming her and I didn't want him to slip and land on them. Or worse, just touch my stuff.

Wow, I hate him.

"You've got three hours."

Before I could turn, he was working his belt.

* * *

The warmth of the black coffee in my hands spread to my fingers. Too many nights I'd sat here, hunched over my kitchen table thinking about escaping Vermont and moving someplace tropical. In the past, I'd be here talking to my uncle. When he died, all I had left were regrets and the voices in my head.

I hadn't thought this through.

The last two online auctions, I'd made close to 20 grand each for a total of $40,000. I could hide that under the metaphorical mattress. I didn't have to explain it. I could spend it on food, a new TV, some new furniture, having some change to spend the few times I could get away during the week.

In the house I'd inherited from my uncle, along with his business, under the kitchen sink, behind the trash was a bag full of money. A few months back, when the devil-worshipping Satan freak showed up with 20 thousand dollars to defile the corpse of a 22-year-old stripper who'd died of a coke overdose, it didn't faze me.

I didn't feel like I'd given up a piece of me.

At the same time, I had no connection to strippers.

I'd made a mistake.

This was gross.

As a child, I was in the other room listening to my father and uncle talk about killing a man while they sat at this table. My father plotting his great mistake.

"He's my son, I don't think a court in the country would convict me."

"I think you'll find yourself with fifteen-to-life at Southern State in Windsor and you'll never see your son again."

"Defending your child is what a parent is supposed to do."

"Then call the police."

"What, and have him go to court? Have him relive and explain to the whole world what he came to me in tears about? You think I want him talking about this ever again?"

"Before you do anything rash, think about it. Think about him. He needs you."

"I am thinking about him."

About a year before this conversation, my mother died of stomach cancer.

About five years after this conversation, my father died shivved in prison.

Escaping from memory, I poured my coffee into the sink, rinsed the cup, and left it in the dish rack.

I opened the cupboard and pulled the trashcan out from under it.

* * *

Descending the stairs, I heard him.

Not moaning or grunting or huffing; instead, he repeated, "Oh Jessica… Oh Jessica…"

He'd stripped off everything but his black socks and tasseled loafers. He'd draped his clothes over the embalming pump. A bad choice to hang his clothes on, if he knew how temperamental and expensive it was.

The old man stroked her hair with one hand and stroked himself with the other.

I gave him my best polite mortician's cough. The one I use to prompt the grieving.

I'm sure he'd used the same cough at funerals as well.

"I don't get hard the way I used to. Granted, this is my third dead child. Something about the safety of the situation makes me struggle for arousal. I thought I could do the gentle thing, but she didn't suffer enough. It diminishes the experience if you can't hear them cry or choke the life out of them and then get down to business."

His words gagged me.

He said, "You've been there for a few minutes, is there a problem?"

"No."

"I'd like to get started and you're standing there with the bag I gave you, what's going on?"

"I need you to get dressed and leave. You can have your money back."

Dropping his soft penis, he straightened his back and squared with me.

"If the police are on their way, I am friendly with the state's attorney in Montpelier. I'm sure we can be presentable before—"

"No, I just need you to leave."

Raised eyebrows wrinkled his forehead.

"You have crisis of conscience written all over your face, I see it all the time. Look, son, she's dead. She's more or less a thing at this point. I'm no more harming her than if I were sticking it in a plastic vagina." His nose angled up at the ceiling. The arrogance of a Sunday school teacher correcting a child's questioning of a god filled the pauses between his words.

"I need you to get out."

He circled the metal table.

He got close enough for me to smell the stink of his breath. A mixture of brandy, cigars, and old man halitosis that could strip the paint off a barn.

"Make me."

My rage was supersonic.

My fist connected to his face.

His wrinkled flesh undulated.

Knocked a step back, he laughed.

"I'm going to sue you, I came here to speak with you about grief counseling methods and you attacked me, or at least that's what it will say in the papers."

On the overbed table, I'd set up the trocars I'd need to take care of Annabelle. I remember the first time my uncle asked me to get a trocar, "It's like a thick needle with a handle." I kept saying *trocar* all day. Looking for excuses, like "this *trocar* is hooked up to the embalming machine, and when the embalming machine is on, it sucks blood through one *trocar* and pumps embalming fluid out another *trocar*…"

I love the sound of that word…

Trocar…

"No, the papers won't say that."

Grabbing a *trocar*, I jabbed it into the old man's neck.

I'd done this more times in my life then I'd shaved my face. The embalming process begins with inserting a trocar into the side of the neck.

Without trying, I'd hit the carotid artery.

My first time with a living person and bullseye.

He made an all teeth donkey face. His hands trembled inches from the trocar's handle. There was no blood, no mess, the hose hadn't filled with fluid. Then I turned the embalming machine and his blood rocketed through the hose faster than anything I'd seen before.

An *eeertp* noise escaped his mouth.

The old man pulled the trocar up and out of his neck.

Sucking air, it hissed.

In perfect beats, blood bolted from his neck.

It covered Annabelle, the tile floor, the embalming pump, the tile walls. He turned and I moved back, not wanting to get sprayed. Wobbling on weak legs, he tried stopping the red flow with his fingers.

"Help me, please, I'll give you more money, I have access to millions, the church has infinite funds... anything you want..."

The words faded to mumbles, as the spray became spurts and the spurts became a flowing trickle.

Maybe I'm sick, but my first thought was, this couldn't have happened in a better place. The room and the equipment in it were mess proof.

Years ago, my uncle and I had to prepare a man who got the bright idea of heating his cast iron bathtub by placing a camping stove under it. The hot water raised his blood pressure and he passed from a stroke. His wife found him after he'd been slow cooking for hours. When we received him, he leaked from everywhere. His flesh came off at the touch. He was worse than a drowning victim who'd been in the water for days.

This guy leaked and leaked.

When my uncle and I finished, this room was spotless, and the deceased had an open casket funeral.

In less than an hour, this room would be spotless and I'd have buried The Father below a grave dug for a funeral for tomorrow morning. Before noon, a casket would be lowered on top of him.

It was riskier than cremating him, which was also an option, but I wanted him rotting. I wanted him covered in filth and dirt. I wanted him stinking in the earth and devoured by worms.

* * *

I figured, I'd be done cleaning everything in time to catch Stephen Colbert; that included figuring in taking a shower.

I didn't get to Colbert.

I fell asleep during the news.

I know you're supposed to feel awful after killing someone. Maybe I would have, if I weren't exhausted. Being out in the cold night air digging a shallow grave inside a deeper grave drained me. And autumnal chills always make me sleepy. I think some of it is also as you get older you build up defenses to the rougher aspects of life. Had I done this as a young man, I'm sure it'd mess me up for the rest of my life. Middle-aged, all I've got now is a *meh, so what?* to describe my emotional state.

I woke to Stephen Colbert laughing at an actress's story from behind his desk.

I listened.

I felt the bed for the remote. Thumbing "mute," Colbert went silent mid-question.

I listened, pushing into the absence of noise, waiting.

Every now and then I get kids messing around in the graveyard at night. I've even caught them making out. But this wasn't in the graveyard; this was closer.

I grabbed my aluminum Louisville Slugger from under the bed. It was a small bat. My uncle got it for me when I played little league baseball. I leaned it on the side of the dresser as I changed into jeans and a t-shirt.

I didn't want intruders murdering me in my pajamas.

Death is undignified enough.

I listened, picking the bat up.

Cracking wood sounded from below.

The logical thing would be to call the police.

Adrenaline doesn't always fuel logic.

I sprinted downstairs.

In the kitchen, there was a mess of glass on the floor. The backyard door opened over the clear shards on the floor. A light breeze nudged the curtains on the door where a window used to be. The draft filled the kitchen. This door wasn't opened with a bang. That came from the caving in of the basement door.

"Oh yeah, how do you like that, Jessica? Yeah, you little fucking whore. Oh god, oh Jesus, you take it all…"

I guess when I drained the blood out of The Father I didn't kill him. I only thought I'd killed him. Exsanguinated, he looked dead. I buried him. He got up and came back here…

…to fuck the corpse of a five-year-old girl.

I crept down the stairs.

He was too into his passionate frenzy to notice me, but still, I did my best to be quiet.

The Father wore his loafers, black socks, and the filth I'd covered him in. He hadn't gone to a hospital or called the police. He came here, to climb up on my dissection table and call Annabelle Jessica Montgomery a whore as he slammed his hips between her legs that were as thick as his arms.

Sneaking behind him was easy. Seeing his pasty, dirty, wrinkled ass jiggle was not.

"Oh God, Jessica, be purified by my holy seed inside you…"

The ding of the bat knocked him square off the table.

I'd hit him so hard, his scalp ripped open. A chunk of bone stuck to the skin flap bending off his head.

Nothing bled out of the hole.

The mortician in me thought, *I'll get some crazy glue and fix that right up*.

He'd gotten dirt all over Annabelle.

In all my years around dead bodies, I'd never defiled a corpse. I've taken money from people to allow them to defile corpses, but I'd never done it myself.

I don't get it.

And now, I have to clean her.

Dropping the bat, I reached for the overbed table.

Scalpel in hand, I cut The Father's dick off and threw in the trash. If I was wrong about him being dead this time, at least I'd taken his instrument of harm.

I cleaned off Annabelle. I swept up the glass in the kitchen. I dragged The Father back to the same grave.

I tossed him in the grave and covered him with dirt.

Again.

Inside, I washed off my hands and lay down to rest with my clothes on. I was too exhausted to bother changing. Tomorrow I'd have to hit the hardware store and get a new pane of glass and a replacement door for the basement.

The television's soft illumination filled the room.

I fell asleep to muted infomercials.

I couldn't breathe.

Someone was on top of me.

"Where's my dick?" The Father shouted.

Pulling at the hand clutching my neck, I sipped the air.

"Go to hell."

He struck me, and I thought I'd been punched.

With his hand up, the TV's light silhouetted my kitchen knife. It came down again. The stabs came in rapid succession. One, two, three, four, five holes in my side.

Clutching my lacerated ribs, I felt cold.

He'd gotten me good.

I wheezed.

One of my lungs was flooding. Coughing hurt, but I couldn't stop it. My body was trying to force the blood out of where air should be.

I wanted more covers but convulsed instead.

I was going into shock.

He left.

Death is not blackness, and neither is nothingness blackness.

There just isn't.

I regained awareness.

The bed sheets felt like sticky crushed cardboard. I peeled them off, breaking the crust of my dried bodily fluids. Getting up, my cuts seeped black clotting blood. I took a T-shirt from the dirty laundry and pressed it to my side, stopping the mess.

I couldn't have a messy funeral home.

The wounds were there, but they weren't debilitating.

I listened, for the sound of my breathing or my heartbeat.

Nothing.

I listened, waiting.

Nothing.

I listened.

Groaning, two floors down.

He'd taken a knife from the kitchen.

I went to my maintenance shed. I figured I needed something heavy-duty for a guy I'd thought I'd already killed, twice.

Equipment in hand, I returned to the house.

I felt purpose, real purpose, for the first time in a long time.

But, he got me, I was going to die—or maybe I was already dead? No, I was getting stupid from the blood loss…

At the top of the stairs, I heard his ugly blissful moaning.

At the bottom of the stairs, I flipped the chainsaw's switch to *on*.

I looked up, searching for my target.

His hands were under Annabelle's knees, holding her legs up and spread. His face buried between her thighs. Working his head up and down, he lapped and whimpered. Lying beside Annabelle was the kitchen knife.

A stainless-steel blade resting on a stainless-steel table.

I pulled the chainsaw's cord. It rumbled but didn't start.

Straightening his back, he turned.

"You threw my dick in the trash. Now, look at what I had to do." He pointed with his hands at his penis.

He'd reattach his member using surgical staples. If he were alive, he'd get a bad infection from not cleaning it.

Palms facing upward, he said, "I can't get hard."

"So?"

"Fix this."

"That's what the chainsaw is for."

Kneeling, I put the chainsaw on the floor.

I pulled the cord, more rumbling but it didn't start.

He squinted, "How would a chainsaw fix anything?"

I realized what I was doing wrong.

I use the chainsaw once or twice a year. When a large tree branch falls and I need to cut it up for firewood. Beyond that, it sits in the maintenance shed untouched. I do this every goddamn time I go to use it. Without fail, I'm always pulling the cord and the thing isn't starting. I'd forgotten to prime it. I gave the bulb a few squeezes.

"You bastard," he said, grabbing the knife.

I guess he figured out how the chainsaw would fix things.

He ran for me.

I pulled the cord.

The chainsaw jumped to life with a vicious buzz.

Feet away from me, his charge made me tense.

I clutched the throttle.

The chainsaw jolted.

Engine revving, it displaced his skin, flesh, muscle, and bone, right where the leg meets the hip. The chain's rotation sprayed mess across the room with geyser force. With the knife in hand, he clutched the wound. Pulling the saw back and up, it caught the middle of his hand. The saw traveled between his middle and ring finger, eating some of the knife's handle.

He dropped the knife and fell.

His leg was deadwood attached to his body.

"Look at what you did to me." He supported himself with one hand.

"Did? I'm not done."

Nudging him, he toppled onto his side. A kick put him on his back.

I pinned him with a knee on his chest.

His bucking to get free was like being on a bumpy car ride.

I began at the mouth.

The chainsaw bisected his cheeks and obliterated his teeth. His free hand went wild. His legs kicked. Bits of teeth ricocheted from the chain and bounced across the floor. The saw reached the fulcrum of the jaw. I guess it was instinct to get the pain away that made him attempt grabbing the blade. The line from his wrist to the inside of his thumb divided what stayed and what hit the floor.

At his ears, he stopped fighting. Here the sound of the saw got lower, reaching substantial bone at the base of his skull.

Working fast and sloppy, reducing him to little pieces didn't take long.

Less than ten minutes.

Vivisecting him in the embalming room felt like I was on the clock.

I packed the meat on the floor into a body bag—I needed an easy way to get it to the furnace.

I don't know if my mind was playing tricks on me or if the bag was twitching.

When I got him in the furnace and fired it up, a drunk disoriented feeling moved over me.

For whatever reason, this piece of shit needed to come back to life to screw a dead girl. I guess Jessica, whoever she was, meant something to him.

At least enough to be an excuse.

Watching him burn through the glass, I felt weak.

Maybe I was dying.

Maybe I was already dead and I'd come back only to end him…

IT TAKES ONE
By Scot Carpenter

Danner frowned and moved the pencil a half-inch to the left so that it lined up with the legal pad. He stared at the spreadsheet on the computer screen. It didn't balance by exactly 1 dollar and 47 cents. He absent-mindedly scratched behind his left ear. Any other accountant in the office would have called it a rounding error. He finally left the office at six-thirty after clearing his desk and wiping it clean with a paper towel that he then folded and placed in the trashcan. The report balanced to the penny.

The kitchen was spotless, of course. He took a small tenderloin that he'd thawed the day before out of the refrigerator and set it in the middle of the cutting board, then sliced it into one-half inch cutlets. He followed the recipe exactly and cut each bite into precisely the same size. After finishing supper and washing the dishes twice, he brushed his teeth, paying special attention to his prominent canines, then changed into a jogging suit and running shoes. He left by the back door, checking three times that he'd locked it, then trotted into the nature preserve his house abutted.

The preserve was several hundred acres of dense woods interrupted by jogging and hiking trails, small clearings and picnic tables. Some of the jogging trails were lighted but there were often dark areas between the lights. The preserve also had a substantial number of homeless people scattered deep inside it.

Danner stopped at an especially dense grove, looked around, then pulled a large bandana from his pocket and spread it on the ground. He undressed, revealing a surprisingly hirsute body, and folded his clothes neatly before he laid them on the cloth. He looked toward the eastern sky where the moon had just fully risen, raised his head and howled.

Several people passed along the path that Danner lurked beside in the darkness. The dark hair covering his body helped conceal him. He sniffed the air and the hair along his spine rose. The faint footsteps of a lone walker grew louder as the plump young woman approached. He crouched in anticipation.

As she passed he slipped out the darkness and circled her soft neck with a chokehold. She struggled for a few moments as he dragged her into the woods, then her body went limp as she lost consciousness. Danner laid her on the ground and stared at her. Her heavy legs were exposed below her walking shorts and her large breasts stretched her tee shirt. He knelt down beside her, pulled her head back and began salivating as he looked at the white expanse of her neck.

As always, the first gush of arterial blood gave him an erection. He tore at the flesh in a frenzy, ripping out mouthfuls at a time and swallowing them whole. She'd regained consciousness at the first bite and thrashed on the ground as he tore her throat out, then became still.

He effortlessly picked up her body and trotted deeper into the woods, holding it in his arms. At a secluded place he stripped off her clothes and buried them in a shallow hole he dug with his hands, his thick nails making the job easier. He took a circuitous route as he carried her back to his clothes. He used the bandana to wipe the blood from his face and hands.

Danner carried the body through his dark back yard, then took it to the basement where he laid it out on a stainless steel autopsy table. Butchering it and wrapping the meat took him half the night. He wrapped each portion into a rectangular block, the larger ones sized in multiples of the smallest so that they would stack neatly. Each package had its weight, date and cut written neatly with a marker. The marker slipped on one package leaving a streak. He re-wrapped it, carefully folding the used paper before he set it aside. Putting the meat into the large top-opening freezer took half an hour, as he first emptied it, then put the fresh meat at the bottom before he arranged the rest in date order with the oldest at the top. Once he was satisfied that the freezer was properly filled, he closed the lid. Then he reopened it to check that it was properly arranged. He did this twice more. After he had put the meat into the freezer he put the discarded paper, bones, entrails, head, hands and feet into a small gas crematory that he'd built and lit it. Then he showered, made a bucket of popcorn and spent the rest of the night watching reruns of *Gilligan's Island*.

Two days later, as Detective Sergeant Hernandez walked into the bullpen, familiar smells greeted him. When he passed Johnson, he detected a shot of bourbon in his Starbucks coffee; Veronica wearing Chloe meant that she was meeting someone after work; deodorant didn't conceal that Roberts was wearing the same shirt as yesterday; and Phelps hadn't showered after sex this morning.

He sat at his desk, turned on the computer and looked around the room. Kavanagh and Smith were huddled in the corner, Kavanagh describing her new boyfriend's penis. Johnson held his cell phone close to his face as sotto voce he assured his girlfriend that his wife didn't know.

The conversation that interested him was Polasky and Voightlander discussing an animal mutilation two nights before. A farmer found a calf with its throat torn out. They thought it was probably a feral dog as wolves hadn't been in this part of the country for decades and mountain lions killed their prey by biting it in the back of the neck. Hernandez unconsciously licked his lips.

He tuned out the buzz of conversation and started going through the pile on his desk.

Lieutenant Ross appeared. "How are you doing, Frank?"

"Didn't get to sleep till four. I can't get the Harris case out of my mind. How anyone could do that to a seven-year-old?"

Ross nodded. "That's a bad one. Sorry it got thrown at you. At least the stepfather confessed. I've got something else for you. A woman's roommate reported her missing two days ago. Yesterday a hiker's dog dug up bloody clothes in the Baker nature preserve. The roommate identified them as hers."

Ross handed Hernandez a file folder, then she sat on the corner of his desk.

He opened the folder. Rebecca Noonan, age twenty-eight. Roommate Abigail Circe filed a missing persons report but no action was taken until the bloody clothes were found.

He looked up at Ross. "I'll get on it as soon as I've cleared my desk."

"Sounds good. I hope it's not another Harris case." She turned and walked back to her office.

Hernandez took a fingernail file from the top drawer and began filing his thick nails. The hair on the backs of his hands contrasted with his pale skin. The file that Ross had given him was sparse, containing a photograph of a woman in her mid-twenties with a smiling, pleasant face, short blonde hair and a thick body that still had some shape. She was standing in front of a mountain overlook. Other photographs showed a shallow hole next to a tree with a pile of clothes in it, three were of the surrounding area and the final one showed a bloody tee shirt and bra, panties, walking shorts, socks and athletic shoes spread on a table. A missing person report, a statement by the man who found the clothes and a brief report by the detective who responded to the call completed the contents.

Hernandez sighed. He finished the report on the Harris case and turned off his computer. Then he took an electric razor to the men's room and ran it over the dark stubble that went from high on his cheeks almost to his collarbone. He'd shave again in mid-afternoon.

He checked out a car and drove to the nature preserve. The detective's report gave clear directions to the scene. He walked down the trail until he came to a light pole that caught his attention. He bent down and sniffed it intently, then unzipped his pants and urinated on it, scuffing his feet backwards when he finished. Further down the trail he stopped at another pole.

At the location indicated in the report he turned off the trail and walked seventy-five yards into the woods where he found the hole that had contained the clothes. He sniffed around the area but it had rained the night before and all scent was washed away. Hernandez turned and looked back toward the trail, then took the most direct route to it. He ended up in a gap in the thick foliage that opened onto the trail. The nearest light was around a slight bend, so anyone standing a few feet back from the trail couldn't be seen. He carefully walked back into the woods examining the ground closely. Twenty-five yards in he found a disturbed area in the leaves. Despite the rain there was a barely perceptible odor of blood. Following faint tracks led him back to the site of the clothes. He picked up the tracks again and followed them for half of a mile. They wove around and at one place circled back on themselves where he lost them. He made his way back to the car and decided to interview the roommate.

She lived in a small two-story frame house in an old neighborhood that somehow hadn't deteriorated into short-term rentals, crack houses and gang hangouts. Hernandez knocked on the door and the woman who answered was the opposite of her roommate, with long brown hair, a petite figure, high cheekbones above a slightly aquiline nose and a wide, full-lipped face. She had a pale complexion but rosy cheeks and dark pink lips.

"May I help you?" she asked.

Hernandez introduced himself and why he was there. She invited him in but he stopped two steps into the living room. A large white cat with raised fur hissed at him. The hair on the back of his neck rose and he suppressed a growl.

She looked at him, curiously. "Is something wrong?" she asked.

"I'm allergic to cats. Could we talk on the porch?"

He asked her the typical questions about Rebecca: did she have a boyfriend, what was she like, did she often walk in the preserve, and so on. When he was finished, Abigail looked at him with wide-open pupils.

"I'm scared. What if this person comes after me? Is there anything you can do to protect me?"

"I can ask for increased patrols of your neighborhood."

She played with her long hair. "Could you check my house to see if it's secure? Maybe there's something I can do to make it safer." She smiled up at him with half-lidded eyes.

Christ, he thought, *a cop groupie.* He made it a rule never to have sex while on duty. His lunch hour didn't count as duty.

"I can walk the house and check the general security, locks, windows, that sort of thing. Just put the cat away."

She followed him as he went through the downstairs, pointing out things that she could do to make it more secure against a break-in. After he finished she stood closer to him.

"Would you check the upstairs, too?"

Hernandez groaned inwardly but said, "Sure."

She led him upstairs. "This is my bedroom. I'm afraid someone might come through the window." She stood back as he walked over to the window and examined the lock.

When he turned around she was in a half-crouch, her eyes tight and feral, a snarl on her mouth revealing canine teeth even bigger than his. She took a step, then launched herself across the room at him. He managed to turn to one side and grabbed her outstretched left arm. She wheeled around and dug her long fingernails into the back of his neck. He elbowed her in the ribs and threw her backwards where she crashed into the wall.

Hernandez took two steps backward. "What the fuck?"

She said nothing but opened her mouth and snarled again, her tongue flicking like a snake's. This time she came at him with her arms half extended, fingers stiff. He caught her left hand as she jabbed at him but barely ducked in time for her right hand nails to rake his forehead instead of his eyes. He grabbed her right hand and pushed her back, holding her hands up in front of her.

She was incredibly strong. He could barely hold her arms up. She kicked him in the crotch and he bent over as she pulled her right hand free. Again she raked her nails across his face, trying to get his eyes. Still bent over, Hernandez punched her in the ribs, once, twice, on the third strike he heard bones crack and she pulled away. He stepped back across the room, holding his crotch with his left hand.

She's a fucking vampire. Why didn't I sense that?

The source of the natural, rather supernatural, enmity between werewolves and vampires is lost in history. One reason may be because the blood of a single werewolf can sustain a vampire for a year. In addition, for vampires, werewolf semen is like uncut heroin. A blowjob from a vampire can drain more than a load of spunk.

In any case, a meeting between the two usually ended with either the death of the werewolf or temporarily debilitating injury to the vampire. Hernandez had no wish for either outcome.

He straightened up. "You killed her! How many others have you killed?"

Her face softened slightly. "I didn't kill her. She was my friend. She didn't know. I don't kill. Anymore, at least."

"Then how do you get the blood?"

She shrugged. "I work at the Red Cross."

"We can end this now, you know."

She touched her broken ribs. "OK. But nothing's changed."

Hernandez backed away and down the stairs. At the bottom he heard a yowl and the white cat dug its claws into the back of his leg. He turned, picked up the cat and threw it to the top of the stairs. It yowled even louder when it hit the landing. The vampire appeared at the bedroom door.

"You bastard!" she screamed as she headed for the stairs.

Hernandez turned and fled to his car. She didn't follow. He looked at himself in the mirror, then used his handkerchief to wipe the blood from his face. The wounds had stopped bleeding and would heal by tomorrow. He called the office and said he wouldn't be back that afternoon.

After Hernandez ran out of the house, Abigail slammed the front door and went into the kitchen. Soon she was on her third Bloody Mary—Stoli and O positive. She saved the A negative for special occasions, which this certainly wasn't.

Fucking werewolves and their PMS. Fucking animals, tearing out a throat and leaving the body. Pissing on trees and shitting in the woods, nothing smells worse than a werewolf turd. And then they go to McDonald's for breakfast.

The cat jumped into her lap, rubbed its face against her neck and began purring.

"Hey, Sweetie. What a good pussycat, warning me about that bad old werewolf. Did he hurt you when he threw you up the stairs? Let me see."

She held the cat up and examined it. When it quit purring and began to squirm, she brought it to her chest.

"You are such a sweet girl? Do you miss your mommy? I'll take care of you as well as she did."

Poor Becky. She was so sweet. If anybody deserved to die, it's me. I loved her like a sister.

Tears welled up in the vampire's eyes. She looked up at the calendar on the refrigerator.

Shit. It was a full moon when she went missing. I wonder if that werewolf killed her. Maybe he came to kill me. I didn't ask to see his badge; what if he isn't a cop? Now he knows what my house is like and how to get into it. Shit, shit, shit.

She put the cat down and went around the house checking all the doors and windows, then made another drink.

I need to get out of town. Stay at a motel for a few days.

She rushed around, packing a bag, putting the cat's litter box and food in the back of her SUV, blood into a cooler, six bottles of Vodka, everything she could think of. She backed the car out of the garage, swerved off the driveway onto the lawn and over the curb, finally straightening it out and weaving down the street.

* * *

The next morning Hernandez chewed his Egg McMuffin and considered the Noonan case. His thoughts were on the vampire, whether she had in fact killed her roommate.

Why would she bury the clothes but not the body? All vampires care about is the blood. If she was turning Rebecca, there was no reason for her not to be at the house.

Half an hour later he sat down at his desk and his eyes fell on the calendar. There was a little picture of a full moon on the day Rebecca disappeared.

Shit. Maybe it wasn't the vampire.

He went to records and started going through missing persons reports. There was nothing for the previous two months but the month before that a teenage girl was reported missing two days after the full moon. She was known to run away, probably spending the nights in the nearby preserve. Given that history, the detective thought she had probably run away again and just filed the report.

Hernandez went back in the records for two years. There were five reports of people who frequented the preserve who had gone missing on a full moon. A considerable number of homeless people lived in the preserve; there wouldn't be reports filed on them if they disappeared. But no bodies had been found. Most people killed in woods and similar areas were buried in shallow graves that were frequently discovered after they'd been dug up by animals.

He strummed his fingers on the desk as he thought. *What if it is a werewolf? The timing of those five makes sense but why aren't there more reports? Could all the rest have been homeless? And werewolves don't usually take the bodies. Why would it have stripped Noonan's clothes and buried them? But five disappearances in two years in one place can't be a coincidence.*

He went home and changed into blue jeans and a polo shirt, then drove out to the preserve and spent the rest of the day talking with people living there. They weren't hard to find given the smell of their camps. His story was that he was a new social worker and was meeting the people he'd be working with. He talked for a while about the program, then led the conversation into people who'd disappeared. The dates were vague but he found another eight people who fit the pattern. Everyone assumed that they'd just taken off.

After he returned home, Hernandez poured himself three fingers of Jim Beam and sat in his recliner.

If it is a werewolf, I've got a problem. It's one thing to identify it, another to apprehend it. And then there's the other problem.

Capturing or killing a werewolf is not an easy task, one similar to getting a job paying a decent wage with an art history degree, except that it is possible to kill a werewolf. Since werewolves retain most of their strength and resilience at all times, killing one that has not changed is virtually as difficult as during a full moon. But the commonly believed methods are useless; five silver bullets to the heart just give a werewolf angina. The only ways for a human to kill a werewolf are burning them to ashes, running them through a wood chipper, or locking them in a cage. Without the ability to feed every lunar cycle they go insane and eventually kill themselves.

The fact that decapitation doesn't kill a werewolf was occasionally exploited in times past. The immobile head is not dangerous so long as you keep your fingers away. The well to do would keep a werewolf head on a shelf, covered with a hood, to entertain visitors. When the hood was removed the head would howl, snap and snarl madly.

But one other way to kill a werewolf exists: the bite of a vampire. Vampire saliva contains a potent toxin to werewolves; the slightest penetration by a vampire's fang will introduce enough poison to paralyze the werewolf for hours, giving the vampire the opportunity to drain it of its living blood before finally giving it a fatal bite. Slightly more brings on convulsions and death yielding the less nutritious lifeless blood. But vampires are rarely willing to risk going *diente a diente* with a werewolf.

The other problem Hernandez mentioned had to do with the *code du loup*. Certain imperatives guided werewolf behavior. Not taboos or rules but behaviors that they could not violate. The most notable ones are that a werewolf cannot kill another werewolf; they are solitary for the most part, coming together only to mate, or for the males, to watch spectator sports; they won't kill dogs unless they are Chihuahuas, which are really just barking rats; and they are very irritated if another werewolf is wearing the same clothes at a social occasion.

Abigail rolled off the worn-out motel bad and lurched to her feet. As she made her way unsteadily to the bathroom, her left foot discovered that the cat's litter box needed cleaning. Continuing the rest of the way on the ball of her left foot, she spent the next fifteen minutes puking into the bathtub as she sat on the toilet. After showering, she stood in front of the mirror, not liking what she saw. She closed her eyes and concentrated before she opened them again.

Much better.

She'd run out of blood three days before and vodka last night after watching *Nosferatu* on Turner Classic Movies. Luckily the hangover overcame the hunger pangs as she looked at the cat huddled in the corner, hissing with its fur up.

She made a vague attempt to comb her hair and then, sans underwear, pulled on a pair of jeans and a Grateful Dead tee shirt. She smeared her face and arms with sunscreen and, with her billfold and room key in her pockets, walked out the door. She'd gotten thirty feet from the door when she realized she'd forgotten to put sunscreen on her bare feet and broke into a stumbling run as she crossed the motel parking lot to the adjacent Ponderosa Steakhouse.

She walked past the woman at the register and collapsed into the first booth she came to. After a brief conversation with the greeter, a server approached her, warily.

"Hi. My name is Landry and I'll be your server today. Here's a menu and I'll get you some water right away."

Abigail kept her head in her hands. "Coffee. Leave the pot. A Porterhouse steak, raw. I don't mean rare, I mean at room temperature. No sides. Coffee ASAP."

The server said, "OK, that's coffee and a Porterhouse, no sides. How would you like your... oh, never mind. You said room temperature. Coffee will be right up."

When the steak arrived, Abigail cut a large piece, chewed it until all the bloody juice was drained, then spit the remnant on the plate. After several bites she finally looked around. A man sitting at the table across from her stared with a frown of disgust. She snarled at him as only a vampire can, lips curled to reveal her canines, irises turned blood red with pinpoint pupils and an almost subsonic growl. Disgust turned to terror and the man bolted from his half-finished meal. She finished the steak and belched, left enough cash for the meal and tip, and walked out the door. A collective sigh of relief ran through the restaurant.

She ran across the parking lot and hopped from foot to foot as she fumbled for the room key. As soon as she was inside she soaked her reddened feet in the bathtub hoping that they wouldn't blister.

I can't stay here any longer. Got to get back to work before I do something someone will regret. Fuck that werewolf. If he comes around, I'll have his blood and his balls for dessert.

Twenty minutes later she was on the road leaving only the cat's litter box.

Lieutenant Ross made her morning rounds, arriving at Hernandez's desk while he was looking at the Noonan file. She glanced down and saw it.

"Any leads on it yet?"

"The roommate looks clear, nothing useful from her. I talked to some of the squatters in the area and they didn't notice anything that night. I'm looking for similar ones in the files but haven't found anything. There was other DNA on the clothes but it's not in the system. Got any ideas?"

"Nope. If something doesn't break pretty soon it'll go cold. After you get done looking through the old files concentrate on your other cases."

He nodded and closed the file folder, setting it to one side and selecting one about a gang related drive-by but not opening it, instead looking at the desk calendar.

Next full moon is a Thursday in about three weeks. I'll have to convince the vampire before then.

After sending an email requesting personal days for that Thursday and Friday, he went outside to the parking lot and pulled an unfiltered Camel from a soft pack. He lit it and took two deep breaths while looking at the overcast sky. He finished the cigarette and went back to his desk and reopened the Noonan file, then punched in Abigail's number.

"Hello?"

"It's Hernandez, I..."

"Fuck you," she said and hung up.

He waited five minutes then re-dialed her number.

"Fuck you, Hernandez and fuck your mother with a hoe handle because that's what she is, a butt-fucking, asshole licking..."

This time he hung up.

The next morning he drove to Abigail's Red Cross blood bank, arriving at seven-fifteen. He parked a half block down the street and walked to the nearby parking garage. He kept walking until he found a section of parking spaces reserved for the Red Cross, then found the nearest elevator and stood next to a column near the stairs where he was hidden but could see anyone approaching the elevator.

She arrived at a quarter to eight in a blue Honda CR-V. Hernandez stepped away from the column as she approached the elevator. Thirty feet separated them.

"Hello Abigail."

She started, then crouched, the snarl coming unconsciously.

He said, "It's OK. I'm just here to talk. I don't want us to get any closer."

She straightened up, the snarl replaced by a scowl.

"As I said before, fuck you."

"How would you like a werewolf's blood? I've got one for you to kill."

She looked puzzled. "You're offering another werewolf to me? I thought you guys were loyal to one another."

He nodded. "As a werewolf, I can't kill another werewolf. But as a cop, this one needs to be taken out. He's the one that killed Rebecca. I thought you'd be interested."

"Shit. Is this for real?"

"I can tell you more later. If I call again, will you take the call?"

She nodded. "This better be real or I'll get your blood instead."

"It's real." Hernandez turned and walked down the stairs.

He called that evening.

"I wondered when you'd call." Her voice was slightly slurred.

"Wanted to wait till you were off work. Is this a good time?"

"Better than later. Talk to me."

"Rebecca's murder happened during a full moon."

"I know. That's why I thought it was you."

"No, I was busy elsewhere. Not a person. I don't kill people. Anymore. I found a pattern of missing people during the full moon going back two years, maybe more. All of them in the preserve. Most of them were homeless people and no report was filed. If we hadn't found

Rebecca's clothes we wouldn't have classed it as a homicide."

"So who is this motherfucker?"

"That's the problem. I'm ninety-nine percent sure it's a werewolf but I have to wait until the full moon to catch him or her in the act."

"What do you want from me?"

"I can't explain it all over the phone," he said. "We'll have to meet in person. Can you do that?"

She said, "I'll be sure to have had an extra pint before we meet. And a drink."

"Do you get mean when you're drunk? I don't want to deal with an angry, drunk vampire."

She laughed. "No, I get all maudlin. But make the meeting early, preferably before noon."

"How about the Pig and Whistle at eleven this Saturday? Shouldn't be many people there."

"OK. See you there."

They waited outside without speaking until the Pig and Whistle opened at five after eleven, then took a booth in the far corner.

Hernandez ordered a Coke, Abigail a vodka Martini.

"How are you doing?" Hernandez asked.

"Same as any morning," she replied. "Tell me about this plan."

Hernandez sipped his Coke, then said, "As you know, I can't kill another werewolf. Putting one in prison is the same as killing it because they go insane and kill themselves. But I can let someone else kill it.

"It's only killed in the preserve, but that's several hundred acres. Lots of area for it to use and squatters are spread all over. It spaces out the kills on the paths, usually kills the squatters. Since it just killed Rebecca, they're who it'll go after. That makes it harder as we'll have more ground to cover."

"What *we*, White man?"

"A vampire's bite is one of the few ways to kill a werewolf. That's why I need you. We'll be in the preserve before the moon rises and will find him before he kills. You'll follow me. I'll distract him with an attack. He'll be surprised when I attack him and that'll give you an opportunity to bite him as we're fighting."

"So how are you going to find him?"

Hernandez said, "A werewolf howls when the moon rises. We can't help it. We'll go to the middle of the preserve before moonrise and wait for the howl and then take off toward it. Once we get close I'll be able to smell it. We'll come from downwind. How fast are you?"

"I can keep up with a werewolf. I've done it before. Won't he hear you howl?"

"I can suppress it if I have to. I've got a question."

She said, "Fire away."

"I can detect vampires. But I didn't detect you when I came to your house. Why?"

Abigail smiled. "I was a witch before I was turned. Not a young one." She waved her hand in a circle around her face. "This is a glamour. It also hides my aura. That's why you didn't recognize me. It also allows me to be irresistible."

She smiled and gave him the same look that she had at her house but even stronger. He felt a stirring between his legs and desire that he hadn't felt for years. Then her expression changed and he was utterly repulsed by her.

She laughed. "Settle down there. It works both ways and both are useful."

Hernandez swallowed and took a sip from his Coke. "I wasn't sure if that shit was real. So you can do spells?"

"On humans. Most of them don't work on magical creatures. So you're safe from being turned into a toad."

"That's a relief. OK, so are you in?"

"I think it's a shit plan, but yeah, I'm in."

"We'll meet at the north parking lot an hour before moonrise. I'll call to confirm. Be sure to be in shape to do this."

"Don't worry. I've got this under control," Abigail said as she ordered another Martini.

Hernandez paced around the parking lot. Forty-five minutes to moonrise and Abigail wasn't answering his calls.

This is what I get for trusting a drunk, especially a vampire drunk.

He heard a car approaching and watched as Abigail's Honda made a sweeping turn into the parking lot and ended up straddling two spaces. The door opened and she clambered out, swaying slightly as she approached him.

"Sorry I'm late," she said in a surprisingly clear voice. "Cat got out and wouldn't come back in. Some smoked salmon finally did the trick."

"Are you ready for this?" he asked.

"Fucking A-OK, ready to rock and roll. Let's do it."

Hernandez sighed. "We've got forty minutes till moonrise and we need to be at the center of the preserve where the two main trails converge. We need to hurry."

"I gotcha. Let's make tracks."

She kept up with him as he trotted down the path. They passed a couple jogging together in identical suits, two men standing just off the trail kissing, a fat woman walking a Chihuahua that skittered to the other side of the trail when Hernandez looked at it, and a dwarf walking a Great Dane. The dwarf was the only one to greet them as they passed.

They reached the junction of the two main paths at ten minutes to moonrise. The exertion seemed to have sobered up Abigail.

"So we just listen for a howl?" she asked.

Hernandez nodded. "It should be about 8 minutes until the moon appears." He pointed to the east. "That's where the moon will rise. He...we, will howl as soon as the bottom edge clears those trees. I'll make sure I don't make any noise. We need to be quiet till then."

Abigail drew a finger across her lips and nodded.

They both stiffened when the top of the moon appeared over the treetops and watched silently as it rose surprisingly quickly. Abigail looked at Hernandez just as the moon was about to clear the trees. He had his left arm in his mouth and when the moon cleared the trees he bit down on his arm just as a faint howl came from the south.

Abigail pointed in the direction of the sound. Hernandez turned his head toward the howl.

"When we get close you'll need to stay about a hundred feet behind me so that he doesn't see you. When I come up on him, circle around so that you can hit him from behind."

Abigail nodded. Hernandez turned toward the sound of the howl and set off at a run through the woods. She kept up with him easily as her night vision was even better than his and she had indulged in three A negative Bloody Marys before leaving for the preserve. A negative blood was her cocaine; every vampire had a particular blood type that was special.

As Hernandez approached the location of the howl, he tested the slight breeze and veered to the left to stay downwind. Soon he caught the scent of the other werewolf and adjusted his course accordingly. He suddenly stopped and motioned to Abigail to stay farther behind. She waited until he was a hundred feet ahead and then followed.

The other werewolf's scent became stronger and another scent was added to it, that of a female human who hadn't bathed for a considerable length of time. He slowed to a walk and began stalking the source of the scents. Two minutes later he glimpsed the other werewolf fifty yards ahead of him carrying a small, clothed figure. He couldn't tell if she was alive. He turned and saw Abigail behind him and signaled that the other werewolf was just ahead. She nodded and moved off to the left, still downwind.

When Hernandez had closed within fifty feet of Danner, he stopped and turned, sniffing the air. Hernandez froze. The breeze picked up slightly, enough to blow Hernandez's scent away from Danner. He turned back and resumed his slow trot.

Hernandez looked to the left. Abigail appeared from nowhere and signaled him, then disappeared again. He continued to close the distance to Danner, Abigail flitting in and out of view as she paralleled his path.

Danner trotted into a small clearing when Hernandez was thirty feet behind. Hernandez saw

Abigail about fifty feet to his left. He gathered himself and charged, covering the thirty feet in less than a second. He tackled Danner at full speed. The woman in his arms flew off to one side as Danner went down but the element of surprise Hernandez had counted on wasn't there. Danner turned over and threw Hernandez off with his left arm, then pushed himself to his feet with his right. Hernandez was able to roll away and get to his feet just as Danner came at him and grabbed him in a bear hug.

Shit, he's stronger than I am and just as quick.

His right arm was free and he stuck his thumb into Danner's eye as he slipped his leg inside Danner's and pulled it back. Danner recoiled from the blow to his eye, releasing his grip and falling on his back. Hernandez backed away and prepared for the next attack.

Danner rose with a piece of a tree limb in his right hand. Hernandez saw Abigail over his shoulder, coming fast from behind. Danner saw her reflection in Hernandez's eyes and whirled, swinging the limb like a baseball bat at Abigail's head.

The crunch of shattered bone accompanied Abigail's fall to the ground. Danner allowed the momentum of the swing to carry him around to face Hernandez. He approached Hernandez with the limb held high, then stepped forward and down, swinging it toward Hernandez's left leg, hitting the side of the knee. Hernandez collapsed with a howl of pain. He rose, then collapsed again as he put weight on the injured leg. He watched from the ground as Danner picked up the woman and took off at a run.

He managed to get to his feet and carefully stand, then turned to look at Abigail. She lay supine, her arms spread, eyes closed. He hobbled over to her. The left side of her head was crushed, brain matter slowly oozing from the cracks. Her left eye lay on her cheek, the eye socket shattered. He knew that vampires couldn't die from injuries but he had no idea how she'd react to this. As he watched her, her right eye opened and slowly focused on Hernandez.

"How bad is it?" she asked.

"The left side of your head is crushed. Your brains are leaking out. And your left eye..."

"You, know, the funny thing is that I can still see out of it."

She reached over and gently picked it up off of her cheek, then slowly moved the eye around.

"That's really weird, seeing a different thing with each eye."

"For God's sake, quit doing that. You're freaking me out."

She laughed and turned the eye toward him, then shut the other eye.

"I can still see you," she said in a lilting voice.

She set her eye back on her cheek and bones cracked as she used her hands to reshape her skull. When she began to reinsert her eye, Hernandez turned away.

"I hate to leave you but I need to follow him."

"Go ahead. I'll put myself back together."

"I'll be back as soon as I can."

Hernandez could faintly see Danner's tracks from the heat his feet left on the ground as well as from the shallow indentations. He limped as fast as he could, his leg slowly able to take more weight. After a mile he was able to walk, another mile and he could trot. The tracks meandered through the woods, twice circling back on themselves. Danner was moving through the preserve in a manner meant to throw off Hernandez but he couldn't conceal his tracks. The prints slowly became less faint and began edging more and more to the east. Hernandez pushed himself as fast as his knee would allow. Soon the trail made an almost straight line to the southeast.

Hernandez saw the glow of streetlights ahead and slowed as the tracks became more vivid. He followed them into a neighborhood adjoining the preserve where they paralleled the backyards of the houses until they turned directly toward a brick house with an immaculate yard enclosed by a low chain link fence. They crossed the fence and ended at the backdoor where a small pile of clothes lay.

Got you, you bastard.

Hernandez walked along the edge of the preserve, counting the houses until he came to a cul-de-sac. He carefully approached the circle until he could read the name of the street, then turned back toward Abigail and set out at as close to a run as he could manage.

She sat with her back against a tree, hugging her knees and humming a song he'd never heard. Both eyes turned toward him as he approached.

"About time. What's the verdict?"

"I found his house. We've got him."

"Since your brilliant plan didn't work tonight, how are you going to get him?"

"Give me time. And it looks like you're not going anywhere for a while."

Abigail felt her head. "I've had worse. It'll take a week or so for me to be back to normal. The glamour helps."

She stood up. "Let's get going. I brought a couple of pints for you. Thought it would help since you missed a kill tonight. I really didn't want to bring the cat."

"The blood will be fine. Missing one kill isn't the end of the world."

When they returned to the parking lot, Abigail opened the rear of the Honda and handed two plastic bags to Hernandez.

He ripped open the blood bags with his teeth. That made it seem more real.

After emptying the bags, he said, "I'll be in touch early next week. We'll go from there."

Abigail nodded and eased into her car, her head tilted at a peculiar angle, then slowly drove off.

Vampires are just fucking weird, Hernandez thought, *bat shit crazy weird.*

A week later they sat in The Pig and Whistle at the same booth as before. Hernandez had his Coke, Abigail, the usual vodka Martini.

"I found his address and all that we need to get him. His name is Reed Danner. He's an accountant at Dewey & Howe, lives alone, no priors. He's basically off the radar."

"It's always the quiet ones. So, do you have a plan?"

Hernandez shook his head, "Not yet."

Abigail reached across the table and put her hand on top of his, then gave him one of her most alluring looks. "Maybe I don't need you to get to him."

He withdrew his hand and sat back. "I hadn't thought of that. Would it be safe?"

"Safer than being with you."

Hernandez winced. "Good point. What do you have in mind?"

"Leave it up to me. This isn't the first time I've seduced a victim."

Hernandez pulled out his notebook and wrote for a moment. "Here's everything I have on him." He stood up. "Be careful."

He walked away as Abigail ordered her third Martini.

Three days later at five o'clock, Abigail stood outside the entrance to Dewey & Howe. She'd retrieved Danner's photo from an Internet sex-meeting site. As he came out the door she strode forward looking straight ahead and bumped into him, spilling the contents of her purse on the ground.

"I'm so sorry. I wasn't looking where I was going." She bent down and began retrieving the items scattered on the sidewalk.

"Let me help," he said and bent down beside her.

She gave him The Look and softly said, "Thank you so much. People are so rude today. It's good to find a gentleman."

They stood up together when they finished. Abigail stepped close to him. She'd brewed her perfume the night before. It did what women hoped perfume would do and it did it to an extreme. Danner's pupils widened and his breath quickened.

Abigail said, "I'd really like to buy you a drink in appreciation. There's a bar just down the street." She put her right hand on his forearm and brushed her hair back with the other hand.

Danner swallowed and said, "Sure."

They sat together at the bar, Abigail with her Martini, Danner, a Manhattan. Her hand was on his thigh. They said the things people usually say the first time they meet at a bar.

After fifteen minutes Abigail said, "This place is so noisy. I'd like to find somewhere quieter. Do you live nearby?"

"I have a house about twenty minutes from here."

She slid her hand farther up his thigh. "I'd love to see it."

Danner opened the front door and let Abigail precede him. As soon as he had closed the door she went up to him, put her face close to his, closed her eyes and opened her lips. Danner clutched her to him and kissed her, sticking his tongue deeply into her mouth, then he pulled back, putting his hand to his mouth.

"You bit me!"

"I like it rough," she said and laughed.

"So do I," he said and grabbed her again, then staggered backward.

She had dropped her glamour and Danner looked at her in horror as he collapsed to the floor. She bent over and her yellowed eyes bored into his as she parted her withered lips.

"You said you like it rough," she said before she tore at his throat.

After she drained him, she explored the house. When she reached the basement she brushed her hand across the autopsy table and examined the crematory. When she opened the freezer it took her a moment to realize what she was looking at. She began furiously emptying it until she reached the bottom and found the packages with the date of Rebecca Noonan's murder.

"You motherfucker," she said aloud.

She emptied the trashcan of its neatly folded contents and placed Becky's remains into it, then searched the basement until she found a shovel inside a neatly arranged cabinet of garden tools. She walked half a mile into the preserve carrying the shovel and trashcan until she came to a large oak tree.

Abigail dug the hole six feet deep, then lowered the trashcan into it and carefully arranged the rectangular packages on the bottom of the grave. After filling the grave and tamping it down she drew a series of symbols in the dirt, then stood facing the east and chanted an incantation. She carried the trashcan and shovel a quarter of a mile away, then returned to Danner's house.

Taking a large carving knife and a Trader Joe's grocery bag from the kitchen, she walked into the living room. She efficiently decapitated Danner's body and placed the head in the grocery bag. Then she pulled down his pants.

"This is for Becky," she said aloud before she ripped off his testicles and threw them into the bag. "I'll have them for dessert."

The next day Abigail called Hernandez and arranged for him to meet her that evening at her house. When he arrived at seven she answered the door, then pointed to the grocery bag sitting on a table.

"I have a present for you."

Hernandez crossed the room and lifted Danner's head from the bag, then turned to her.

"Good job. Everything go OK?"

She nodded. "I found out what happened to the bodies. The son of a bitch butchered them in his basement, put the meat in a freezer and cremated the rest. I found what was left of Becky and buried her in the preserve."

"Holy shit. I've never heard of a werewolf doing that. I guess it's technically not cannibalism but still..."

She said, "Anyway, it's over." She gave him a look of pure camaraderie and opened her arms. "To a job well done."

He hesitated, then stepped forward and hugged her. He felt the slightest prick on his neck and recoiled from her. "What the fuck?"

She smiled ruefully. "I can't deny my nature; it's like the scorpion and the frog. I didn't reach this age by being sentimental."

Hernandez stared in disbelief as he fell on his side. Abigail rolled him over on his back and looked at him with a mother's loving eyes.

"Don't worry," she said. "I'll be gentle."

THE BEAST OF BOWERY'S END
By Norris Black

Gerard felt the beast's presence the moment it crossed the threshold of his apartment building.

Twelve stories separated him from the building's lobby. Floor after concrete floor, each filled with people going about their daily routines inside little boxes. All that space, filled with concrete, carpet, blood and bone. Filled with the hopes and fears of dozens of faceless neighbors. Through all that, he still knew the exact moment the beast took its first step onto the cracked and broken tile floor. It howled. He felt it more than heard it, like a blast of hot air carried up from the depths on malignant currents. It made his skin crawl and his soul shiver.

He had run out of time.

He dumped the headless rooster he had been waving through the air just moments before onto the tabletop, heedless of the spray of bloody drops splattering against the far wall. The bird, too, had run out of time.

Wiping his hands on his pant legs, he quickly crossed the room to check again a series of rough symbols scratched into the thick layers of white paint covering the frame of the apartment's main door. It looked like a blind man had hacked them into being with a dull butter knife. His eyes caught sight of the bent and battered butter knife he had used, lying amongst a debris field of white paint chips scattered across the floor. Hastily, he scooped it up and deposited into a pocket. You never knew when you might need a butter knife.

More than a hundred feet below him he could feel the beast move, closer now. He guessed it had found the staircase. While its long, sinewy limbs and wicked talons are excellent for say, tearing a man apart, they're not well suited to the pressing of elevator buttons.

He concentrated. North. It was coming up the north side of the building. If he moved quickly, he might be able to get down the hall and escape down the south staircase.

He had just grasped the brass doorknob, the metal cool in his hot, sweat-covered hand and was prepared to make a run for it when an unexpected voice behind him caused him to freeze in place.

"I don't think that's a very good idea."

He turned slowly, reluctant to let go of the doorknob on the chance the word 'bad' joined the words 'mysterious' and 'startling' to describe the advice he had just received.

Sitting on the windowsill on the far side of the room was a small man in a big suit. Gerard figured he wasn't much over five-foot tall and willow thin.

Slicked-back blond hair framed a smooth pale face and a set of eyes the color of freshly turned dirt. He was dressed in baggy white dress pants, a black button-down shirt and a crushed velvet red sport coat with padded shoulders and ridiculously wide lapels. The points on the lapels looked so sharp you'd want to count your fingers to ensure they were all still attached after getting dressed in the morning. He looked like a boy who had gotten into his uncle's clothes closet. An uncle with absolutely atrocious fashion sense.

"I'm sorry, what was that?" Inwardly Gerard complimented himself on how calm his reply sounded. At least he thought he did; it was a little hard to be certain with all the other internal screaming he was doing right then.

The small man smiled. It was the type of smile a shark might give moments before ripping the limb off an unsuspecting surfer. The part of him that was internally screaming found a new octave.

"You definitely don't want to open that door," the man nodded to where Gerard's hand still gripped the doorknob.

The man tilted his head to the side. "It knows you're here but doesn't know exactly where. Your... sigils are confusing it." The pause before the word 'sigils' was just enough to convey the man's contempt for Gerard's work. "But the moment you break that seal it's over, it'll know exactly where you are and then," he spread his hands and the predator smile made another appearance, "that dog will definitely have his day."

Gerard snatched his hand away from the doorknob like it had burned him and stepped cautiously away from the door and into the center of the small apartment. Somewhere far below, though still too close for comfort, he felt the beast pause as if it had momentarily lost the scent.

"How do you know that? Where did you come from? Who are you? And, most importantly, why are you wearing that ridiculous coat?"

The small man tilted his head to one side as if listening to an unseen voice.

"No, no, pay him no mind," he said, soothingly, as he stroked one of the coat's lapels like it were a family pet. "Of course, I don't think you're ridiculous. Now don't pout, its okay. Once this business," the word laced with distaste, "is over with I'll give you a nice relaxing steam and de-linting; you'd like that right?"

"And you," he continued, voice hardening as his eyes locked eyes with Gerard. "Just because you've chosen to lose your mind doesn't give you an excuse to forget your manners. Words hurt."

The man glanced at the nearby table where the formerly living farm animal had pumped out its last few ounces of life. Blood pooled in designs similar to those ringing the doorway. The symbols were arranged in an unstable pattern that squirmed and shifted when looked at too closely.

"Speaking of which, you didn't really think that would work, did you?" he said incredulously. "You must be desperate indeed to even attempt that old witch's tale. I hate to break it to you, but just because you've locked away that deal of ours somewhere inside that soft head of yours doesn't make it any less binding. You owe me, and I will have my due."

The last sentence was spoken in a sepulchral growl that reverberated through the air and set the window's glass rattling in its casing. As if in response the beast gave out another silent howl.

Somewhere below, Gerard could feel it on the move again. He could almost hear the clicking of its hooked talons on concrete steps as it came ever closer. He imagined those same talons tearing into his flesh and shuddered.

The man slapped his hand down on the tabletop with a thunderous clap, blood splatter flying up from the impact. Time slowed, then stopped. Droplets of blood hung suspended in the air like tiny, perfect rubies.

One of the droplets hung suspended a few inches in front of eyes, reflecting his own face back at him like a funhouse mirror. The droplet slowly rotated then stretched, blotting out the rest of the world in a sea of red.

Slowly the color faded, and he saw an image of himself but much younger, well dressed and sharp-eyed. He stood below a streetlight in a yellow pool of electric light surrounded by a sea of black.

Gerard watched, bodiless, as his younger self paced back and forth impatiently for several minutes, stopping every now and then to check his watch and squint out into the velvety darkness.

The small man, still wearing the ridiculous coat, appeared without warning, materializing out of the blackness so suddenly it was as if the darkness itself took form and stepped into the light.

The man strode up to the younger Gerard with a smile and a greeting on his lips. His younger self had his back to him, but Gerard could guess from the stiff set of his shoulders that the reply wasn't near as friendly. The two spoke for a time, the words inaudible to Gerard's formless self, before the small man finally barked a laugh and extended his hand for a shake. Gerard was certain the man looked directly at him, merriment dancing in those grave-dirt eyes as his younger self took the proffered hand.

The colors of the world ran and smeared together before resolving into a new scene.

He saw his younger self again, this time standing on what appeared to be a film set. He was screaming, red-faced, at a young man wearing a headset and carrying a clipboard, the words BOWERY STUDIOS emblazoned across the back of a blue windbreaker. Gerard watched as his younger self turned away to address a pair of actors standing in front of a green screen. Behind him, the young man set down his clipboard and stumbled shakily away. Gerard knew with a certainty he couldn't explain that the young man would be dead by the end of the week, laying in a pool of his own blood as the life leaked out of his wrists.

Red swirled in, blotting the movie set out before receding and revealing a new scene. He was resting on a couch inside a lavish apartment. Beside him sat a young girl, barely out of her teen years. He watched as he placed a hand on her knee and whispered something in her ear. She laughed nervously and tried to brush his hand away, but he just gripped harder. He spoke again, the words lost in the gulf of time, but the expression on his face was expectant, demanding. He stood and took her hand, leading her from the couch to an open bedroom door set in the far wall. She followed, halting, hesitant. She glanced over her shoulder at the apartment's main door across the room. He tugged her hand again, leading her into the bedroom and closing the door. The last thing Gerard saw before the door clicked close and the vision dissolved was the raw animal fear in her eyes.

One by one scenes faded, only to be replaced by the next. He watched as he crept guiltily out of a motel room while his oldest friend lay sprawled on the couch, dried vomit running from the corners of his mouth and glassy eyes staring sightlessly at the ceiling. He witnessed his own descent into poverty and desperation as money ran out and newfound friends deserted him. Saw as that desperation turned to fear and a seemingly never-ending string of self-proclaimed mystics and shamans as the deadline on the deal he had made loomed ever closer.

The last vision was of him arguing with an old woman in a rundown shop surrounded by shelves overflowing with all manner of trinkets and oddities. The old woman had, at most, two teeth to her name. Her dirt-brown eyes twinkled in amusement as he angrily snatched a rooster's cage from her claw-like hand and threw a handful of bills onto the crowded shop's grimy countertop.

As the final scene faded from view, Gerard found himself sprawled, cheek pressed to the dusty wooden floor of his apartment. As he began to rise the door behind him exploded into splinters.

The beast had found him.

Gerard had barely managed to get one foot under him when the behemoth slammed into him from behind. The impact tossed him across the room and into the far wall with a sickening splintering sound as the ribs along his left side give way. He slumped to the floor, breathing suddenly difficult. Blood frothed on his lips.

The malevolent presence of the beast washed over him in waves as it paced back and forth in front of him, all sinew, bone and violence.

Gerard laboriously reached into his pocket and pulled out the battered butter knife.

The beast blurred as it rushed him again. He felt an awful pressure as needle-like teeth clamped down on his arm. The beast shook its head like a dog with a toy and Gerard felt the bones in his arm give way with a sound like snapping twigs. He faintly heard the clatter as the useless knife tumbled away into a far corner of the kitchen.

The beast released him and quietly slunk away, only to turn quickly and launch itself at him again, this time catching him under the armpit, teeth scraping on broken ribs. He felt hard talons tear at his soft belly. It planted its paws and pulled hard, once, twice, then let go.

The agony was unbearable. Gerard's breaths came quick and shallow, each sending a lance of pain through his chest. His vision darkened to a tunnel, the lambent yellow eyes of the beast staring at him like a train rushing down the tracks. He was going to die.

Without warning the beast's eyes were replaced by a pair of soft brown ones. The small man with the silly coat had stepped between Gerard and the beast and was looking at him with a tiny smile on his lips.

"You remember me now, don't you?"

Gerard nodded weakly, too far gone to give voice to words. Even the effort it took to nod very nearly sent him spiraling into the darkness.

"And you remember our deal?"

Another nod, a spark of panic as the darkness pressed in even further.

"Good," he said with a hint of satisfaction. He glanced down at Gerard's chest. "That certainly looks like it stings a little. Tell you what, I'm not an unreasonable man and I think you've learned your lesson here. If you're interested, perhaps we can make a new deal?"

Gerard's vision had narrowed so all he could see was a pair of expectant brown eyes. The rest of his world had been swallowed by darkness. He managed to nod feebly one last time.

The small man leaned down and whispered the conditions of the deal into Gerard's ear, but he barely heard them. He didn't care what the deal was, he'd do anything to make the pain stop, anything to spend just one more moment in the light.

He felt a small soft hand grip his and heave. He felt himself pulled from the wreckage of his body, felt himself torn asunder and remade anew. The last of the darkness rushed in and carried him away.

The beast entered the lobby of the run-down apartment building, black talons clicking on broken tiles. Up above somewhere he could feel his quarry; he could almost smell the blood and the sweat. The fear.

Gerard howled. The hunt had begun.

BREAKOUT FROM HELL
By J Louis Messina

Breaking out of Hell warn't gonna be easy.

First off, Jesse James, a Southern peacock, insisted that whore Belle Starr come with us, jus' 'cause they'd rode together once. She warn't nothing but a lowdown horse thief, and as ugly as sin, and Hell was a mighty fine place for her. I might've stoled a horse or two in my lifetime but didn't make my living off it. Didn't rob no banks, stagecoaches, or trains, neither.

And Jesse said he don't take no orders from a kid, even if it's the notorious Billy the Kid; and, by the way, I died at twenty-one, and he was just thirty-four when he was murdered.

Also, Jesse and Belle got better press than I did. Robin Hood? Ha! Take from the rich, give to himself. Bandit Queen my ass! Least ways, the newspapers made me famous. No matter. Jesse wanted to plan the whole escape, but it was my idea, and I set things in motion, and I had the most infamous jailbreak amongst them. Said if he don't like it, I'd go it alone. That shut him up. But I needed Jesse in case we ran into trouble.

Hell had plenty of fire and brimstone, torture and such, pretty goddamn hot, never stopped sweating, and my old clothes stank all the time. But it was mainly the absence of things you craved for, tobacco, whiskey, fornication. You'd think sex be big down here on account it was so sinful. Or was that the point? Plenty of bad women, but you can't do nothin' with them, if you get my drift. You're hungry all the time, too, but you don't get no food, and you can't eat, but there was a passel of cooking smells to drive you plumb loco. Mixed with the rotten eggs' stench, I smelled beef stew and cornbread, almost tasted it, and they knowed it was my favorite, but there weren't none to be had. Pure misery.

You're allowed to roam free, as you can't go nowhere, and it was awful big down here, lotta sinners, never come to the end of it. You'd think you wouldn't feel lonely, but most kept to themselves, and some I don't wanna have nothin' to do with, mean, filthy sons-a-bitches.

But after I explored the place awhile, I found me an escape route. Demons guarded us, mostly poked us with their pitchforks; a few ate your flesh and organs, too, and it stung like blazes, except they always growed back so's they can eat you again. One choked on my big pecker once, and, despite the spurting blood and agony, laughed my ass off, and that gratified me. But demons weren't concerned about anyone escaping. Hell's biggest weakness? Eternal damnation. Lax on defenses. Not expectin' it, see?

One thing fer certain, you can breakout near anyplace, if you've a mind to. I didn't much like being cooped up, and was most dangerous when cornered. My pal Sheriff Pat Garrett knew that. Garrett had hidden in the shadows as I ate a late-night snack. Shot me down in the bedroom without me pulling my gun. Course, jus' killed two of his men, so reckon I deserved what I got.

I recalled my last words, "*¿Quien es?* Who's that?" as much as I recollected how many men I killed. Really wished I'd come up with a more memorable exit line. "Who's that?" *Bang!* You're dead. Damn fool.

We got the news from *Hell's Gazette* down here regularly; more to make us long for living again, make us suffer. This one was dated 1885. My murdering had been ruled justifiable homicide. There was a story of me telling a judge, after he'd said I'd hang until "You are dead, dead, dead!" that I fired back, "You can go to hell, hell, hell!" All true. Press rarely got the truth straight. Seemed I arrived at both, though, dead and in Hell. Then I read: "After Pat Garrett served as a lieutenant in the Texas Rangers, he moved back to his ranch in Roswell, New Mexico." That one interested me most.

Back to this here route. The walls teemed with yellow brimstone, red-hot and burning of sulfur. Easy to dynamite. Then I got to wondering where the mail come from. It didn't appear out of nowhere; it was hand-delivered by these green, horny toad critters. They bit your hand when you took it. Caused blisters. Hurt like the devil, as they say. By the way, none have seen the real devil, Satan. Never visits. Too busy topside.

Anyhow, I planned a stakeout. Watched them little critters. Marked where they'd come from. There was a way out back in one of the caves. I calculated it. We don't have days and nights here, just endless torture, but I learned to count. I mean, I got me ten fingers, ten toes; that was twenty, and I didn't have much else to do, all the time in the world, so when the mail was delivered, I figured in finger, toe time.

It was that time now.

In every prison, there was that guy that kin get you things you need, smokes and such, and Hell weren't no different. This man might've been the first person in Hell for all I knowed, but he could be mighty helpful.

"We need guns," I said. "And dynamite."

The man, an apish feller and hairy all over, sat naked and reached back into a big pile behind him, brought the items out, and plunked them in front of him. No doubt stuff he'd saved from the dawn of creation.

"What you trading?" the big ape grunted.

"My black bowler hat, my most prized possession." I handed it to him. Sure hated to part with it. "Died with it on."

He inspected it and weighed it in his hand, like he was a judge at a best hog contest, and shoved it on his head. He appeared satisfied.

"Take," the hairy man said. "What's it for?"

"Don't spread this around. Gonna breakout."

He tilted the bowler to look stylish. Didn't help. "Punishment great for trying. No one escapes Hell. Wander the Earth forever, but can die by Hell's Night Riders or the same way you were killed. So beware."

"Good advice." I would of tipped my hat, but for obvious reasons, couldn't.

I bundled up the trade and headed over to Jesse and Belle, weaving through the caves, easy as hiking through Ten Rocks Slot Canyon, New Mexico. Chased there a few times. Jesse and Belle were in a heated argument when I arrived. They were always fighting 'bout some business, usually me, as Belle didn't like me much, neither. She was always causing problems between me and Jesse, and I guessed since they couldn't touch one another for fun, probably frustrated as all get out.

"Howdy!" I said. "Got what we need. Let's get this done."

Belle could pass as a man, no matter what dress she wore, that's how plain ugly she was. She'd married a lot, bore kids, but I couldn't rightly see the attraction. But she was refined, as was Jesse, so that must be the connection.

"Howdy, Kid," Jesse said, pulling out of the fight, one he never won. "What's the plan?"

I crouched down and drew a diagram in the dirt with my finger. "Here's the escape route, commencing soon. We dynamite it, making it possible to slip through. If the demons come after us, we shoot our way out."

Belle put her hands on her hips and her snooty nose in the air. "How do we know it will work?"

"Don't," I said. "It's the best plan we got. If you don't like it, you can stay behind and wait for the next guy to bust you out."

"Don't get cantankerous, Kid," Jesse said. He looked to challenge me and poked me with his finger. "A gentleman doesn't act impolite when a lady asks a question."

I rose and hitched up my pants. "I ain't no gentleman, and she ain't no lady."

Jesse took a swing at me and grazed my chin. We could hurt each other, and a fight was the closest to feeling alive, and why I threw the insult. I jumped onto him, and we tussled on the ground. Belle hit me over the head with a rock, and it smarted some, but nothin' could knock you out, so we just caused each other a bushel of pain.

I rolled off him, dusted my pants, and helped Jesse up. That was the end of it, and I led them to where we'd plant the dynamite.

"Here 'tis," I said. "The critters be comin' soon." I lit the dynamite (plenty of fiery places), and lodged it into the brimstone. "Hide behind those steaming boulders."

We skedaddled. The dynamite blew. A booming sound shook rocks from the ceiling and crashed down onto us. No one took notice or cared.

"There," I said, pointing at the horny toad messengers. "The critters be spittin' out, and the hole's big enough to fit us. Go now."

When I popped up, a demon, an unpleasant bastard with brown scales, like a huge Texas horned lizard, had come over to see what all the commotion was. It saw me and raised its pitchfork to skewer me with. I drew my gun and shot its fool head off. It toppled over, like the town drunk on Saturday night.

"Your dynamite and gun will bring all those demons down on us, Kid," Belle said, cranky-like.

"What'd you want me to do? Give it a kiss? I know you'd kiss anything."

She slapped me. I made to backhand her, but Jesse caught my arm.

"Stop!" Jesse said. "We don't know how long we have."

Grindin' my teeth, I narrowed my eyes at him. "Then let's get outta here before more come."

We rushed over and shimmied up into the hole one at a time, me first, then Belle, then Jesse. The tunnel sucked us up, and we screamed our way to the top. I'd seen a shack caught in a twister before do the same thing.

Since we were in Hell, it took a spell, might've seemed a week or more to us, but we no longer had a sense of the seasons. There warn't much to do, and the trip was as long and boring as a politician's speech, but it beat gettin' skinned and roasted alive.

"See light!" I shouted.

I felt like a geyser as we gushed out into a showery downpour and severe thunderstorm, high into the sky, then plummeted smack into the mud. We rocked to our feet, slipped around, and breathed in the fresh air and Earth. Lightning blazed across the night and the rain hammered down onto my head—and me without my damn hat.

We whooped and hollered, and Jesse swung Belle around, as if at a barn dance, and then we stumbled onward. Jesse wrapped his arm around Belle, planted a sloppy, wet kiss on her, and, realizing he could do more now, reached a fever pitch.

"No time for that," I said, shaking Jesse's shoulder. "We need horses."

"Where are we?" Belle asked, coming up for air.

"New Mexico," I said. "I knowed this here territory like the back of my hand. Yonder's the Chisum ranch."

We trudged some and arrived at the ranch. Because of the storm, the horses had been corralled in the barn. It was easy pickins, and we saddled up and rode out, but we run into Chisum and his ranch hands.

"Halt!" Chisum aimed his Winchester at us. "No good horse thieves. Fire, men!"

They shot their guns and the bullets ripped through us. The horses bucked and whinnied, but we weren't hurt none. I searched myself, but there warn't a scratch on me.

A ranch hand crept forward, looking as scared as a man buried alive. "Who the devil are ya?"

When they got a good look at us with their lanterns, Chisum cried out, "Can't be! You're all dead and buried four years ago."

"You still owe me 500 dollars, Chisum," I said, failing to mention I'd rustled his cows for payment due.

They dropped their guns and scampered, frightened as pups.

Jus' when we thought we was safe, shadowy men in black attire on dark, beastly horses galloped at us. The rain sketched their gruesome figures, and the lightning flashes bared their skull faces.

"What in tarnation are they?" Jesse said, slowing his steed.

"Some of your friends, Kid?" Belle asked in her nasty tone.

I whoa'd my horse and peered at the gang. "Posse from Hades! Hell's Night Riders. I was warned they'd come after us. We better make a run for it."

"Thanks for not informing us beforehand," Belle said.

Really wanted to shoot her off her saddle but had more pressing issues.

We turned and sprinted. Gunfire spat at us, kicking up at the horses' hoofs. I whirled and fired back to let them know we was armed and dangerous and wouldn't be an easy catch.

"Cross the Pecos River!" I hollered and spanked the reins onto my horse.

A bullet whizzed over my head, partin' my hair. Closest shave I ever had. When we got to the river, I faced the posse.

"What are you doing, Kid?" Jesse said. "Trying to make a name for yourself?"

"I got me business in Roswell. You two head for Texas. If we split up, we half their forces."

"Knew you were up to no good," Belle said, slapping her thigh. "Told you he needed us for a diversion, Jesse."

"Shut up and ride!" I said.

"Good luck, Kid!" Jesse said with a soldier's salute and a cowboy's wave.

"*Adios, amigos*!"

I reared my horse and charged away. The posse split up, like I figured, and 'bout fifteen of the fiends chased Jesse and Belle. The posse blasted away at them, and Jesse and Belle returned fire. One slug struck a phantom skeleton and knocked it off its perch. The posse didn't let up, though, but roared over the fallen creature, crushing it into mangled bones. The things fired off another round of volleys, as loud as the thunder. One fortunate bullet hit poor old Belle in the back. She yelped, dropped, and before she thumped the ground, gone to dust. Jesse shrieked in anguish but rode faster. If matters went badly for us, I'd see him in Hell again.

Vengeance drove me on, and the thought of Pat seeing my ghost sprang into my mind. He'd probably keel over from fright before I had a chance to exact my revenge. Don't think he'd go to Hell, as he lived a decent life.

I had to lose the posse or pick them off one by one. Neither be easy. Roswell was less than 3 miles away.

I decided on a trick I'd done to another posse hot on my tail. I was well ahead of them, so I crossed a shallow spot in the river and circled 'round. It was easy to spot the muddy horse prints, and they followed my tracks in pursuit. Before they had a chance to figure my plan, I'd showed up behind them.

Drawing both guns, I shot four down at once, riddling them with bullets. They scattered a might, but reformed and faced me, shooting like happy hunters in a buffalo herd. I dodged and bucked, then fired off more rounds, killing six more. Only two left.

I kicked my horse and stormed into them, hootin' and a hollerin'. My luck held out. They missed. I had a bead on them horrible faces and drilled them clean through their bony heads. They fell off their horses, and I trampled and stomped them into the muck.

Without lookin' back, I headed to Roswell.

* * *

I rode all night, soaked to my skin. No lights in the house. Pat and whoever were in there were well asleep and not expectin' company. Least ways, not a dead man come back from the grave.

I snuck up the porch. It creaked. The storm had subsided some, down to a trickle, and the lightning storm had moved on, so my sounds could be heard. Don't know if Pat was a heavy sleeper or not but couldn't take a chance. Didn't know who else was with him, if he had a wife or family, and didn't want to make a mistake of killing the wrong person. I ain't no murderer.

Pulled on the front door, but he'd bolted it from inside. A broken window would alarm him, and I'd lose my surprise attack. I snuck to the back. Same there. Couldn't shinny down the smokestack, and, anyhow, I'd make too much clatter on the roof. The house was sealed tight.

Slunk 'round to the other side. He'd left a window open by mistake. He had a big ranch house, and I hoped I didn't drop into his bedroom; didn't want to start shootin' without him knowin' it was me first. I found a few crates and stacked them up. I pulled myself up, wiggled 'round, and slipped feet first through the window.

I lowered myself to the floor, careful-like not to make a noise. I'd stepped into a pretty big kitchen with a table long enough to feed ten people. Then the smells hit me, like a punch in the face from Tom "Big Foot" O'Folliard. He could pack a wallop. Thought I was back in Hell at first. Stew and cornbread.

Glory be! I'd struck gold. The pot on the stove had the beef stew. It drove me outta my head, like I was crazy drunk. A heap of cornbread invited me to the table.

But could I eat? Could I taste it?

I shuffled over to the stove and grabbed the pot. My hand shook. I sweat some, and my heart beat like an injun war drum. Pushed my face into it and breathed it in. Heaven on Earth.

Seizing a wooden spoon, I collapsed in the chair at the table and swiped a big piece of cornbread. Trembling, I brought it to my mouth, slowly, watching it, makin' sure it didn't disappear, that it was no mirage in my mind.

Took a bite. Ecstasy. Better than Millie's Cathouse outside Fort Sumner. I dug into the pot and shoveled in the stew, chewed and swallowed. Praise the lord, I could eat! I ate so fast it filled my cheeks. Some stuck in my gullet, and I had to cough it out and down, makin' a racket.

I thought 'bout how nice it was for Pat to leave the grub out. I'd pay him a visit in bed, and before I put a bullet in his head, I'd thank him kindly, as I had manners, and chuckled at the stupefied look I'd see on his face.

I'd been so busy with my eating that I hardly heard the feet enter behind me. Took another mouthful of stew and cornbread, wiped my lips with my sleeve, then looked over my shoulder, slightly, the spoon in my hand, the gun in my holster.

Someone stood in the shadows in the doorway.

"Who's that?"

"Like the chow?" Pat stepped out. "Hell warned me you were coming, Kid."

Bang!

Damn fool.

REUNION
By Chisto Healy

As the guillotine slams shut behind me and I jump despite being safely past it, I think to myself about how this is the last place that I want to be. I wish I felt like I had a choice. The Crenshaws took my choice away a long time ago. This has been in motion since I was six years old. I always knew it would come to this. I just tried to avoid the realization until it was actually upon me, to pretend I could lead a normal life, but I always knew in my heart that he would come for retribution eventually.

Twin sense is real, you see. My sister Tara is in pain and I can feel it in my bones. She's been in pain every day for the last twenty years... but this is different. This pain is fresh, raw; not an old scar that scabs and reopens year after year. Something has happened to her. He has taken her.

I know that she's alive though, at least for now. If she were dead, I would feel it. It would be an impossible to fill hole in my soul, a void in the center of me. No. She's alive, but I don't know for how long and that's why I came back to this treacherous place. If he needs his revenge, he can take it out on me, and leave Tara out of it. She saved me from his wicked family and now I will return the favor.

I couldn't go to the police and deal with paperwork and questions and disbelieving people thinking I'm crazy or telling me that they already searched this place. Depending on how badly she is injured, she could be dead by then. It would be a long delay and give the last surviving Crenshaw the time he needed to find retribution.

I swore that I would never come back here, but that was foolish because I have always known that Tara would. I also knew that he would. I knew the game would have a second act.

I spot the tripwire just centimeters before hitting it. I knew it was there, but I could have sworn it was further in. He must have moved it as if he knew that someone aware of the traps was going to be going through these tunnels. Maybe he knew exactly who. He wanted us to come. All of this was for us, for Tara and I. He wants his revenge. I always knew he would.

I close my eyes and take a deep breath, my body trembling. In my mind I remember all those years ago when Tara and I stood together and watched in horror as another child, a boy of nine named Samuel, ran through the wire. He made it three more steps before a giant steel block fell on him and crushed him. It was big enough to cover him entirely. There was nothing left to see. It was as if he just disappeared, like he ceased to be and in his place was an enormous safe—a safe I would never want to open.

The Crenshaws' ranch was in the middle of nowhere. When there were no solid leads to the child abductions, the police did come out here to investigate, but they never would have found the man-made tunnel system beneath the place without knowing it was there. The rescue at the hands of the FBI came much later and way too late for so many, but not too late for us and I know he remembers.

"Tara!" I call out, waving my flashlight over the dark walls and ceiling. I don't care about giving away my position because I'm not a child anymore and the 9mm Glock in my other hand will be proof enough for anyone that wants to test it. I've been training to shoot since I turned 21. I almost never miss.

My sister and I were just six years old when the Crenshaws brought us to their house of horrors. We were the youngest of the abducted children. They locked us in cave-like cells with television screens that showed the surrounding tunnels. Each day, they would unlock one cell and allow someone the chance to escape, with the rest of us watching on our screens. The tunnels were lined with traps, each deadlier than the last. We only saw one person make it out, an older girl named Melissa. When all was said and done, they found her body outside. Making it through their nightmare obstacle course didn't lead to freedom. It was all just part of their game—the game I have returned to play as an adult. For Tara, I would do anything. I owe her everything.

They tried to separate Tara and I back then, but we screamed and clutched each other and refused to let go even when they beat us. As my mind replays the memories of their savagery, I kneel before one of their puzzles, trying to remember the solution. Tara was the smart one. She was the one that figured out the puzzles when it was our turn to go through. Then she would let me go first so if it re-set, she could just solve it again.

She was my big sister by seven minutes. I should have reached out to her last week. I knew it was the twenty-year anniversary, and when the children started disappearing, I should have known how it would affect her. I should have called her, but I couldn't. I wasn't strong enough. I couldn't handle that my worst nightmare was actually becoming a reality, that it was happening again. I couldn't face the fact that he was back. I would have ignored the whole thing if it hadn't been for Tara.

When I first arrived I wondered why the police or the FBI didn't come here first, why they didn't automatically target this place. Was twenty years so long that they had forgotten what had happened to us all out here?

Then I saw the abandoned police cars out front and realized they had come. Seems like Crenshaw was prepared this time. He had plenty of time to plan. He was waiting for this day as long as I had been. He must have worked out every little detail, corrected the mistakes, found ways to succeed where his family failed.

I didn't find any bodies at first, but there were blood trails across the floor and walls and they all led to the trap door to the tunnels. Of course they did. Why would I have expected any different?

My heart pounded and I couldn't breathe. I immediately withdrew my gun and made sure the safety was off before re-entering this hell.

As I went through the first part of the maze, I found the bodies. They were hanging from the ceiling like Halloween piñatas, a distraction from the traps and puzzles beneath them. When I didn't pay attention to which stones I was stepping on because my eyes were on the bodies above me, my misstep opened a door in the wall and two snarling starved and wild dogs hellbent on ending their hunger came charging at me. That's how I expended my first two bullets.

I love animals far more than people and I hated putting them down but they were far beyond reason. I couldn't die before I found Tara. As much as I love animals, I love Tara more. I love her and I owe her my life.

I was far more careful after that, my mind showing me that filthy television screen and the live footage of the boy that had become dog chow all those years ago, a vision that has never left my nightmares.

Tara and I hugged each other and screamed and refused to watch once it had begun, but the monitors came with audio and the sounds were as horrific if not more so than the imagery. There was no escape from the horror. The Crenshaws had made sure of that. I can still hear it if I close my eyes.

I knew that it couldn't have been the same dogs twenty years later, but it couldn't be the same killers either. They were all either locked away or dead, and whoever arranged this twenty-year reunion had plenty of time to plan, to starve and beat new dogs and set new traps. This wasn't a spur of the moment decision; of this I was sure. Someone had been waiting years for this moment, and I knew exactly who it was.

When the agents came and saved us, back then when we were kids, there had been talk of a missing member of the Crenshaw family, a child who should have been the same age as Tara and I, but they never found him. Now he found us.

Either that psycho family had hidden the child away somewhere spectacular or he had already gotten out. Maybe it had been a safety measure. Maybe those sick bastards had told the child to return in twenty years and start again. Maybe that was all part of the plan. This revenge plot was his destiny, just as it was mine to stop it.

Some people speculated that one of the surviving children that had been saved was actually the Crenshaw boy, but if that was the case than he had to have slipped away once they got us all outside. Every child that made it back was identified and returned to their families, although not all were in one piece. My poor sweet Tara.

We had reached one of the guillotine puzzles. There were a series of statues in boxes. You had to move them around and get the right statue in the right box to stop the blade from falling. It took her a minute with me hanging on to her and crying, but Tara solved the puzzle like she did the rest and the blade came to a sudden halt at the top. I was staring at it, eyes wide with terror and Tara pushed me and yelled at me, hurrying me through.

I saw one of the Crenshaws waiting on the other side, a huge massive man in filthy bloodied overalls, smiling at me with broken yellowed teeth and I panicked. I reached back and grabbed Tara. I was trying to go back, to get away from the scary man but Tara wouldn't let me. The blade came down between us and I was left still holding Tara's arm despite being on the opposite side of the trap. She turned ghostly white and collapsed. I turned towards the bad man, still clutching my sister's severed arm in my hand, and his disgusting smile widened. He had an arm in his own hand, a mechanical one. Apparently the traps could be controlled manually as well. I was six years old. How could I have known that? I thought it was disarmed. I thought it was safe. I made a mistake and Tara ended up maimed for life.

When I fell to the floor, sobbing loudly, that was when the FBI burst in. They took down the bad man, who was still laughing as they cuffed him. Someone ran to Tara and screamed for a medic. If only they had been just a few minutes sooner, my sister would not have been permanently maimed and I would not have to have carried that guilt for so many years.

She lived of course, but she was never the same after that. She never left this place, not really. I went on with life, putting as much distance between myself and the memories of this house of horrors as possible, but Tara never could. Her missing arm was a constant reminder that she couldn't escape. She had no choice but to remember.

Of course when it began again she felt the need to come here, to try to save those children, to not allow them to suffer as she had. It made perfect sense. It was Tara. She has a prosthetic arm now and does pretty well with it. She was perfectly capable, and she had a hero's heart.

She saved me all those years ago. Tara has always been a hero. It was in her very nature, to survive and protect. I was ignoring the news, trying to pretend this wasn't real and wasn't happening. I was being the opposite of Tara. I was living the coward's life when I felt her pain. It dropped me to my knees. I couldn't ignore it any longer. I had to come. It was my turn to save her this time, to end this once and for all.

I haven't seen any sign of Tara since I arrived here though. The traps were all set and waiting for me. If she had already gone through, the Crenshaw boy must have put her somewhere; locked her away and reset the traps. Maybe he knew I would be coming. Maybe that was what he wanted.

I was the one that got away unscathed. Maybe he wanted to change that. Maybe he was waiting for the others, the ones that had still been locked in their cells, awaiting their turn at this horrific maze. Maybe the biggest trap was yet to come. It didn't matter. I had to find Tara and get her help. She was the reason I survived this place, the reason I got to leave without injury, and I was the reason she didn't.

I haven't seen anything living at all since I got here, aside from rats and cockroaches big enough to be mistaken for rats, but I know she's in here somewhere. She's in here and so is he.

Surely, the dead officers would be reported missing and more would be coming. Maybe the full SWAT team would come or the FBI again. I just need to find Tara and keep us both alive until they get here. I can and I will. Failure is not an option. I'm not the weak little girl I was last time. I knew this day would eventually come and I have trained my whole life for it. Crenshaw thought he would be getting revenge today but I am the one who will see retribution. I will make him pay for what his family did to us, for Tara's arm, for whatever he has done to her now.

I turn left down a new tunnel and the lights go out. Suddenly it's pitch black as opposed to the dank and dim of before. I come to a stop and hold my breath though I can hear the pounding of my heart in my chest like a marching band's bass drum. I can't see anything. If I step on the wrong stone or hit a tripwire or move past a puzzle I'm supposed to solve it will be over before I even have a chance to regret it. This is new. We were never in the dark when we were kids. It feels unfair, extra cruel; something twenty years of building hate would conjure.

It makes me angry so I yell to him in case he can hear me. I yell profanities and hatred and about how I am going to kill him for what he did to my sister, whatever that was.

It's all bravado and he probably knows it. I haven't taken a single step. I'm terrified of making a mistake, and if this is anything like the old days he can see and hear exactly what is happening in these tunnels. He's probably waiting, smiling like his old man, teeth just as bad. Then I remember the flashlight in my hand. Terror makes you irrational. Surely he's laughing at me now. "Screw you!" I yell.

I wave the light around searching for a trap. It truthfully doesn't help much. Either the darkness is so deep that the beam can barely penetrate it or the batteries are on their way out. Still, it is going to have to do, as it is all I've got. I just have to look closely, step carefully, and hope my eyes adjust to the darkness. Without breathing, I make my way forward, one step at a time. The dim beam of the flashlight catches a glint of something and I make me way over to it. It's a key but I don't yet know what to. What do you have planned?

Keeping my eyes peeled and the beam moving, I continue on. Eventually I come to an empty metal box. Behind it I can hear more than see, saw blades going in the darkness. I need to put something in this box to stop it, but what? I can't remember this puzzle from last time. It's possible it wasn't here then. I begin to wish that Tara was here to help, but Tara is somewhere beyond those saw blades and I won't ever see her again if I can't get past them. I look at the key in my hand and know it has to be the answer so I double back and start scanning the ground. I don't find anything so I head back towards the grinding, singing saw blades, but this time my light is focused on the ceiling above. It has to be here.

Then I see it.

There is a locked box hanging from a rope a good fifteen feet overhead. I use my third bullet and after a rare miss, my fourth, to sever the rope. The box falls through the dark and lands ahead with a clatter. I just hope I didn't break whatever was inside it. If I can't complete the puzzle then Tara is lost.

I scan the ground with the flashlight until I find it and then I hurriedly use the key to unlock it. Inside is the final statue to the puzzle that took my sister's arm. Now I know for sure that this is personal. He knew she would come and I would follow. He planned this. He probably thought it would elicit fear but it only serves to make me angrier.

With a sigh and a deep breath to steady my nerves, I put the statue in the empty box and I can hear the saw blades grind to a halt. I don't know if they're on a timer or if the Crenshaw boy has a way to manually restart it so this time I don't hesitate. I know there's no time. I take off running, navigating my way through the giant circular blades. As I pass the last one, they come to life with a whir and start viciously spinning again. I was a split second from death or dismemberment and that knowledge brings me the need for a break. I lean against the wall and thank God while working to catch my breath. Once I've regained composure I head to the end of the corridor and turn left.

The new hall is so well lit that it's blinding after the total darkness. I click my flashlight off and shield my eyes. I know there must be another trap in here, something I'm expected to miss while blinded, something lethal. Hand over my eyes, I squint through the light and strain to see. Up ahead is finally something familiar. It's a door. A door that I will never forget. The door to the cells. Tara has to be beyond that door. I'm so close now that I feel a surge of adrenaline. I'm also painfully aware that I have yet to see the Crenshaw boy and I must accept that he is probably waiting for me beyond that door too. I check my gun and make sure that I am ready for that confrontation. I am. I think. I hope. God, the lights are so bright.

With my first step I feel my foot press down into the floor and I know I made a terrible mistake. The hallway starts to become narrower as the walls begin to literally close in. They're coming towards me fast. There may be another trap between the door and me but it's a chance I have to take. If I wait, I will be crushed for sure.

I take off running and sprint for the door, praying silently that it isn't locked and that's not the final cruel trick to end this little game. The walls are constricting to the point that it's actually hard to run, hard to breathe. I'm not going to make it. Tara, I'm so sorry.

Then the door is there. I grasp the handle with hope in my heart and it comes open. I squeeze through the now narrow opening and the walls complete their course, crushing the open door between them. I drop to my knees in the familiar hallway lined with cells on both sides. I am shaking with fear and adrenaline. I don't call out for Tara as much as I want to because I know that he has to be here somewhere too. He's in one of the cells most likely, watching and listening, waiting and laughing.

He knows exactly where I am but I have no idea where he is. The only option I can see is to check the cells one at a time. I will have to be careful to watch my back, to make sure he doesn't come from behind me as there are cells on the left and right. I feel the weight of my disadvantage and hope I have what it takes to save my sister. I tell myself I do. I have to.

I look from side to side and decide to start on the left. I tuck the flashlight away and then slowly grasp for the first door handle, gun raised in my other hand. I glance over my shoulder at the door behind me before I tug the cell open. My nerves are going haywire.

The door comes open and I can't help but sigh and bow my head. The very agent that held me in his arms and carried me out of here twenty years ago is lying dead against the back wall. Two others are slumped nearby. They're still wearing their protective vests. I frown at this. They were prepared and ready and it did them no good. Seeing the dead agents makes me nervous again. I spin around, gun raised, but everything is just how I left it. For some reason that leaves me more frightened than at ease.

I step back into the hall and move up to the next door, eyes pinned to the door on the opposite wall. I'm afraid my aim will be off if Crenshaw comes for me. My hands are shaking so badly.

The door is locked. It's a simple bolt lock so I try to pop it with one hand but it is stuck and won't budge. I have to put my gun away to open it. I don't like it. I contemplate skipping it and going to the next one but something nags at me. If the door is locked, it may be for a reason. Tara could be inside. I think about my options for a moment. There's no point in being quiet anymore. He's probably watching and listening anyway. "Tara! Tara, are you in there?" I yell. "It's me. I'm here to get you out!"

I don't hear words from the other side of the door but I can hear crying. It could be one of the abducted children. Maybe they weren't dead yet. Either way, I know I need to open the door.

I take a deep breath and stare hard at the door behind me. Then I tuck my gun in my pants and get quickly to tugging at the lock. The hairs on the back of my neck are standing up. I feel like he is going to come up behind me, kill me before I can save my sister or whoever is on the other side of that door.

The lock pops and I tug my gun free and spin around.

There's no one there. With another deep breath I turn back and open the door. My heart almost stops. Tears well in my eyes. Tara is laying on the floor. Her prosthetic arm has been removed and by the looks of it, forcibly. "Tara, I'm here," I tell her. "I'm going to get you out of here. I'm going to save you like you saved me. It will all be over soon."

I'm stunned by the anger in her eyes when she stares up at me. "Stop it! Just stop it! Why are you doing this?" she yells. "Why couldn't you just let it go?"

I shake my head, confused. Could she have been drugged? How did Crenshaw turn her against me? That would be the ultimate revenge, wouldn't it? "You need to get up," I tell her. "I haven't seen Crenshaw. He could still be in here. We need to go. Please."

"Stop it!" she screams, bounding to her feet and lunging towards me. "You have to stop it!" She's pointing at me angrily now with her one and only hand. I stumble backwards away from her and then glance nervously over my shoulder to make sure that Crenshaw isn't behind me.

"I know you blame yourself," she says to me. "You always have. I know you have never let it go and the guilt has eaten away at you our whole lives and I know the anniversary was a trigger for you but please stop it. I can't believe you would go this far. How could you do this?

You took those children. You killed them just to get me here so you could save me. It's insane. You're insane. Those police officers. The agents. Yes. You're one hell of a shot. You trained for this. You needed to relive it, to be my hero and save me and you couldn't do that if I wasn't a victim first. You had to recreate everything."

I shake my head. Why is she saying these things? I didn't do this. Crenshaw did. I'm a survivor, not a killer. "I had a good life," Tara says to me. "I moved on. I was happy. Then you ruined it. You brought me back to hell and you took my arm. It's over. I'm not going anywhere with you. You hear me? It's done. It's done!"

I can feel someone behind me. I spin around but it's too late. I hear the pop after I feel it. My gut burns red hot and I collapse to the floor. There is a man standing over me. He steps on my gun and tugs it out of my grip with his foot. My crying sister asks who he is.

"My name is Billy Crenshaw," he tells her. "It was hard enough to live all these years with the terrible things my family had done. I couldn't allow it to happen again. I'm so sorry I didn't get here sooner. I've spent my life hiding away, avoiding reality. I came as soon as I realized what was happening. The children?"

"They're gone," Tara tells him, her voice sullen.

I watch him help her up and start down the hall with her good arm around him. I don't understand. This was not how things were supposed to go. He's one of them. How could she leave with him after all they did to us? He shot me. He shot her sister, and she's leaving with him. It doesn't make sense. I was supposed to save her this time. It was supposed to be me. "It was supposed to be me!" I scream at them. "You can't do this! It was supposed to be me!"

CHRISSIE DATES AMERICA
By Clark Roberts

Chrissie Templeton waltzed through the door, her unexpected entrance bringing the lunch rush to a grinding halt.

Matt finished ringing up the family's order in front of him before his eyes slid to see what the excited murmuring was all about. The family's order consisted of a number one with an extra-large soda and onion rings for the father, a side salad with extra cheese and two additional ranch packets for the mother, and a kid's Wacky Sack complete with a toy for their little brat. All of this quickly became a side note though, as the line of customers parted like the Red Sea as Chrissie Templeton approached.

There were three others with her. Two men, lugging on their shoulder the largest cameras Matt had ever laid eyes on, stayed close to the reality star's sides and tracked her every movement. Both cameramen dipped, dived, and swooped with the type of urgency that spoke volumes towards professionalism—neither willing in any way to allow the other to invade their shot angle.

A third man, a bona fide celebrity in his own right, called out directives to the customers waiting in Matt's line.

Matt immediately recognized the perfectly groomed man as producer and acting host of the hit show, *Chrissie Dates America.*

"Pardon us!" the man barked. He grabbed some old-timer by the shoulders who hadn't budged and gently nudged him aside. "Reality star coming through."

The old-timer curled one Parkinson's shaking hand into a fist and slowly turned on the producer. Old-timer's face knotted into a grimace indicating he wasn't about to put up with any of this young whippersnapper's shenanigans—popular culture be *damned!*—but when Old-timer's eyes fell upon Ms. Templeton, his jaw dropped almost as quickly as his indignation. He didn't say a thing. Instead, mouth still gaping and revealing toothless and denture-less gums, he reverently stepped aside and shot a hand up to comb what was left of his stringed out hair.

Old-timer was the only soul in line that offered up even an ounce of resistance to Chrissie Templeton and the television crew's cutting to the front. Not that Matt could blame any of them. After all, it wasn't every day when a stone cold beauty of this magnitude showed her face in this town—heck it wasn't *ever* as far as Matt knew. *Chrissie Dates America* hadn't simply dethroned *The Bachelor* from its reign in the primetime slot; it absolutely annihilated it from the rankings.

As the reality goddess approached the counter, Matt readjusted the uniform cap on his head. Why management required them to wear such a ridiculous add-on Matt couldn't fathom. It wasn't like other fast food joints were doing that nowadays, but maybe that was the point. Still, being twenty-two he felt absurdly juvenile each time he groomed the tip-top of his uniform to start his shifts.

Stay calm, dude, a voice whispered in his head. *Don't make a fool of yourself.*

As cool as he could keep it together, Matt said, "Welcome to Barmy Burgers, home of the world famous Quadruple Barmy Beastburger. Can I take your order, please?"

"You... are... adorable," Chrissie Templeton said warmly. She smiled, causing butterflies to flutter from Matt's skin. "I love those dimples."

Remain professional. Women like a man with the confidence to perform his duties in any situation.

"Thank you, Ms. Templeton," Matt said. "May I please take your order? You're holding up the line."

"Hey now, buddy!" the producer cut in. "Nobody talks that way to Chrissie Templeton! No-bod-y!"

"It's fine, Jon." Without looking away from Matt, Chrissie waved the producer silent. She teased a smile at Matt before facing the camera to her left. "I love it. He doesn't think stars should be put on a pedestal. It's beyond cute."

"That's nice and all, Ms. Templeton," Matt said, "but I really do have a job. To be perfectly honest, a performance eval. is in my near future. Average wait time at my register is a major factor in quarterly evaluations. So again, your order?"

"Oh my, you're being serious." Chrissie scrunched her face.

Matt stifled a laugh, because for a moment, the world's sexiest reality star resembled a chipmunk.

"Let's see..." Chrissie Templeton drummed her hands on the counter. "What was that burger you pitched when I walked into your life?"

"The Quadruple Barmy Beastburger. It's huge, Ms. Templeton. I sincerely doubt you could even finish one." Gosh darn it if he wasn't impressing himself with this bold machismo shtick.

"Sounds like a challenge..." her eyes flicked down to his nametag, "...*Matt*. I'd also like to make that a meal."

She winked at him.

Typically, a wink from anything on two legs would've floored Matt, but the sheer absurdity of the moment—*Chrissie flipping Templeton had just ordered a Quadruple Barmy Beastburger from him*—for whatever reason couldn't shake him. He one-upped her wink by actually blowing her an air kiss before he said, "You want waffle fries or onion rings with that?"

Chrissie Templeton burst into laughter, and it emboldened Matt even further.

Half playing, but also half serious with this Joe Cool act, he leaned an elbow on the counter and propped his chin in his hand. Exactly where this macho behavior bloomed from he'd never be able to explain in a million years. He said, "Chrissie-baby, I can do this all night. But right now I got to know what's it gonna be—waffle fries or onion rings?"

"I'll do fries," she said after regaining composure. "Oh, and one more thing, I'll also have a date with you when your shift is over. You're going to be on *Chrissie Dates America.*"

"Nice, that'll be $9.59."

* * *

"Can I ask you a personal question?" Matt said.

"Sure."

Their date hadn't been much up to this point. After his shift, he'd offered to take Chrissie up to the local watering hole for a quick dinner and drink, but Chrissie had insisted on dinner at Barmy Burgers despite having it earlier for lunch. Matt had shrugged, and Chrissie had totally floored him by consuming two more Quadruple Beastburgers with a side of waffle fries. Eating with the cameras trained on him, and also while his co-workers jeered and not so surreptitiously offered joking thumbs-ups and air high-fives, had been awkward. He had a feeling this episode of *Chrissie Dates America* would be edited in a manner to depict him as the bumbling fast food worker all starry-eyed by the breathtaking celebrity.

After dinner he'd wanted to go home, shower, and change, but Chrissie was persistent that she loved a man in uniform, and she was too convincing with those come-hither eyes for Matt to defy her wish.

Word must have traveled quickly because, every now and then, passers-by would catcall Chrissie or even yell words of encouragement to Matt.

Chrissie took it all in stride like a true professional.

The one constant annoyance of the evening was Producer Jon's pleading that they *please just do something interesting already!*

As far as Matt was concerned, they *were* doing something interesting. They were getting to know one another.

Now, Matt was guiding Chrissie on a walk through the town's park. They circled the small pond with the cameramen swarming their every move.

"No, I mean it's really personal," Matt stressed.

Chrissie laughed. "I'm the star of a reality show. Not only that, but I completely interrupted your day. I think it's only fair that I answer one personal question."

"When you put it that way," Matt shrugged. "Do you ever have to protect yourself from the creeps on the show? I mean you're something else, drop-dead gorgeous and a wonderful personality from what I can tell, and sometimes you have to hang with some real losers."

"Sometimes I do," Chrissie acknowledged.

"Is it ever scary?"

"Not really," Chrissie said. "When I was on *Miss America*, my talent was knife-wielding. I've no doubt if I'd chosen a skill the judges accepted as a bit more ladylike, I'd have run away with the crown. But whatever, nobody remembers the cow that won, and I'm worshipped wherever I go."

"Yeah, I get it," Matt said and gave a nervous laugh, because really he didn't get it at all. Wanting to change the subject, his impulse took over before he could think to stop himself from blurting out his next question. "Do you ever sleep with any of the random dudes on *Chrissie Dates America?*"

"Turn the cameras off," Chrissie ordered the cameramen.

Both men quickly dropped the shoulder cameras.

"Whoa, whoa!" the producer called out from behind them. He trotted up, turned his palms to the sky. "What gives? Things were just getting good, now get those cameras up and continue rolling."

Oh boy, Matt thought, fearing he'd made a drastic mistake.

"No," Chrissie demanded. "I want this off camera. This is personal business between me and my boyfriend."

Boyfriend? Matt's mind reeled. *When the heck did that happen?*

"This is going to be the most boring episode ever," Producer Jon griped. He steeled himself, locking his eyes with Chrissie. "I'm getting sick and tired of your diva behavior. For starters, this joker here isn't your boyfriend." He jerked a thumb over at Matt.

"Come on, man," Matt whined. "There's no reason to insult me."

"Listen to me, kid," Producer Jon said, now regarding Matt. In the producer's eyes was a dog-tiredness that was impossible to deny. They were ringed red, and below were heavy bags of exhaustion. "You don't know what it's like—the pressure from the fans, the pressure to keep the show at number one. Always walking on eggshells to keep this snob satisfied." This time he thumbed at Chrissie. "You want my advice, kid. You run.

You run and you don't look back. We'll record you in full sprint and I'll salvage the show with some editing magic. Hell kid, you'll have girls crawling to your front door all because you had the spine to turn away from Chrissie Templeton. The single most important key is you have to *run like the minions of hell are chasing you down!"*

Chrissie Templeton reached into her side pocket. She flicked her wrist and suddenly a butterfly knife expertly clicked into attack mode. She moved swiftly, faster than Matt had ever seen a person move in his life.

In the next instant, the producer was stumbling backwards with both hands at his neck in the universal choking sign.

But Producer Jon wasn't just choking; the man was dying before Matt's very eyes.

It took a few seconds, but eventually blood began to bubble out and over the producer's hands. He gargled and fell flat on his back, his head pounding against the sidewalk. His legs stiffened with jitters.

"Holy Toledo!" Matt gasped. He'd never seen so much blood in his life.

"Matt, I'm going to be straightforward with you," Chrissie said. She closed the butterfly knife as swiftly as she'd opened it and slid it back into her pocket. She grabbed Matt by the hands and faced him. "I'm not exactly a virgin, but to answer your question, I've never slept with *any* of the contestants on *Chrissie Dates America*—that is, until tonight."

"You just wasted that guy!"

The dying producer coughed a splatter of blood, and then went silent.

Dead silent.

"That little thing," Chrissie giggled. "Thanks for your concern, but nothing will come of it. I'm a celebrity, an A-lister. Trust me, when I say Jon was only going to put a wedge between us. All he ever cared for was the success of the show, and if I get serious with someone, the show is kaput."

"Yeah, but golly, the man didn't deserve to die!"

"Don't be mad at me." Chrissie reached up and wiggled his nose. "I love you... and I love Barmy Burgers."

* * *

"You're in a predicament," his father admitted. Frank popped a top and handed the beer over to Matt before picking his own up from the small workbench and swigging deeply.

It had been a week since Matt's first date with Chrissie and somehow she'd convinced him to introduce her to his parents. They'd had a pleasant enough dinner, even with Chrissie insisting they provided Barmy Beastburgers and waffle fries rather than enjoying his mom's home cooking.

It was beyond weird how Chrissie wouldn't even sniff any foods at this point unless they came directly from Barmy Burgers.

It was also beyond weird how Matt's life had been completely flipped upside down by a woman who seemed to have absolute impunity from the law.

The door adjoining the garage and the house burst open with alarming suddenness. Matt's mother poked her face into the opening.

"Frank," she said, and scowled at her husband. "You're not out here sneaking a smoke are you?"

"Oh for Christ's sake, Cathy," Frank said. He regarded his wife with scorn. "Last time I got to enjoy a cigarette I was coaching Matty's shitty Little League team."

"There's no need for that type of language around our boy," Cathy said.

"It's alright, Mom," Matt said. "I'm not in grade school anymore."

Cathy turned her attention to Matt. She beamed a smile that was all pride. "By the way, Chrissie is just lovely. I knew submitting your name to *Chrissie Dates America* was the right choice. The two of you are perfect."

"Thanks," Matt said, not knowing if he meant it, but unable to think of anything else to say. He wondered if his mother would feel the same if she'd actually witnessed Chrissie so easily slit a man's throat rather than get the report from the local news. Matt raised and tipped the beer at his mom, took a small sip.

"Matty Joseph, is that alcohol?" His mother regarded him sternly.

"Cathy," Frank cut in, saving Matt from having to answer. Frank began using his hands in great gestures to emphasize what he said next. "We're in the garage. It's guy talk out here, and sometimes guys enjoy a beer together. I haven't had a cigarette. Matty's gonna have one beer. Please, go back inside and keep Chrissie company."

Cathy's lips thinned. Her eyes turned to slits and switched on Frank. Slowly, she shut the door, all the while lingering her gaze on her husband. Footsteps thundered away from the door and then faded.

Frank immediately opened a drawer beneath the workbench and pulled out a pack of cigarettes. He shook one loose and lit up.

"Don't you dare look at me like that, son," Frank said. He leaned against the workbench, knocking a couple dirty wrenches clanging to the concrete. Smoke drifted lazily in front of his face. "I didn't lie to your mother. I said I hadn't *enjoyed* a cigarette. For the last 15 years I've been sneaking around and hiding out for this one small pleasure, and let me tell you, that ain't the same thing as enjoying."

Matt put a hand up saying, *not my place.*

"Alright then," Frank said. He chugged what was left of his beer, wiped his mouth on his sleeve, and fished another can from the twelver on the floor. "Back to your situation, you say you're not sure if Chrissie is the one. Maybe she is; maybe she isn't. When did you first start questioning the relationship?"

Relationship? That particular word hadn't yet crossed Matt's mind, but there it was in its naked glory and out in the open. As he'd already confessed to his dad, Chrissie had moved her essentials into his apartment just two days after their recorded date. And then Wednesday night he'd come home from work and found boxes upon boxes upon boxes stacked in the cramped apartment. Thinking of it that way, it wasn't just a relationship; it was a *committed* relationship.

Okay, so to answer his dad's question.

"To be honest, Dad, I was somewhat second guessing things in the midst of our first date, you know when she killed Producer Jon."

"That's a red flag for sure." Frank raised his eyebrows. He blew a few smoke rings and punched them out with his finger. "But that's a woman for ya. You probably don't want to hear this but your mom can go a little loco from time to time. What I'm saying is, don't jump ahead of yourself. That circumstance doesn't necessarily mean Chrissie can't be the one."

"I'm not talking about whether or not she's the one. I'm just confessing that I'm extremely confused. Call me crazy, but I was sort of hoping you could offer some fatherly advice for once. I don't know what to do; I've only known her for a week, and she already forced herself into moving in with me."

"Yeah, well," Frank managed a bemused smile. "A good woman will do that." He slammed the second beer and pitched the empty with the others piled in the corner. "I don't know what to tell ya, son. I mean she's cute, seems pleasant enough. You say her bank account is filled with enough bills for a king's ransom. But when the sun sets, every man's gotta make their own decisions in this life."

And that was when they both heard Cathy's terror filled scream from inside the house.

"Christ on his throne, what now?" Frank grumbled. He dropped the half-finished cigarette and in no great rush grounded it out with a boot. "Your mother... always making something outta nothing."

Matt tore inside, slamming the door open so hard it punched a hole through the drywall. He ran straight to the kitchen.

The horrifying scene stopped him in his tracks. There were great arcs of blood splashed against the kitchen's cabinets, walls, and even up to the ceiling. On the other side of the center island, his mother's legs were visible, and her feet pointed directly to the ceiling.

Chrissie was at the sink whistling. She turned the butterfly knife's blade over, and crimson ribbons of water slipped down the drain.

"You killed her," Matt whispered.

"I did," Chrissie stated, matter-of-factly. She continued to wash the knife. "She told me next time we visited we couldn't bring Barmy Burgers, that she would have to cook. I tried to explain to her, Matt, I really did, but she wouldn't have it. In fact, she actually *demanded* she do a home cooked meal for us next time. She said you thought her meatloaf was—and I quote—*'Da Bomb.'* That it was ten times better than any Quadruple Barmy Beastburger. So I did the only sensible thing." Chrissie shut off the faucet and flicked the knife closed. "I slit her throat and slashed her face."

Time slowed as the gravity of the situation weighed on Matt's mind. He stepped slowly to lean over his mother.

Cathy's face was so doused in blood it was impossible to count how many times she'd been cut.

"You killed my mother, you – you – you…" The anger boiled up so fast for a moment it dissolved his thoughts. Matt rushed forward with outstretched arms, fingers taught and splayed. Screaming, he wildly finished his thought, *"You bad person!"*

Something solid blocked his path. Matt looked up.

His father, nostrils flaring, glared down at him.

In a low, serious voice Frank said, "A man never overreacts to any situation."

* * *

She lightly bounced up and down on him. Nothing too dramatic, actually, this so far had been their most normal round of sex in their short relationship.

Somehow Matt's dad had talked him around to accepting Chrissie's half-hearted apology for slaughtering his mother.

Honestly, Matty, it isn't really that big of a deal. Ya know, sometimes in this life a man's gotta take the good with the bad. Look at it this way, your mother's death frees me up a bit, so if you need a hand working on the car or hanging some drywall or maybe ya just want some company while your checking out engagement rings or just whatever, well shit, now I'm always available. You two lovebirds run along, and I'll get in touch with the proper authorities. Chrissie, really, like my beloved and soon to be rotting wife said of you earlier—you're just lovely. I'm forever indebted to you.

And now here Matt was again doing the dirty with Chrissie.

It was pleasurable to Matt, all this kinky sex, but truthfully it was also getting somewhat tiresome. If asked this just a month ago he would've scoffed at the idea, but right now he wanted *lovemaking* and not whatever their bedroom escapades could be called. Not only that, but he was wholly convinced Chrissie's gluttonous hunger for Beastburgers was starting to take its toll. Her hips were feeling considerably softer than they had just the previous night, and making the matter worse was the body sweat pouring out of her in buckets. The sweat was slick and somehow even thick, and it covered every inch of Chrissie's body as Matt massaged with his hands like working a lather.

Still, he'd take what he could get, beggars can't be choosers and all that jazz.

Maybe they could both orgasm in the next couple minutes or so and be done with it. Maybe she'd be content and let him cuddle her, hug her close like the lifelong companion he now so desperately wanted. So far, so good, so normal.

Except, was she panting something under her breath?

It was dark. He couldn't see her lips to tell if they were moving, but he swore there was a chant being whispered to the rhythm of her bounces. He turned an ear, focused on her whispering voice.

Yes, there it was again, and again. One word over and over and over, and it was so odd it jarred him right out of his sexual bliss.

"Milkshake…" —*up, down*— *"milkshake…"* — *up, down*— *"milkshake…"* —*up, down.*

He wasn't one to swear, could probably count the number of times he'd cursed his entire life on his toes, but this was so peculiar that what he said next was purely instinctual. He asked, "What the fuck are you talking about, Chrissie?"

"Tell me…" she panted from the darkness above him. "Tell me… oh God… tell me about the… oh this feels so good… tell me about the milkshakes."

"Milkshakes?" he asked. He halted his hands from rubbing.

She slapped him hard, right across the cheek, and instantly he could feel the burning imprint of her palm. Next, her fingernails were digging into his chest like talons and her light bounce intensified into a pile-driving grind. At the top of her lungs, she shrieked, *"TELL ME ALL ABOUT THOSE DIRTY MILKSHAKES YOU MAKE!"*

"Fine!" he yelled in desperation. "Just take it easy; you're breaking me."

She slowed her motions, even stopped bouncing and took up an even grinding. "The milkshakes, baby, tell me how you make the milkshakes."

"Yeah, the milkshakes," Matt said, trying to gather his thoughts. He'd never felt so on the spot even going back to his school days and presentations. "So there's this machine and uh…"

"Machine? I like where you're going with this, Matt. What about the machine? Tell me more about the machine."

"So this machine, it's got these three levers, and…"

"Three levers…" Chrissie repeated after him, sounding like she was intentionally gathering all of her sexual energy for one final explosion. "I love levers. Are they shiny, Matt? Please tell me they're shiny."

"Oh baby, you know they're shiny." What the hell? Lord, was he getting into this too? "We polish 'em up every night after we close to keep 'em shiny."

"And why are there three levers, Matt?"

"Because there are three flavors—chocolate, vanilla, and strawberry."

"That's what I like to hear, three flavors. And what do you do with the levers?"

"Well, we put a cup beneath 'em and pull the levers down."

"Tell it... tell it... tell it..." Chrissie was chanting again, and her rocking motion built back into the grinding.

"Yeah, baby," Matt cooed. "We put the cup underneath and the liquid ice cream oozes out and into the cup."

"It oozes, huh?"

"You know it oozes. It oozes like nobody's business." The sweat was back and cascading downward like water squeezed from a sponge.

"And then what...? Tell me more... *TELL ME MORE!"*

"We cap the cup and hand it over to the customers with straws!"

"AND WHAT DO ALL THOSE NAUGHTY CUSTOMERS DO WITH THEIR DIRTY, DIRTY MILKSHAKES?"

"They drink 'em, Chrissie! They put their naughty lips on those straws and..."

"YES... YES... OH, MATT... MORE ABOUT THE MILKSHAKES!"

"... they drink those milkshakes down! They drink every last drop down!"

Deadly serious, Chrissie said, "I want my own milkshake."

She once again geared down her movements and shifted back to the light bouncing. Her breathing became more controlled.

"No problem, baby," Matt replied, but thought, *Criminy, this stuff is getting out of control.* He certainly appreciated all the wild sex, but the fast food pillow talk was unnerving. He'd heard of people with some strange fetishes, but gol-dang this one took the cake home. This was out of the ballpark strange, but the intensity of her voice convinced him to stay in the game for now. "I can bring home a milkshake tomorrow night, whatever flavor you want."

"I don't care about the flavor, Matt, but it better be big." She slapped him a second time, even harder than the first.

"It'll be big!" Matt cried out, desperate to satisfy his girlfriend's desires if only to end it. He could sense her building, gathering to climax. "It'll be the biggest milkshake ever!"

"IT BETTER BE, MATT! IT BETTER BE!" She was grinding into him harder than ever before. It'd be a miracle if she didn't break his pelvic bone.

"I'll mix all the flavors together—how's that for kinky? I'll mix 'em all together in the largest cup we have!"

"OH YEAH YOU WILL! MY GOD I WANT A GIANT MIIIIILKSHAAAAAKE!"

And then she collapsed, panting so hard she drooled on Matt's chest. She rolled off of him and was sleeping in under a minute.

For Matt though, sleep was elusive. His mind raced trying to formulate a plan. He had to get out of this somehow, but knew if he mentioned second thoughts about their relationship, Chrissie would *not* have second thoughts about using her blade and doing away with him. He couldn't put his finger on it, but something told him Chrissie might be the jealous type. Not only that, but Chrissie could slit his throat at high noon on Main Street, and not a soul would care—not the cops, not his father, heck probably not even the town's gossiping social media page.

Chrissie was a wealthy celebrity, and apparently that made her untouchable.

Matt stared into the dark and conceded he was stuck. This was no way to navigate life, not allowed to shower, only eating fast food, being forced to place his hands on a woman that was feeling more and more like lard grease with each passing day.

The surrounding air was thick and sticky. God, this was gross. The bedroom didn't even carry the aroma of sex. It smelled like—*oh come on, just admit it.* It smelled like Barmy Burger's kitchen after suffering the onslaught of an all-timer lunch rush.

Matt physically felt disgusting, like he'd just worked a double shift at the height of summer and a twenty-minute steam shower wouldn't wash away the thick layer of grease suffocating his skin.

He stepped into his boxers.

Chrissie turned over in her sleep and moaned about double extra-large waffle fries.

In the bathroom, Matt immediately turned on the faucet, leaned to splash cool water on his face.

He paused, breathed heavily.

No, this couldn't be possible.

His hands were slathered creamy white. He sniffed at his shaking palms, wanted to puke.

With morbid curiosity, he stuck his tongue out. Licked.

And then he did puke.

When he finished retching in the sink, he took a look at his reflection in the mirror. He was completely slathered in the shit. He crumpled to the floor and cried. There was no denying it now; his girlfriend snoring from one room over was a murderer that sweated like a pig—*sweated grease.*

Matt sobbed.

He had to get away from her somehow.

He sobbed.

My girlfriend is actually becoming what she eats!

He sobbed, and sobbed, and sobbed.

And then, like a processed patty slapped to the griddle, a plan sizzled to life.

* * *

Matt bounded up the apartment complex stairs as fast as he could. He carried a cardboard box filled to the brim. Five days prior he'd pleaded and convinced the closing manager to let him take home all of the "waste" food that typically went to the trash. The first night that had been twelve Quadruple Beatburgers, seven orders of onion rings, two pounds of waffle fries, two cherry turnovers, and a crispy chicken salad minus the dressing.

After making short work of the meal, Chrissie had then forced her tongue down Matt's throat. Her breath smelled like trash, but when Matt tried to wiggle away she'd slammed him down to his hand-me-down sofa and rocked her semi-flesh body atop of him.

The buttery sweat had showered down on Matt.

Sleep was a long time coming that night.

The next morning, the change in the former reality star was undeniable. Her complexion had seemingly overnight turned from a healthy golden tan to something off-white, waxen even. It looked as if her top layer of skin could be peeled off with fingernails.

He did not touch her before leaving for his afternoon shift. That night he brought home another massive meal for Chrissie.

By the third night, it was no longer Chrissie at all. It was a thing—a mass of textured blob that he'd sickeningly rolled into the bedroom corner and fed. When he'd put the Beastburgers down next to the blob, an appendage had slowly formed, and with it, great sucking sounds that had Matt thinking of mudslides.

Matt stared wide-eyed as the thing absorbed the fast-food dinner, cardboard box and all.

An inhuman sound came from it—deep, bubbly, demanding.

"MAAAAAWWWWWRRR, MAAAAAWWWWWRRR."

More.

The thing couldn't be satisfied. Matt had locked it in the bedroom that night. He'd stayed on the couch and listened to its god-awful calls. At times, the bedroom door seemed to bulge outward and he'd feared for what was to come.

The fourth night had basically been a replay.

Now, on night five of the plan, at the top of the stairs, Matt hesitated. The rank stench had grown and pervaded every inch of the upstairs hallway. He was astounded the neighbors hadn't reported him to the main office.

As if on cue, the door nearest him opened and Old-lady Nancy peered out at him.

"You better fix whatever that problem is, Sonny," Old-lady Nancy said, and then sharply slammed the door.

Fix the problem. Yes, that's what he had to do. Fix the problem, and as disturbing as the last four nights had been, his plan had so far played out exactly as he'd predicted.

Matt went to his door, leaned an ear into it. From the other side, he heard terrible and rotten noises.

"Chrissie!" he called out.

"MAAAAAWWWWWRRR BEEEAAASTBUUURRRGERRR!"

"Just keep your pants on for the moment."

Balancing the box of fast food, he shouldered open the door.

The foul odor intensified ten-fold.

Matt's bedroom door was splintered and hung askew from the bottom hinge, the two upper hinges broken off. Somehow the bulbous thing had squeezed through the doorway. A trail of slime led right to the small kitchen where every cupboard had been ransacked.

And there it sat, pulsating with hunger.

Matt could see no eyes, but the thing seemed to be aware.

The thing had grown both thick and fibrous tentacles. The ropy tentacles whipped about in a frenzy while the fleshy ones flopped at the floor, searching.

A hole opened and it spoke one more time, *"FEEEEED MEEEEE!"*

Matt threw the box of food at the grease-creature.

Ropy tentacles instantly found purchase and yanked the box towards it. A new growth formed, bulging around and engulfing the food. An unearthly light began to strobe like a pulse and illuminated the thing from the inside. It released a noise that was squishy, nearly orgasmic in nature.

This is my chance, Matt thought.

He pulled out the candle lighter and hairspray stuffed in his back pocket and rushed forward. He triggered the lighter while simultaneously discharging the hairspray.

The grease-thing caught like gasoline. In seconds, giant flames reached for the apartment ceiling.

Matt backed away, but not before the intense heat singed his eyebrows. He stared through the flames, and for a split moment saw Chrissie Templeton's face form in the burning grease ball.

"You were supposed to be the one, Matt. I gave it all up for you!"

That was enough for Matt. He turned to leave but something caught his eyes. He grabbed the object off of his nicked up dining table.

Ten minutes later when the firemen rushed onto the scene, they found Matt on his rump, propped up against the apartment door with smoke rolling out from beneath the crack.

The first fireman ran up to him, got right down in Matt's face.

Through the clear protective face shield the man wore, Matt saw the fireman's eyes pop wide with recognition.

"You're the lucky bastard that got a date with Chrissie Templeton," the man gasped. He dropped his gaze and saw what Matt held in his hand. The man's face grimaced and he growled, "You better not have hurt her. There'll be hell to pay if you did." He thrust Matt to the side and barged into the blazing apartment all chest and brawn.

Cast aside like a piece of trash, Matt smiled the smile of a lunatic. He repeatedly flicked open and closed the butterfly knife, practicing with the memento.

RUN, RUN, RUN
By Max Carrey

"You got two more years, and then you'll be a big enough girl to sit on your own," I say, catching her reflection in the mirror. The car lurches through the dip in the driveway, Nia thumps in her booster seat, and she tugs on the straps with a scrunched up face.

"But I'm a big girl *now*."

"I know that, baby, but Mommy doesn't need a big ticket, and don't you mess with those!"

Nia glares and she crosses her arms over her chest with a huff.

Turning off the car, the engine's rumble dies, and the locks automatically release. Flicking off the headlights, the darkness surrounds us, the nights coming earlier now. As I step out, the air slices at my bare skin with an icy chill.

"Why don't we get your jacket on you?" I say as I unlock her harness, and grab her jacket among the grocery bags littering the floor.

"Ahhh!" Nia screams.

Suddenly arms are reaching around me as I turn on my heels. A shadowy form smashes a cloth into my face, a sickly sweet order stings my nostrils.

"Mommy…" she cries.

Our feet scuffling against the cement, the figure tries to pull me down, but I hold my breath and shoot out an elbow. The person crumples inward with a moan, dropping the cloth.

Turning back around, my body swimming in adrenaline, my heart beating sharply, I see another figure grabbing hold of my daughter, who kicks and wails against the shadow.

I scream and lurch myself forward, tackling the person to the ground, Nia squashed between us. I claw to tear her from their grip.

Something cracks against my head and I slam to the ground. Pain throbs inside my skull; my vision flickers, reaching out for Nia, tears streaking down her face. She's yanked away, her muffled voice crying out for me.

"Night night," a man's voice grumbles into my ear.

I try to muster up the strength in my limbs to fight, though I stagger about uselessly as the cloth is placed back over my mouth, and I unwillingly inhale, the chemical sweet overpowering my lungs. Then nothing…

* * *

My veins are on fire, every muscle spasms tightly, my body jerking up. *Clang…* I hit my head against the metal bars.

"Wakey, wakey," a balding man exclaims as he removes the cattle rod through the cage...*my* cage...sitting atop a wooden slab, so I'm almost eye level with him. I'm crunched in a cage much too small, housed in a big dilapidated barn with stereotypical red paint peeling off the wooden boards.

"Where the hell is my daughter!"

"Why, she's just right there," he replies with a smile pushing up his leathery cheeks, pointing behind me with the cattle rod.

I pull my legs into my chest and pivot around, spotting Nia splayed out in a cage, unconscious.

"Nia? Nia!"

But she doesn't stir. I focus my eyes on her and notice her chest rising and falling gently.

"What did you do to her?" I scream, as our captor strides around the edge of my cage.

I throw out an arm, lashing out a claw, but he sidesteps it. A laugh erupts, echoing flatly in the stale air. His eyes are a watery blue, with aggravated red veins popping against cloudy white.

"You're a fighter, I like that... Don't you worry, your little kitten is sleeping soundly."

Bringing my arm back through the bars, I clutch at them desperately, but they're too strong to bend. White knuckling the tarnished iron, my voice growling, "What do you want with us?"

"Why, we're going to have a celebration!" a shaky woman's voice sounds from behind me.

Jerking around I find a plump middle-aged woman with an apron tied around her waist, and splaying an eager smile.

"Let us go!"

"We couldn't do that," she says as she cocks her head to the side. "We don't have the time to catch anyone else, and we've never had *your* kind before."

"Oh great, we've been kidnapped by white supremacists," I spit at her, but she just chuckles jovially.

"My, oh my, you're a special one aren't you?" she asks, with a sparkle in her eye, looking over my dark skin. "Rabbit silly... we've never had rabbit before."

"Last year was deer season," her husband remarks, wrapping his thumbs around the straps of his overalls.

"What the fu-"

The woman clucks her tongue, wagging her index finger in the air, reprimanding in a motherly tone, "Now, now, now, no cussing. That's a horrible vile habit."

"Kidnapping and holding people in cages... children no less...that's not vile at all."

I seem to have ruffled her feathers for a confounded expression droops her smile as she mumbles, "It's an honor really. You've got the kind of pluck we look for."

"I'm so glad-" I begin to say sarcastically, but am cut off.

"Mommy..." Nia's weak voice murmurs. "Mommy?"

"Baby...baby!" I shriek, twisting back around in my cage, seeing my daughter stir and rub her eyes. "It's okay baby, everything's going to be okay."

"What's going on?" she asks as her voice raises an octave in panic, eyes stretching to saucers. She tucks her knees to her chest and shuffles until her back hits against the bars.

"I'm Jordan," he says as he approaches her cage, then motions back to his wife, "And this is Martha."

"Don't you go near her," I threaten. "Don't you touch her!"

He steps back, a chuckle reverberating, jiggling his belly. "I ain't gonna do anything...at least not yet."

"Mommy, I'm scared."

I hate to see her little hands trembling, and her face twisted in fear. My whole body aches, and itches to be with her. "I know baby, I know, but don't worry-"

"Yes baby, don't worry," he interjects, mimicking my tone.

"You shut up!" I shout, but startle Nia. I stretch my hand toward her, though I know the distance is too great, trying nonetheless.

A swift movement shifts out of the corner of my eye. The cattle rod streaks through the air and pings off my radius bone. I shriek, my arm going limp as it dangles over the side. My entire forearm throbs, yet I'm able to withdraw it back into my cage, though I do so with gritted teeth, panting heavily.

Jordan wears a satisfied smirk, smacking the rod into his palm, toying with me.

Looking to Nia, I notice she's pulled her braids forward in front of her face, hanging like a curtain to block everything out, and I can hear her sob behind it.

"I'm okay, Nia. Don't you worry baby... Mommy's fine, Mommy loves you."

Her glistening eyes, wet with tears, peek through, but she's frozen in terror.

"Let us go! Let *her* go at least..." I plead desperately, turning to the wife, clutching my sore arm. "Please, she's just a child."

"I'm sorry, but that's just not possible" she says all too sweetly. "If you want to be free, you're going to have to escape."

My mind muddles with confusion, and I sputter, "W-what do you mean? You *want* us to escape?"

"*Try*, try to escape," she corrects. "You see, you're our little rabbits for our anniversary pie, but that is if we can get you once we're on the hunt."

"You...you want to *eat* us?"

Horrified, my stomach churns and acid fills my mouth, my body begs to vomit, but I choke it back down.

"Yes...and I imagine you'd be so, so tasty."

A tongue darts out of her mouth and she wets her lips with anticipation. Her husband Jordan comes up beside her. Placing an arm around her waist, he pulls her in and she delightedly squeals as he places a kiss upon her cheek.

"It's been our tradition ever since we got married... Steak pie, chicken pie, fish pie, pigeon pie, pie, pie, pie, pie, pie!"

They laugh in jangled maddened unison, then kissing again, this time slopping spit on each other's mouths, already looking hungry for flesh as they suck on their lips.

"You disgust me," I remark as my face curls into a snarl.

Martha pulls away from him in a sudden sickening snap, her eyes locking furiously onto mine as her usually light tone darkens. "You disgust me too...until you're gutted, skinned and chopped up into fine little morsels, then tossed in a delicate array of herbs, spices and vegetables, until browning into succulent bites inside flaky pastry!"

I bare my teeth, staring them down, as my fingernails scrape ear-splittingly across the iron bars. Their muscles twitch to wince against the noise, but they both just smile at my feeble attempt to get under their skin.

Jordan saunters up casually, pointing the cattle rod in my face, though I refuse to pull away. It crackles with a pop of electricity, and my facade trembles, but I stay put nevertheless.

"We'll be coming to get you soon, little rabbits," he says, his empty hand flexing with anticipation. He tries to peer around me to Nia, but I sway in the same direction to block his eye line. His smirk deepens. "Then we're going to play a game of hide and seek, because what's a celebration without some fun and games?"

"A lawful one without attempted murder," I utter with venom.

"We never *attempt* anything… and you'd do well to watch your tongue."

"Why, too tough? Afraid you'll choke on it?" I reply sarcastically. "Please do."

Jordan goes to speak, his harsh angular features flaring in anger, but Martha stops him with a calming hand upon his own. "We'll be back. You should prepare yourselves," she says with a wink.

They turn to leave, seeming like an innocent pair of middle-aged farmers from the back, with muck-stained Wellie boots and meager clothing, yet from the front it's obvious they're anything but normal. It's their eyes and the way they hold their smiles that unnerve and cause a chill to nip at me, even amongst the nauseating warmth.

The old barn door creaks and I catch a slight glimpse of the world outside: A plain field, a forest, a night sky filled with stars—things that would make a beautiful evening, but now appear daunting and evil.

Once they're gone I swivel around and whisper, "Nia...Nia, it's just me. It's just Mommy. Talk to me Nia!"

A chin pokes out from under her braids, then thin lips, the tip of a nose, and her dark eyes. Her face is so wet with tears it causes them to form in my own eyes. I gnaw on the inside of my cheek, worry churning my gut.

"We're going to get out of here. *I am* going to get us out."

She's frozen, petrified as a statue.

"Trust me Nia... all right? I need to hear that you trust me," I half order, half beg.

"I trust you Mommy."

I feign a smile, because guilt crashes down on me heavily, constricting my chest. I feel like I'm lying, as I barely believe my own words.

"I trust you," she repeats, her voice trailing off softly.

My mind growing determined, fists clenching, and feet twitching to escape, I decide it is true too. I am going to get us out of here... because there's no other option.

I nod my head, trying desperately to think and not become overwhelmed.

"When they come back..."

Nia twitches and I grimace.

"If they come back, and we go to play a game, you've got to give it your all, baby. All right? There's only one rule: listen to me…"

Nia moves her head slowly up and down, shaking loose some more tears.

"I love you baby," I choke out, biting my bottom lip to keep from breaking apart into sobs.

"I-I love you too Mommy," she whispers bravely, and I give her a reassuring smile.

Every second after is filled with anticipatory tension. Nia's fiddling with the ends of her braids, while my mind is flustered with plans of escape.

I body slam against the bars, but I simply clang off them helplessly. I can't rock the cage or shuffle it, in the hopes to make it tumble off the platform, because it's too heavy, and the cage door doesn't even budge on its hinges. Wrapping my hand around a bar on the door, I can feel a sort of pad behind it, and I begin to fiddle with it, trying to find some sort of button or keypad, but it's strangely smooth.

A speaker system crackles on, causing me to jump and Nia to let out a little shriek.

"Hello…hello?" a male voice bellows out, patting against an unseen microphone, testing it with a laugh, and our hands go up to our ears as the sound snaps and pops before clearing. Jordan continues, "So…eager to start the game are you?"

My heart sinks, blood rushing wildly through me. I look to the corners of the barn, trying to spy the cameras they must be watching us with, but they're well hidden.

"Once the doors open and the music sounds, you'll have a head start of exactly two minutes and forty-five seconds. I suggest you use them wisely, because once your time is up, we're coming to get you… so get ready to run, run, run!"

I inhale sharply then hold it, the silence palpable, and my eyes burn, refusing to blink.

A metallic *click*, and suddenly the doors pop open by themselves.

I fling myself from the cage, falling to the ground, stumbling in the dirt with numbed legs. Growling against it I force myself to stand, hobbling toward my daughter's cage; she's still wedged up to the back of it, an ashen, sickly gray tinting her skin.

"Come on baby, remember what I told you?" I ask with a shaky voice, already feeling the time tick away.

Suddenly the scratch of a record blares and then the voices of Flanagan and Allen start to sing…disgustingly, morbidly, the song *Run Rabbit Run*.

Nia stirs, launching herself forward and I help her down. Taking her hand we run to the barn doors, finding they push open easily. The fresh cold air wafts against us, burning my lungs. To the right of us is the blinding porch light of a little house, with Martha's silhouette standing out in front with a shotgun raised in the air.

"Get a move on!" she screams, then *Bang!*

Nia falls to the floor, shaking violently, but I haul her up into my arms and run, run, run… to the left toward the forest. Stumbling over gopher holes in the lumpy field, and we close in on the trees.

Half the song over with, I urge my legs to move faster. Nia's crying against my shoulder, and I'm puffing white smoke as we enter the fold of trees. Weaving around their massive trunks I can feel my pace slow. Searching for a straightaway to dash forward in any direction as long as it puts distance between us and *them*.

The song becomes more of a whisper but I can hear it begin to fade out. Dropping to my knees I put my daughter before me, raising her chin up so her eyes meet mine, I fight to keep my voice strong, for her.

"I need you to be Mommy's little spider monkey," I point to the gnarled branches of an oak tree.

She nods her head, running over to it, clasping at the bark with firm grips she begins to climb. I come up behind her, holding out my arms in case she should fall. She stops abruptly, glancing back.

"Mommy? Come with me…" she cries.

"I'm staying down here, but I'm not going anywhere. Now climb…climb!"

She scurries up the length of the tree.

"Go as high as you can. Hold on, and stay quiet no matter what," I whisper up to her, just as the song cuts out.

I pinch my lips together and gnaw on them nervously… *they're coming.*

Nia disappears within the foliage. The branches stop yawning and the leaves stop swaying. She's good and hidden, for now at least.

Hearing noises in the distance, snapping twigs and crackling leaves, I slink behind the tree. My veins throb, blood pulsing furiously, as I try to focus, mumbling, "Think, think, think…"

My eyes dart around the forest, trees and trees for miles… The echo of the shotgun rings out in my brain. Weapons… we've got nothing. I can feel myself slide into the swirl of madness, as if tumbling down a vertigo spiral. I shake my head, snapping myself out of the trance of fear. *Think!*

Steak pie, chicken pie, fish pie, pigeon pie, Jordan's words come back to haunt me. How many people had they killed and stuffed into pies? No one must have escaped, as they're settled comfortably in their little rundown hell farm, continuing it year after year.

I inhale, feeling tears well at the edge, ready to fall over, but I hold still until I come into my realization... statistically we're going to die. But if we're going to die, I'm not going out without a fight.

I grit my teeth. Ripping off my shirt, I step down on one side of the seam, balling up the other side in my fist and stretch the fabric. Threads popping until the shirt's tension suddenly gives and tears in half.

Wrapping the shirt several times around both my hands until it is a taut band between them. I plant my feet, ready, waiting quietly, but it isn't long before footsteps are shuffling in our direction.

My breathing so erratic that I try to hold it until I absolutely need it.

The footsteps intensify, edging closer, and my body feels afire with the strain of ridged muscles that beg to snap.

Rustling and murmurs travel from across the line of trees. The *other* one is sweeping the land not too far from here, and I realize they're trying to push us out.

"Where are you, little rabbits?" his gravelly voice drags over the air, close to me.

Peeking around my tree I see a puff of breath swirl into the air not more than a foot from me.

Boom! A shot fires. I jump, throwing a hand over my mouth to keep silent. Then panic sweeps through me and I look up, but Nia's still hidden and quiet… *good girl.*

My hands sweaty, I tighten my grip. Time feels slowed.

CHK CHK

He pumps the shotgun, expelling the used shell, the new one still loading.

I spring out, taking him by surprise. I wrap my shirt around the barrel of the shotgun, he fires, but it's too late, as I twist it out of his grip and it falls to the ground.

I dive for it, but suddenly a searing pain slashes into my arm. Crying out, I tumble too far away to reach the gun. Spotting blood running from a slash in my upper arm, I try to ignore it to help block out the pain, but Jordan splays a maniacal grin upon his face as he tosses his field knife from hand to hand. It gleams threateningly, catching the moonlight, the blade painted in crimson.

"Come on little rabbit," he jeeringly says, jerking forward with a step before pulling back, making me unsure when he'll strike.

I stumble to my feet, keeping my shirt pulled tightly between my hands.

Thundering footsteps approach from behind, closing in…Martha. Two against one.

My heart sinks, but my feet spur onward. Ignoring the flaring pain, I leap forward, sidestepping quickly as Jordan plunges the blade forward. The edge grazes my shoulder, but before he can swivel it down into my flesh, I kick out at his knees.

He screams, falling forward. Stepping behind him I wrap my shirt around his throat and heave up toward myself. The blade drops from his hand, and he gurgles as he chokes. His stifled breathing only gets more fervent as I cross my hands to create a suffocating twist. My muscles shake against the weight, and he twitches violently underneath me.

A scream cuts through the air.

Glancing behind myself I see down the barrel of a shotgun, and I drop to the ground.

Boom! Right over my head, but instead of reloading she swiftly brings up the butt of the gun and smashes it against my temple.

Too dazed, my head a swirl of agony, I turn to crawl away.

Jordan stirs beside me, clutching his throat as he heaves dryly, coughing raggedly.

"Say goodbye, little rabbit," Martha says.

CHK CHK

I totter against the ground, as if it moves. Collapsing to my side weakly, I await another gunshot, the *final* gunshot.

A high-pitched squeal resounds throughout the air. Nia leaping from a tree branch overhead lands down upon Martha's back. The shot fires into the night sky as she's hurled backward, Nia wringing her neck with her arms and clawing into her chest with her fingernails, causing Martha to thrash against her.

"Leave my mommy alone!" she cries, before sinking her teeth into Martha's neck.

"Ahhh!"

Blood runs down her neck, but her eyes flare wide with rage. She lets go of the gun, grabbing onto Nia and flings her forward. Nia flies through the air until smashing into the ground with an excruciating thud.

I lurch forward, the world still upon its tilt, trying to grab the gun, but Jordan wrests me to the ground. Putting his full weight upon me, digging his knee into the small of my back, I drop with a hopeless thump, wriggling helplessly.

"Go!" he shouts.

I stretch my arm farther; still trying for the gun that Martha's hurrying to seize back. I can feel the cool metal touch my fingertips. Suddenly the field knife sinks down into my hand, pinning it to the ground. I wail as my fingers spastically spasm, and Jordan drives the knife in further.

"I'll take care of her, you take the girl back!"

Martha retrieving her gun saunters over to Nia, who's moaning and holding her head in her hands, eyes rolled back into her skull.

"Yes dear," she chuckles with an elated smile stretching across her bloodied face. Snatching her off the ground, Nia weakly kicks, but Martha's arm is too tightly wound around her.

"No!" I cry, watching uselessly as Martha disappears in the thick cropping of trees, back toward the farm.

His tongue drags across my cheek and he says with a hoarse voice, "You're gonna be mighty tasty."

Withdrawing the knife, my hand tremors in pain, a slit cut all the way through, from the knuckle to the top of my wrist.

I can feel pressure release as Jordan sits up on his knees, and picture him raising the knife into the air over my head.

Fighting against the haze and burning cuts, I heave, rolling onto my back, kneeing Jordan in the gut. He curls inward, his arm drooping, but his grip on the blade firm.

I scurry out from under him, hearing him clamber after me. The knife comes down licking at my heel, but I kick away. Throwing myself forward I'm at his shotgun, my hands clasping it, despite my slippery grip and my wound screaming at me.

I fling myself unto my back, the barrel pointed up at Jordan who staggers to a halt, his eyes going wide

"No dinner for you," I say, pulling the trigger.

BAM!

It blows a hole in his chest, big enough to see through, and a smile creeps up on my face as he falls over dead.

I exhale roughly, trying to catch my breath, but there's no time... *Nia!*

Pocketing the field knife, I then take my torn shirt and wrap it around my hand, tying it tightly to stop the bleeding.

CHK CHK

The spent shell tumbles to the ground.

Ready, I fumble back the way we'd come, though this time it takes longer and my nerves burst afire. Praying Nia's ok and I'm not too late.

I blunder out into the field, leaving the trees behind me. Trudging up to the house, the bright light shut off, Martha must think he's killed me. Good, I've got a surprise for her.

Stepping up onto the creaky porch, I fling open the screen door and barrel into the house, causing a huge racket.

"You're back quick…" Martha shouts through the house.

My ears prickle with the noise, following the trail. I stomp through the weathered living room set up with laptops splaying video feeds from the barn, and a record player with *Run Rabbit Run* still set up for play.

Treading into the hallway, frames cover all over the peeling wallpaper. They're pictures of the happy couple on their anniversary each year, holding up pies. Young faces, old familiar faces… frames by the dozens…. *dear God.*

"Why don't you take her out back and get to prepping her?" she continues, as I march into the kitchen.

Nia's tied down on the kitchen island, gagged, crying and wriggling against her restraints. Her eyes go wide when she spots me, and her body freezes up.

Martha's in front of the kitchen sink washing dishes. A pie tin with dough spilling over the edges, filled with vegetables, sits waiting upon the counter next to her. Heat rises in my cheeks, my blood boiling, as I raise the gun, aiming over my prone daughter.

"I don't need you bringing your muddy boots through-" Martha stops, catching sight of me in the reflection of the window just as I pull the trigger.

She drops to the floor, and the glass shatters where she stood, missing her entirely.

CHK CHK

Panicking, as Martha pops up from behind the island whipping out her own shotgun, I yank back the trigger, but it just clicks…empty.

"Aw, what a shame…" Martha says with a smirk.

I drop the gun and it clatters to the floor. My arms hang at my sides, though I'm slowly reaching into my back pocket, and as my heart pounds against my ribs I throw a smile onto my face.

"You don't get it yet do you?"

Martha squints her blackened eyes curiously, her grip loosening somewhat, the color returning to her knuckles.

"That was Jordan's shotgun...but where oh where is Jordan?"

Martha's mouth opens in shock, her eyes going distant for a moment.

I take the advantage by grappling the knife from my pocket, and I quickly raise it, thrusting it forward.

Martha snaps back to focus, reaffirming her grip.

The knife flies from my fingertips.

Martha fires.

The blade slices through the air.

The pellets hurtle toward me, and I go to move.

The knife sinks into Martha's chest.

I sidestep, too slowly, and a wad of pellets lodges into my shoulder.

Our cries echo out, clashing against each other.

Martha falls backward onto the counter, and I fall forward onto the island. Nia filling my vision... *my* Nia, *my* beautiful strong Nia. She tugs against the ropes, muffling cries for me. Suddenly the pain, which had been seemingly insurmountable, becomes a door I can close. Adrenaline surges through me, and I catapult around the island.

Martha's trying to pull herself up from the counter, bent over wretchedly. Her shotgun on the floor, but I don't risk it. In a split second upon spotting a butcher's block with an assortment of knives, knives she was going to use on Nia, I snatch the biggest blade, a chopper, swinging it forward with a mighty roar.

I plunge it into her neck where Nia's teeth marks are dug into her skin, a large cut splitting them open further, blood spurting out splattering my face. She squirms against it. Twitching spastically, her eyes clouded with untamed fear, she burbles blood.

I heave it out then slam it back, a sickening snap and a thud as it slashes through bone. Her head flies off her shoulders, popping up into the air, landing with a soft thump amidst a bed of vegetables. Her head resting inside her homemade pie.

I leave the chopper stuck into the linoleum countertop, a waterfall of blood seeping off it. Grabbing another knife out of the block, I saw away at my daughter's constraints.

"We're okay," I tell her, my voice shaking as the realization of it begins to wash over me. "We're okay baby, we made it!"

The ropes all cut, Nia wriggles out of them, and upon pulling the gag from her mouth, she cries, "Mommy!"

Lurching forward, she wraps her arms around me. I wince, the pain coming back once more, crashing into me like waves. But still I fight against it and hug her back, as tightly as I can. Tears fog my vision, sobbing so profusely.

"I love you baby…I love you."

"I love you too," she whispers.

"But," I begin, pulling away suddenly, though still clutching onto her hands with my good one, "I told you to listen to me, and you didn't. You did a very, very dangerous thing." Thinking back to her coming to my aide in the woods, a smile erupts onto my face, "And I couldn't be more proud."

Nia bursts into a fit of giggles as I help her leap off the counter.

"Look away baby," I tell her, trying to cover her eyes from Martha's headless body slumped onto the floor, lying in a pool of her own blood.

"But I'm a big girl...I can handle it," she replies confidently.

I chuckle, curling inward with a sharp pain. "I know that," I remark as my smile begins to slide off my face wearily.

I want to be rid of this place, this horrible disgusting hellhole, itching to take Nia as far from here as possible.

Looking around, I spot a pair of keys lying on a side table in the living room, and point to them.

"We're getting out of here. Be Mommy's little helper and grab those will you?"

Nia spiritedly dashes away, full with life...alive; we're alive... We did it.

Despite the awful, agonizing wreck my body is in right now, I'm happy, because I know we're all right.

She snatches the keys, jangling them, excited to go. But before I leave the kitchen, I grab the pie tin off the counter, my hand dipping from the weight of Martha's head, and put it in the oven. Turning it on to two hundred and fifty degrees I leave it to cook, *bitch*.

Taking Nia's hand in my own, we step outside, the cool breeze wafting over us with the sweet scent of freedom. Loaded into the pickup truck, the engine rumbles to life, and we drive on out of the farm. Finding a road, I gas it as the sky breaks into dawn.

SKELETONS

By Frederick Pangbourne

I couldn't say why the day was different this morning, but there was an unknown change in the air itself. Though I could sense this hidden alteration as soon as I had awakened, I could not for the life of me put my finger on the source. The day just felt... different.

I rolled my head about in circles on my neck and felt the soft popping of the vertebrate. Sighing, I gazed back down at the laptop resting on my lap. I had only managed to write one paragraph in the last thirty minutes while I sat on the back deck. Not my usual speed of production when it came to my writing but the difference in the way the day felt had also appeared to be affecting my thought process. I again sighed heavily and placed the open laptop on the small table next to me. My imagination was bogged down and sitting here trudging after elusive ideas was mentally draining me. I picked a tall glass of vodka and orange juice off the same table and took a deep sip. Probably not the best way to start one's morning off but I found that just the right amount of alcohol could rejuvenate my creative juices faster than spinach to Popeye.

I shielded my eyes from the rising sun as it made its way over the distant trees across the lake. My cabin was backed up right to one of the narrower portions of Nantahala Lake's shore and sitting on the back deck, especially during sunrises and sunsets, always evoked my writings to be more powerful and flowing. That was unfortunately not the case this morning, for whatever reason. Like I said, the day felt different... unusual. It was at this point that I noticed that there were no sounds. The woods surrounding both my cabin and the lake were eerily silent. None of the usual bird chirping or any insect stridulation filled the air. Nothing. I looked out to the few other homes that were also along the lake. They too seemed empty and silent, even though I knew they were occupied. My gaze then caught a canoe out in the distant water. Someone in a red shirt and matching hat was casting a line into the lake's clear waters. I guess the day wasn't totally void of life.

I took another long sip from my glass and set it back next to the laptop. I could feel the alcohol starting to take effect as it took advantage of my empty stomach. Good. After this glass, I should be ready to go. I do a lot of writing these days. More of a hobby than a career. I retired early in life. Put my years in as a desk jockey in the Air Force and could call it quits at fifty-one. Now, with a little help from the funds willed to me by departed grandparents some years ago, I sit out here in peaceful solitude and write. Mostly dime store novels and a few short stories here and there.

Between that, my military pension and my inheritance, I do okay for myself.

I figured I'd go for broke and picked the glass up again and tipped it back, downing the remains of the screwdriver. As my head was tilted upwards, I glimpsed the clouds overhead. They were darker than I initially remembered them when I first came out onto the deck. Dark and with an odd coloring to them. Almost like an orange hue was mixed into the dreary grays and whites. As I pulled the empty glass from my lips, I continued to stare up into the strange colored cloud masses that were gathering. Gray clouds with a bright orange touch to their linings. Strangely fascinating they were.

I was pulled from heavenly observations by the faint and distinct sound of the doorbell. Taking my glass with me, I sat up and made my way inside the house. Leaving the glass on the kitchen counter as I passed, I went to the front door.

"Mike, Good morning. What do I owe the pleasure?" I said, running my hand through my disheveled head of hair.

"Morning, Dave," greeted my usual mailman, Michael Dane. Briarsville, North Carolina was more of a hamlet than a town and had only three mail personnel delivering mail. Ninety percent of the time I had Mike dropping parcels off to me. "The package was too big for your mailbox out on the road so, I'm hand delivering it." He pulled a brown cardboard box, slightly bigger than a shoebox, from his mailbag and handed it to me.

"I wonder if these are advanced copies of my book?" I said more to myself as I accepted the package.

"Got me. All I know is that it's addressed to one David Bissett."

"Well, that is certainly me as far as I-" My words were interrupted by a deafening blast of thunder that shook the very air. The two of us jumped at the unexpected explosion of sound. Suddenly the clouds opened up and released a torrential downpour of rain. There was no forewarning of a few advanced drops, just an immediate cascade of water. Luckily, the two of us were beneath the cover of the porch roof.

"Jesus Christ. Didn't see this coming," I said as I watched the pouring rain.

"You and me both. Shit, I left the windows open. Catch you later," Mike said over his shoulder as he scurried off the porch to his mail truck. Not only were the windows down, but also the passenger's door was wide opened. I smiled as I watched him rush across the gravel wrap-around driveway to his truck near the stairs. I hoped there wasn't any mail near those open windows. He was instantly saturated with the orangish rain as he…. orangish rain? It took a second for me to acknowledge what I was witnessing: the rain was not clear but had an orange color to it. The puddles that were already forming had an orange oily looking tinge on their surface. Without subjecting myself to the rain, I leaned on the porch railing and looked up to the sky. The oddly colored clouds seemed to pulsate with a strange light that remained hidden deep within.

I turned my gaze back to the mail truck and saw that Mike had collapsed in the driveway only a few feet from the truck. He lay face down in the gravel with his arm outstretched to the open truck door. "Mike!" I yelled from the safety of the porch, daring not to venture out into the bizarre rainfall. "Mike! You okay?"

As if in response, Mike rolled over onto his back and groaned. Wisps of white steam were rising from him. His eyes were rolled up into his head and his mouth hung open. It was then to my horror that I saw the unthinkable. Mike's flesh was melting from him like liquefied wax. Areas of skin, portions of muscle and clumps of his hair slid off the bone and were dissolving at an incredible rate. His eyes melted and bubbled up as they sank deep into their sockets. The rain was acting as some powerful corrosive acid that was liquefying the soft organic tissue, causing it to drip into pools of a slimy fluid that collected in the driveway. His postal uniform remained unscathed by the water, as did everything surrounding him. The grass on my lawn, the wood of my cabin and the mail truck itself. They all seemed unaffected by the acid like rain. The acidic destruction of the man was over within a minute and apparently without any indication of pain, as Mike never cried out in agony. Only that one final drawn-out groan was all that escaped his lips.

Then, as abruptly as the mysterious rain had started, it ended. Like a faucet high above in the clouds was promptly turned off, leaving pools of orange water and a lone skeleton in a postal uniform laying in my driveway.

My legs felt weak and rubbery and I surrendered into a sitting position on the porch, my back resting against the front door. All I could do was stare at the bleached white skeleton that was only a minute ago my mailman. Though this was the most shocking thing I had ever been subjected to in all my life, I somehow remained calm. There was no panic or the slightest amount of stress wracking my body. I would like to chalk it up to the alcohol but who can say? After about five minutes of just staring out at the skeleton, I decided it was probably best if I went inside and called the police. Briarsville was so too small of a town to have their own police department, so we relied on the State Highway Patrol for any type of law in the area. They had a barracks about thirty minutes out of town and they would roll through about half a dozen times during the day just to make sure the town hadn't run amok.

I was mentally preparing my end of the phone conversation before I made the call when a faint droning hum began. The sound seemed to come from no particular direction, but seemed to be emitting from everywhere. The sound grew in intensity until I had to cover my ears. I tightly closed my eyes and palmed my ears as the volume of the droning hum became painful. Then, just like the rain, it halted. I opened my eyes and lowered my hands. Nothing had changed. I wasn't sure what would have changed but, the way the day was going, I was ready for just about anything at this point. Almost anything.

I heard the gravel in the driveway stir and looked up to see the skeleton sitting up straight. The unexpected sight had now evoked a flicker of panic within me. My legs instinctively pulled in closed to my body and I pressed my back against the closed door. The skull then turned in my direction, and the skeleton was now on its feet, facing me. It stood at attention with its arms hanging at its side. Without Mike's fleshy waistline, the uniform trousers fell from the bony pelvis to the ground, the belt buck clanging on the stone. It then stepped from both its shoes and discarded pants and proceeded to rip the front of the uniform shirt open before that too was cast aside. My hand reached up for the doorknob with trembling fingers. It was when the skeleton started taking steps toward the porch that I turned my head and all my attention to the doorknob.

I fell through the threshold and quickly closed the door behind. Again, with trembling fingers that barely responded, I managed to lock the door and latch the security chain. I then crab walked backwards on all fours until I was practically in the kitchen. I stopped once I backed into the refrigerator and watched. The skeleton proceeded up the stairs and stopped at the door. I could see its skull and black hollowed eye sockets staring through the glass pane in the door. It did not attempt to enter. Instead, it simply stood facing the door.

With the front door now secured, I turned and got to my feet as I rushed to the sliding glass doors to the back deck. As I locked the door and dropped the security bar in place, I looked out to the lake. There was no movement from the other houses that I could make out from this distance but I could see the lone canoe that was afloat earlier far out on the water. It was now capsized and drifting about aimlessly on the lake's smooth surface. As I stared out at the water, something broke that glass-like surface just offshore. It only took a moment before I realized another skeleton was emerging from the water as it walked onto the stony banks. As it walked, it was tearing off a red shirt and leaving it behind on the ground as it neared the cabin. It was just making its way up the deck stairs when I hurried from the glass doors and retreated into the bathroom down the hall.

Once inside, I promptly closed and locked the door. I then pushed away the shower curtain and crawled into the tub where I sat balled up with my knees against my chest. There was only one small window in the bathroom, and it was set high, restricting anything from outside from looking in, so I stayed seated in the tub proclaiming the bathroom as my safe room. I couldn't say how long I sat there trying to calm down and collect my thoughts but when I did finally slide back into a partial state of sane normality, I began to collect the evidence that I had witnessed, and after a long deliberation between my thoughts; I had come to two possible conclusions to the reasoning behind today's freakish and fantastic events.

The first was that the government was conducting some type of secret military experiment. Briarsville was a tiny and insignificant enough town that it could easily be isolated and subjected to some bizarre secret government experiment. Were they testing some synthetic chemical agent on us? Some chemical that rapidly dissolves the flesh from people, harming nothing else, and then using some sonic stimulant (the droning hum) to stimulate the skeletal remains, somehow animating them? My second theory was just as outlandish. Were we in the process of being invaded by extraterrestrials? The strange lights in the clouds and their discoloration would point to some hidden spacecraft initiating the events. Again, using some alien chemical to mix into our rain that would easily wipe out anyone that it came in contact with, then again, using some futuristic sound machine to raise and control the deceased remains? Both possibilities were as far-fetched as the other but, from what I had seen, I could form no other explanation. I told myself that the two scenarios were at least something I could use to plan my next course of action.

The first thing to do was to see if the two skeletons were still at the doors. Using the sides of the tub for support, I pulled myself out and opened the bathroom door. The house was deathly silent as I crept quietly into the hall. I peeked around the corner and saw that the one at the sliding glass doors to the back of the house was still standing there at attention. As I changed angles, I saw that the skull at the front door window also remained. At least they showed no intention of coming inside. It almost seemed as if they were being posted at my doors in case I tried to leave.

To test that theory, I stepped out into plain view of them both. Neither reacted. I waved my hands over my head to get their attention and still they stood unresponsive. Satisfied that they had no desire of entering the cabin, I moved to the television and turned it on. Something of this magnitude must be on some news channel. Unfortunately, I would never find out. There was no power going to the set, and I soon discovered that the entire cabin was without electricity. I tried my cell phone. That too was a dead end. No Internet either. Both scenarios I had put together were now slightly solidified. An interruption of communication and electricity surely pointed to an invasion and/or cutting the town off from the outside world. With my two undead sentries content only at guarding the cabin's exits, I poured myself a strong drink and sat on the couch, mentally scheming on a way out.

The large circular wall clock over the television ran on AA batteries and was still showing the time. Everything that had happened since I answered the door until now had taken just over an hour. It was now 10:23, and I sat there for close to another hour and two more drinks before I came up with an escape plan: I would use the crawlspace beneath the house to sneak invisibly from here so my departure would go unnoticed by the skeletons, if they could even see. Their limitations were still unknown. For all I knew, they still possessed hearing and sight. I would then drive the mail truck out. I could only assume that the keys still had to be in the ignition. I doubted Mike would have turned off the truck and taken the keys out just to make a quick drop off. With the plan now completed, I gathered the supplies I would need for my jailbreak. I changed into jeans, a t-shirt and sneakers. Filled a large shaker cup with vodka and orange juice and lastly pulled an old wooden baseball bat from the back of my closet.

I had opened the trap door and swung my legs into the hole in the floor when a cannon-like blast of thunder erupted. It shook the cabin and, as before, was immediately followed by a downpour of rain. I sat at the edge of the trapdoor, listening to the rain falling heavily onto the roof. After it had suddenly ceased, I continued to wait for what I believed would be next. After several minutes, the droning hum originated once more until it hit a painful level, then that too abruptly stopped. Whatever was being conducted was repeated. I could only guess that another wave of acidic water was being dropped to catch anyone who had avoided the first rainfall. Whoever was behind this was making sure that no one survived. Without thinking too much into the matter, I slid into the trapdoor and underneath the cabin.

The stony earthen floor beneath the house was cold to the touch as I maneuvered past support beams and the network of PVC piping through the dark confines toward the outline of the outside door to the crawlspace. Crawling up to the door, I paused and listened. When I was satisfied, I slowly pushed the plywood door outward. I half expected to see a pair of skeletal feet in front of me as I climbed out but, thankfully, there was none. I avoided touching the wet grass and soil as I emerged into the sunlight with the use of the bat as leverage.

I stood up straight and stretched my back as I looked around. The air was still muted and void of the usual nature sounds. That was until I heard a scream. It was a woman and seemed to come from one of the homes across the lake. I froze and threw a glance across the water. The scream came once, echoing from the far shore before it fell silent. I decided that I should keep moving and carry out my plan before I was the next one screaming. I stopped at the corner of the house and peered around its edge. The skeleton continued standing a few inches from the door. I turned my gaze to the mail truck. It stood as before, with its passenger's side door open and facing toward the cabin. I pulled a quick swig from the shaker cup and crept out from the house.

With that bat in one hand and liquid courage in the other, I slowly moved in a wide arc toward the front lawn. My plan was to move unnoticed and place the truck between the house and myself. When I reached the driveway, I crept even slower and more carefully as I crossed over the graveled stones. When I arrived at the side of the truck, I exhaled and took another swig from the plastic cup. So far, so good. I peeked through the open driver's side window and across the opened door. The skeletal sentry had not moved and continued facing the door. I then turned my gaze to the keys, which hung from the ignition. The gas gauge showed the fuel level to be three quarters full. Perfect! I nearly completed my plan. Once inside, I would drive out to town and possibly to Route 1310 if necessary, where the trooper barracks were. I pulled myself away from the window and rested my back against the side of the truck, mentally preparing myself for the next phase of my grand scheme. When I deemed myself ready, I began to slowly make my way around the front of the truck. I turned my attention to the front porch as I moved and saw that the skeleton was no longer on the porch. I froze and caught my breath in mid inhale.

The sound of gravel shifting came from behind me and I whirled around. Before I could react, bony fingers were around my throat and it pushed me up against the front of the truck. The shaker cup fell from my fingers. The emotionless expression of the grinning skull met me socket to eye as the being of nothing more than bone structure attempted to strangle the life from me. Though there was no longer any muscular tissue, the skeleton still possessed a sense of strength. I gagged at the pressure being applied to my windpipe and pushed the bat horizontally into the face of the skull. I continued to press the slender end of the bat against its teeth as hard as I could until the front teeth gave way and shattered as the handle of the bat was now pushed into its open mouth. My struggling managed to push me off the truck as the two of us fell forward to the ground. My weight in the fall was to my advantage as I tumbled on top of my assailant. With the skull still biting down on the bat, the weight of my body forced the bat deep into the mouth, taking out all the teeth as the wooden handle was pushed deeper, and once the bat could go no further, it dislocated the mandible, popping the jaw off the skull.

It released its grip and frantically clawed at its face. Its bony fingertips scraping across the skull face. I quickly pulled myself to my feet and commenced to bash the skull. The tiny bones in the hands exploded with the first couple of blows and the skull was soon bashed into jagged fragments from the remaining strikes of the bat. When I had finished, the head was nothing more than an opened cranium with no face. It reminded me of fractured eggshell. I heard something near me and spun around to see the second sentry racing around from the back of the house toward me. Leaving my cup of courage behind, I jumped into the truck and slammed the door closed and cranked the window up. Instantly the skeleton was pounding on the side of the truck and window. I turned the key and started the truck. It was in gear and tearing around the loop of the driveway, kicking up gravel as I steered it away from the cabin and toward the road. In the rearview mirror, the skeleton was still pursuing but was soon left in the distance.

I gently rubbed my throat as I could now feel the pain as I tried to swallow. How had it gotten the jump on me? None of that mattered now as I cut the turn out of my driveway tight and took out my mailbox as the truck was now on the paved road and headed east toward town.

I found myself laughing hysterically as I raced along the road, and once I heard how insane I sounded, I dropped it down to an irresistible snicker. I was a genius! No secret military experiment or even an alien invasion could contain or outwit me. As I neared Briarsville, I saw no other cars on the road except one. A red pickup truck was embedded in a ditch off the roadside. The driver's side door hung open but I saw no one as I sped by. I tried to decide what to do once I entered town and what I would see. I wondered how many people in town had been caught out in the unexplainable rain and were subjected to the same fate as Mike Dane and were now skeletons awaiting my arrival.

As I entered the outskirts of town, I found most of the homes apparently deserted. How did I know this? Because the ones along the road that weren't empty reminded me of the one I just left. Skeletons stood on porches and on lawns awaiting the helpless residents inside to emerge. I glimpsed two homes where motionless bodies lay sprawled out on the grass or in the driveway. Skeletons lingering over their lifeless forms, ensuring that they remained where they had died. Waiting for the coming of the next wave of acidic rain. Each wave adding to their growing numbers.

The center of town was a scene of utter chaos. Unlike the sporadic homes along the road further back, downtown Briarsville was at the opposite end of the spectrum. Skeletons were everywhere and not just standing about like back at my place. No, there were dozens upon dozens of them running all over the place. Some were chasing screaming people who had avoided the rain and still had flesh on their bones. Others were attacking the ones they cornered and fell upon. Choking the life from them or pounding on them with their bony fists. I caught sight of a couple running around with long knives in their hands. Vehicles were run up on the curbs and a few into store windows. The diner on the corner was in flames.

Fleshy bodies littered the roads and sidewalks. Victims to the undead onslaught. I'm not proud of my actions as I roared into the center of town and plowed through both the living and the dead. The mail truck was no tank by any means and I dared not to slow down regardless of what stood in my way in fear of the tiny truck being stopped. Skeletal bodies shattered on impact as I barreled through the masses and a few unfortunate towns folks as well, including poor old Ms. Wagner. She worked over at the drugstore down on Tobias Street. She came running across the road, trying to wave me down with two of those bone fiends chasing right behind her. I closed my eyes just before hitting her and unfortunately running her over. I opened them to find blood splattered across the windshield in a sickening display that was dripping down the glass. As you can imagine, I wasn't laughing anymore at my self-proclaimed genius.

As quickly as I had entered the center of town, I was now leaving it behind me. As I had stated earlier, it was more of a hamlet than a town. Now that there was no reason to remain there, I was now setting my sights to the State Trooper barracks. I figured it was about twenty minutes away. I looked about the inside of the truck for my shaker cup and cursed out loud when I realized that it was sitting back in my driveway. I could have really used a drink right now. I was only about three or four miles out of town when, to my amazement, a patrol car appeared just over a rise in the road as I was ascending it. We passed each other quickly and I hardly had time to react to its presence. By the time I pumped the brakes and slowed down, I glanced into the rearview mirror in time to see the patrol car also braking and cutting into a U-turn. "Thank Christ," I said aloud and quickly pulled the truck over off the road onto the dirt shoulder.

Almost immediately, the car's overhead lights came on as it sped up behind me and eventually stopped behind the truck. I exhaled loudly as good fortune had found me and I had the chance to forewarn the trooper about his trip into town. As the trooper emerged from his car and slowly approached the mail truck, I looked ahead through the blood-streaked windshield and noticed something in the road ahead of me. Maybe about fifty yards away I saw that the pavement was discolored. The portion closest to me was dark from the rains that had fallen while the other half of the road was bone dry. I had come upon the perimeter of the experiment or the furthest the invasion had advanced. Everything beyond the saturated part of the road was unaffected and free of danger.

My attention was abruptly diverted when the sliding door to the mail truck was suddenly slid open and the patrolman's SIG Sauer pistol was pointed at me.

"Sir, place your hands on the steering wheel!" he shouted. I did as he ordered.

I wasn't sure why I was nervously trembling. I had done nothing wrong. I mean besides murdering Ms. Wagner and a couple of other folks on my way through town, but that was more out of survival than pure malice. I looked out to the wet and dry section in the road and wanted to suggest that we move forward onto the dry area, but I lost my words as my thoughts were all jumbled about now. I didn't know where to begin explaining everything that I had just gone through.

"Sir, why are you in a government postal truck and why is there blood all on the front of the vehicle? Explain, please!"

"I-I was just t-trying to, uh…" My mind was being overloaded as the reality of today's experience was finally sinking in.

Before I could calm myself and gather my thoughts to explain the situation transpiring in town, I was forcibly pulled from the truck and placed on the pavement. I felt the trooper's knee in my back as he pinned me down and was having restraints placed on my wrists behind my back.

"Headquarters, I have a possible 10-54, hit and run out on Stadler Road, just before

Briarsville. Request an addition unit. Copy?" the patrolman was speaking into his radio mic.

Still, I was unable to explain myself, let alone form a sentence. I couldn't stop myself from shaking. As the trooper repeated the transmission on his radio, I realized that he would get no response. All communication within the perimeter would be useless. A movement then caught my eye as I laid face down on the pavement. I looked to the wooded tree line. Just before the woods near the road thickened, a skeleton stepped out from behind a large tree. It stood motionless, watching. I started stammering unintelligently as I squirmed to get up. I felt the knee press harder into my back and his hand pressed my head firmly to the pavement. "Sir, stay where you are."

Behind the lurking skeleton, another appeared farther back in the trees.

"Sir, I'm going to need you to-" His words were cut short by a thunderous crack of thunder. I craned my head beneath his hand and looked out to the dry portion of road only a stone's throw away. If only I had pulled over fifty more yards down the road. I unknowingly resumed my hysterical laughing again as the downpour of orange rain fell upon us.

THE ARCHIVIST

By Juliana Amir

Varo's house was his personal museum where no one was ever invited. Neighbors had reached into his mailbox pretending his letters were wrongly delivered to their address. Varo studied his admirers from the window, shifting their weight, waiting for his door to open, ready to feign a parched throat, hoping to peer into his house of wonders.

All left disappointed.

They tucked his mail back where it belonged before returning to their normal homes full of bedrooms and bathrooms. Boring homes well suited to the boring minds inhabiting them.

He sensed they were lonely, unlike Varo who never was.

His mother was rich and his father fine-looking... well, he hoped so. It was uncertain which of her many husbands was his father. Varo always insisted it was the cheese connoisseur with the strong jawline who played steal the cheese. Cheese, wrapped in cloth, was kept in the father's suit jacket, and if Varo could pickpocket it, it was his to eat. He'd pop it into his mouth whole in a single greedy gobble. He loved when it was Gouda, hated when it was Baby Swiss, but the delight of unwrapping it to find out was always the best part.

All the husbands were buried in the backyard gardens, and flowers bloomed as if longing to be the brightest and most desirable. Encased behind a stone wall were rolling grounds with willful perennials surviving amongst countless weeds and a weeping willow to mark the resting place of Varo's temporary fathers. Varo's mother no longer ventured out to her gardens, but remained in the wine cellar where the temperature was a chilly forty degrees.

Varo's friends were aware of his mother's fragile condition and inquired thoughtfully after her health. Varo loved making new friends. He made them quite easily.

To bland eyes, his gallery might appear motionless, but Varo's eyes were those of an artist's. With his brushes and oils, he swept faces onto canvases. Some faces were calm like his relatives in their caskets. Their complexions gray as if storm clouds had gathered beneath their skin.

Others presented curves of happiness with upturned mouths and crinkled eyes. All of the cheery faces had golden hair like his aunt who harnessed the firelight. He longed to wed her, but she chose an ice-sculptor whose tributes soon melted. Varo's endured. His walls, frame-to-frame with faces, stared vacantly at all strangers. For

Varo, the portraits rose to life, ever grateful for his return.

They appreciated his company far more than Maple. In the walk-in closet, surrounded by all Varo's beautiful clothes, shone a metal hook. Maple hung there now as Varo had once been hung by his suspenders when his cigar-smoking father deemed it necessary. The closet was even soundproofed, so while Varo threatened to send the devil after him, only the devil could hear. It was okay. The devil's ear was all he needed.

Now that Varo was older, the hook appeared empty with nothing adorned there, so he filled the void with Maple, the wooden marionette in the ruffled dress given by the father who pretended his mother had a daughter rather than a son. The marionette had two copper braids made from real hair and glass eyes glued into their wooden sockets.

How her scrawny legs kicked when she sang: "Lemme out, lemme out. Before I send the devil after you." It was odd how whenever he entered the closet, just to let Maple know she was remembered, the stale scent of cigar-smoke filled him clouding his senses and making the air thicker, harder to breathe.

The cigar connoisseur was among the meanest of the temporary fathers, but not the strangest. No. When he wanted to think of the strangest, he went to the trunk room on the third floor. It had wooden floors and shelves of luggage as well as one large, locked trunk. That father loved modesty and cleanliness. He met his mother in winter when she was bundled in her fur coat, gloves, and boots. He seemed average, but his personality toward her changed by spring when layers were peeled off.

"Why aren't you wearing gloves?" He'd chase after her with a pair, perhaps blue or silver.

He loved gloves and bought them both many pairs. They had to eat with gloves, touch nothing without gloves, and Varo even had to play in gloves.

"What if…" he asked Varo one bright day. "You were playing. And a tiny speck of dirt lodged itself beneath your fingernail. Just there." He gestured to his own immaculate finger. "And in the dirt hid a microscopic insect and it burrowed under your skin." His mustache danced when he said burrowed. "And it multiplied. Yes. All those little crawling critters squirming along, multiplying in your bloodstream. Multiplying. Sucking up the nutrients in your body. Until one day… they sucked you dry until you could play no longer. The only way you could see the sun was if someone rolled you by the window or wheeled you outside in your chair. And what if there was no one to wheel you out that day?"

It sounded far-fetched to Varo, but he believed what he wanted and hated playing in gloves. He relished feeling the crumbliness of the earth, and ripping up blades of grass, and tossing smooth stones into the creek. He couldn't feel the world the way he wanted to while wearing gloves, so he'd leave with them on and soon stuff them into his pocket. But one day, the cool shade of a shadow eclipsed the sun. The noise around him dimmed as he stared up to see the temporary father.

The temporary father made no scene. No.

He waited.

Until one night when Varo was done brushing his teeth, heading off to bed. Varo saw it in his room. Shadowy with only the nightstand lamp casting its glow on the black leather and the shiny wheels of the chair with two handles for someone to push him as if he were Maple. As if he too were made of wood.

The wheelchair, rising before him, made Varo's legs begin tingling. He collapsed onto his knees and jabbed at his foot wondering if he could feel the flesh or was it all in his imagination? The tears started, his breath hitched, and for sure he thought a curse would paralyze him by morning. He screamed.

His mother swept in and pulled him into the slippery softness of her silk robe. She held him for a short while, wheeled the chair away, and then returned to tuck him into bed. She tickled his feet to reassure him before she turned out his light. When he woke, his tear-stained pillow had dried and the sweet scent of pancakes wafted.

The glove connoisseur sat before his heavily buttered pancakes. At the table, his eye and his moustache kept twitching. He swallowed another butter-drenched bite and then another. Fork still in hand, his gaze froze.

His eyes were like glass, reflecting but not seeing, and yet his head turned slowly from Varo to his mother.

His entire body, rigid, slid from the chair with a thud. The fork clattered, escaping his gloved hand.

His mother stabbed a blueberry and chewed it thoughtfully. "No weeping willow for him," she said. "The trees are our memories of those we love. They flourish. But he should shrivel."

Varo nodded.

"Good, he was stranger than you will ever know." She winked as if Varo understood the inside grown-up joke. At the time, he winked too.

But the glove collection remained in the trunk room. Varo thought the gloves: black, blue, silver, plum, charcoal, all looked deflated with no hands to wear them, so he ordered mannequin hands, promptly delivered in brown boxes. The female hands were less expensive than the male hands, which he thought was sexist, but also a good deal, so he ordered accordingly. He fitted them inside the gloves and arranged them on top of the trunk.

One night when he was sleeping in his room on the second floor something drew him from his dream into the waking world. A noise. A scuttling.

Creatures, it seemed, were trapped in the ceiling, clawing. Varo wished it would stop. It didn't. The noise, scraping against the magnetism of his dreams, descended from upstairs. He tiptoed through the dark mirrored hallway, following the sound. He opened the door. Something soft grazed his ankle. He pawed for the matchsticks, singed the candlewick until it burned, and revealed gloved hands strewn across the floor, everywhere, but all was quiet.

He blew out the light. The scuttling began. When his eyes adjusted to the gloom, white gloves crawled ghost-like, on the edge of imperceptible. He struck another match and pressed it to the wick. Silence. Stillness. He unlocked the trunk, flipped open the lid, and roughly threw all the hands inside, slamming and locking the trunk before they could crawl out dragging their weight, finger by finger.

He took the candle with him, but the flame flickered and vanished before he reached his room. He hurried.

Safe in bed, as the house fell silent, Varo fell also, drifting into a deep sleep. No sooner did color begin to take shape, did his dream begin to tell him a story, that a sound jolted him awake. The sound of dishware shattering cut sharp, echoing.

"Go to sleep!" Varo yelled, but he himself had to watch the rising sun brighten his own wall.

He padded barefoot to his favorite room. His trunk room wasn't favored, not like the butterfly ballroom. Oh yes, he trapped the butterflies in jars waiting for them to suffocate, or broke their little thorax with a pinch and preserved them forever. One looked like Christmas—red and green. Another was a mysterious blue. There was a happy yellow. A vibrant orange.

His best capture was one that reflected an entire rainbow in its delicate wings, but amongst his collection it was nowhere to be found. It had flitted frantically in its glass prison, the colorful flash of its wings, mesmerizing.

Varo, as a teenager, hurried to the cheese connoisseur to show him his new treasure. He didn't beam like Varo had hoped he would. No. He snuck into his room while Varo was cuddling with Mother and let his prize escape.

When Varo noticed the glass jar empty, unenchanted, he wailed.

His mother pulled him into the scratchy fabric of her lace gown and kissed his head.

Soon afterwards, the cheese connoisseur became ill. A little more tired he grew with each day. The tender skin under his eyes turned sallow and his cheekbones, prominent. So tired. He took supper in his room.

One night, in a strange fit of strength, the cheese connoisseur hurled his bowl of supper, shattering it against the wall, splattering gray paint with cinnamon porridge. Under the moonlight, while the cheese connoisseur slept, Varo split the earth and dug deep.

The next night, Varo crept to his bedside and loomed over the sick man. "Mother knows best," he said consolingly.

Eyes closed, he smiled just then, slowly, but said nothing, as if he knew a joke, but Varo didn't.

When the moon was scarcely visible, a weeping willow was planted for him. Mother's willows always matured faster than ordinary.

But even with the greatest of butterflies gone, he had collected dozens upon dozens. In the ballroom, also on the third floor, was a vintage record player and heavy velvet curtains, which were drawn to keep his masterpiece from fading. Each preserved butterfly attached to a clear thread was fastened from the ceiling covering the entire room. Once upon a time, fans blew gently creating a swirl of movement and color. As he danced, colorful flashes filled his peripheral vision reminding him of his childhood when there were parties full of family and friends. The women had worn vibrant dresses and now, when Varo danced around the room, it was as if all those vivid dance partners moved from the corner of his eye.

Varo remembered the languid notes of the violins and the music played seamlessly in his mind. Now he glided around in a crisp white shirt, grey trousers, and imported leather shoes, but there was no longer a breeze because, like the lights, the fans no longer worked. He assumed they would come back on, but he was mistaken. The electricity had been turned off. But in the bunker by the wine cellar were hundreds of boxes of candles nestled amongst the jarred peaches and green olives.

Candles were lit, but the ballroom wasn't the same with no breeze. Varo headed to his gallery to find cheer and conversation. He was unsure where amongst his friends to stop. All eyes followed after him trying to peer beyond their frames when he entered their peripheral.

Katrina with golden hair and crinkly eyes, said: "Darling, how is your mother?"

"My love," chimed Darla, also golden-haired. She was the jealous-type. "You look stunning. Is there nothing you don't model well?"

He winked, just as he'd seen his mother do many times. He greeted his houseguests, basked in their attention, and when he had his fill of adoring company, he swept out to the sounds of many voices asking him to soon return.

Varo sliced a hunk of aged cheddar onto a black cocktail napkin outside. He crossed the yard and ducked under the long tendrils. In the dusky hour, under his favorite willow, he left the cheese by the roots of the one who remained his best father, even after the butterfly incident.

Less friendly eyes seemed to watch him here.

The fathers, for one reason or another, did not like Varo. Flashes of silhouettes darted from one tree to the next.

A child-sized glove blew on the evening breeze onto his shoe. Varo pinched it between two fingers, walked it to the creek and tossed it in. He watched it float for a while, strolling along side it, until thoughts of guilt for not visiting Mother began to nag. He pressed on as fireflies glowed and colorful weeds bloomed amongst the rocks, imagining all that he would tell her. When he turned, pressed flat upon a rock, air-drying, was a glove.

The willows' tendrils rustled in the breeze sounding like a smoker's asthmatic laugh.

Varo no longer enjoyed playing outside his house. With shadows and a cool, unseen touch tracing his skin, he cut across the yard and opened the sliding door to reenter when a pressure settled upon his shoulder.

Cold touched his ear and it ached deeply.

"You sent the devil after me? No. He sent me after you."

Varo whipped the door closed behind him to choke out the sound of asthmatic breathing. All was quiet. He locked the door to be safe. He closed his eyes and his shoulders sank in relief.

A sharp thud struck the door. Varo skittered back. Nothing was there. It was the front door. It came again and Varo waited. Screeching tires peeled away.

A foreclosure notice was tacked to his door. The bank would seize his property. His friends, his butterflies, his childhood—they would seize it all.

"Curse them," Varo ordered. "Curse anyone who enters Mother's house."

He needed her council. Off the kitchen was a hidden door. Down a dusty, creaky staircase was the wine cellar. Varo brought a candlestick that lit his path, one wooden step at a time. Wine, for the days he wanted to preserve the rations of food, lined the walls. Once the walls were abundant, but now empty pockets were everywhere.

He took his candle and lit the lanterns that hung from the ceiling. His mother was never fond of electricity. It was the natural light she loved. "It glows warm," she said. "Technology, even if it glows, glows cold." She was bright in many ways.

Propped up in her rocking chair sat his beautiful mother. Her hair grew longer but also more brittle, so he wrapped it in a white scarf. She waited for him in her burgundy dress. An empty glass was balanced on the arm of her chair.

Varo filled it for her, knowing she liked to have a full glass before a serious conversation.

"Mother, you're so lovely," he complimented.

He thought he saw her chair rock a little in approval.

"Something terrible has happened." Mother's sight was going, so he read the foreclosure notice. "The common folk will force us out. All you built for us. Mother, please."

Her gaze directed him to the secret hatch in the wall. Servant tunnels ran under the house from the olden days when it was first built, so the help could move invisibly. The passages were clandestine, kept from sight.

"You're right, but it will be dark. So dark, Mother." He stood and walked to the square barely visible in the wall, and pushed gently. "But they can't force us, if they can't find us."

Varo brought all the candlesticks and the lanterns down to begin lighting the creaky wooden tunnels. He explored them, but was never as comfortable navigating them. They were not at all like the rest of their spacious house, but narrow and sometimes even crooked. There were so many spiders; gossamer threads clung to him as he ventured from one passage to the next. Spiders, unlike the hands, at least scuttled in silence. One room was filled with moth-eaten blankets, but still they would be warmer than nothing.

He took all the golden-haired women from the gallery and brought them into the tunnels. The other portraits he cared less for. Who could join and who could not had to be decided. The gloves would remain on the third floor. Maple on her hook would be granted safekeeping even though she reeked of cigar smoke. He placed her, still tangled on the hook, in the cobwebbed-corner.

His mother remained optimistic.

Varo agreed. "Having a host family means the rest of the house will be lit. And they'll stock the cupboards for us. We'll eat well again. And when they sleep, we'll come out to enjoy what's ours."

Varo brought his mother into the safety of the halls. She didn't smell her best, so he fetched her perfume. He had never changed a thing in her room, but left it just as it was in case she wanted to return.

That opportunity was gone.

The perfume, French, smelled of lilac gardens. He spritzed and spritzed, so everything would have the scent of Mother. When he walked by the hook, he noticed Maple was gone. The strings floated barren attached to the controller. No longer was she tangled or confined by cords.

Now that she was freed, she could go anywhere at anytime.

"Just don't bother our host family," Varo warned, hoping she could hear him wherever she was hiding.

The host family became exciting. Though he liked no one in his home, finally his art would be adored by more than just him and Mother.

Perhaps, they too could become part of the exhibit. They would be living pieces of art inside his museum.

Varo was liberated. He had once feared parts of his house. He had feared people that once walked through. He had feared that undetectable parasite in his bloodstream, but now as the door opened above and he heard people milling around as if moving inside him, inside the place he knew and loved so well, he knew that there was no reason to fear.

"No one should ever be afraid in their own home," Mother once told him, looking out upon all the willows. "And to never be afraid, you must know the most treacherous being inside of the walls is you." Her voice, always with Varo, was why he at last released his every fear, closed his eyes, and smiled.

GEMLOCH DEMANDS SACRIFICE

By Matt Bliss

With the reoccurring agony that was office work, Timothy hardly thought about the itch on his back. Each day had become an echo of the last and the irritation he felt behind his left shoulder seemed to have always been there. Like the electric hum of the air conditioner or the *glub* of bubbles in the water cooler, the itch had become part of the background. So when Timothy stretched a ruler over his lopsided shoulder to scratch it, it was just another annoyance of his employment.

Other than the faint smell of mildew, the small cubical held no personal artifacts to identify its occupant. The only unique thing in the myriad of khaki and gray was the thin, oddly shaped man who sat hunched over his desk. Timothy made an effort to remain unmemorable in hopes of avoiding the unwanted attention that his misshapen form usually attracted, however this didn't stop the people in the office who took advantage of Timothy's submissive character.

"Timmy," said Brad with a smug grin leaning around the cubical wall, "how are we coming along on that report?"

The report you were supposed to do that you dumped on me? Timothy thought before giving a reluctant smile. "Just wrapping it up now, and uh, call me Timothy."

"Great! You're the best at this man, I really appreciate it," said Brad. He started to walk away thoughtlessly before his conscious, however limited it was, caused him to pivot back. "Thanks, again Timmy! Anytime you need a favor, I've got your back." His eyes shifted to Timothy's misshapen spine and let out a brief laugh at his poor choice of words.

"It's Timothy," he said, but Brad had already left. Timothy was used to harmful jokes at his expense but each time they came, they would still sting with an all too familiar pain. Growing up with scoliosis wasn't easy. All his life he was picked on and laughed at for his twisted shape. Even as an adult in a so-called professional setting, he couldn't escape the assholes like Brad, who, for some reason, he allowed to walk all over him.

Timothy turned back to his computer, reached over his shoulder, and worked at the itch while finishing Brad's work.

* * *

Each overstuffed chair in the wood paneled conference room was filled with an impassive face. All eyes were fixed to the enlarged spreadsheet projected on a drop down screen hanging from the far side of the room. The very same spreadsheet that Timothy painstakingly assembled over an entire week of long days and late nights. Now he watched as Brad basked in the praise of another's work.

"Nicely done Brad," said the manager after reviewing the report. "I don't how you pulled it off this time, but color me impressed!" He reached across the table to clap Brad on the back with a thick hand.

"Thank you sir but I'm just doing my part for the team," feigned Brad. He smiled across the table while raking his blond hair to the side. "Nose to the grindstone as always." He smiled in his best humble impersonation.

Timothy's insides raged like a furnace. *The only part the bastard had in this was throwing it on my desk,* he thought as his thin crooked frame began to tremble with irritation.

The urge to scratch returned.

"Everyone in this room could take a page out of Brad's book here. It's his hard work that is carrying the rest of you right now," said the manager. He looked straight at Timothy.

The itch grew worse.

Not only was Timothy forced to witness his nemesis enjoying the commendation *he* so rightfully deserved, but when the next impossibly difficult assignments were dealt out with a twenty-four hour deadline, Timothy knew he would expect "The Golden Child" to pass the buck to him. His whole body urged him to stand up, claiming the work to be his while calling out Brad for the liar and bully he was, but Timothy's inherently meek character simply wouldn't allow it. Instead he watched both angry and heartbroken while scraping his nails over his shoulder.

Before long the meeting came to a close and Timothy raced to leave, feeling he had endured enough torture for the moment. As he shuffled from the room, he overheard Brad whispering to another coworker behind him, *"Don't worry, I've got the hunchback to help me…"*

His heart dropped and a lump formed in his throat. It didn't matter how much he did for these people; he was still seen as a sideshow freak. He reached over his shoulder and dug his nails into his skin, clawing at the now unrelenting itch.

* * *

Timothy pounded keys and answered phones for the remainder of the day, waiting for the blue-eyed Brad to finally throw this new assignment on his desk. He kept watching the cubical entrance as the day wore on, all the while still picking at the itch on his shoulder.

The word "no" kept repeating in his head as he prepared himself for the encounter. *This time*, he thought, *I'm actually going to stick up for myself and not get pushed around.* But just when he thought his bully wasn't going to come, Brad finally worked his way to Timothy's cubical.

The man had coldly dropped the file on top his in-box and said, "You heard the boss, tomorrow morning," without even a glance before he turned to walk away.

The itch on his shoulder was screaming to be scratched.

Suddenly all of his rehearsed refusals had vanished and the words wouldn't come out. Something else came out instead, something that surprised him.

"I heard what you said," said Timothy in a calm voice.

Brad stopped dead in his tracks. "What?" he said, tilting his head slightly without turning to face him.

"About my back," said Timothy. "I heard it." He was suddenly feeling less brave. This was the big moment he always dreamed about, except now he was shrinking.

Brad turned around slowly, with a look of eager malice in his eyes. "Let's get something straight," his finely polished shoes stepped slowly and methodically forward until his toes were nearly touching the desk. "I need *you* to handle the crap like this, because *you* make me look good. And you need *me* to be the face and charisma you so desperately lack because *you* look like a freak. The sooner you get this through your head, the better." He sat on the desk and combed his fingers through his thin hair. "We need each other Timmy. The company needs us. Alone, we're nothing, but together it's a complete package." Brad stood and adjusted his tie. "Oh," he said, remembering one last thing, "you will keep your mouth shut about this, or we're both fucked. I'll make sure of that."

Tears began to fill Timothy's eyes as he watched Brad leave. He rolled his chair back slightly and turned to face his computer before jamming his hand under shirt to attack the itch.

* * *

By the time Timothy had arrived at his one bedroom apartment, the itch had become unbearable. What started as a minor irritability had now become insufferable pain. As he stretched his tricep to claw at the hard to reach itch, his fingers explored the tender area. The back of his shoulder was severely inflamed and his fingers soon discovered a mass the size of a golf ball protruding. He prodded it inquisitively and winced at the pain.

What the hell? he thought. *When did that get there?*

He ran to the bathroom mirror and hastily disrobed, eyeing himself in the reflection. Craning to look at his back he saw the area was now red and raw; a hard growth with veiny skin stretched tight at the center. The lump throbbed with pain and felt warm to the touch. Thoughts of cancer came to mind with a worrisome dread.

I need to see somebody about this, I've got to call in to work. The lump would clearly be visible even through clothing, sticking out on his already over-pronounced back, his *hunchback.* The memory of Brad's comment suddenly filled his thoughts. Sometimes an insult is more than just words, and *that* word brought back some of the most painful memories he had tried to bury. Every crude joke. Every pointing finger and disgusted stare. Brad suddenly represented every bully Timothy encountered throughout his life.

The lump shifted.

Timothy eyed himself in the mirror. Flexing his fragile pale arms and offset shoulders. The lump that stood atop his curved shoulders only highlighted his abnormalities.

"Just another thing for them to laugh at," he said aloud in the mirror before letting out a defeated sigh. "This is the last thing I need right now. Why is it always me?" Watching himself in the mirror, a sudden urge overtook him.

He walked to the kitchen and removed the shears from the knife block. He placed the shears on the bathroom counter next to a hand mirror, and a number of white washcloths. He placed one in his mouth and clamped down as he lined up the two mirrors to see the red lump in its reflection.

This red lump had suddenly become more than a lump. It symbolized the misshapen spine he was so unfairly cursed with. It was the kids that picked on him for being different. It was the disgusted stares. It was the ones who pointed and laughed. It was Brad, sitting on his desk, calling him a freak. *Here we go,* he thought as he placed the open scissor blades on either side of the growth. He huffed three times in rapid succession and let out a muffled growl through his gritted teeth, and squeezed the handles together.

Timothy howled as pain shot through him. The sharp blades cut through his flesh with ease sending the malignant chunk falling to the floor. He dropped the scissors and gripped the counter as he screamed towards the ceiling. Snatching a cloth and pressing it to the wound, he waited for his vision to clear. He rotated his body towards the mirror and saw blood streaming down his translucent skin from under the cloth. Nervous laughter spilled out between pain-filled moans at the sight.

I did it! he thought, feeling rather pleased with himself. Timothy removed the blood soaked cloth to the see the damage he had created in his back. He wasn't surprised by the wound itself; however, it was what was inside it that made his stomach lurch. Inside the hole, buried beneath his skin, was the unmistakable shape and movement of a small red eye. A bloodshot eye that seemed to flick from object to object around the room with rapid succession, as it was seeing for the first time. The skin around it began to pulse and ooze as the eye flicked up to meet Timothy's horrified stare.

Timothy jumped back from the mirror with utter shock at the sight, sending him tripping over the tub and hitting his head on the cold tile floor, sending him into darkness.

* * *

Timothy woke in a haze and peeled himself from the bathroom floor with an audible rip. The blood, now dry and brown, had stuck him to the tile flooring like a mouse in a glue trap. *What the hell happened?* he thought as his eyes adjusted to what looked like a crime scene around him. He hung over the sink, drinking water from his cupped hands when he glanced at his watch. He was late.

Although Timothy had a number of flaws, his work ethic was not one of them. The only way he was able to get ahead in life looking the way he did was to be the smartest and hardest working person he knew. No matter how early another coworker would arrive, Timothy had somehow gotten there first and remained hard at work. With only the thought of his unfinished work in his mind, Brad's work, he hurried off without even a thought as to why he woke on the bathroom floor.

What will I tell Brad? I didn't finish the assignment, he told himself as he flew to his closet and began pulling his slacks and usual button down shirt from hangers with unprecedented speed. He hadn't even stopped to think about the wound he had created as he winced slightly, pulling on the bright white shirt. Files and folders spilled from his arms as he sprinted to the parking garage, barely managing to close his front door on the way.

The mid-size sedan lurched forward from its numbered parking space and raced toward the exit. The roads were free of traffic, which was unusual for this time of day, and Timothy felt a glimmer of hope as he found a parking space near the front of the building. He thought he'd made it, until he heard the voice.

"Let me see, let Gemloch see…" whispered a gurgled voice in his left ear.

The memory of the eye in the mirror came flooding back to him. He refused to believe it was real. "Just a weird dream," he said aloud, trying to convince himself. "You're not hearing voices; the stress is getting to you."

"Let me see again, Chosen One. Gemloch wants to see…" The voice was small but throaty, as if spoken through gurgled blood.

"This… isn't happening!" Crippling fear surged through him as he sat in his car, straining his ear to hear the disembodied voice once more.

"Gemloch demands sacrifice. Gemloch wants blood."

It wasn't until then that he realized the voice was coming from inside him. The voice was coming from the back of his shoulder, the spot he had opened up last night.

* * *

Sprinting into the office as quickly as his condition would allow, Timothy ignored both the security guard and the receptionist on his way to the bathroom at the back wall. He kept his head down and prayed no one would notice him while he navigated the maze of cubicles and filing cabinets. The bathroom door slammed shut and the lock slid home before Timothy frantically stripped off his shirt to stare into the mirror.

He turned and saw the swollen red hole with an eye inside his shoulder. The red iris glistened as the vertical pupil darted around the room expanding and contracting.

"Yes. Yes. I see. Gemloch sees," said the twisted voice in his ear.

The hole had grown larger and swollen, making his small hump appear even larger while the redness around it had spread into a spider web of swollen veins.

"Oh my god!" Timothy became filled with dread at the sight of it. "What is happening?" he shrieked with a quaver in his voice. Struggling for breath, Timothy began to shake uncontrollably as every preconceived notion of reality was shattered by the thing watching and speaking to him from inside his own skin.

"Gemloch sees you, Chosen One. Show Gemloch his sacrifice. Give Gemloch blood," the eyehole grew wide as the voice spoke.

The shirtless man fell to the floor holding his knees as his eyes welled with tears. "Please! Please leave me alone," he cried as he rocked slowly. "It's not real, it's not happening!" His mind had finally snapped, and all these years he assumed it would have been his spine to snap first.

"We shall dine on the flesh of our enemy's chosen one."

"No! Please stop talking! Please!"

"Rise, Chosen One. Bring Gemloch his sacrifice," the voice continued to whisper when suddenly, someone knocked on the door and startled the both of them.

"Uh, I'm gonna be a minute!" Timothy shouted as he jumped up in a panic.

"Yes, Chosen one. Let them enter so Gemloch can tear into their insides."

"No! Just stop it! You have to go away! Please! I… I got to get out of here!"

He paced the room trying to figure out what to do when eyes landed on a ballpoint pen sticking out of his notebook. He cringed when he turned to see the red eye glaring at him from his hump in the reflection before removing the cap with his teeth and spitting it to the floor. His hand trembled as he tried to convince himself of what he was about to do.

"What are you doing, Chosen One?" said the voice. *"What tiny weapon is this?"*

Timothy yelled as he swung his arm over his shoulder and stabbed the pen into his own back. The pen had all together missed its target and sunk full depth into his skin slightly to the left of the eye. As it turns out, stabbing yourself in the back is a difficult thing to do. Confusion had washed over him rather than pain, as the pen seemed to pierce into a hollow spot under his skin. Once the pen was removed a loose flap of skin now remained near the eye that watched on with palpable excitement. This flap moved in and out, breathing, before rows of tiny sharp teeth jutted out from it, moving up and down forming words.

"Yes! Yes, Chosen One!" they said. *"Free Gemloch!"* The loud foreboding voice echoed in the small bathroom as the thing was pressing outward, flexing against the skin of his hump, trying to break free. As it pushed and twisted, bits of rubbery green flesh escaped through the tearing skin with a coating of blood and viscera. Timothy's eyes widened as a mouth full of yellowed teeth lay fully exposed in his shoulder blade next to the watching red eye.

"FREE GEMLOCH! Gemloch wants BLOOD! Gemloch wants his SACRIFICE!" The throaty voice screamed so loud Timothy held his hand to his ears to lessen the volume.

He stood petrified for a moment before fearing the noise would send someone to investigate. He then threw on his shirt and buttoned it up in an attempt to hide the creature that was spawning from his back.

"Step one: leave the office. Step two: figure out if I need a doctor or a priest."

* * *

The office was bustling with its usual fervor when Brad spotted the bathroom door open to reveal Timothy's panic stricken face. His walk seemed more askew than usual as he hurried towards the exit. Brad couldn't help but notice his hump had almost doubled in size. He quickly traced a path to intercept him as their meeting was moments away from starting and Brad still hadn't got his report back from the man.

"Timmy!" Brad said jovially as he swooped in to place himself in directly in his path. The panic-stricken man swiveled his head around looking alarmed while avoiding Brad's eyes. *This is not a good sign,* thought Brad. "I haven't heard back from you Timmy. I need that report! The meeting's about to start," he smiled but held the edge in his voice. *Is the freak finally standing up to me?*

"What? The report…" Timothy seemed surprised and confused by the question and quickly tried to work his way around Brad. "I'm not sure what you mean." He moved in place like a trapped animal.

"The report that *you* said *you'd* do!" Brad moved in close and grabbed Timothy by the shoulder, causing him jump like scared cat. "Don't fuck with me you little geek," he said in a hushed voice. His normally cool eyes were wild and dilated.

"Yeah, I uh… got it right here. Just like you asked," he motioned to his folder before trying to dodge around Brad.

Brad blocked him once more giving him a curious look, "Great, then let's head into the meeting shall we?" He grabbed hold of the petrified man and steered him into the conference room. "It's your time to shine Timmy! It's your time to shine!"

* * *

Sweat poured from Timothy as the meeting worked its way through its usual agenda; all the while Brad's icy blue eyes stared daggers at him from across the conference room table. Timothy was struggling to work out an escape from the situation while simultaneously bracing himself for the voice to speak. Jostling movements from his back sent tremors through his body followed by a smell of rot and decay.

Brad's voice eventually pulled him from his stupor.

"Sorry for not letting you in on this but after the last meeting, Timmy was inspired to step up and he asked me if he could handle the assignment himself. I've been so busy with other projects and I could use the help so I handed it off to him," said Brad with a toothy grin. "So go ahead Tim, I have full faith in you."

Timothy looked like a deer in headlights as all eyes fixed on him. He was at a loss for words, but the creature inside him was not.

"Who dare to speak against The Chosen One? Show him to Gemloch!" the loud voice from his hump seemed to rip through the room.

Timothy looked up wide-eyed and horrified as the room watched him with anticipation. His frail body trembled as he scanned the room, waiting for their reaction.

"Gemloch will RIP OUT YOUR BONES!"

Another pause.

"We're waiting," said the manager after a long silence.

It suddenly occurred to Timothy that the room didn't seem to notice the horrible voice emanating from his shoulder. Timothy squirmed, sweating in his seat as the room watched him with overwhelming confusion. *It's in my head; I'm going crazy,* he thought as he continued to shake nervously.

"Tim? Are you okay?" said the manager. His mood shifted as the concern suddenly shown across his face.

"Gemloch will destroy the one who speaks against The Chosen One! Gemloch will bathe in his BLOOD!"

"I'm sorry…" began Timothy as he trembled like an abused dog. "I didn't do it."

"What do you mean you didn't do it?" Brad said, jumping eagerly at the statement.

"YOU WILL ALL SUFFER! GEMLOCH WILL DESTROY!"

"Brad threatened me to do it, and I was going to do it, but when I got home I..."

"Yes! Yes, Chosen One!" shouted Gemloch, *"Show him your teeth! Show him the claws you will use to RIP OUT HIS HEART!"* his hump vibrated with excitement.

"That's a lie!" Brad jumped up, slamming his fists on the table. "I would never do such a thing!"

"Gemloch will drink his BLOOD! Gemloch will TEAR OPEN HIS INSIDES!" The hoarse voice was loud enough to tear vocal chords.

"Enough," said the manager. "We will handle this matter in private. I think that's all for today. I want you two in my office in thirty minutes."

"Rip out his throat, Chosen One! RIP OUT HIS THROAT!"

Timothy rose almost immediately and raced to the exit as Gemloch continued to scream in his ear.

"BLOOD! Gemloch demands his BLOOD!"

* * *

Timothy returned to his cubical and after looking around for prying eyes, unbuttoned his shirt. A small, rubbery, green head with wispy white hair had torn itself completely free from the skin and looked around, wildly baring its teeth.

"I want BLOOD! Gemloch wants BLOOD!" the screaming voice reverberated through the office. Its red eyes whipped around the small space, searching for a target as its pointed yellow teeth chattered with anticipation. *"Let us go now Chosen One! Let us bathe in their blood!"* It snarled into Timothy's face just inches away.

The man was quite a sight. Sitting in an office cubical with no shirt, and a small green head with red eyes resting next to his, demanding blood.

"Shut up," said Timothy in a defeated voice. "Just shut up. Jesus, I've finally lost it." He lowered his head into his hands. "Why am I the only one who can see or hear you? What the hell is happening?"

The pointy-eared creature turned his head slowly towards Timothy's ear before snarling its lips back to speak.

"Gemloch wants his sacrifice..." it whispered with rancid breath into Timothy's ear. *"Chosen One, push the tiny sword used to*

free Gemloch into the soft part of their necks. Put your claws inside to work them like puppets." His face had become calm and serious.

"What the hell are you talking about? I don't even know what you are. Are *you* Gemloch?" Timothy turned to face the creature just inches away. "Why are you doing this to me? What's happening?" His eyes were glassy and pleading.

The creature cocked its head slightly while blinking its red eyes at him before screaming into his face. *"Gemloch wants BLOOD! Gemloch wants TO WEAR THE FACE OF THE ONE WHO SPEAKS AGAINST THE CHOSEN ONE!"*

Timothy dropped his head into his hands once again. "I'm doomed," he said as Gemloch continued to scream.

* * *

The two heads that was now Timothy walked into the manager's office and took a seat in the only available chair. The other was already taken by Brad, who sat wearing a smug grin. Timothy's shirt was only half buttoned and stained with blood and bile; but, along with the creature spawning from his shoulder, this seemed to go unnoticed by the others.

"Show him your claws Chosen One! Gnash your teeth to strike fear in their hearts that we will soon feast upon!" shouted Gemloch as they arrived. His red eyes jumped between Brad and his manager while baring his teeth.

"Gentlemen," said the manager as he leaned forward placing his forearms on his desk. "I want to know who was responsible for this. What the hell is going on between you two?"

"Go ahead Tim," Brad quickly replied, "tell him how you begged me for your chance to shine before dropping the ball." He shook his head at him waiting for a response.

Whether it was the possibility that this whole situation was a delusion of his now fractured mind, or the anonymity provided by being the only one able to see and hear something, in that moment Timothy was a different man. He no longer cared about being labeled a freak, or being different. It was impossible to worry things so insignificant when a creature's head was birthed from your shoulder.

"Shut the fuck up!" Timothy finally snapped at Brad. "I've had enough of you!"

"Yes, Chosen One! Yes!"

Brad's eyes went wide with shock.

"I have been doing *your* work for years because I let you bully me into it! In fact, I've let everyone bully me my whole life because I was afraid. I was afraid of being different. Afraid to be me! But guess what?" he turned to his manager, now screaming, "I'm the best damn employee you've got in here!" His face burned a bright red.

"Destroy him, Chosen One! Make him SUFFER!" Gemloch's voice screeched like a locomotive of broken glass.

"Take it easy Tim," said the manager, holding his hands up in a pleading motion.

"It's Timothy!"

"KILL HIM! KILL HIM NOW!"

"I bust my ass for this job, and if you can't see the crap this guy's been up to, well then fuck you too!" Timothy's thoughts raged like a rabid animal.

"YES! Tear off his face! Gemloch wants to wear his pretty face! GEMLOCH WANTS BLOOD!" Gemloch was squirming at the thought.

"And you," he said, turning to Brad, "I-will-never-" Timothy shouted as he raised his finger to point in the man's shocked face when, suddenly, Gemloch burst from Timothy's shoulder with a loud sucking noise. The small sinewy creature sprinted across the room and jumped onto Brad, feverishly shredding the man's face with its tiny razor sharp claws. Brad's arms flailed wildly as Gemloch pulled bits and pieces from the man. Screams of both pleasure and pain rang out from the two as warm blood sprayed onto the surrounding men.

In a moment's time, Brad's body fell limp to the floor and Gemloch stood panting over it, covered in blood and gore. Timothy was still standing in surprise with his finger raised in the air, before he smiled at the scene in front of him.

He turned to his manager, who remained frozen with terror.

"Maybe it's time we talk about the terms of my employment," said Timothy as his lips curled back into a sinister smile.

* * *

Uneasiness washed over the manager as he rounded the corner towards Timothy's office with the new hire in tow. He had given the man the raise and promotion he so rightly deserved; however, the conditions of which they were given still terrified the man. He knocked rather cautiously before entering.

Timothy rose straight as an arrow to greet the two of them with a smile and a firm handshake. The majority of the office couldn't help but notice how the once crooked man somehow now stood tall and proud.

It did take some time for Timothy to adjust to his new shape, however. He would walk in a terribly awkward manner for a number of days while his shoulder healed, but true to form, he refused to take any time off.

Gemloch seemed to have disappeared in the pandemonium that followed Brad's *dismissal.* Although he never spoke of the events of that day, Timothy assumed Gemloch had returned to whatever lost realm he came from. He didn't know how or why he had become "The Chosen One" but hoped that someday he would return so he could thank him. However brief it was, Timothy had come to miss having the wicked little creature living inside him. After Gemloch left, Timothy found himself feeling incomplete, as his inner voice was now far too tame for his liking.

But right then, as the two men stood in Timothy's office, they could have sworn they saw red eyes glaring back at them. This would happen quite a bit and sometimes they would wonder if the look in his eyes had always been there. Just like the electric hum of the air conditioner, or *glub* of bubbles in the water cooler. They were just another part of the workplace.

ABOUT THE AUTHORS

JULIANA AMIR

Juliana Amir is a graduate of the NEOMFA. Her work appears in places such as: *Enchanted Conversations*, *Fantasia Divinity*, and *Grimoire*. She enjoys exploring trails and teaching at The University of Akron.

ROSS BAXTER

After thirty years at sea, Ross Baxter now concentrates on writing sci-fi and horror fiction. His varied work has been published in print by numerous publishing houses in US and UK short-story anthologies. He has won a number of awards, including the Horror Novel Review.Com best creation short fiction prize, and had a short story on the 2017 HWA Bram Stoker recommended reading list. Married to a Norwegian and with two Anglo-Viking kids, he now lives in Derby, England.

NORRIS BLACK

Norris Black is a Haudenosaunee/mixed-blood author, originally from Tyendinaga Mohawk Territory and now living in the city of Belleville, Ontario. He spent several years as a print journalist where he garnered a handful of Ontario Newspaper Awards for both writing and photography before retiring from the industry. His first foray into fiction writing, a short story in *Dark Lane Anthology: Vol.9*, is scheduled for publication in the fall of 2020.

MATT BLISS

Matt Bliss enjoys spending time with his family in Las Vegas, Nevada while working, writing, and slowly releasing cosmic monsters on the unsuspecting public.

SCOT CARPENTER

Scot Carpenter is a writer living in Arizona, who comes in from the desert occasionally to write crime, horror and speculative fiction. His stories explore the often perverse and absurd nature of life, featuring characters defined more by their flaws than their attributes. Humor, frequently dark, is an intrinsic part of dealing with the human experience and his stories often reflect this. His work has been published in *Switchblade Magazine*, and numerous anthologies, including *The Sharpened Quill* and *Blood and Blasphemy*.

MAX CARREY

Max Carrey currently lives in sunny California, but will be moving to a gloomier location much like the settings in her stories (hopefully without the tragedy and mayhem involved). She's had stories appear in Zimbell House's *The Dead Game* and *Spirit Walker,* Chipper Press' *The Princess,* Temptation Press' *Marked,* Impulsive Walrus' *The Quarantales,* and *PCC Inscape Magazine*'s "Dark Minds & Light Hearts" issue. To stay up to date, follow her at: instagram.com/maxcarrey/

JOSH DARLING

Born on Long Island, Josh Darling started writing poetry and horror fiction in his teens. After dropping out of college, he bummed around America, before making ends meet by ghostwriting self-help books. His published works include poetry, non-fiction, and fiction, and they span the genres of fiction, crime, and horror. He's served as a judge for the Northern California Mystery Writer's Association's short fiction contest. His stories have appeared in various literary journals, including *The Bookends Review,* and he was the Editor's Poetry Pick in *The Horror 'Zine*. He currently lives in Tampa, Florida, with the love of his life and their son.

JAMES DORR

James Dorr is an Indiana-based short story writer and poet. His most recent book is a novel-in-stories from Elder Signs Press called *Tombs: A Chronicle of Latter-Day Times of Earth*. He works mostly in dark fantasy/horror with some forays into science fiction and mystery. His book, *The Tears of Isis*, was a 2013 Bram Stoker Award® finalist for Superior Achievement in a Fiction Collection. His other books include: *Strange Mistresses: Tales of Wonder and Romance*, *Darker Loves: Tales of Mystery and Regret*, and an illustrated all-poetry collection, *Vamps (A Retrospective)*. He has also been a technical writer, an editor on a regional magazine, a full time non-fiction freelancer, and a semi-professional musician, and currently harbors a Goth cat named Triana. An Active Member of SFWA and HWA, Dorr invites readers to visit his blog at: http://jamesdorrwriter.wordpress.com

GERRI R. GRAY

Born and raised in the Chicago area, Gerri R. Gray is an American novelist, short story writer, and a lifelong aficionado of horror, dark humor, and all things bizarre. She blames her twisted sense of humor on a wayward adolescence influenced by the likes of *Monty Python's Flying Circus*, Charles Addams cartoons, Frank Zappa records, and John Waters films. Her debut novel, *The Amnesia Girl*, was published by HellBound Books in October of 2017, followed by *Gray Skies of Dismal Dreams* (a collection of dark poetry and prose), *Graveyard Girls* (an all-women anthology of horror), *Blood and Blasphemy*, and *The Strange Adventures of Turquoise Moonwolf*. Gerri's interest in writing started early on in life, and she began writing poetry, music, short stories, and plays while a teenager in the 1970s. Her work has appeared in numerous anthologies and literary journals. She lives in upstate New York in an historic nineteenth-century house with her husband and a bevy of spirits. When she isn't busy creating strange worlds filled with even stranger characters, she can often be found rummaging through antique shops, exploring haunted houses, or traipsing through old cemeteries with her camera. Visit Gerri's website at http://gerrigray.webs.com for more information.

CHISTO HEALY

Chisto Healy has been writing since his brother handed him Dean Koontz's *Servants of Twilight* at age 9. His hero and favorite author is Simon Clark, so go read him right now. Chisto's got a lot of great stuff of his own coming out and you can find all the details at https://chistohealy.blogspot.com, which he does his best to keep updated. There are always new books coming out with his work in them. He has a romantic werewolf serial that you can keep up with at : https://www.davidpaulharris.com/2020/07/animalistic-by-chisto-healy.html He lives in North Carolina with his beautiful and wacky fiancée, her chill mom, three of the most creative and awesome kids the world has to offer, and a plethora of kickass pets. Please reach out. He would love to hear from you. You can follow him on Amazon here: https://www.amazon.com/Chisto-Healy/e/B088FV7L44

CARLTON HERZOG

Carlton Herzog works for the United States Postal Service. He is a USAF veteran. He holds a B.A. from Rutgers University, where he graduated *magna cum laude*. He also holds a J.D. degree from Rutgers Law School, where he served as articles editor of the *Rutgers Law Review*. His partial publication history can be found at Carlton Herzog's Amazon Author Page, Not a Pipe Publishing page, and Google Scholar. He is also an artist whose work recently graced the cover of *Schlock Magazine's* 2019 Halloween edition.

SCOTT McGREGOR

Scott McGregor is a Canadian writer based in Calgary. He is also a student at Mount Royal University, graduating with a degree in English and Sociology in Winter 2021. His honors project will explore Marxism in literature and the future of historical materialism. His fiction has appeared in various anthologies by Hellbound Books, NBH Publishing, DBND Publishing, Nocturnal Sirens, The Macabre Ladies, *Schlock! Webzine*, and others. Movies, board games, and Xbox achievement hunting are some of his other passions. Sarcastically appealing and unapologetic, Scott is either drinking tea or sassing the ones he calls friends in the off time he isn't living or breathing stories. You can reach him at www.scottmcgregorwrites.com or on Twitter @ScottMSays.

J LOUIS MESSINA

J Louis Messina is the author of *Strange Tales from a Boy's Life: Fiction Stories Published in Boys' Life and Other Magazines*. He has had short fiction stories published in *Boys' Life Magazine*, *PKA's Advocate*, *The Harrow: Original Works of Fantasy & Horror*, *Cricket Magazine*, and *Discovery Trails*. He is winner of the Paul A. Witty Short Story Award from the International Reading Association, the Association of Educational Publishers Distinguished Achievement Award, the Society of Children's Book Writers & Illustrators Short Story Merit Award, Quarter-finalist in the Lone Star Screenplay Competition, and The Harrow: Original Works of Fantasy & Horror Contest for best horror story. His short horror story "The Chosen" is out in the anthology *Hellfire Crossroads: Horror With A Heart (Volume 7)* in paperback and E-book; His short science fiction story "Switching Worlds" is out in the Hadrosaur Productions science fiction anthology *Exchange Students* in paperback and E-book.

DREW NICKS

Drew Nicks is a writer of horror and weird fiction who resides in Moose Jaw, Saskatchewan. His works have been published by Gehenna and Hinnom Books, The Ghastling, HellBound Books, Oscillate Wildly Press, Dark Corner Books, The H.P. Lovecraft Lunatic Asylum, Vaughan Street Doubles, and others.

COOPER O'CONNOR

Cooper O'Connor has been published in *Dark Moon Digest* ("Room 207"), *Wax and Wane: A Gathering of Witch Tales* ("Hopscotch"), *9 Tales Told in the Dark* ("This World Will Eat You All the Way Up"), *Trysts of Fate* ("Forget Me Not"), *Ink Stains* ("Spouse Swap") and *Skeptics Must Die* ("The Portrait"). When he's not writing short stories, he also produces The Stephen King Cast, a weekly podcast that analyzes the works of Stephen King in the chronological order of publication. This podcast is among the highest rated and longest running Stephen King podcasts and is in the top of the iTunes search engine for Stephen King.

BRETT O'REILLY

Brett O'Reilly. After a nearly thirty-year hiatus from writing, Brett O'Reilly recently found his way back with the publishing of his story *Orpheus Wept* in the Black Quill Editing™ anthology, *Map to Desire*. Brett then followed up with his horror novelette, *Lord of Playgrounds*, self-published on Amazon Kindle and Rokobuten Kobo. Brett lives in Surrey, British Columbia, Canada, with his wife, two children, and feline Lord of the House, Joey Bojangles. His hobbies include golf, board games, and watching horror movies, none of which he has time for; thirty years of not writing means he has a lot of catching up to do.

LISA PAIS

Lisa Pais hails from coastal New England where she lives with her husband, daughter, and cocker spaniel, Buddy. Her short story *Death Broker*, which is included in this anthology, made it to the finals in the Coverfly 2019 Cinematic Short Story Competition. Her work can be found online at *Altered Reality* magazine, *Bewildering Stories*, and in two anthologies: *Beyond the Infinite: Tales from the Outer Reaches* and *What the Fox?!* When not writing, she paints, plays drums, and has participated in the occasional ghost hunt. You can find Lisa on Twitter @LisaPais1.

FREDERICK PANGBOURNE

Frederick Pangbourne is a recently retired native of New Jersey who has loved the horror genre in both film and literature since childhood. He currently has three of his own horror anthologies in publication along with a multitude of short stories published in various anthologies and magazines.

CLARK ROBERTS

Clark Roberts writes horror fiction, which has appeared in over twenty publications. His fiction collection, *Led By Beasts*, pays homage to Stephen King and other influential horror writers from the last few decades. His children's novella *Halloween Night on Monster Island* is intended for a younger audience and is published through Deadman's Tome. Mr. Roberts lives in Michigan with his wife and two children. Besides reading and writing, he enjoys spending time in the outdoors, hunting and fishing. He particularly enjoys fishing in the hours of dusk when trout streams whisper and eyes open in the surrounding woods. Friend him on Facebook using the following link: https://www.facebook.com/clark.roberts.39589 If you friend him, he'll confirm; he won't reject you. You'll be a lot cooler for doing this.

ROB SANTANA

Rob Santana is a filmmaker/writer. His film, *Heysoos* (a Jesus satire) can be viewed on Amazon Prime. His short stories have been published by *Centum Press*, *HP Lovecraft Lunatic Asylum*, *Bon Appetit: Stories and Recipes for Human Consumption*, and *Story Shack*, among others. His three novels are listed on Amazon Kindle. Rob's website is: www.robsantana.org

THORNE & CROSS

Tamara Thorne first published in 1991, and since then she has written many more novels, including international bestsellers *Haunted, Bad Things, Moonfall, Eternity* and *The Sorority. Brimstone* is her latest solo novel. The first horror thriller in her new *Fort Charles* series will debut later this year. A lifelong lover of ghost stories, she is currently working on several collaborations with Alistair Cross, including the next novel in *The Ravencrest Saga* series. Learn more about her at: http://tamarathorne.com

Alistair Cross grew up on horror novels and scary movies, and by the age of eight, began writing his own stories. First published in 2012, he has since co-authored *The Cliffhouse Haunting, Mother, Darling Girls,* and *The Ravencrest Saga* with Tamara Thorne. His debut solo novel, *The Crimson Corset,* was an Amazon bestseller and he's written several more since then. The third book in his *Vampires of Crimson Cove* series, *The Black Wasp,* will be published later this year. Find out more about him at: http://alistaircross.com

Thorne and Cross also host the horror-themed radio show, *Thorne & Cross: Haunted Nights LIVE!* which has featured such guests as Anne Rice, Laurell K. Hamilton, Charlaine Harris, V.C. Andrews, Preston & Child, and Madame Gray herself.

KELLI A. WILKINS

Kelli A. Wilkins likes to scare people. Her short horror fiction has appeared in several print and online anthologies, including *Mistresses of the Macabre*, *Wrapped in White*, *Moon Shadows*, *Dark Things II: Cat Crimes*, *Frightmares*, *The Four Horsemen*, and *The Best of the First Line*. She has authored three horror ebooks: *Kropsy's Curse*, *Dead Til Dawn*, and *Nightmare in the North*, plus *Extraterrestrial Encounters: A Collection of Sci-fi Stories*. Visit her site at www.kelliwilkins.com to learn more about her writings.

SCOTT BRYAN WILSON

Scott Bryan Wilson writes short stories and comics for reading in a dark barn by the light of your digital watch while waiting for the killer outside to go away. His fiction has appeared in *The Horror Is Us* anthology, and journals such as *The Denver Quarterly*, *Pindeldyboz*, *3rd Bed*, *Liquid Imagination*, *Eyeshot*, and *The Mid-American Review*. His comic books and graphic novels have been published by DC Comics, Dynamite Entertainment, IDW, Valiant, and Image, and in many horror anthologies. Find him at scottbryanwilson.com.

ABOUT THE ARTIST

<u>Nirvanah O'Neill</u>

Nirvanah was born and grew up in Shropshire, England, with a keen interest in photography, music, and wildlife. She was diagnosed at a young age with Autism and Tourette's syndrome and being none verbal until age 5, art became a very natural and preferred method of communication.

Despite being told that mainstream school would not be an option, Nirvanah achieved her GCSE levels and progressed on to full-time college spending 4 years studying animal management and behavior.

Nirvanah is now 20 years old and using her year out of education to focus on her love of art. When asked, *"Why do you prefer to draw your feelings?"* Nirvanah simply says,

"Why try to explain emotion when I can show you something beautiful"

Other titles from HellBound Books
The Amnesia Girl

Filled with copious amounts of black humor, Gerri R. Gray's first published novel is an offbeat adventure story that could be described as One Flew over the Cuckoo's Nest meets Thelma and Louise.

Flashback to 1974. Farika is a lovely young woman who wakes up one day to find herself a patient in a bizarre New York City psychiatric asylum. She has no idea who she is, and possesses no memories of where she came from nor how she got there.

Fearing for her life after being attacked by a berserk girl with over one hundred personalities and a vicious nurse with sadistic intentions, the frightened amnesiac teams up with an audacious lesbian with a comically unbalanced mind, and together they attempt a daring escape.

But little do they know that a long strange journey into an even more insane world filled with a multitude of perilous predicaments and off-kilter individuals are waiting for them on the outside. Farika's weird reality crumbles when she finally discovers who, and what, she really is!

Gray Skies of Dismal Dreams

Prepare for an excursion into a gloomy world of shadows, where the days are never sunlit and blithe, and where the nights are wrapped in endless nightmares.

No happy endings or silver linings are found in the clouds that fill these gray skies.

But what you will find, gathered in one volume, are the darkest of poems and tales of horror, waiting to take your mind on a journey into realms of the uncheerful and the unholy.

An amazingly surreal collection of short stories and the darkest of poetry, all interspersed with stunning graveyard photographs taken by the multitalented author herself - an absolute must for every bookshelf!

Blood and Blasphemy

If you enjoy your horror dipped in buckets of blood and sprinkled with generous amounts of blasphemy, then you've come to the right place!

Blood and Blasphemy is a collection of over thirty of the most sacrilegious horror stories ever written.

Within these irreverent pages, you will encounter a priest that keeps his deformed spawn chained in a root cellar, a convent where a poisonous species of salamander is worshiped, a demonic altar boy, possessed religious relics that kill, blood-drinking clergymen, a Son of God who feeds on sin, an unsuspecting couple who run afoul of religious lunatics in a small town, the divine (and deadly) turd of Christ, and other terrifying tales guaranteed to make church ladies faint and nuns clutch their rosaries.

Featuring stories by: Aron Beauregard, George Alan Bradley, Cardigan Broadmoor, Scot M. Carpenter, Myna Chang, Clay McLeod Chapman, Nick Dinicola, Jude M. Eriksen, Michael Martin Garrett, Gerri R. Gray, Christopher Hamel, Carlton Herzog, B.T. Joy, A.L. King, Daryl Marcus, Jeremy Megargee, Donna J.W. Munro, Hari Navarro, Trevor Newton, Drew Nicks, C.C. Parker, Wolfgang Potterhouse, J.L. Shioshita, J.J. Smith, Henry Snider, J.B. Toner, Sheldon Woodbury, Ken Goldman, and Shawn Wood.

Graveyard Girls

A delicious collection of horrific tales and darkest poetry from the cream of the crop, all lovingly compiled by the incomparable Gerri R Gray! Nestling between the covers of this formidable tome are twenty-five of the very best lady authors writing on the horror scene today!

These tales of terror are guaranteed to chill your very soul and awaken you in the dead of the night with fear-sweat clinging to your every pore and your heart pounding hard and heavy in your labored breast…

Featuring superlative horror from: Xtina Marie, M. W. Brown, Rebecca Kolodziej, Anya Lee, Barbara Jacobson, Gerri R. Gray, Christina Bergling, Julia Benally, Olga Werby, Kelly Glover, Lee Franklin, Linda M. Crate, Vanessa Hawkins, P. Alanna Roethle, J Snow, Evelyn Eve, Serena Daniels, S. E. Davis, Sam Hill, J. C. Raye, Donna J. W. Munro, R. J. Murray, C. Bailey-Bacchus, Varonica Chaney, Marian Finch (Lady Marian).

The Strange Adventures of Turquoise Moonwolf

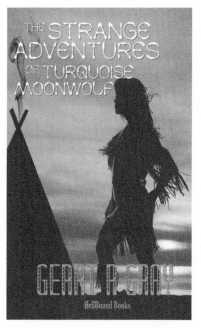

In Turquoise's first strange adventure (Twisted Teepee), a tornado carries Turquoise Moonwolf off in a teepee trading post to a bizarre world of human oddities after incompetent Grandfather Fukowee's rain dance goes awry.

Pursued by an evil shape-shifter and accompanied by two escapees from a circus sideshow (one a human ferret and the other a strongman with an abnormally long penis), Turquoise's only hope of returning home is a mysterious medicine man. But a plethora of perils lie in wait along the twisted red road she must follow to get to his reservation.

When Turquoise and an assembly of very weird relatives arrive at the Chateau Catatonia for the reading of eccentric Aunt Uvula's will, sanity takes a holiday. The chaos that erupts in this second strange adventure (Wigwam, Thank You Ma'am) is further compounded by an explosion at a nearby chemical plant that mutates the residents of an adjoining nudist colony into flesh-eating hippies. Wearing nothing but love beads and ravenous appetites, the cannibals run amuck. Will Turquoise become an heiress of a bed and breakfast, or a menu item of a naked lunch?

In Turquoise's third and final strange adventure (No Happy Medium), Grandfather Fukowee undergoes a bizarre transformation during an exorcism gone wrong and Turquoise is kidnapped by conjoined twins, Russ and Ross Gonzalez, each of whom have changed their first name to Tania after becoming self-brainwashed revolutionaries of the Siamese Liberation Army. However, things get even worse for Turquoise when a wormhole created by a strange comet sucks her into a perilous parallel world.

**A HellBound Books LLC
Publication**

www.hellboundbookspublishing.com

Printed in the United States of America

Made in the USA
Coppell, TX
15 December 2022

89185719R00239